YET A STRANGER

THE FIRST QUARTO: PART II

GREGORY ASHE

H&B

Yet a Stranger
Copyright © 2020 Gregory Ashe

Published by Hodgkin & Blount
https://www.hodgkinandblount.com/
contact@hodgkinandblount.com

Published 2020
Printed in the United States of America

Trade Paperback ISBN: 978-1-63621-009-4
eBook ISBN: 978-1-63621-008-7

FALL SEMESTER
SEPTEMBER 2014

1

Auggie and Fer had been driving for three days when they reached the Sigma Sigma fraternity house, which sat on Frat Row on the south side of Wroxall College's campus. For the last hundred miles, the Civic had been chugging and croaking, and it made a shrill, despairing noise every time they went up a hill—which in this godforsaken corner of the Midwest was about every fifty yards. Auggie was pretty sure he could smell something burning. It was better than the day and a half of Fer's cheesy-tater-tot farts, though, that he'd experienced in the middle of the trip.

"Be fast, dick drip," Fer said as he pulled into the Sigma Sigma parking lot. "Or I'm going to miss the shuttle."

"I know."

"So be fast."

"I know, Fer."

"So don't sit there scratching your pubic lice. Get a fucking move on."

"I hate you so much," Auggie said as he jumped out of the car and ran toward the move-in tables set up in front of the fraternity house. It was mid-afternoon because they'd left Amarillo later that morning than they had planned, and Auggie guessed the rush of move-ins had already happened. A couple of guys around his age—they were sophomores too, he guessed—were lugging plastic totes toward the red-brick house, and another guy was folding bedsheets while he argued with a girl—sister? girlfriend?—at the back of a station wagon. No parents. No older brothers.

Fer laid on the horn, which was actually pretty pathetic because the Civic just squeaked a few times. Then he shouted, "For fuck's sake, imagine some dude is jackrabbiting your hole and move your ass, Augustus!"

Auggie's face was hot as he approached the move-in tables. He found the L-R sign and felt his face get even hotter. The guy sitting there was gorgeous: big, brawny, in a tank and shorts and Adidas slides, with blond curls spilling over his forehead. He was grinning as Auggie moved forward.

"Lopez," Auggie said.

"Hi," the guy said, shuffling the papers. He glanced up. He had blue eyes. "Dylan."

"No, August. But I go by Auggie."

The guy laughed.

"Oh," Auggie said. "Got it. Hi."

Dylan laughed again. He had a nice laugh. He had very white teeth. When he handed over the paperwork and a key, he said, "You know everybody's talking about you, right?"

"No, I definitely did not know that."

"Yep," Dylan said. "They are. I like your videos. You're super funny."

"Thanks. I'm always looking for people who want to be in them."

"Nah, man," Dylan said. "Not really my thing. It's cool, though. I'm following you on Instagram and Snapchat. dylan_j199. Add me back."

"Cool," Auggie said.

"You want a tour?" Dylan glanced at the other guys manning the table, who were all trying incredibly hard to pretend they were doing something else. "Someone can cover for me."

The Civic squeaked again, and Fer roared, "Jesus Christ's bloody tampon, Augustus, either go down on him or don't, but hurry it the fuck up!"

"Maybe another time," Auggie said.

"Hit me up."

"Do you live here?"

"No, man. Senior. Some buds and I have a place off-campus. You should come over sometime. Hang out."

"That'd be cool."

"Hit me up," Dylan said again, but this time with a lazy smile that Auggie felt low in the belly.

As Auggie jogged back to the Civic, he could hear conversation buzz to life behind him. One guy said, "Jeez, Dyl, let the kid take a breath before you bend him over," and another guy said, "Dylan, you are such a fucking perv," and Dylan just laughed—a low, rumbling sound.

"Did you get your complimentary scissoring?" Fer asked as he got out of the car. They had different dads, and Fer was taller, darker, and bigger—muscle that was softening as Fer spent more and more time at business lunches and meetings. The taller part, that was what irked Auggie. Of course, sometimes the bigger part was pretty fucking annoying too.

"For the millionth time," Auggie said, "I didn't need you to drive out here with me."

"And let you go by yourself and give blowjobs to truckers for almost two thousand miles? Yeah, right, Augustus. Great idea."

"And for the millionth time, I didn't want you to drive out here with me."

"Pay for your own fucking education then."

"Just unload the stuff in the parking lot, and I'll get some guys to help me carry it inside."

Fer ignored him. He was working the biggest piece of luggage out of the trunk, grunting at the weight. "What the hell do you have in here? Your stainless-steel dildo collection?"

"Oh my God," Auggie said, covering his face.

The unloading and moving-in process went relatively smoothly. The Sigma Sigma house was a massive, three-story Colonial with red brick and gleaming white pillars. It was relatively new construction, with high ceilings and big windows. Auggie's room was on the third floor. The walls were a grayish brown, and someone had clearly patched and painted over the summer because there were no nail holes or broken plaster. Twin beds took up one side of the room, and matching desks occupied the rest of the space. One wall had been given over to two closets, which was where Auggie was going to have to store all his clothes—apparently, a dresser was not part of the standard package.

"This is worse than your last place," Fer said on their third trip upstairs.

"No, it's way better."

"Do you have a roommate?"

"I don't know; if I do, he hasn't moved anything in yet."

"He'd better not be a fucking psycho like your last one."

"I think that's everything, Fer."

Fer grunted, hands on hips, still studying the room.

"I guess you can go now," Auggie said.

"I want to see the bathroom. Your last place, you had that private bathroom."

"You can't just wander around the bathroom."

"I'm going to take a leak."

"You can't."

"I can't take a leak? Jesus, Augustus, I don't even know if you hear yourself sometimes."

Fer left, and Auggie considered whether or not it would be better just to die right now rather than dragging it out for the rest of the time Fer insisted on staying. Instead, he rearranged some of his luggage and the moving boxes, snapped a selfie, and pushed it out on Instagram with the caption: *The eagle has landed at Bro Central. Wish me luck!* He repeated the process with Snapchat—he was still feeling out the relatively new platform, but he thought it had a lot of possibility. Almost immediately, he got a snap back: it showed a quarter of Dylan's face and his mop of blond curls, and then grass, trees, and a swatch of asphalt. Dylan was grinning, and he'd scrawled a message on top of the picture: *welcome to Bro Central, little bro!*

Auggie added him as a friend so fast that he almost sprained his finger.

"Private showers," Fer reported, adjusting his junk as he came back into the room. "But it's just curtains, so you could still get ass raped."

"Go home, Fer. Go catch your shuttle. Go stand in the middle of the street until someone runs you over."

Instead, Fer shut the door. "You and I are going to have a talk right now, Augustus."

"Oh God. Hold on. I should probably record this."

Fer pushed Auggie's phone down and shook his head. Then he said, "Condoms."

"What?"

Taking a foil-wrapped condom from his pocket, Fer said, "Condoms." He pronounced each syllable distinctly, wagging the packet for emphasis. "Your fuck-up father isn't around to give you the talk—"

"Fer, no. Please. No. Please. You already gave me the talk. You gave me the talk when I was thirteen. You used a cucumber. Please don't make me go through this again. I'll never earn enough money to be able to pay for the therapy I need to get over this."

"That was the straight-Auggie talk. This is the flaming-homo-Auggie talk. I've been doing some research because I wanted to get this right."

Auggie groaned.

"You're young. You're an ugly little fucker, but you're still probably going to get some dick."

"I will use a condom. I will be safe. End of discussion."

With his free hand, Fer jabbed a finger into Auggie's chest to punctuate each word. "Every. Dick. That. Goes. In. Your. Ass. Suits. Up. Do you understand me?"

"Suits up?"

"Rubbers up. Learn the fucking lingo, Augustus. And I'm not fucking kidding with you right now. I don't care if he's your little fancy man and you think you're head over heels in love. Rubbers. Rubbers. Rubbers. I will buy you a lifetime supply if you want, but you use a rubber every fucking time. Same goes for you if you decide to stick your Vienna sausage somewhere."

"What do I have to say so that you will leave? What do I have to do? Is it money? Do you want money?"

"Save it for your fancy boys," Fer said. Then he wrapped Auggie in a huge hug, squeezing him tighter and tighter until Auggie grunted.

"I can't breathe."

"I love you. You're basically just one really fucking annoying snipping of ball hairs, but I love you, and I want this year to be better for you. I want you to be safe, and I want you to find some stud who can cornhole you all night long."

Black specks danced in front of Auggie's eyes, which was probably why he had such a hard time fighting off Fer when Fer started kissing him all over the face like a lunatic.

"Go home," Auggie said, shoving Fer away, laughing and wiping his face. "God, you are so weird sometimes."

"Fine. I'm going. Now you can hunt down that guy you were throwing a bone for and deepthroat him or however you gay guys say hello to each other."

Auggie found a sneaker and pitched it; it caught Fer in the shoulder, and Fer stumbled back, laughing.

2

Theo sat in Dr. Wagner's office, flip phone at his side, trying to look like he was paying attention to whatever Dr. Wagner was saying. The office was cramped, and it felt even smaller because the walls were lined with books. They made the space smell like moldering cloth and old paper. Dr. Wagner currently had his red, bulbous nose buried in the Riverside Shakespeare; he was looking for a specific passage that he had suddenly decided to add to the lesson plans.

Tell him you've got a sister you want to set him up with.

The text was from Howard Cartwright. Cart was a police officer, and he had been partnered with Theo's husband, Ian, before Ian died in a car accident. In the year since that accident, a lot had changed between Theo and Cart—some of it good, some of it . . . well, Theo couldn't quite tell. One thing that hadn't changed was that Cart was a redneck pain in Theo's ass.

Aren't you supposed to be working? Theo had gotten pretty good at texting on the flip phone. He still didn't understand the rush to get a smart phone; he was just barely getting the hang of this one.

I am working.

Really working.

I am really working, dumbass.

"Mr. Stratford," Dr. Wagner said, lifting himself up from the pages of the Riverside Shakespeare with what looked like a great deal of effort. The booze on his breath when he faced Theo directly was strong enough to overpower the smell of the old books. "It's lost to me now. I suppose I'll have to find it later."

Then he stared at Theo, his head bobbling on his neck, his eyes cloudy with cataracts and drink. Theo wouldn't be surprised if the horrifying old fossil just dropped dead—the female grad students would probably have a parade out of pure relief.

Wagner was still staring.

"We were going to talk about grading expectations," Theo said.

"Well," Dr. Wagner said, his jaw working soundlessly for a moment. "I don't know if that's really necessary."

Tell him you've got an eighteen-year-old cousin who will do things to his limp little lizard that Shakespeare never dreamed of.

Theo fought to hold back a smile.

"It was your idea, sir."

Last year, at this time, Theo had been planning his own class. Last year, Theo had worked out an entire semester's worth of material exploring adaptations and versions of *Lear*. Last year, he'd gotten some major work done on his thesis, and he'd also had the highest instructor evaluations in the department—for graduate students and professors. He'd turned some of his course materials into an article that was in the second-round review at *Shakespeare Quarterly*. This year, though, Theo was a teacher's assistant. He was going to shuffle papers, sit in on discussion groups, make copies, and scratch his balls. He'd be lucky if he didn't have to carry Dr. Wagner's briefcase and mop up his drool every time a co-ed bent over.

"I believe I do have a rubric," Dr. Wagner said, hoisting himself out of the seat and tottering toward the filing cabinet.

Stop a crime. Shoot up a bank robber. Get in a car chase. Rescue a kitten from a tree if you've got nothing better to do than bother me.

Gotta leave the kittens up there or the FD won't have anything to do.

Theo smiled in spite of himself.

"Here it is," Dr. Wagner said, holding a yellowed sheet of paper between two fingers. He waved it around and then blew dust off it. "Yes, I remember this. '59 was an excellent year for rubrics."

Kill me.

Not until you buy me that burger you owe me.

Mother. Fucker. You are one miserable son of a bitch. I was joking. It wasn't a real bet.

A bet's a bet.

"You can take a look at it for yourself, but I think you'll find it's perfectly up to snuff. I don't understand why there's all this rush to innovate these days. I really don't. Edwin Markle developed the six-point rubric in 1959, and it's just as good in 2009."

"Or 2014," Theo said.

"I'm very well aware of what year it is, Mr. Stratford. I was waxing poetic."

That wasn't all he was waxing.

Ok, I kind of cheated, Cart texted. *I already knew you were ticklish.*

Bastard.

Can't help it. You're just too cute when you laugh.

That one sentence was evidence of how very far things had shifted between them.

"Mr. Stratford, there is something that I think we need to discuss."

"Yes?"

"I understand that in the past you were found to be having inappropriate relationships with students."

Theo tried as hard as he could to keep his face smooth. His first year as a graduate student at Wroxall, the evening of the department's welcoming social, he had watched Dr. Wagner pursue Grace round and round the cheese table. Finally Grace had retreated to the bathroom. Dr. Wagner had followed. Theo had pushed open the door, rapping loudly, asking if anyone was in there. Dr. Wagner had stumbled out, his cheeks almost as red as his nose, smelling like he'd been swimming in a distillery. He'd mumbled something about getting turned around. Grace had been holding a can of pepper gel, so she would have been fine, but Theo hadn't forgotten.

Now, looking at those cloudy eyes, the glint in them, he realized Dr. Wagner hadn't forgotten either.

"No," Theo said.

"Excuse me?"

"I said no. That's not true. I had a relationship with an undergraduate student who had been my student previously. There was never any suggestion that the relationship had taken place while we were teacher and student." Theo struggled for a smile. "And relationship is really too strong of a word. We tried something, and it didn't work."

Wagner huffed. "Well, that's certainly not how I heard it."

"You're hearing it right now. From me."

"Yes. Well."

"And I'm sure you understand how appearances can be misleading."

Wagner huffed some more. "I certainly hope there won't be any further misunderstandings, Mr. Stratford. No more misleading appearances. As instructors, we have a sacred trust to shape young minds. We are responsible for their wellbeing. I hope I make myself perfectly clear when I say that nothing less will be tolerated."

Gin, Theo thought. He couldn't be sure, because all he was getting was the reek of alcohol, but Theo would have put money on gin being the drink of choice.

"Of course," Theo said.

"I think that will be all, then."

Dismissed, Theo limped out of the office, collecting his cane as he went. His knee was much better, and he had been consistent with his exercises even after physical therapy ended. He carried the cane, though, because his knee stiffened after he sat too long, and it still gave out at the weirdest times. And, if he were honest, because he found the cane comforting. You could really mess somebody up with a cane if you needed to.

He was unlocking the door to the office he shared with Grace and Dawson, a cubbyhole of a room at the far end of Liversedge Hall, when his phone buzzed again. He fanned the door back and forth to clear the toxic musk of weed (Dawson) and chai (Grace) from the closed-up room. Another message from Cart.

Have you talked to him?

Just got out of the old fuck's office.

Theo was just settling in at his desk, cane propped against the window, when the phone buzzed again.

You know that's not what I meant.

Theo looked at the message for almost a full minute. Then he closed the phone, put it in his pocket, and started up the ancient desktop computer. It was none of Cart's fucking business if Theo had talked to Auggie yet.

3

Auggie ran into Orlando, literally, on his second day in the Sigma Sigma house. Auggie was naked except for a towel around his waist, and he was rushing because he'd overslept and they were having a house meeting in half an hour. He yanked open his door, charged into the hallway, and crashed straight into his roommate from freshman year. They both went down in a tumble.

"Oh my God," Orlando said, "I'm so sorry—Augs?"

Auggie grabbed the towel, which had ripped free in the fall, and covered himself awkwardly as he stood. Orlando picked himself up too. He'd been carrying a box, and now it lay on its side, spilling sneakers and tie-dyed jockstraps across the carpet squares. Auggie forced his eyes up, away from the jocks, to meet Orlando's eyes.

His former roommate hadn't changed much: the same thick eyebrows, the same heavy scruff, the same strong jaw. He looked both thinner than Auggie remembered and like he'd packed on even more muscle. It seemed impossible but made sense in a way—Orlando was a star on Wroxall's wrestling team, and he'd doubtless worked hard over the last six months to recover from the terrible stab wound he'd taken in the winter. He was staring at Auggie, and Auggie had to fight the urge to cover his bare chest.

"Hey Augs," Orlando said. "Umm. Hi. Hello."

"No. Absolutely not. Whatever this is, go away."

"This is crazy, right?"

"Yep. Crazy. Totally batshit. Bye, Orlando."

Then the door next to Auggie's opened, and Ethan Kovara, a junior and one of the few other Cali boys in the frat, poked his head out. "Hey, Auggie. You met my new roommate? Orlando, this is Auggie. Auggie, Orlando."

Orlando smiled uncertainly. "How have you been?"

"You guys know each other?" Ethan asked.

"Could you give us a minute?" Orlando said.

"Yeah, man. Oh, dude, raunchy," he said, laughing as he looked at the jocks, and then he shut the door.

Orlando stooped down, gathering up the jocks and sneakers. Auggie grimaced and struggled with a growl and then squatted—which was weird as hell in a towel—and helped. It had been his fault, after all.

"I, uh," Orlando said, "didn't know you were going to live here. You said you thought you were going to get a place with Tyler and Chris."

"That didn't work out."

"I wasn't trying to, you know . . ."

"Stalk me?"

A huge grin broke out on Orlando's face. "Something like that."

For some reason, Auggie found himself smiling too. "God, I'm an asshole. I'm sorry. I just didn't expect—I mean, it's good to see you, but things just ended kind of weird."

"Yeah, I didn't like how they ended. I'm really sorry, Augs. About all of it. I—I'm on a new med, and I'm seeing a therapist, so, you know, you don't have to worry."

"I wasn't worried." Orlando's smile got a little bigger, and Auggie heard himself adding, "I could have handled things better too."

"Nah, man. It was all me. Sorry again."

They were still hunkered down, and Auggie was still in a towel, and Orlando's dark eyes were staying painfully fixed on Auggie's face like he was fighting the desire to look.

"Are you ok? I mean, the recovery and stuff."

As they both stood, Orlando tugged up his tee to expose dense muscle covered by dark hair. Low on his stomach, a shiny scar ran for four inches; it still looked inflamed

"Shit," Auggie said.

"I might be out this season. The doctors really don't want me wrestling; they already think I might have to have another surgery, and they're worried I'll do more damage."

"I'm so sorry."

"It's ok. If I creep you out again, just don't punch me in the stomach."

"Orlando, you didn't creep me out. It just . . . it just didn't work."

"Yeah," Orlando said, "well, you're a nice guy for saying that."

Down the hall, somebody was blasting Korn, and two guys stumbled out into the hall headbanging and screaming.

Over the blare of music, Auggie said, "I guess we're neighbors."

"I'm not going to bother you, Augs."

"That's not what I meant."

Orlando's dark eyes fell, and he fiddled with the flaps of the cardboard box. "Ok, well, I gotta finish bringing up my stuff."

"By yourself?"

"Yeah, I mean, sophomore year. Last year, my parents, my brothers and sisters, they all pitched in. This year, I guess I'm an adult and I'm supposed to handle things myself. You know how it is."

"Yeah," Auggie said, but he was thinking of Fer driving halfway across the country with him. "Let me put on some clothes and I'll help you."

"No way."

"Yeah, it'll just take me a minute."

"Augs, that's weird. You don't have to be nice to your psycho ex-roommate."

"I'm not being nice. I mean, I guess I am. But you're not psycho. And you're not just my ex-roommate. I thought we were friends."

Orlando played with the cardboard flaps. When he looked up, his eyes were dark and heavy. "God, you want me so bad, don't you?"

Auggie stared at him.

A tiny grin played at the corner of Orlando's mouth.

"You are such a dick," Auggie said.

Orlando burst out laughing.

"Let me change. Oh, hold on. Do you want to do something fun? Like a move-in video? We could do like . . . well, let's see if Ethan wants to be in it. We could have him move your stuff every time we bring up more boxes. Or something like that."

"And I have to pretend to be mad," Orlando said.

"You're shit at being mad. Maybe you should just pretend to be dumb."

"Hey!"

Auggie grinned.

"Go change," Orlando said, "before I forget how generous I'm being by providing you with free content."

Over his shoulder, Auggie flipped him the bird as he went back into his room. He changed and went next door. As soon as Ethan heard their plan, he wanted in on it. He was good looking, too, which helped—dark brown skin, huge eyes, a nervous smile that Auggie's audience would eat up. Not as good looking as Orlando, and that was a good thing too. You had to balance that kind of thing, or it started looking like a Gap commercial.

They were on their third trip up, both of them with arms full of boxes, when a familiar voice called out, "Little bro, you're missing the house meeting."

Dylan was leaning against one wall, blond curls spilling over his forehead, an unreadable smirk on his mouth as he watched Auggie. He was in a blue paisley tank top that showed blond stubble on his chest. He had massive legs.

"Hey," Auggie said, smiling—too big of a smile, he realized. Then he stumbled, and he would have fallen except Dylan caught his arm and steadied the tower of boxes. Dylan's grip was solid. He still had that smirk that Auggie couldn't decipher.

"Careful," Dylan said.

Sweat beaded on Auggie's nape.

"Augs," Orlando said from the stairs.

"Yeah," Auggie said. "Coming."

"You're a fucking killer," Dylan said, squeezing Auggie's bicep. "Please God tell me you're trying out for lacrosse."

"Augs," Orlando said again.

"Don't fuck my life," Dylan said with a grin. "Come to tryouts."

"Yeah," Auggie said, holding back an answering smile. "Maybe."

"Who's that douche?" Orlando said when they were passing the second-floor landing.

"He's actually pretty cool. His name's Dylan."

Orlando shook his head.

"What?"

"I just forgot that sometimes you're kind of dumb."

4

Theo lived in a small brick house on the western edge of Wahredua. It was barely inside the city limits, in what his husband had called the boonies—small houses on big lots, where neighbors minded their own business. Ian had needed to live in the city because he was with the Wahredua police, but in some ways, he was even more of a country boy than Theo, and he'd wanted his space. This house, which needed the tuckpointing done, which needed a new chimney, which needed a lot of patches or, better, a completely new roof, and which cooked like an oven from April to November, had been the compromise.

Saturday afternoon, Theo picked up after himself. He took the dirty clothes to the basement and started the laundry. He swept and mopped the living room and kitchen. He ran the dishwasher. He fiddled with the window unit; he had long suspected that machines only responded to bullies, and so he hammered on the A/C until he thought it was chugging slightly cooler air into the baking heat of the house. He cleaned the bathroom—not that Cart noticed things like that—and then he showered and put on a linen shirt and a pair of what Cart had taken to calling his booty shorts. They were just khaki shorts that came to mid-thigh, but Cart really got a kick out of calling them that. He ran a comb through the bro flow of strawberry-blond hair, wondering if he needed to get it cut, and he was considering his beard, patting it, trying to determine if it was really as fluffy as it looked— and, if so, how to fix that in the next thirty seconds.

Cart's footsteps moved outside the bathroom, and liquid heat ran through Theo.

"Hey," Theo said as he went into the kitchen.

Cart was opening a Big Wave, and he glanced over his shoulder. The bottlecap clinked into the sink, and then he took another longer, look back at Theo. He was skinny in the wiry, country-boy way that Ian had been skinny, the hair on his head perpetually buzzed at zero, a little bit jug-eared, a little goofy when he got those huge, shit-kicker grins on his face. He'd changed out of his uniform, and he was in mesh shorts and a Cardinals t-shirt. He licked his lips and wiggled his eyebrows.

"Perv," Theo said.

"You just get me all hot and bothered."

Theo crossed the kitchen and pretended not to notice Cart's moment of hesitation when Theo leaned in to kiss him. Then they were kissing, one of Cart's hands at the small of Theo's back, his fingers cold and wet from the beer and pressing hard through the linen.

In spite of Theo's best efforts to keep things between them at the level of friendship, their relationship had accelerated quickly over the summer. Cart had wanted things to move forward. Theo had, ultimately, allowed things to move forward. He thought about that sometimes when he was up at night, about why he'd let this happen. He thought about the fact that Auggie had stopped answering his texts after Theo told him that he and Cart had begun seeing each other romantically—he refused to call it dating yet. But during the day, it seemed to make sense. Right now, with Cart's firm touch juxtaposed to gentle, questioning kisses, it made sense.

"You look good," Cart said quietly when Theo pulled back from the kiss.

"So do you."

"Nah, I look like white trash. You smell good, too."

"Thanks."

"Let me see how you taste," Cart whispered, and then he kissed him again. He always said those things quietly. He set the beer bottle down, the glass clunking on the counter, and then he had both hands on Theo's hips, rutting up against him.

"I haven't started the coals," Theo said when the kiss broke.

Cart was biting his lip as he shook his head. He undid the button on Theo's waistband. "Lose the booty shorts."

Theo forced them down and kicked his way free. He hadn't bothered with underwear—he knew Cart's routine pretty well by now—but he still gasped when Cart took him in hand. He had workman's calluses, and he had strong fingers. Theo moaned when Cart slid a hand under the linen shirt and twisted a nipple hard.

"Fuck yeah," Cart whispered. "Fuck yeah."

He manhandled Theo to the couch in the living room, hopping the last few steps so that his shorts and underwear fell around his ankles, and then they made out on the couch, trading hand jobs until Theo got on his knees to give head. Cart didn't last long after that—he never did, he just gasped and muttered, the words growing louder and more forceful as he lost control, those strong fingers clutching Theo's long hair. Then Cart screamed, "Fuck, fuck, fuck" and came, and Theo finished himself off with his hand.

Cart helped him up onto the couch, pulling Theo onto his lap, those callused hands tracing Theo's hip, his belly, his thigh. He kissed Theo's temple.

"God, I'm so fucking crazy for you."

Theo just looked up at him and ran his fingers over the buzzed hair. He had learned with Cart not to lean in for a kiss until he'd brushed his teeth.

"You don't have any idea what you do to me," Cart was saying, the words rumbling in his chest, vibrating into Theo. "I wish I weren't such an ignorant fucking redneck so I could tell you how you make me feel." One of his hands cupped Theo's dick and balls, and Cart made a noise in his throat.

"How about a practice run?" Theo said.

"Yeah?"

"I think so. You won't get better if you don't try."

"You know how when you're fishing—"

Theo couldn't help himself; he burst out laughing, burying his face in Cart's bony shoulder.

"Well, fuck you, then," Cart shouted, slapping Theo's ass a few times.

"I'm sorry, I'm sorry, God, my poor ass, ok. I'm sorry. Tell me how my blowjobs are like fishing."

"Not your blowjobs, you hoosier fuck-for-brains."

Theo rolled his eyes. "You're losing me."

With a huge sigh, Cart settled himself, his hand stroking lightly over where he'd spanked Theo. "You know how when you're fishing, like early, you go out on the water and it's just barely light, the sun not even up yet, and everything's quiet, and you think, 'Yeah, this is it, I could do this for just about forever.'"

"I couldn't," Theo said. "I don't know what it is about skinny country boys, but you're killing my jaw."

Cart tried to push him off his lap.

"I'm kidding," Theo said, laughing as he fended off Cart. "I'm kidding."

"You're a rude, uneducated, uncivilized—"

Theo put his hand over Cart's mouth until Cart settled down. Cart's dark eyes stared at him.

"That was really sweet," Theo said.

Cart mumbled something behind Theo's hand.

"Yep," Theo said. "It really was. You don't need any practice. That was perfect. Tell me things like that, and we're going to do just fine."

Cart mumbled something else.

Theo kissed the side of his neck, then where his neck joined his shoulder, pulling the Cardinals tee aside so he could kiss lower.

"Am I supposed to be feeling this much?" Cart whispered after pulling Theo's hand away. "It's so much sometimes I get scared."

"You feel what you feel," Theo said. "It doesn't have to be anything but what it is. And you don't have to be scared of it."

"I am, though," Cart said, and then he kissed Theo's temple again.

"Let me brush my teeth," Theo said. "And we'll get dinner going."

In the shorts gathered around Cart's ankles, his phone buzzed. Theo fished it out for him and passed it over.

"Yeah?" Cart answered. "For fuck's sake. Are you fucking kidding me?" He listened for a moment. "I'm at the grocery store, dumbass. I'll be there in five minutes." When Cart disconnected, he gently nudged Theo off his lap, and then he stood and pulled up his underwear and shorts. "Work," he said as he adjusted himself. "Another goddamn demonstration."

"They've got a right to be upset," Theo said. "I've been to a few of them myself. We should all be upset."

"I'm not saying they shouldn't be upset," Cart said a little too loudly. "But could they fucking do it when I'm not having a night off?"

"At the grocery store," Theo said.

Cart wiped his face, staring at his feet.

"I shouldn't have said that," Theo said. "Sorry. I wasn't trying to pick a fight."

"Well," Cart said, heading for the door, "you still said it."

21

5

On Sunday, Auggie had just finished editing another video when the knock came at his door. In the video, he, Orlando, and Ethan competed to do the best version of the dancing-in-underwear scene from *Risky Business*. Auggie had to give himself credit—he was a way better dancer than the other two, and, of course, that was the whole reason he'd wanted to do the scene. But Orlando stole the show anyway. He was just too hot in nothing but briefs and white socks. At the end of the video, the camera panned to show three bored girls sitting on a sofa. They got up to leave, totally unimpressed, while the boys were still arguing about who had won. Auggie posted the video, rolled off the bed, and answered the door.

Orlando was standing there, his eyes red, a hangdog expression on his face.

"I just posted it—" Auggie began. "Hey, what's wrong?"

"Can we come in?"

"Um, sure. Ethan—"

"No, not Ethan. Billie, come on."

A girl sauntered into view. She was clearly Orlando's sister—the same dark, curly hair, the same strong jaw—and Auggie imagined that only ferocious waxings kept her unibrow-free. She moved with a casual grace, shaking out her hair, turning her head to wink at someone down the hall. A moment later, Ethan came into sight, practically drooling. The button on her white polo was undone, and she wasn't wearing a bra. Her shorts left about a mile of tan thigh exposed. Auggie wondered if there was anyone normal in Orlando Reese's whole clan.

Moving to one side, he waved for them to step into his room, and then when Orlando looked at him, he shut the door.

"No roommate?" Billie asked, flopping onto the unmade bed. "Lucky duck."

"This is my sister Billie," Orlando said. "She doesn't want me to do this, ok? So just ignore her."

"What's going on? I just saw you a couple of hours ago for the video, and you seemed fine. You—have you been crying?"

"I guess so," Orlando said, pressing the heels of his hands to his eyes.

"He's overreacting," Billie said. She worked a scrunchy off her wrist and put her long curls into a ponytail while she talked. "He's always been a crybaby. That's because he's spoiled."

"Sit down," Auggie said, guiding Orlando to one of the desk chairs. Orlando dropped into it heavily, still covering his eyes. "Why don't you tell me what this is all about?"

"It's Cal," Orlando said, and then he started to cry.

"Oh Lord," Billie said, rolling her eyes while she adjusted the scrunchy. "I have not missed this, I can tell you that much."

"Who's Cal?"

"Our brother."

"He's missing," Orlando said, his voice rising with anger. "And nobody told me!"

"We don't know that he's missing," Billie said. "You need some posters and stuff. Oh, you know what you should get? You should get a hookah. That's such a frat boy thing to have."

"I don't understand," Auggie said. "Your brother is missing?"

"Yes," Orlando said, wiping his eyes.

"No," Billie said.

"And they've been lying about it for almost a week."

"Orlando, you are such a baby about things. We weren't lying to you. We just didn't tell you. Honestly, it's because we didn't want to deal with this. You're a total drama queen, and it's exhausting."

"He's really upset," Auggie said. "Maybe you should go easy on him."

"Go easy?" Billie tugged on the polo, studying her boobs. "Everybody goes easy on him. He's the youngest. That's the whole problem."

Orlando sniffled, and Auggie found a tissue in his backpack and passed it over. After blowing his nose and wadding up the tissue in one hand, Orlando said, "Augs, I want you to find Cal."

"Oh my God," Billie said.

"I know you can do it, Augs. I know you can."

"Orlando told us about you solving that murder last year." Billie shrugged like she could have done it herself if she hadn't been busy with something else. "But it's not like this is your job or anything. I think it's silly to ask someone like you. No offense."

"I thought he wasn't missing," Auggie said. "Why do you care if I look?"

"Well, he's not missing missing. He's just not, you know, where anyone can find him." She must have recognized some of what Auggie was thinking in his expression because she blushed slightly and said, "I mean, it's not like we need the police or anything. Cal's probably on a bender again. He'll come back and clean up. That's all."

"On a bender?"

"Oh my God, you're almost as bad as Orlando."

"We'll pay you," Orlando said, snuffling into the back of his hand. "Two thousand dollars."

"Jeez," Billie said. She threw him a dirty look. "Mom and Dad are going to shit bricks, Orlando."

"Butt out," Orlando said. "Just go away, Billie."

"He's probably having his period," Billie said with a smile for Auggie.

"Get out!"

Stretching as she rose, Billie said, "This is a waste of your time, Auggie. Cal will come back; he always does." She tugged on the polo one more time, considering her boobs, and then she flashed a Miss America smile and headed out the door.

Auggie heard Ethan and Orlando's door open, and then Ethan saying, like it was a magical coincidence, "Oh hey, you must be Orlando's sister."

Orlando groaned and covered his eyes again.

"My brother Fer would call Ethan a dripping dick with legs or something like that," Auggie said.

Orlando gave a wet laugh. "I'm sorry, Augs. I shouldn't have bothered you."

"You didn't bother me." Auggie dragged out the other desk chair and sat. "Why are you so worried, but she's not?"

"Because she's a bitch."

Auggie leaned back.

Wiping his face, Orlando said, "Ok, she's right. Cal goes on benders. He's got . . . he's got problems. But he's never been gone like this before. I mean, a day, tops. And we could find him because he was always somewhere in town—one of the bars he likes, with one of his dumb friends, that kind of thing."

"Your family lives in Wahredua?"

"Just outside the city limits, so it's technically just Dore County."

"So you grew up here?"

"Oh yeah. Wahredua High."

"Why didn't I know that?"

"Well, we didn't really talk about that kind of stuff last year."

And Auggie was surprised to realize that Orlando was right: they hadn't talked about that kind of stuff.

"You really think this is different?" Auggie said. "Serious, I mean?"

Orlando nodded. He was still trying to dry his cheeks.

"Don't you think you should go to the cops?"

Blowing out a breath, Orlando nodded again. But he said, "Augs, it's not just, you know, alcohol."

"Oh."

"So if they pick him up, I mean, he'd probably get charged with possession at the minimum. And he's got a business. And my parents would honestly shit bricks, like, a whole stack of them. All they care about is what people think, and this would be awful."

"We should still go to the police."

"Augs, please. I will do whatever you want. I will—I will find a way to get you more money if that's what it is. I'll be your wingman. I'll get you the hottest ass in town. I will do your homework for the rest of college."

Auggie let a little grin break out. "I saw your Intro to World Literature paper last year, Orlando. 'The symbolism of black is death.' Four pages like that."

A blush crept up behind the dark stubble, but after a moment, Orlando smiled. "Ok, smartass. Not all of us were getting private tutoring and boning sessions from the professor."

"I wish that's what I'd been getting," Auggie said, and then both of them burst out laughing.

"Please, Augs," Orlando said when the laughter faded. "Please."

"Promise you won't go anywhere near my homework."

"Promise."

"Promise you will not try to be my wingman."

"Swear to God."

"Promise you will never, ever, ever try to get me the hottest ass in town, which sounds a little rapey."

Orlando rolled his eyes and put his hand over his heart. "Never, ever, ever."

"If things get weird, we're calling the police. Ok?"

"Of course. I trust you, Augs. I know you'll do the right thing. And my parents really will pay you."

The two thousand dollars would be a huge help; Fer liked to rub Auggie's face in the fact that he was paying for his education, but the reality was that Fer was stretched pretty thin financially, even if he wouldn't admit it. And although Auggie kept hoping for a marketing or advertising deal that would help him break out as an influencer, his agent told him that many big companies were still shy of alternative lifestyles—queers, in other words—no matter how many followers they had.

And then Auggie realized that this might be the perfect opportunity to deal with the other man in his life who perpetually made things more difficult for him.

"You're not going to like this next part," Auggie said.

It took a moment; then Orlando's eyes widened. "Augs, no."

"I didn't solve that murder alone."

"Not him. Please."

"I'm going to at least ask him. If Theo doesn't want to help me, I won't bother him again."

But Auggie didn't think that would happen. Theo Stratford had an annoying—and occasionally breathtaking—protective streak. Auggie was smiling as he pulled on his sneakers.

6

After his morning visit to Downing to see Lana, Theo sat on the relatively new couch in his relatively new living room, ignoring his phone. The window A/C was making a pathetic yowling sound, like a cat was caught in the fan, and the house was hotter than hell. Theo had stripped down to a pair of jersey shorts, and he was still sweating.

He had planned on replacing the air conditioner before another Midwestern summer, but all of his savings—and then some—had gone to restoring the house. Much of the home's interior had been destroyed earlier that year by desperate people looking for something they thought Theo had; after the chaos had ended, Cart had helped Theo repair the damage. Or, better said, Cart had fixed everything, and Theo had specialized in carrying things and opening beers. Since then, Theo had been slowly buying furniture at thrift stores and from garage sales, whenever his grad student budget allowed.

His phone buzzed again; Theo refused to look at it.

The night before, Cart hadn't answered any of Theo's texts. Theo had simply been checking in—was Cart safe, had the demonstration been peaceful, things like that. It was one o'clock in the morning when Theo had finally put the phone under his pillow, and it was almost two by the time he fell asleep. If Cart wanted to talk today, well, he could wait until Theo was ready to talk.

A part of Theo thought about the Bluetooth speaker with its removable panel, the picture frame with the gap between the glass and the backing, the light fixture that was loose in the ceiling. Lots of hiding places Cart never thought to look. Lots of opportunities to feel better for a little while.

Theo flipped through the Riverside Shakespeare he'd borrowed from the library, examining the prefatory material for their edition of *Romeo and Juliet*. Dr. Wagner's class was one of the literary themes lectures that the department offered—every year, different themes. Dr. Wagner, big surprise, had chosen Adolescence and Erotic Love as the theme for his course. They were using anchor texts and then shorter companion pieces; *Romeo and Juliet* was the first anchor text, and even though Theo doubted he'd be in charge of anything besides turning on the projector, he wanted to be prepared. Besides, he was still considering a chapter on *Romeo and Juliet* in his thesis, and he wanted to read the play once more before he made that decision.

He was just finishing the scholarly introduction to the work when someone knocked on the door. It was Cart; he knew it. The dumb hoosier had come over to apologize and get a blow job—probably not in that order. Rolling off the couch, Theo dropped the Riverside Shakespeare on the coffee table and padded toward the door. In the heat and humidity, his feet made sticking noises on the floorboards.

"Listen," Theo said as he pulled the door open, "if you can't be bothered to answer one fucking text when I'm worried about— Auggie?"

"Um, hi."

Auggie looked good. Auggie looked fantastic. His dark hair was still in the same short crew cut, and his soft brown eyes were exactly the way Theo remembered them. The combination of tank top, shorts, and sneakers left very little of Auggie covered. Very, very little. Auggie was still lean and toned, although his shoulders looked a little broader, and he had a scattering of chest hair that hadn't been there a few months before. Even his legs looked more muscular.

Then Theo remembered he wasn't wearing a shirt, and he slammed the door. He stared at the door for a minute, not quite believing what had just happened. Then he stumbled over to the sofa and wriggled into the washed-out Lambert's Cafe t-shirt. He turned toward the door. No. He turned toward the bathroom. His knee had stiffened up, but he hobbled as fast as he could. He pushed his hair behind his ears. He patted down his beard. Why the hell did it have to be so poofy? Then he hobbled back to the door.

When he pulled it open, he said, "I'm going to try that again."

"Try what again?" Auggie said, his eyes wide and innocent.

"Hi, Auggie. I didn't expect—I didn't know—Jesus Christ, is that Orlando?"

"Yeah, he's hiding over there because he thinks you're still mad at him. I told him you weren't. You aren't, are you?"

Orlando peered around the corner of the house and gave a tiny wave.

Theo decided not to answer that. "Auggie, it's nice to see you, but this isn't a good time."

"Because you're having sex?"

Theo choked on something—he wasn't sure what, maybe just spit. "No, I'm not—"

"Because you're all sweaty, and your nipples look kind of bruised."

"Just a second," Theo said and shut the door again. He leaned his head against it. And then he pounded his head against the wood several times. Cart and his fucking needle-nose-plier fingers.

"Theo?" Auggie called from the other side of the door. "Are you all right?"

"Yep. Just give me two more seconds to cut my throat and you can come in."

The handle turned, and then the door popped open an inch.

"Theo?"

"Let's do this another day. I want to see you, Auggie, but maybe now isn't—"

Auggie pushed, and Theo allowed himself to be forced back, and then Auggie was standing inside his house, young and beautiful and smiling.

"Can I give you a hug?" Auggie asked.

"Yes. Yeah."

"Cart won't be mad?"

Dragging Auggie into a hug, Theo said, "Who the fuck cares if he gets mad?"

He'd forgotten this, how Auggie felt in his arms, the smell of his hair, the sound of his breathing. Not forgotten. Blocked away.

Tightening his arms, he said, "Why the fuck did you stop answering my texts?"

"Ow, ow, ow, ok, God, you're going to puncture a lung." Auggie stumbled free, grinning, a blush darkening his light brown skin. "Because I'm a stupid kid and I got mad at you. Because I was super jealous of Cart. And because I'm petty as fuck."

Theo crossed his arms.

"I, uh, I know I laid a lot on you at the end of last semester." Auggie copied Theo's pose, folding his arms. "I just want you to know, I realize that was really immature, and I've done some growing up, a lot actually, over the summer. If you could, you know, forget that stuff?"

Forget it, Theo thought. Forget being told that Auggie loved him, that Auggie wanted to be with him. He nodded mechanically.

"Forgiven?" Auggie said.

Theo managed, "I'll think about it."

"You got a new couch."

"Semi-new. A widow died in it."

"She died on it?"

"No, Auggie, she died in it. Don't ask me what it means, but they were very specific when I bought it."

Auggie's grin got bigger. "Do you have any Doritos?"

"I don't keep them stocked just on the off chance you might decide to start talking to me—don't go back there!"

Auggie ignored him and headed for the kitchen. Over his shoulder, he said, "See if you can convince Orlando that you're not going to skin him alive and eat him."

Theo limped out onto the porch again and stood at the rail, stretching his knee. "Orlando, get your ass over here."

Orlando emerged from around the side of the house. He gave another wave. The dumb fuck had packed on more muscle, but he still looked thin from the injury he'd taken earlier that year.

"Why are you hanging around Auggie?"

"I'm not. I swear! I just—he'll tell you. And we're neighbors."

"Neighbors?"

"I didn't know. I swear! It was just chance."

Theo stared at him.

"Oh my God," Orlando muttered. Then, louder, "I swear to God!"

"Orlando, you don't strike me as the smartest guy in the room, so I want something to be really clear. I need you to understand that I will literally—this is not exaggeration, this is not hyperbole—I will literally murder you if you hurt him again. Do you understand me?"

Orlando swallowed and whispered, "Yeah."

"Good. Come inside. I've got to save my kitchen before Auggie starts ripping out the drywall to find those chips."

Auggie had already gotten the bag of Cool Ranch Doritos that Theo had purchased on Thursday. He was stretched out on the couch, his bare feet resting on the Riverside Shakespeare, his sneakers fallen on their sides on the floor next to him.

"God damn it," Theo said.

"Theo," Auggie said, pausing to crunch a Dorito extra loudly. "Orlando needs help finding his brother."

"No. No way."

"I promised to help him."

"You will not. I will call Fer, and I will put you on a plane back to California before you get into another mess like last year. Hell, I'll put you in a straitjacket if it comes to that."

"Fine," Auggie said, a little pout manifesting before he snapped his teeth shut on another chip. "I guess Orlando and I will just find him ourselves."

"God damn it," Theo said again because he knew that somehow, he'd already lost the argument.

7

"This is your car?" Theo said when he saw the Civic. "This?"

"It's a car. What's the problem?"

"But it's your car?"

"Yes."

"Yours?"

"Oh my God. Orlando, you're sitting in the front seat. I already can't handle this."

Auggie wasn't sure, but he thought Theo was smiling as he slipped into the back seat. It was hard not to keep checking the rearview mirror. Hard not to keep stealing looks. Theo looked better than ever. The hollowness in his face, the dark circles around his eyes, even most of the limp—they'd all vanished, as though the summer had been a magic cure. Or Cart, a treacherous part of Auggie's brain suggested. Maybe being with Cart had made everything better. Theo was staring out the window, pushing the flow of strawberry blond hair behind his ears. His beard had copper in it where the sun struck just right.

"Umm," Orlando said.

Auggie jerked the wheel to keep from hitting a mailbox.

In the back seat, Theo made an amused noise, and Auggie resolutely refused to look in the mirror.

"I didn't know your family lived in Wahredua," Theo said.

"Just outside the city limits," Orlando said.

"Wahredua High?"

"Yup."

"I knew," Auggie said.

"You found out, like, an hour ago," Orlando said.

"But I still knew before Theo."

Orlando looked over his shoulder, obviously trading glances with Theo, so Auggie gave him a dead leg, driving his knuckle into Orlando's thigh.

"Jesus fucking Christ," Orlando shouted.

"No more talking until we get to Cal's apartment," Auggie ordered.

"Thank God I got the back seat," Theo murmured.

"What was that?"

In the rearview mirror, Auggie caught Theo's too innocent smile.

Orlando rubbed his leg the rest of the drive.

The apartment building that Orlando directed them to was situated on the northeast side of town. Although there were some signs of revitalization—hipster cafes, a bike repair shop, a narrow brick house called, creatively, the Redbrick Bed and Breakfast—much of this area looked older and run down. Frame buildings were desperately in need of paint and, in some cases, structural support. Cinderblock strip malls displayed cracked foundations and empty storefronts.

"I've never been over here," Auggie said as he parked.

"Really?" Orlando said. "The Pretty Pretty's a couple of blocks that way."

"What's the Pretty Pretty?"

"The only gay club in town. You haven't been? Oh my God, we've got to go sometime."

Theo didn't do anything. He didn't even move. But suddenly Orlando's face was red, and he said, "Um, you know, um, um."

"Oh my God," Auggie said.

Orlando was still stammering.

"Did you threaten him?" Auggie said to the rearview mirror.

Theo just rolled his eyes.

"I can go to a gay club if I want," Auggie said.

"Be my guest," Theo said. "You'll get eaten alive, and not in a sexual way. Well, not exclusively in a sexual way."

"What does that mean?"

"Go to the Pretty Pretty and find out."

"Maybe I will."

Theo rolled his eyes again.

"And I can go with Orlando if I want."

Sighing, Theo just unbuckled his seat belt and got out of the Civic.

The apartment building had clearly been extensively renovated: the brick was clean, almost new looking, but its dark red color matched the other brick buildings in the area; the windows were definitely new, the energy-saving kind that Fer had bitched about putting in the house in California; in the exterior corridors, the stairs and railings had glossy black paint, and the outdoor carpet tiles were a bright, yellow-and-blue check that the sun hadn't faded yet.

"That's Wayne's." Orlando pointed to a blue BMW. Then, gesturing to the empty stall next to it, he said, "That's Cal's spot. He drives a yellow Mustang, and I'll text you the plate number in case it helps." He led them up the stairs, down one of the exterior corridors, and stopped at the door marked 3F. He knocked once.

The man who answered had to be related to Orlando. He had the same scruff, although his was so thick that it was almost a beard, the same lantern jaw, the same thick brows. He was bigger than Orlando, taller and wider, and although he had the first hints of a gut pulling at the rugby shirt he was wearing, he still had an athlete's build. His eyes were red, and his gaze drifted over them until settling on Orlando. Then he turned and shuffled back into the apartment, the door hanging open behind him.

"He's not handling this nearly as breezily as Billie," Auggie said.

Orlando just shook his head and went inside, and Auggie and Theo followed.

The apartment clearly belonged to bachelors. The living room furniture consisted of a pleather loveseat and matching pleather recliners, all three pieces arranged to face an enormous television. Auggie could see into the kitchen from where he stood: a Vitamix blender, tubs of protein powder, a frying pan and plates in the sink. The only ornamental items were a poster with the 2012 Mizzou Tigers football roster, a sepia-tone map of St. Louis, and a framed baseball card featuring Mark McGwire, first base, in a USA uniform—Auggie didn't know baseball well enough to know if the card was valuable, but it looked old, and he guessed it hadn't been framed for purely sentimental reasons. A short hallway led off the living room; Auggie could glimpse a bedroom through a partially closed door.

"I thought we were going to Cal's apartment," Auggie said.

"This is Cal's apartment," Orlando said. "He and Wayne live together." Then he said, "Wayne, this is Auggie and Theo. They're the ones I told you about."

Wayne dropped into a recliner. The chair had a built-in cupholder, which was currently occupied by a can of Pabst. Wayne chugged the beer, crumpled the can with one hand, and tossed it. It made a cheery, clinking rattle as it joined the pile of cans next to the chair.

"Hi, Wayne," Auggie said.

Wayne's gaze finally moved to him, but his eyes were bleary and unfocused, and Auggie couldn't tell how much Wayne was really seeing.

"What are we doing here?" Theo asked in a whisper.

"Trying to find out what Wayne knows," Auggie whispered back.

"They're helping us look for Cal," Orlando said a little too loudly. "They want to talk to you."

"So let them fucking talk to me," Wayne said. He rubbed his big hands along the recliner's arms. "Peepee, get me a beer."

Orlando's face turned to fire, and he very obviously tried not to look at Auggie as he headed to the kitchen.

"You don't look so good," Theo said.

"Right back fucking at you."

Theo shot Auggie a look.

"I think he's just asking if everything's ok," Auggie said. "You seem upset."

"Upset?" Wayne said. "No, I'm not upset. I'm pissed off. And I'm drunk. My brother's been gone for over a week. We've got a business to run. Personalized coaching. So I'm going to be doing double the work until Cal decides to show up. My sisters want to pretend nothing is wrong. And my other brother is such a royal fuckup that I can't ask him for any help." Orlando had come back with the beer, and when he held it out, Wayne snatched it from his hand and said, "Isn't that right, Peepee?"

Orlando stared at his feet.

"He's been gone for over a week?" Auggie said. "I thought it hadn't been quite a week."

"Nobody knows, really," Orlando said.

"What? How is that possible?"

"I was out of town," Wayne said. "When I got back, no Cal."

"How long were you gone?"

"Weekend. Left Friday night, came back Sunday night."

"Cal didn't have any appointments over the weekend?" Theo asked. "Training sessions, practices, nothing like that?"

"Right before Wroxall starts up, we take a week off. Like a summer vacation for the kids who have been training. Cal was going to stay here and jerk off all weekend." Waving lazily with the beer, he added, "We go back tomorrow, just like you."

"He didn't have a girlfriend? Someone he might have spent time with, I mean."

"Cal and I are building a business. We didn't have time for stuff like that. Not everybody's lucky enough to go to school on Mommy and Daddy's money, nights and weekends free to suck a few cocks. The rest of us, even the girls, we had to go on scholarship. We had to work hard enough to make the right team. We had to work our asses off to get a chance. Not baby Peepee."

Orlando's face, if anything, got redder.

"What's that like, Peepee?"

"Maybe you should wait outside," Auggie said to Orlando.

Orlando shook his head.

"Could I use your bathroom?" Theo asked.

Wayne waved at the hall, and Theo moved out of sight. A door clicked shut.

"Pretty sweet life, huh?" Wayne said, and then, faster than Auggie could believe, he slapped Orlando's stomach. Orlando let out a grunt and stumbled back, both hands pressed over his abdomen. His face was white.

"What the hell is wrong with you?" Auggie said, putting an arm around Orlando. He could feel Orlando shaking. "He's still healing."

"What a fucking crybaby. This is why you're going to take a year off? Because your tummy hurts?"

"He got stabbed, you dumb fuck," Auggie said.

"You know why we call him Peepee? I bet he didn't tell you that story."

"Wayne, come on," Orlando said, but he was still trembling, and he was still holding his stomach.

"Sit down," Auggie said.

Orlando just shook his head.

"He was, I don't know, three or four. Mom and Dad were having a dinner party. The Joneses were there, remember?"

Orlando stared blankly.

"And he comes out of his room in his pullups, you know, what kids wear so they don't piss the bed, only he's got them around his knees, and he's saying, 'Look at my peepee, look at my peepee.'"

Orlando swallowed. His eyes were shining, and he blinked rapidly. "You're such an asshole."

Wayne burst out laughing, but the laughter ended almost as abruptly as it had begun. Then all the energy seemed to drain out of him, and he lay back in the recliner, his eyes half closed. His breathing evened out.

"So you can't tell us anything?" Auggie said. "You didn't talk to Cal all weekend? You didn't text? Nothing?"

"Nothing," Wayne said. "I saw him Friday night. I left. When I came back Sunday night, he wasn't here. Monday morning, he still wasn't here. That's when I started texting. We looked all the usual places."

"Where?"

"Flaherty's, Saint Taffy's, Meramec Maniacs. There's a girl he hooks up with sometimes. Jessie something. Then I noticed stuff was missing."

"What stuff?"

"Collector's items. Autographed bats, limited-edition jerseys, a puck from Game 3 of the 2008 Stanley Cup. Probably more, I just haven't noticed it's missing yet."

"Somebody broke in and stole your stuff? And you didn't report that to the police?"

Wayne grunted. "Nobody broke in. Cal took it. He sells it, and then he scores, and then he's on a bender. Notice he didn't touch any of his own shit." He gestured at the framed baseball card.

Theo came back, and when Auggie shot him a look, he gave a discreet shake of his head.

"Is that all?" Wayne said. "Because I want another fucking beer."

Orlando turned toward the kitchen, but Auggie caught his arm and steered Orlando to the door.

"Get it yourself," Auggie said as they left.

8

Theo followed Auggie and Orlando down to the parking lot. The August day was boiling hot, the air shimmering over the asphalt, and sweat broke out on Theo's face and back. The smell of hot tar came in on each breath. Theo felt dizzy from it.

Auggie kept his hand on Orlando's arm, and when they got to the car, he gestured to his stomach and said, "Are you ok?"

"Yeah. It just hurt."

"You don't think you need to see a doctor?"

"He didn't hit me that hard. He's an asshole, but he's not a monster. Come on, I want you to meet the rest of my family."

"Maybe we should drop you off at Sigma Sigma," Theo said.

Auggie glanced over, his expression impossible to read.

"No," Orlando said. "I want to be there."

Auggie was still looking at Theo.

"Orlando," Auggie said slowly, "it might be easier to ask them some questions if you're not there."

"No," Orlando said. "I'm going with you. Can we please go? It's hot, and it smells like ass out here."

So they got in the car, and Auggie followed Orlando's directions out of town.

"Could you turn up the A/C?" Theo asked.

"It's all the way up," Auggie said.

"Of course it is."

Theo had meant it as a joke, but Auggie glared at him in the rearview mirror.

They were driving past block after block of tiny frame houses, most of the houses with chain-link fencing, all of them with steel mailboxes that had wonky numbers running along the side. In one yard, some sort of terrier mix was chained up. The dog had run to the end of its chain, and now it stood on its hind legs, yapping at cars. In another yard, ancient patio furniture cooked slowly in the sun. A woman with the skinniest legs Theo had ever seen was sitting under an umbrella, drinking what looked like lemonade.

"That's not how Wayne usually is."

"Ok," Auggie said.

"I mean, he's always kind of a bully. But he's just mad today."

"I get it," Theo said. "Jacob, my brother, he's a complete prick. Of course, he's a prick with the Bible in one hand, so it's kind of a different tone."

"Fer likes to give me shit," Auggie said. "It's just a brother thing."

"Yeah," Orlando said, resting his head on the window.

Auggie reached over and squeezed his leg. Then Auggie's eyes went to the rearview mirror, and Theo realized that he'd been caught watching Auggie, watching him touch Orlando. Busted, Auggie's eyes said. More sweat broke out across Theo's back, across his chest, under his arms. He looked out the window. When he looked back, Auggie was still watching him.

Orlando took them out of the city, and they followed a narrow blacktop road behind a Baptist church, across a one-lane bridge, and over a wooded hill. On the other side, the ground sloped down into a field of chest-high Indiangrass. A storybook house stood in the middle of the field: frame with gray siding and blue shutters, a wraparound porch, dormer windows. Flowerbeds full of echinacea, catmint, and the billowing flames of bougainvillea gave way to a perfect lawn. A diamond cutting pattern was visible in the grass. Three cars were parked in the circular drive—two Audi sedans and a Mercedes coupe.

"You grew up here?" Auggie said.

"Yeah," Orlando said, his head still resting on the glass.

"It's beautiful."

"Yeah," Orlando said.

They parked in silence.

Instead of approaching the front door, Orlando led them around to the garage. He keyed in a code, and after the door had rattled up, they snaked past a huge gray Silverado and a Lexus crossover. The third bay of the garage held two four-wheelers. Orlando walked into the house, wiped his feet, and shouted, "We're here."

Theo had been in nice houses before. He'd been in nice country houses before. But the Reeses' home wasn't like any house he'd been in before. Some of the stuff was what he'd expected: high ceilings, wood floors, an open floorplan, granite and stainless steel in the kitchen, thick rugs and swimmable leather sofas in the living room.

What made the home different from everywhere else were the pictures. He recognized Wayne in several of them. Others featured another man. One, a newspaper clipping, had his name in the caption: Calvin Reese. He had a slimmer build than Wayne, but otherwise they could have been twins. Three girls with softened versions of the same family features filled the other frames. All of them were dressed in uniforms or sporting apparel. All of them had at least one picture that showcased them as part of a university team—Cal, for example, was featured with a Mizzou tennis uniform. Not a single picture of Orlando.

They found Orlando's family in the living room. A middle-aged man with thick, salt-and-pepper hair bounced to his feet and shook hands with Theo and then Auggie. "Jerry Reese," he said as they shook. "Reese Automotive." Then he said it again for Auggie's benefit. Orlando's mother, Cathy, was trim, and her hair was dark—expensive coloring, Theo thought, because it looked natural and she didn't have any roots showing. Then the three girls: Chris, the oldest of the girls; Pam, a middle child; and Billie, who was just older than Orlando. All three of the girls had dark, curly hair that they wore long, all three had the strong features that made them handsome instead of beautiful, and all three of them had the strong, firm bodies of athletes.

"We told Mom and Dad that we had to do this," Chris kept saying, laughing between rounds like she was making a joke. "We told them we just had to do this."

"No," Orlando said. "Don't lie. None of you wanted to do this."

"It's not a bad idea," Jerry said. "I never said it was a bad idea."

"It's just so much fuss," Cathy said. "It's a great deal of fuss when he'll be back any day now."

"We don't know that, Mom," Orlando said. "We need to make sure he's ok."

"Oh, Orlando," Cathy said to the rest of the room, rolling her eyes like he wasn't there.

"You know how it is with the youngest," Jerry said to Theo. "Spare the rod, spoil the child."

Theo kept his mouth shut. He wanted to see how far this crazy train could run on its own.

"Don't be rude, Orlando," Billie said. "Offer them something to drink."

"Yeah, Pee—" Pam said, and then she cut off, her face reddening.

"How about a beer?" Chris said. Her voice was deeper than her sisters', and she rose from the couch with easy grace. "Theo will help me. Come along, Theo. Mom, I'll freshen that up for you." She took her mother's glass, hooked Theo's arm before he could say anything, and tugged him toward the kitchen.

"So," Chris said as she filled her mother's glass with fresh ice, "you're the sleuth."

"Not really," Theo said.

"Grab something to drink for you and your—" She hesitated. "Boyfriend?"

"Friend."

"But you are gay, right?" The question was delivered with a kind of frank wonder that almost made Theo smile. "You just don't seem, you know." She flopped her wrist, laughed, and reached past him to retrieve a bottle of Skyy vodka from the freezer.

"Very gay," Theo said. "Extra gay. Like I got a double helping."

"Would you ever consider fucking Orlando?"

"Excuse me?"

"Just theoretically, I mean. I know he's a total wipeout with girls. He's just such a loser. But I thought maybe gay guys had different standards."

Theo forced a smile and opened the refrigerator. He was surprised—and pleased—to see four-packs of Perennial, a craft brewery in St. Louis that he liked. He took a can of their pilsner, and then he spotted a Coke and took that for Auggie.

"He can have a beer," Chris said as she added tonic water to her mother's glass. "Nobody's going to say anything."

"He's nineteen."

Chris beamed at him. "Oh God, you really have a thing for him, don't you? I thought Orlando was just jealous."

"I'll take Auggie his drink."

"Don't run off; I wanted to talk. Just us girls." Chris laughed. "Orlando didn't really promise to pay you, did he? Dad blew his stack when he heard that."

"I don't know anything about that. I'm just helping because Auggie and Orlando asked."

"It's so silly. This whole thing is just so silly."

"Orlando doesn't think so."

"Drama." She sang the word in lilting syllables. "He's just tired of not getting any attention. He thinks this is his chance to shine."

"Is it true Cal has a problem with drugs?"

"Oh my God," Chris said, laughing again. "You're really serious about this, aren't you? You look way too old to be caught up in this kind of thing."

"Where do you think Cal is?"

"Sleeping one off. Probably with that girl."

"What girl?"

"Jessie something. Oh, you're playing detective. You want her last name. Hold on." She took her phone out and tapped the screen. "Jessie McEwen. If you want to talk about drugs, you should take a look at her. That girl." She shook her head. "Can you believe she and Pam were friends in high school? Gross."

It was getting harder and harder to keep the smile in place.

"Just think about it," Chris said, taking the Perennial from Theo and popping it open. She slurped foam and then took a long drink before handing it back. "Preferably before you get dragged upstairs. You'd think the boys were still in high school, with how much time they spend in those old rooms."

"Think about what?"

"Fucking Orlando," Chris said with another husky laugh. "Honestly, I think Dad would pay two thousand dollars just for somebody to pop his cherry."

9

They were there two hours before Auggie finally managed to get Theo alone. Two hours of the Reese Family Everything's-All-Good-Sunshine-Hour-and-Alcohol-Poisoning Show. When they finally got away, Orlando was leading them to Cal's childhood bedroom, and Auggie stopped on the stairs and caught Theo's wrist.

"These people are fucking nuts," Auggie whispered.

Theo nodded. His face didn't change as he reached down and removed Auggie's hand.

"Are you listening to them? They all insist everything's fine. They're all pretty and polished and slightly drunk and evil."

"Ok, they're not evil."

"They're evil."

"Well, maybe Chris."

"All of them. They're like those super bitchy girls on *Pitch Perfect*."

"What?"

"Never mind," Auggie said, thumping his head against the wall. "I forgot you're a million years old."

"Ok," Theo said, starting up the stairs again.

"And why do you get a beer and I have to have a Coke?"

"I'm not doing this with you."

"I've had beer before."

Theo kept going.

Auggie went after him. "Fer lets me have beer."

"Bull."

"Ok, but he pretends he doesn't know I sneak them when he's not home."

"We're not talking about this anymore."

Orlando emerged onto the landing above them and said, "What's taking you so long?"

"Theo was just offering to grab me a beer," Auggie said. "Want one?"

Theo shook his head and kept going.

Auggie laughed and shot past him, taking the stairs two at a time.

"You guys are so weird," Orlando said.

Auggie followed Orlando into the first room off the landing. It was a shrine to Cal: pictures of Cal, tennis whites that had presumably belonged to Cal, trophies with Cal's name on the plaques. The few items that didn't feature Cal in some way were obviously his teenage relics. A 2006 Cardinals World Series poster. An autographed baseball—Auggie couldn't decipher the scribble. A spool of hot pink grip wrap, the kind he must have used on his racquet. A pile of tennis shoes.

"Wow," Auggie said.

"Mom and Dad like to leave our stuff exactly the way we had it."

Theo came into the room at the tail end of Orlando's comment. He was standing behind Orlando, making a *gee! wow!* expression, like Orlando had just unraveled another mystery for him. Auggie had to fight to keep his own face smooth.

"So can we see the Orlando shrine?" Auggie asked.

"If you want to," Orlando said, "you'd better hurry. Mom's been talking about turning it into her craft room, and I have the feeling she's going to do it soon. They already moved my guns down to the basement."

"I thought they left the room exactly the way you had it," Theo said.

Discomfort and embarrassment on Orlando's face made Auggie ask, "Why do you have guns?"

"Hunting," Orlando said, rolling his eyes. "Do you want me to show you? I've got a Savage 110 and a Remington 870."

"No, thanks."

"If you change your mind, I could teach you."

"Thanks, Orlando."

"Sooner is better than later. Mom's going to make me move everything to the basement, or else I'll have to figure out a storage unit."

Auggie examined the room and shrugged. "It's cool to see Cal's stuff, but why'd you want to show us this? Is there something you think we need to see?"

"Oh, I just thought you might be getting a little bored." Then Orlando blushed, huge spots of color in his cheeks. "My family talks a lot."

Downstairs, a loud voice rang out, although the words were muffled. Theo cocked his head and said, "Is that Wayne?"

Orlando nodded. "I figured he'd come over. He usually shows up for Sunday dinner."

"So he'll be here for a while?"

Orlando nodded again.

"I think we should go back to Cal's apartment," Theo said.

"Ok. I'll ask Wayne—"

"Without Wayne."

Orlando's thick brows drew together. "I don't know." Then, as though he were testing thin ice, "I mean, I would, but the apartment is locked."

"You are a bad liar," Auggie said.

The color in Orlando's cheeks darkened.

"You have a key," Theo said.

"No."

"You know where the spare is."

Orlando stared at his shoes.

"Come on," Auggie said. "You'll feel better once we find Cal."

Auggie steered Orlando by the shoulders toward the stairs. They left the house by the front door to avoid passing Orlando's family, and Auggie drove them back toward Wayne and Cal's apartment on the northeast side of the city. The Civic sounded like it was whining more than usual, and once, after turning left, Auggie caught a whiff of something that made him think of overheated wires. In the rearview mirror, he caught Theo looking at him.

"What?"

"Nothing." A block later, though, Theo said, with a painful attempt at sounding casual, "You know, you're welcome to borrow the Malibu. If you ever need to."

Auggie drove two more blocks. He tapped the brakes a little harder than he needed to. He almost missed a turn. He was thinking about Fer driving all the way across the country with him, Fer insisting on carrying everything up to his room, Fer unable to even consider the possibility that Auggie might be able to do things on his own. And overlaying those thoughts was Fer insisting on this piece of shit car, and Theo's little jokes about the Civic all day, and the nice truck that Cart drove. And overlaying that was the way Theo had said, *This is your car? This?* And then his brain ran wild with it: Theo and Cart holding hands, Theo and Cart kissing, Theo telling Cart about the Civic and Auggie and then Theo and Cart laughing like crazy.

"Where's the Pretty Pretty?" Auggie asked.

"Huh?" Orlando said.

"Really quick, just so I know where it is. Let's swing by."

"I'm sorry," Theo said. "What?"

"Orlando?"

"Just turn up here. No, the next one."

"We don't have time for this," Theo said. "Wayne—"

"Wayne's at Sunday dinner," Auggie said. "He's going to be gone for hours, right, Orlando?"

"Well—"

"See?"

In the rearview mirror, Theo opened his mouth and then shut it again. The tendons in his neck looked strained. Finally, he said, "Yep. I see."

Auggie refused to ask what that tone meant.

"It's on the corner there," Orlando said.

"Is it open?"

"Stop it," Theo said.

"I just thought I'd poke my head in. You know, so I'll feel a little more comfortable when I come next time. Do you think you could come with me, Orlando? So I don't feel awkward?"

"Yeah, I mean, I guess."

"Wouldn't it be super weird if we ran into Theo and Cart? Do you ever go to the Pretty Pretty, Theo?"

Just the shrill answer of the Civic's belts and fans.

"Maybe the four of us could go together."

Auggie stopped and pretended to consider an open parking spot along the curb. He let his eyes drift up to the mirror.

Theo's dark blue eyes always made Auggie think of wildflowers. They were wide now, and Auggie couldn't tell if the emotion there was shock or pain or anger or a brew of all three.

"Stop it," Theo said again, quietly.

The flush ran through Auggie's whole body, sweat prickling across his chest, down his belly, up his neck. He shifted the car into gear and followed Orlando's directions the rest of the way to the apartment. He couldn't bring himself to look into the mirror again.

At Wayne and Cal's building, they got out of the Civic, and Theo said, "Orlando, go find the spare and wait for us. Not you. You stay."

Orlando shot a look and said, "Augs?"

"It's fine."

"Um, yeah. Right."

When Orlando's steps were ringing out on the metal stairs, Theo said, "What was that?"

"What was what?"

"Don't do that. If you've got a problem with me, tell me. Don't pretend to be fine and then go out of your way to upset me."

"Why would I want to upset you?"

Theo scratched his beard. Hard scratches. "One more chance."

"I don't know what you're talking about. Did I do something wrong?"

"The other stuff I can let slide, Auggie. I said something dumb. I pissed you off. You came back at me. Fine. But this, this kind of thing. Just so you know, I don't put up with it."

Auggie opened his mouth, speechless, and held up his hands.

A truck blew past them, kicking up the cardboard sleeve from a Wendy's five-pack of nuggets. It skittered across the asphalt.

"Ok," Theo said, nodding. "So that's how it's going to be."

"How what's going to be?"

But Theo was already moving toward the stairs. Auggie waited, letting Theo get a head start, and tried not to be sick.

When they got to the apartment, Orlando had unlocked the door, and he was wiggling the knob. His expression was transparently relieved when he saw them. "Hey Augs, everything—"

"Yep," Auggie said.

Theo didn't even slow down; he just pushed past Orlando and headed toward the back of the apartment. Auggie followed with Orlando, and they found Theo in the second bedroom. It wasn't much different from a lot of the rooms in the Sigma Sigma house, or from the rooms Auggie remembered from the dorm the year before. It had a twin bed with the sheets in a tangled mess, a dresser with chipped paint, a bong that looked like a baseball bat, socks and shirts and underwear in random piles on the floor. On the walls, posters of Rafael Nadal, Andy Murray, and Maria Sharapova hung in an uneven line. At some point, at least one other poster had been displayed in that row, but now only a pair of tacks and a scrap of torn paper marked where it had been. Theo was already pulling out dresser drawers.

"This is Cal's room?" Auggie asked.

"Yeah," Orlando said.

"I'm searching in here," Theo said as he pulled out another drawer and inspected the back and bottom. "You two go work somewhere else."

"Ok," Orlando said.

"We should probably all search in here," Auggie said. "Since it's Cal's room, and we're looking for Cal."

"I don't think so," Theo said, yanking out another drawer so hard that the dresser rattled and the baseball-bat bong toppled over.

"Agree to disagree," Auggie said, moving to the closet.

"Fine," Theo said, tossing down the drawer. He pushed his hair behind his ears, took a deep breath, and said again, "Fine." Then he walked out of the room.

When the sound of cabinet doors opening and closing came from the kitchen, Auggie said, "What's his problem?"

Orlando just shook his head and began digging through the drawers Theo had pulled out.

Auggie opened the closet. A tennis racket stood in one corner. There was a hang rod and a single shelf. Auggie pawed through the clothes—two button-ups, a single polo, and the rest jerseys and t-shirts—and then began removing the shoeboxes that lined the shelf. Nike. Adidas. Saucony. A lone pair of Reeboks.

"I know he thinks he's in charge because he's older than us," Auggie said. "But that's not how this works. We're partners. The three of us."

"Augs?" Orlando said from the pile of clothes he was sorting.

Auggie made a questioning noise as he reached for the next box. He was on the back row now, and he was starting to wonder what Cal had needed with all these shoes.

"You're kind of being a dick," Orlando said.

"Jeez, everybody's so—" Auggie began.

Then he stopped and stared at what he was pretty sure was a bag of cocaine.

10

"Theo," Auggie shouted from Cal's bedroom.

Theo ignored him, pulling out breakfast cereals, toaster pastries, individual packets of oatmeal—the kind with the dinosaur eggs that 'opened' in hot water. He had the vague idea that he would pull everything out of the cabinets first and then search each box more carefully. At that particular moment, though, he was mostly focused on slamming each cabinet door as hard as he could.

"Theo!"

Then footsteps.

"Theo," Auggie said. He and Orlando stood at the edge of the kitchen's tile. Auggie was holding a shoebox. "I think we found something."

"What?"

"Drugs."

Theo dropped a box of Honey Smacks and went to look. In the shoebox, a small plastic bag held off-white powder.

"Is it cocaine?" Auggie asked. "I think it's cocaine."

Orlando was pale under his scruff, his dark eyes huge.

Using the hem of his shirt, Theo opened the bag.

"What are you doing?" Auggie said.

Theo stuck a finger in the powder, smelled it—no odor that Theo could detect—and rubbed it on his gums.

"What are you doing?" Auggie shouted.

"It's cocaine," Theo said. The rush was barely anything, but it was there.

"What the fuck is wrong with you?"

Theo raised his eyebrows.

"What the actual, living fuck," Auggie said, "is wrong with you?"

"Do you have a chem lab?" Theo said.

"Do you have any idea how stupid that was?"

"Or were you going to call the police and ask them to test it?"

"I cannot even believe what I just saw you do."

"Because I thought I remembered Orlando telling us he didn't want to take this to the police precisely because Cal had drug problems."

"Are you kidding me right now? What is going on with you?"

"Auggie, it was a tiny amount that I dabbed." Theo paused, hovered on the precipice, and then it was too late. "Grow up."

Auggie looked like Theo had slapped him.

"So," Orlando said, "you guys are shouting really, really loudly, and I think maybe we shouldn't, you know, shout so much. Not right now."

Auggie was still staring at Theo.

"I'm going to talk to the neighbors," Theo said.

He didn't look back as he left; he didn't think he could stand it.

The neighbor in 3G didn't answer, although the lights were on and Sam Smith was playing inside. The neighbor in 3E kept the door on the chain. She was thin, with stringy gray hair, and she could have been any age between forty and seventy. When Theo mentioned Cal's name, she shut the door, and he heard the bolt go home.

The day was impossibly hot, and sweat made Theo's shirt stick to his back. He walked to the end of the corridor and leaned on the railing. Below him, heat shimmered up from the asphalt. Sunlight ran across the cars, gleaming back from chrome trim, warping along glass. The hot tar smell still hung in the air. Theo clutched the rail with both hands, his knuckles white, his heartbeat pounding in his ears.

Then he went down to the second floor and tried 2F. The woman who opened it was in scrubs, and she was hopping on one foot as she pulled on a sneaker. She smiled when she asked if she could help him.

"This is kind of strange," Theo said, "but I'm trying to help Wayne Reese track down his brother. Do you know them? They live above you."

"I probably know them better than anybody else in the building," the woman said as she switched feet. "Not that that's saying much. Their arguments are my personal soundtrack at this point. Well, all the ones I've been home for. I work second shift at the hospital."

"Do they argue a lot?"

Her smile got a little bigger. "You don't know them very well, do you?"

"I guess not. Any chance you saw Cal last weekend?"

"A week ago? I can barely remember yesterday. And I'm going to be late, so I've really got to go. I'm sorry."

"That's ok. Thanks anyway."

"I hope you find him. Is he ok?"

"We hope so."

Theo moved down the hall, and behind him, he heard the woman's keys as she locked the door. Then the woman said, "The fights get pretty bad, you know. I've had to call the police twice. Just noise complaints, but honestly, it's because I've been scared."

Turning back, Theo said, "Any idea what they fight about?"

She shook her head. "Money? Everything? I can't hear clearly enough to make out the words, but it's been worse lately."

"Mind if I ask you one more question?" Theo said.

"Besides that one?"

Theo smiled. "Yeah, kind of a bonus. Memory is a funny thing, and sometimes one thing will help you remember another. Do you remember anything about last weekend? Anything at all? Did you have a visitor? Go clubbing? See a movie?"

"Clubbing?" She shook her head and laughed. "No, sorry. I've got a boring life. The big thing for me is when I order a pizza." Then her mouth widened into an O. "Oh my God, you're going to think I'm insane."

"Nope," Theo said. "I love pizza."

"You're right: I do remember something. It's a tiny thing, but I remember it. I ordered a pizza on Friday; I was off work, so I was home that evening. I always get Gianino's—"

"Because their crust is the best," Theo said.

"Exactly. Only their delivery guy isn't, well, the sharpest. More than once he's taken it to 3F or 1F instead of 2F. So I poked my head out a couple times, hoping I could catch him. And I saw him."

"The pizza guy?"

"No, Cal. He was hanging around on the stairs, and I waved at him."

Theo waited.

"That's it," she said. "I mean, we didn't talk or anything. But he looked like he was waiting too."

"What makes you say that?"

"I don't know. Maybe just because I was waiting."

"That's fantastic," Theo said. "Do you remember what time that was?"

"No," she said with another laugh. "But my phone does." She checked something and said, "I ordered the pizza at 6:07pm, and it usually takes them a solid half hour. So I was looking out my door around 6:30, 6:40."

"Any chance you saw him after that? Saturday? Sunday?"

She shook her head. "Sorry."

"Not at all; you're amazing. Can I get your name and number in case I need to follow up?"

She laughed and blushed, but she gave him her name, Vicki Miller, and a phone number. She threw sidelong glances at him until they parted at the stairs, and she went down, and Theo went up.

He found Auggie and Orlando in Cal's room, shoving clothes back into the drawers and straightening up as best they could. Auggie refused to look at Theo. Orlando gave him a single glance and then blushed and looked away.

"A neighbor saw Cal waiting outside around 6:30pm last Friday night," Theo said.

Auggie nodded.

"She saw him on the stairs," Theo said, "which makes me think he was nervous or anxious or excited. Otherwise, why wouldn't he wait inside, where it's cool? Combined with the drugs, it sounds like he was going to score."

"Drugs on demand," Auggie said as he stuffed a sweatshirt into the dresser. "Personal delivery. But why does he need to buy drugs when he's got cocaine in a shoebox?"

"Maybe he didn't want cocaine. Maybe he wanted something else."

Auggie made a face; Theo refused to react to it.

"What do we do now?" Orlando said.

"Nothing. You guys are done."

Auggie shook his head.

"Is there a problem?" Theo said.

Auggie said nothing.

"Then let's go."

They walked outside. Orlando locked the apartment and replaced the spare key under the doormat. Not a great hiding spot, Theo thought. Anybody could get inside. Anybody could get in while Cal was asleep. Or somebody might have thought both brothers were out of town. Somebody who knew they kept drugs and cash and valuable memorabilia in the apartment. Somebody who got frightened when he realized Cal was there, and then an accident happened. Lots of ways things could go bad.

As they went downstairs, the sound of chanting voices came from a distance. Theo could see a crowd moving up the street toward them.

"What's that?" Auggie said.

"Another demonstration," Orlando said.

"Demonstration for what?"

Theo and Orlando traded looks.

"What?" Auggie said.

"It must have happened before you got here," Theo said. "A girl was shot."

"Oh my God. But what are they demonstrating about? Gun control?"

"A black girl," Theo said. "She was unarmed, walking alone. A police officer shot her. With everything going on in St. Louis, the Michael Brown shooting, it's—well, it's stirred up a lot of powerful feelings."

"Oh my God. It wasn't Cart, was it?"

Theo stopped.

"I'm just asking if he's ok," Auggie said.

"You're unbelievable."

"He's the only cop I know. It just—I just thought of it. I wasn't trying to say he'd actually do something like that—"

Theo headed for the sidewalk.

"Theo, come on. It's a million degrees outside, and you're going to hurt your knee. I'll drive you home and I won't say anything and I'll apologize as many times as you want."

Orlando said something Theo couldn't hear.

"Theo," Auggie called, "don't be stupid."

Theo shook his head and kept going, and after a while he couldn't hear Auggie anymore. He ran into the crowd of demonstrators, standing to one side as they marched. Men and women, mostly black but with a sprinkling of people from other races. Their banner said *JUSTICE FOR DEJA*. When the crowd had moved on, Theo started limping toward home again.

11

Monday was Labor Day, and a knock at the door woke Auggie. He stumbled out of bed and answered.

"Get your ass up, little bro," Dylan said, shoving a blender bottle at him. "Lacrosse tryouts."

"What?" Auggie rubbed his face, considered the blender bottle, and realized he was wearing nothing but a pair of boxers printed with unicorns. A guy whistled from the hallway, and Auggie groaned. "I don't—"

"I'm not taking no for an answer," Dylan said. "Shorts, t-shirt, and the best athletic shoes you've got. Let's go!"

"Don't I need—"

"Yeah, we'll buy you the rest of the gear later. Move your ass, bro!"

The protein shake was awful. Tryouts were even worse. It wasn't that Auggie was uncoordinated. And it wasn't that he was out of shape. He could run, and he could pass—well, he didn't humiliate himself anyway.

He was just too fucking small.

By the end of tryouts, the other guys had turned it into a joke, keeping score every time a guy body checked Auggie, laughing every time he was sent flying.

Auggie was picking himself up while a gang of guys walked away, slapping each other on the shoulders. One of them said, "Let's see him make a jerkoff video out of that."

Auggie started after them. He was surprised when someone caught his arm, spinning him around.

"Get the fuck off me," Auggie said.

"Cool it," Dylan said. His blond curls were dark with sweat and clinging to his forehead. His pinnie and shorts and hell, just about every inch of him, was covered in dirt from when he'd taken a bad fall earlier.

"That dickwad thinks—"

"What? He thinks you're a joke? He thinks you're an internet kid? A one-trick pony?"

Auggie ripped his arm free.

"What are you going to do?" Dylan said. "Go get your teeth knocked out? That'll show him."

"Fuck off."

"You're going to prove him right. You're going to prove you just care about being the center of attention, having a million fans stroke your ego."

The September sun was hot on Auggie's neck. He wiped sweat from his eyes. "So what am I supposed to do?"

"Find your fucking center, little bro. And work your ass off in the gym this year, come back next year, and show that dildo what you can do." Dylan studied his face, laughed, and wrapped a big hand around the back of Auggie's neck. "Come on. We'll get you some decent gear, we'll get you set up at the gym, and we're sure as hell going to get you meditating. Your chi is wack as hell."

Three hundred and twenty-seven dollars later, Auggie had plenty of gear. He also was pretty sure he could hear Fer screaming all the way from California.

Tuesday morning, someone knocked on Auggie's door.

Auggie was in boxer briefs, staring at two outfits on the bed: a tank top that showed a unicorn punching an elephant, paired with running shorts and high-tops; or a pink polo, blue chinos, and penny loafers. It was the first day of school because Monday had been Labor Day, and he was trying to figure out who he wanted to be.

The knock came again. Then Orlando's voice: "Augs?"

Auggie groaned and opened the door a quarter inch.

"Good," Orlando said, pushing into the room. "You're up. We need—oh."

It shouldn't have been weird because they'd been roommates and Auggie had changed clothes plenty of times while Orlando was in the room. But when Orlando's eyes moved up and down, taking in Auggie, Auggie crossed his arms and stared over Orlando's shoulder at the dresser.

"Sorry, I can come back."

"What do you want?"

"This is weird. I'll come back."

"Jesus, Orlando, you're making it so much weirder. What?"

"We need Theo."

"No, we don't. Theo was a bag of dicks yesterday. I don't want anything to do with Theo."

"Well, we need him. If Cal is involved with drugs—"

"If?"

"If he's in trouble, I mean, I don't know who else to ask."

"We go to the police."

"Augs!"

"You said you trusted my judgment. You said if I wanted to go to the police, we'd go to the police."

"Ok, right, but just listen—"

"And Theo was fucking awful to me yesterday."

"Look—"

"And if Cal disappearing is connected to drugs, then you need the police. There was this one detective who seemed all right. Somerset. I think he gave me his card. Hold on."

As Auggie turned toward his desk, Orlando caught him by the arm. When Auggie glanced back, Orlando's face was bright red, and he looked like he wanted to retreat. But he didn't. His touch was light but firm.

"Augs, please don't make me go to the police yet. My family is—well, you saw. And if I go to the police, they will never forgive me. Please don't make me do that. Please."

He'd forgotten that Orlando's hands were soft and strong. Goosebumps worked their way across Auggie's chest.

"Well, what are we supposed to do?" Auggie asked. "I mean, I don't know anything about drugs. I don't know anything about this town, really, except for the college."

Orlando's thick brows came together.

"No," Auggie said.

"I tried to ask Wayne but he just—I mean, it was Peepee this, Peepee that, like I'm too stupid to hold my own dick."

"No, Orlando."

"Please."

"He was a bag of dicks." Auggie couldn't seem to think of another way to phrase it. "You saw how he treated me."

"Yeah, well, you were—" More red moved into Orlando's face. "You were provoking him."

"Excuse me?"

"You know you were. You didn't like when he said you could borrow his car, and then you were—well, Augs, you were kind of mean to him."

Auggie ripped his elbow free.

"And you know what?" Orlando said. "You picked him—"

"We're not doing this, Orlando. We're not going to talk about why you and I didn't work out. You won't like it if we do."

"That's not what I'm saying. I'm saying you picked him, though."

"I said something to him, yeah. But I don't even know if I meant it. I had a lot going on, and I wasn't thinking clearly."

"You'd better figure it out; you made some pretty big decisions about your life because of him. If you're serious about that, if you still feel that way . . ." Orlando hesitated and then, in a rush, said, "Well, maybe you need to do what he said and grow up."

The worst part was that Orlando wasn't saying anything Auggie hadn't thought to himself over the past day and a half. After the lacrosse tryouts, he'd spent most of Labor Day with the Sigma Sigma guys, barbequing on the back patio, playing a pickup game of frisbee, and then following the party to a junior's apartment where he could score a few beers and two shots of tequila. And the whole day—sprawling in a chaise next to the grill, smelling the burgers sizzling, or getting cornered in the kitchen by a twinkie senior who kept touching Auggie's arm, or throwing back the next shot of Milagro—the whole day, Auggie had been trying to figure out why he'd been such a shit to Theo.

He covered his eyes and groaned.

For some reason, this seemed to encourage Orlando because he said, "And you should apologize."

"Ok."

"And you really need to mean it."

"I said ok. Good God, what has my life come to when you're the one giving advice?"

When he peeled his hands away, Orlando had a nervous smile. "So you'll ask him?"

Auggie groaned again.

Orlando's smile firmed, and he said, "And you should probably shave your chest because those little hairs are cute, but I don't think that's the look you're going for."

"Oh my God," Auggie said, trying to shrink behind his folded arms.

"And you only have three of them, so it's not like it'll take very long."

"Get out."

"And Theo is obviously into tweeny hunk Auggie, so maybe trim under your arms because you're getting, you know, a little bushy. And if you aren't already trimming down—"

Auggie shoved him out of the room.

"Shave your pits and wear the tank," Orlando suggested from the hallway.

Auggie shut the door and leaned against it in case Orlando tried to come back with more advice. He spent almost fifteen minutes considering his armpits and trying to decide if he had too much hair, and then he spent another ten minutes looking at the chest hairs from various angles with a mirror. And fuck Orlando, because there were four of them, not three, marching down his breastbone. He wondered if maybe he should just skip classes and figure things out tomorrow. Then he pulled on the polo and chinos and loafers, because he remembered how Theo always dressed for school. He adjusted the lights, took a selfie, and posted it with the tag *Mortal Kombat: Round 2!* And then he took another picture with one arm behind his head, drew a circle where a few dark hairs poked out from under the short sleeve, and posted it with *Be honest: too much?* Then he considered pulling the picture down, killing Orlando, and killing himself.

He was still trying to figure out what was wrong with him as he walked across campus. Morning classes were a bitch, but Auggie had needed to take a full course load, and he was glad to see that he wasn't the only one out and about. Students filled the quad: walking, running, biking, two girls at a stand giving away free first-day-of-school hugs, a long-haired boy on an overturned milk crate begging for the sexual liberation of jellyfish. Many of the students, like Auggie, had dressed up for the first day of classes, but others—usually older students—wore shorts and tees, often looking like they'd just rolled out of bed.

His first class was English, a literary theme class: Adolescence and Erotic Love, taught by Dr. Wagner—Auggie hadn't heard of the professor before, and his ratings were mediocre. The only reassuring thing was the thread that ran through all the comments: just repeat what he says, and you'll get an A. One student objected, saying it depended on the TA, but Auggie wasn't worried about impressing a TA.

The class was located in Tether-Marfitt, a building with flying buttresses and ornamental stonework and stained-glass windows. Last year, it had reminded Auggie of Notre Dame, but now it just reminded him of Theo's Shakespeare in the World class. Inside, the hallways of Tether-Marfitt still had the worn stone and gleaming brass that he remembered. He passed the classroom where he'd met Theo last year and climbed to the fourth floor. Unlike the rest of the building, the classrooms looked like they'd been picked out of an office-supply catalogue: tablet-arm seats, high-traffic carpeting, non-slip rubber treads for even the slightest unevenness in the floors. Auggie found a seat in the back, snapped a selfie with his Riverside Shakespeare—it was going to be a pain carrying that thing every day—

and responded to the comments that were already flooding his earlier posts. Apparently, most guys liked the pit hair.

He decided to give a quick reappraisal, pulling on his sleeve to get a better look at the hair, twisting in his seat to get enough light. A muttered "Oh my God" made Auggie jerk upright.

Theo was standing near the door in tan chinos and a baby blue shirt—something was printed on it, but Auggie couldn't tell what it was from a distance. He had his sleeves rolled up. And his ass. God. The man knew how to fill out a pair of chinos. Theo stared at Auggie, yanking on the strap of his satchel. When Auggie started to get up, Theo jerked his head and moved to the opposite end of the room, where he dropped into a chair next to the blackboard.

The rest of the class filtered in slowly. Auggie pulled out his phone and tapped a message to Theo. *hi!*

Theo had the same edition of the Riverside Shakespeare open on his lap. He was paging through it with what looked like agonizing scrutiny.

Auggie tried again: *hey, I'm really sorry about Sunday.*

He knew the message went through; the class was basically silent, and the sound of Theo's phone buzzing ran through the room. But Theo was still staring at the Riverside Shakespeare like he was deciding if he should rip it apart with his bare hands.

"Theo," Auggie called in a whisper-shout that carried though the room. "Theo! Check your phone!"

Theo didn't move, but Auggie heard again: "Oh my God."

Then the door opened, and a tall, thin man in a dark suit came into the room. He had a bulbous, red nose, and his head wobbled on his neck as he made his way to the blackboard. He scrawled his name, Dr. Wagner, and glanced around until his eyes landed on Theo. Without a word, he handed Theo his briefcase and then shrugged out of his suit jacket and handed that to Theo too.

Auggie had seen that look on Theo's face before. Once, it was when Theo discovered that Auggie had eaten all the rocky road ice cream.

"Oh shit," Auggie whispered.

The girl in the next seat glared at him.

Dr. Wagner was as awful as he looked. He droned on, spending most of the first class reading the syllabus and punctuating his remarks with scathing anecdotes about students who had failed to live up to his expectations. Theo stayed frozen over the Riverside Shakespeare, only occasionally turning a page. After finishing the syllabus, Wagner explained the semester's literary theme—something about nascent ephebophilia and the natural erotic potency of the adolescent, with a charming little riff about the first time he had masturbated. The whole thing sounded misogynistic and a little molesterish. Then a bell announced the end of class, and kids shot to the door.

Auggie waited for the crowd to clear, and then he started toward Theo and Wagner. Theo talked to Wagner in a quiet voice, shook his head to a question, nodded another answer, and then he limped out of the room. Auggie veered after him.

"Mr. Lopez," Wagner called.

Oh shit, Auggie thought.

When he got closer, he could smell something like rubbing alcohol on Wagner. The professor's eyes were whitish with cataracts, but his gaze was unpleasantly sharp as he focused on Auggie. "I understand that you and Mr. Stratford have a previous relationship."

"No—I mean, we're just friends."

"Yes, well, just so we're clear, I will be grading all of your work."

"Yes, Dr. Wagner."

"We don't play favorites."

"I understand, Dr. Wagner."

"I could ask you to drop the class."

And then Auggie understood. "No, please, Dr. Wagner. I can tell this is going to be a really great semester. Your literary theme is so interesting, and it's a perfect fit for what I want to study."

"This is a favor, you know. I have a TA so I don't have to do the grading."

"I know, Dr. Wagner. Thank you so much."

"It's really not fair to the other students."

"I promise I'll work really hard, and I know you'll be tough but fair. All your online evaluations say that you are."

"Yes, well." Wagner stuffed himself into his jacket. "I suppose I am. Dismissed, Mr. Lopez."

Auggie raced out of the room, but the halls of Tether-Marfitt were already emptying. No Theo. Auggie took the stairs down two at a time, thinking he might catch up with Theo because Theo was still limping, but he didn't see him on the ground floor, and he didn't see him outside. He checked his phone and saw that Theo still hadn't replied.

Ok, Auggie thought. We can do it this way.

He went to Liversedge Hall next and took the elevator to the third floor. He passed the main office for the English Department and kept going to the end of the hall. The last door had a plaque next to it that said GRADUATE STUDENT OFFICE. Under the door, the lights were off, but Auggie knocked anyway.

No response.

Ok, Auggie thought. We can do it this way too. He started the route in his head: the library, the student union, Tether-Marfitt again to check the classroom from last year. And if none of those panned out, Auggie would head west to the street with the little brick house. Theo Stratford didn't stand a chance.

12

Theo went to Downing Children's Healthcare Center after Wagner's horrible class. The bus ride gave him time to process the uncomfortable sheen of sexual arousal that had overlain Wagner's lecture. At Downing, he packed up those thoughts and signed in, and then he spent a couple of hours with Lana. His daughter had been seriously hurt in the same car accident that had killed his husband, and although Lana was getting better, the doctors had warned Theo that the most serious disabilities were likely permanent. He held her, her little helmet bumping against his shoulder. He read to her. He checked her for bruises and for signs of bedsores. He didn't cry anymore on the ride home, the way he had for much of the first year. He leaned against the window, watching the city ebb around him. The bus's vibrations passed through his head; they ran all the way through him. Mostly, he felt hollow. By the time he got home, he had almost convinced himself that he had forgotten about Auggie and the shock of seeing him in Wagner's class.

Inside the small brick house, he flipped on the window unit, kicked off his shoes, and carried them upstairs. Two bedrooms were snugged up under the eaves: a larger one, which he had shared with Ian, and the smaller one that had been Lana's. He'd started the process of moving their stuff into the basement over a year ago, shortly after the accident. He'd mostly finished with Ian's stuff—he'd left a few trinkets on the dresser, a few of Ian's shirts that he liked to wear—but Lana's room was still a work in progress. He tossed the shoes in the closet and changed into shorts and an AC/DC tee.

His phone buzzed, and he saw Cart's name on the screen.

"Are you still mad at me?" Theo said.

A slight pause. "Fuck, that's how we're going to start?"

"Yep. Answer the question."

"No, I'm not mad at you. Christ, Theo, I wasn't ever mad at you."

"So, the new routine is that I blow you, and you don't answer my texts for three days."

"I've been busy."

"This is not the day to test my fucking patience."

"I've been busy. Jesus, Theo. Jesus Christ. Is that so hard to believe, that I've been busy? Do you know how they've had us running around ever since these demonstrations started?"

"Ok," Theo said and disconnected.

The phone buzzed again. Theo let it go to voicemail. It buzzed again, this time a text message: *I'm coming over to help with the garage. I'll make it up to you.*

Sticking your knob down my throat isn't a way to make it up to me, Theo texted back. Then he sent a second message: *Don't come over. I'll clean out the garage myself.*

This is fucking bullshit, Cart wrote back.

Theo closed the flip phone. Then he opened it again and powered it off. He stood there, thinking about the line of pills he'd taped to the back of the electrical box of the outlet in his bedroom.

Instead, he went downstairs, got the peanut-butter knife out of the fridge, and was mortaring together two pieces of bread with a good layer of peanut butter when the knock came at the door. His first thought was that it was Cart, driving over here to apologize and, of course, fuck around. Theo was holding the peanut-butter knife in one hand and the sandwich in the other as he marched to the front door. He had the vague thought that he might have to stab Cart to teach the motherfucker a lesson.

With a little juggling, he managed to get the door open, and then he said, "No. Not today."

Auggie was standing there in a pink polo and blue chinos, sockless in loafers, his crew cut perfect as always. He stood with his arms folded, his shoulders hunched, and he said, "Hi, Theo."

"I don't want to be rude," Theo said, "and I don't want you to take this the wrong way, but please go away."

Then he shut the door.

Theo went back to the kitchen, opened a can of White Rascal, and poured it into a pint glass he kept in the freezer. The whisper of cold air made him close his eyes, and he rested his head against the freezer. Then he went back to the front door.

Auggie was sitting on the steps.

"Auggie, come on."

Auggie looked over his shoulder at Theo and shrugged. "I know I messed up. When you're ready to talk to me, I'll be here."

"This is blackmail. This is emotional blackmail."

"Would you feel better if I waited at the end of the block?"

Theo swallowed a scream. When he trusted his voice, he said, "Just get in here."

Auggie's footsteps followed him to the kitchen. Theo took a bite of his sandwich and then a gulp of beer.

"That looks good," Auggie said. "Got one for me?" Then he put up both hands, a tentative smile crossing his face. "Kidding."

They stood there. Auggie wiped sweat from his forehead. He still looked like he was trying so goddamn hard to smile.

"Do you want some water?" Theo asked.

"Sure."

So Theo got him a glass of water.

"Do you want to sit down?"

"Do you want to sit down?"

Theo closed his eyes.

"I mean, whatever you want," Auggie said. "That's all I was trying to say."

"Just sit down."

So Auggie sat.

"Do you want a sandwich?"

"I don't know. Have you washed the peanut-butter knife since the last time I was here?"

Theo stared at him.

Auggie took a sip of water. Then another. He smiled and said, "This is really good water."

"Oh my God."

"Well, I don't know what to say! I mean, you were my best friend before I left, and then you started dating Cart, and I screwed things up because I stopped texting you, and then I screwed things up again by being a jerk when I got back, and I miss you so much that I don't know what to do sometimes, and then I came over here to apologize and you made me drink a glass of water, and I honestly don't know what to say!" Auggie took a deep breath and combed his fingers through his dark hair. "Ok. I know what to say. I'm sorry, really sorry, for how I treated you, and I won't do it again, and I hope you'll forgive me because I was serious about you being my best friend and I don't know how to handle you being mad at me."

Before he could do the next part, Theo had to chug the rest of the beer.

"That bad?" Auggie said. He looked like he was about to cry.

"I'm sorry too," Theo said, wiping his mouth with the back of his arm.

Auggie blinked. "What?"

"I'm sorry. I didn't mean to upset you about the car, but I shouldn't have opened my mouth. I just thought—I mean, I know you like cars, and I thought maybe you'd appreciate it. I realize now that I sounded like a dick."

"You didn't sound like a dick. I was just being too sensitive."

"And I'm sorry about Cart. I mean, I'm not sorry about dating him. Well, today, actually, I am kind of regretting it. But I'm sorry about how I told you. And I'm sorry if I made you feel like I didn't want to be friends with you anymore."

Auggie's dark eyes were fixed on Theo, and as always, Theo felt the same dangerous, prickling heat in his gut.

"You're kind of regretting it?"

"Oh no. We're definitely not doing that."

Then Auggie smiled, a real Auggie smile, the one that was so huge and innocent that sometimes Theo couldn't believe it was real. "So, friends?"

"Friends."

"Friends with benefits?"

"Auggie."

"Kidding! Mostly kidding."

Theo shook his head and cracked another White Rascal, and they moved out to the living room. Somehow, that opened the floodgates, and they both started to talk. Auggie told him about summer, about the weirdness of seeing his ex-girlfriend after he had come out, about his former buddies who avoided him, and about how they'd come crawling back when they'd seen the number of Auggie's online followers surge. Theo found himself talking about his thesis, about short-distance hikes, about his visit home for Fourth of July. He got another beer and talked about things he was surprised he could talk about. He talked about Lana. It was like last year. In some ways, it was better than last year because it was so good to talk to Auggie, because Theo had Cart as a buffer, and he could laugh a little louder, lean a little closer, touch Auggie's arm and leg and smile and have Cart like a safety net. He even heard himself talking about Cart.

"And then he still didn't apologize. He just texted to say he'd 'make it up to me.' Whatever that means."

Auggie's face was unreadable. "It sounds like things are pretty serious. I mean, if you're getting this upset over him. That's not a bad thing. Just an observation. Are you in love with him?"

Theo groaned.

"It's a fair question."

"I don't know. I mean, sometimes I think a part of me is broken, and—" Theo ran a hand through his hair. "And I should not have had that third beer because I was definitely never going to talk to you about Cart."

"You can talk to me about Cart."

"Nope. No." He got up. His knee was still screaming at him from the long walk across town on Sunday, and it had stiffened up again while they sat. A few months ago, he would have been rattling his bottle of Percocet, but Cart had taken possession of the pills—or so he thought—and he was a stingy motherfucker when it came down to it. "Christ," Theo said, massaging his leg. "I've got to finish the garage. That was the only project I wanted to get done before school started, and I didn't do it."

"I'll help you."

"Auggie, come on, it's hot outside, it's crappy work. You've probably got homework."

"No, not today. Just tell me what you need me to do."

"Absolutely not. You'd ruin your clothes."

"So just lend me something," Auggie said, already wriggling out of his shirt. He had small, dark nipples against the light brown of his skin. "There's no way you should be doing that kind of work with your knee jacked up again."

"I don't want you doing manual labor for free at my house," Theo said, trying to keep his gaze at eye level.

Auggie went limp, sprawling on the sofa like he was dead. "You are this unending tangle of drama. You know that right?"

"Ok."

"I'm helping you because you're my friend. That's what friends do."

"Auggie—"

"You let Cart basically rebuild your entire house."

"That was—"

"And don't you dare say it was different."

Theo sighed. "I'll get you some clothes."

He limped upstairs, found a clean pair of mesh shorts and a Nirvana tee with Kurt Cobain on the front. He found socks and an extra pair of sneakers. Then he carried it all downstairs.

Auggie was already in his boxers.

Theo groaned. "We've been over this."

"What?" Auggie said.

"You know what. We've already had this conversation."

"Did you know your floor is sticky?" He lifted one bare foot to demonstrate.

"Since you apparently need a reminder," Theo said, "please keep your clothes on at all times."

66

"You're so weird."

"House rule: at all times," Theo repeated, dumping the clothes he'd collected in Auggie's arms.

Auggie just grinned a huge, goofy grin as he wiggled into the t-shirt. Looking down, he plucked at the fabric and said, "He's kind of cute. Who's he?"

"Kurt Cobain."

"Who?"

"Nirvana?"

Auggie shrugged.

"Never mind," Theo said with a sigh.

They worked in the garage for a while. Although Theo hated to admit it, Auggie had been right: he wasn't up to all the lifting and carrying, so after a couple of trips of hauling junk down to the road, he settled into a lawn chair and directed Auggie. Auggie, for his part, trotted back and forth, sweating and wiping his face with the tee, exposing those faintly defined abs, grinning like this was the most fun he'd ever had in his entire life. Theo went inside and made Country Time lemonade, shook a few ice cubes loose from the tray, and brought out two big glasses.

"Thanks," Auggie said, wiping his face again with the shirt. He took a long drink. Then he said, "In a porno, this is where I'd say something about all the hard, sweaty work I'm doing for you."

Theo coughed lemonade.

Auggie grinned.

"New house rule," Theo said. "No talking about porn. Ever."

"So many rules," Auggie murmured and took another drink. "You're so strict."

"Auggie."

"Well, you are. Last year you got so mad just because I borrowed—"

"Stole."

"—your blender. And I brought it back."

"Two months later."

"But I brought it back."

"Broken."

"But I still brought it back."

Then he grinned, and in spite of his best efforts, Theo burst out laughing.

When he'd calmed down, Auggie said, "Hey Theo?"

"Uh oh."

"I know it's not my business."

"Oh no."

"But just, you know, for the sake of argument, what if Cart really did have a good reason for not texting you?"

Theo blinked a few times. "Are you defending him?"

"No." A faint flush worked its way into Auggie's cheeks. "But I'm saying I think you should hear him out. Give him a chance to explain. And maybe tell him why it upset you that he didn't respond."

"He knows why it upsets me."

"But did you tell him?"

Theo tried to think of a good answer to that. He settled on, "Who are you?"

Auggie smirked. "That's what I thought."

They finished cleaning out the garage. Theo tried to pay Auggie with his last twenty, and Auggie laughed so hard that he had to sit down on the driveway. The swampy Midwestern heat blanketed them, but the sun had started to slide behind the horizon. The air smelled like honeysuckle, and every once in a while Theo got a whiff of Auggie's deodorant. Fireflies had started to bloom in the dusk.

"I made some phone calls," Theo said.

Auggie cocked his head.

"I think I know a few places where Cal might have been scoring. If you wanted any more help looking for him, I mean."

"Yeah," Auggie said, smiling huge and then biting his lip. "Yes. I'd really like that. Thank you."

"It just makes sense," Theo said. "We're a good team."

Auggie nodded. He was still smiling. "Yeah. We are."

13

Auggie was still wearing the tee, shorts, and sneakers that Theo had lent him when they walked toward the Malibu. The sun had stopped just at the horizon, like it was never going to finish setting. That was fine with Auggie. It was a perfect day, even if the air was so thick he felt like he was breathing underwater, even with the mosquitos starting to come out, even with his clothes pasted to him with sweat.

"Do you want to change?" Theo asked.

"Will I blend in better with a polo and chinos and loafers?"

Theo rolled his eyes.

"You just want to see me get naked again."

"I was asking a question. That's all."

"Oh my God, are you blushing?"

"Let's play the no-talking game."

"It's so cute. Your face is the same color as those little red hairs in your beard."

"No talking," Theo said. "Starting now."

Auggie just smirked when Theo handed over the keys.

"Shut up," Theo said.

Auggie gave him his best injured expression.

"You heard me," Theo said.

They drove first to a run-down apartment building south of Wroxall's campus. It was a two-story walk-up with a crumbling brick façade. Someone had papered an entire bulletin board with flyers for FREE KARATE LESSONS – IN-HOME STUDIO – GIRLS ONLY.

"Jesus," Auggie said.

"Please don't call that number," Theo said.

"It's says girls only."

"I know."

Theo led Auggie to a ground-floor unit, 17, and rapped on the door. Only a single light was working in the corridor, and moths bumped up against the milky glass. From inside the apartment came a steady, thudding bass, and then screams of laughter. When the door opened, a girl stood there, her hair fried from too much bleaching, her eyes vacant. A chemical smell, like too-hot electronics, wafted out into the hall.

"Jessie?" Theo said.

The girl turned and shouted over the music, "Jess!" Then she stumbled back into the apartment.

"This is the girl Cal hung out with?" Auggie said. "I remember Wayne saying that name, Jessie. How'd you find her?"

"Chris told me her last name, and then I looked her up in the student directory."

"What's your plan?"

"I'm going to ask her where Cal is."

"Uh huh. And when she doesn't tell us?"

"Why wouldn't she tell us?"

Auggie tried not to groan and said, "Maybe because they're smoking meth right now. How's that for a starter?"

"I'm sorry I didn't come up with a plan that meets your approval."

"It's ok. I've got an idea. Can you butch it up a little?"

"Excuse me?"

"Butch. I'm only asking for a little."

"You're the one who showed up at my house in loafers. Sockless."

"Talk about Monster energy drinks. Stand—no, like this, like you're always trying to make sure she notices your arms and shoulders. Ok. No, not at all. Do you not know how this works? You've got great arms. Killer shoulders. Why are you standing like you're trapped in a paper grocery bag?"

"I'm standing like I normally stand, Auggie," Theo said through gritted teeth.

"Never mind. Just pretend you like the Cardinals and look at her boobs."

"I do like the Cardinals."

"Yeah, like that, only try to be convincing."

Theo was glaring at him, mouth open, when another girl came to the door. Her brown hair had highlights that needed touched up, and she was barefoot in jean shorts and a midriff top. "Yeah?"

"Jessie?" Auggie said.

"Yeah?"

"Where is that cheating motherfucker?"

She blinked. Her eyes were glassy. "Huh?"

"Cal. Where the fuck is he?"

"Listen, you can't—"

"And don't even think about protecting him. Did you know he was cheating on you?" Auggie thumped Theo on the chest. "He's been pumping my bro's girl for weeks now. Did he tell you that? Did you have any idea?"

This was when Auggie looked at Theo.

"And," Theo said in an unnaturally deep voice, "he, uh, took my Axe body spray."

For a moment, Auggie was speechless.

Fortunately, Jessie was already focused on something else. "What the fuck? What the fuck? That cheating motherfucker. I knew it! I knew he was doing somebody else. Where is she? I'm going to cut a bitch. Where is she?"

"He's not here?"

"No. I haven't seen that dickhole for almost two weeks. Who's the girl? Who's this bitch he's been seeing? She's your girlfriend?"

"You haven't seen him for two weeks?"

"No. We did some blow a couple of weeks ago, and he didn't even chip in. I haven't seen him since. I knew that motherfucker was cheating. I knew it!"

Jessie turned away, heading into the apartment with jerkily fast steps.

"Any follow-up questions?" Auggie said.

"No. Is she . . ."

"She's going to cut a bitch," Auggie said. "Do you want to stay around for that part?"

"Not really."

"Axe body spray?"

"Let's play the no-talking game again."

"Frankly," Auggie said, "that would be a relief."

As they backed out of the parking stall, Auggie said, "I thought maybe Saint Taffy's next. That was another place Wayne mentioned."

Theo shook his head. "That's a cop bar. He might have gotten wasted there, and I'd believe he might have started a bender there if it was just booze. Someone would have to be really stupid to try to deal there. And even stupider to try to score."

"So where?"

"Meramec Maniacs."

"Oh, is that one of those urban chic hipster places that are popping up all over town?"

"Less commentary, please."

"You know, like, svelte Missouri movie-star casual."

"Just so you know, this is why nobody likes people from California."

Auggie grinned as he followed Theo's directions out of town. Once they were past the city limits, they followed a state highway into the darkness. The last ember of day was sinking on the horizon. Fields of crops, some still green with big red tassels, some golden-white when the headlights swept across them, were stitched together with long miles of trees or fenced pasture.

"Sorghum," Theo said.

"Pineapple."

Theo smiled. "Sorry. Bad habit."

"I was just teasing. I like when you teach me things. Which one is sorghum?"

"The one with the rust-colored grains."

"Oh. And, just in case somebody didn't know, what's sorghum?"

"It's a grass. Some people eat the grain, and they also make molasses out of it. A lot of it is for animal feed, though."

"Huh."

"As I said, bad habit. I'll be quiet."

"Does your family grow sorghum?"

Theo glanced sideways at him. "Actually, they do. There's been a huge demand for it lately. China is buying a lot of it. Dad and Jacob switched most of the fields over to sorghum last year. They made a killing. Well, relatively speaking. It's not quite movie-star money."

They drove another mile, the headlights carving out parts of the world: a glint of animal eyes, the highway's weedy shoulder, an irrigation pipe, a branch hanging out over the asphalt.

"I don't care about that stuff, you know."

"What?"

"I mean, I'm not a snob."

"I know."

"I just—it's just different from where I grew up."

"I know."

Auggie tried to think of the right way to say what he wanted to say, but they all sounded the same, and they all jumbled together, so he just drove the rest of the way in silence.

Meramec Maniacs was a long, low frame building that had obviously been built in stages and, Auggie guessed, with whatever was cheapest or easily available. In some places, corrugated sheet metal served as siding; in others, strips of what Auggie thought might be tin; plywood, boards, and a few scabs of vinyl siding covered the rest of the structure. Light seeped through a thousand cracks, and when Auggie turned off the Malibu, the twang of rockabilly music filled the car.

"Please wait here," Theo said as he unbuckled himself.

"No."

"Auggie, please. I said it nicely. This place is . . . rough."

"I'm not a kid."

"I don't think you're a kid."

"Yes, you do. You think I'm this naïve, spoiled California kid, and you think I can't take care of myself."

Theo released the seat belt, which retracted with a soft whir, and then he pushed his hair behind his ears. "Where's this coming from?"

"I can handle myself."

"That's not what I asked."

Auggie set his jaw.

"I'll be back in five minutes. Ten, tops. Any longer than that, and I want you to call the sheriff."

"What?"

"Kidding," Theo said with a small smile. "Please stay here. I promise I'll be fast."

The door clicked shut, and then Theo was just a dark shape moving in front of the pinpricks of light leaking out of the bar. Auggie drummed his thumbs on the wheel. Then he unbuckled himself and went inside.

The music hit him like a wall, guitar and banjo and drums, a man belting out something about his dog and his truck. Inside, the bar was darker than Auggie had expected, with exposed bulbs hanging at distant intervals. The floor had been chopped up with shoulder-high walls, creating a maze of nooks and crannies where tables and booths were nestled. Men and women filled most of the available space, and Auggie had to turn sideways to squeeze through the crowd. His borrowed sneakers scuffed through sawdust, and every breath brought the stink of sweat, bodies, and beer.

He made his way to the bar and found an opening at the end. When the bartender looked over, Auggie waved once, and the guy— young, with a flattop and a Harley Davidson t-shirt—nodded before moving to fill two pints at the tap. Auggie used the time to study the crowd. Rough was a pretty good description. Big guys with beards and leather vests, hard-looking women in tank tops and booty shorts.

One of the guys, probably not much older than Auggie, stared back at him. He had on a full leather jacket in spite of the heat, the sleeves decorated with metal studs, and under it he was wearing a grubby shirt that said EAT FUCK KILL. He looked jittery, with a twitch under one eye. When he stood, he bumped the table, almost spilling the drinks, but he didn't seem to hear the shouts and complaints of the people he was with. He kept his eyes on Auggie as he came toward him.

Auggie glanced over at the bartender. Flattop was wiping his hands on a towel, watching, obviously not intending to get involved.

"You're in the wrong place."

Auggie looked at EAT FUCK KILL and immediately regretted it. The guy had obviously been hitting the glass pipe pretty frequently: his teeth were brown stumps, and his breath reeked of decay. Up close, the twitch in his face was more pronounced.

"I'm just getting a drink," Auggie said.

"Get it somewhere else. You're in the wrong place."

Auggie didn't break eye contact, but he was aware that the men and women closest to him were throwing sidelong looks, some of them carrying drinks away from the area as though anticipating a fight.

"I'm not looking for trouble," Auggie said. "I just came in here for a drink."

EAT FUCK KILL smiled, exposing more of the brown mess of teeth. "You got something wrong with your hearing?"

"Go sit down," Auggie said. "You're making a mistake."

"Fuck, kid. The only mistake was you coming in here thinking you were hot shit." He grabbed Auggie's arm, yanking Auggie toward the door. Auggie threw one wild look around the room; nobody would meet his eyes. They all stared at their drinks or had their attention fixed off in the distance.

Then EAT FUCK KILL rocked forward. For a moment, a brief look of amazement crossed his face. He went up onto the tips of his toes and squealed. Releasing Auggie, he stumbled to the side, one hand pressed to his back. Theo was there, grabbing Auggie as the other man fell. Theo's face was hard, almost unrecognizable, and he delivered two brutal stomps—the first one landing mid-thigh on the other man, the second coming down on his chest. EAT FUCK KILL wheezed as he curled up on the ground. Bubbles of spit flecked the corner of his mouth.

Without a word, Theo dragged Auggie toward the door. The music was still blaring. My dog and my truck, my dog and my truck, my dog and my truck. A banjo picked up the melody, notes coming faster than Auggie could believe. Then he stumbled through the door after Theo, the night a dark, humid weight falling on him, the inside of his mouth tasting like cigarettes.

Theo just kept moving, hauling Auggie toward the Malibu.

"Theo, I'm sorry—"

"Be quiet."

When they reached the car, Theo shoved him around the front, and Auggie slid into the driver's seat. His face was hot. His eyes prickled.

"Start the car," Theo said.

"I'm sorry."

"Start the goddamn car and let's get out of here before that son of a bitch's friends decide to even the score."

Auggie's breath hitched, but he started the car, backed away from the bar, and pulled onto the state highway.

"Stay in the goddamn lane," Theo said. "Or do I need to drive?"

Shaking his head, Auggie corrected course.

They'd driven for ten minutes before Auggie tried again. "I was just going to ask the bartender if he'd seen Cal."

"I asked you to stay in the car."

"I thought—"

"I know what you thought. Everybody in that fucking bar knows what you thought. Be quiet, Auggie, and drive the fucking car." After a moment, Theo hammered on the car door. "God damn it."

"I'm sorry," Auggie whispered.

After that, they didn't talk except for when Theo barked out directions. Auggie didn't dare ask where they were going, although he could tell that they were heading away from Wahredua. After a while, he saw signs for Kingdom City, and then a blue I-70 sign. Some of the tension had drained out of Theo, and he was rubbing his knee.

When the sign for a travel plaza appeared, Auggie said, "How bad is your knee? Can I stop and buy some ice for it, please?"

"It's fine." Then, seeming to work for it, Theo said, "Thanks anyway."

At Theo's instruction, Auggie merged onto I-70, and they drove until Theo told him to exit at a rest stop. Sodium lights buzzed high overhead, illuminating a grassy strip with concrete-block bathrooms, men's and women's separated by a few cement benches. An old Chevy with a camper shell slanted across two disabled parking spaces, and a sedan was nosed up to the base of one of the lights. Two tractor-trailers were parked along the edge of the lot. Other than that, the stop was empty. Not a person in sight.

When Theo unbuckled himself, Auggie said, "What do you want me to do?"

"Why does it matter what I say?" Theo said and got out of the car.

Auggie rested his head on the steering wheel, wiped his eyes, and then ran after him. They checked the bathrooms first, Theo calling out, "Cleaning crew," several times before entering the women's. Then they made their way around the perimeter of the stop. Theo halted abruptly. Then Auggie knew why: he had smelled death before, and he recognized it now.

Theo stomped on the tall prairie grass to mat it down, moving a few steps and then taking a deep breath. Auggie crept after him. Then Theo stopped and took out his phone. He swept the light back and forth.

"There," Auggie said, where light gleamed on metal. A belt buckle, Auggie realized when Theo steadied the light. And denim. And legs.

Theo nodded. "Call the police. I think we found Cal."

14

They were at the police station most of the night. Detectives Lender and Swinney took turns asking Theo the same questions over and over again, until the answers started to run together in his head. Swinney was all right, based on Theo's previous, limited experience with her. She had her hair buzzed except for a few longer, reddish-blond strands at the front, and she had the hard look of a woman who had seen too much. The problem was that she was partnered with Lender. Lender reminded Theo of a squirrel, with his big bushy mustache and his huge glasses and the invisible aura that suggested he carried a pocket protector. He was a dirty cop, and the year before, he had threatened Auggie, Theo, and Theo's daughter in an effort to find and destroy evidence of his corrupt dealings.

When Theo finally stumbled into his house, it was past five, and he barely had the strength to get himself upstairs and into bed. His last thought before sleep was Auggie. The police had separated them, and when they had released Theo, a uniformed officer had told him that Auggie had gone home hours ago.

He woke a few minutes before noon, his head pounding, his knee on fire from the way he had moved when he had kicked the guy at Maniacs, and his mouth tasting like he'd been eating cat litter. Theo limped downstairs, drank a few glasses of water, and took ibuprofen. He stretched his knee as best he could. Then he hobbled into the shower and cleaned up.

Wednesday meant no classes; he only had to TA for Wagner on Tuesdays and Thursdays, and he had scheduled his own courses for the same days. In theory, having Monday, Wednesday, and Friday free meant that Theo could do readings and work for his classes, grade papers for Wagner, and make progress on his thesis. In practice, it meant that he stretched out on the couch in his boxers and fell asleep again almost immediately.

A knock woke him. The shadows in the house had shifted, and when he looked at the clock, he was surprised to see that it was almost three. His stomach grumbled, and Theo tried to remember when he had eaten last—the peanut butter sandwich the day before, when Auggie had surprised him?

Another, longer knock came at the door.

Theo got up, grateful to find that his knee, aside from being extra stiff, was already feeling better. He made his way to the door and opened it.

Auggie and Orlando were standing there.

"I know you're probably still mad at me," Auggie said, "but nipples."

Theo shut the door.

"It's ok," he heard Auggie say on the other side of the door. "That's actually a good sign."

Theo limped upstairs, found shorts and a t-shirt that smelled clean, and dressed. When he got back downstairs, he opened the door again.

"See?" Auggie whispered.

Orlando didn't look convinced. He was red eyed, and he sniffled without seeming to realize it.

"I'm sorry about your brother," Theo said.

Orlando nodded. "Thanks for finding him. I don't think my family—I mean, nobody else even tried. The police tracked down Cal's Mustang this morning; it was at an abandoned warehouse, that old place that used to be Sexten Motors."

Theo grunted. "A Mustang, and he ditched it at an abandoned industrial park." Then, to Auggie, "Why do you smell like meatballs?"

Auggie elbowed Orlando, and Orlando retrieved a paper bag from the steps and held it out.

"From Mighty Street," Auggie said. "I know you like their food, and I figured you hadn't eaten."

Theo's stomach gave an ominous rumble.

"And I wanted to apologize of course," Auggie said.

"Of course."

"So I'm apologizing. I apologize. I'm really, really sorry about what happened last night. You're the bravest, smartest, strongest professor in the whole wide world, and you kick ass like Chuck Norris."

"Try a soft open," Theo said, snatching the bag from Orlando. "You do the same thing in your papers: you start off too strong."

Carrying the sandwich, he headed to the kitchen.

"I got a 98.5% in your class," Auggie shouted after him.

"98.5%. Not 100%," Theo said without looking back.

"He's just grumpy because he hasn't eaten," Auggie said. "Those meatballs are going to soften him right up."

Theo had left the door open—by this point, he wasn't sure anything less than an airtight concrete vault could keep Auggie out—and sure enough, Auggie and Orlando appeared in the kitchen while Theo was unwrapping the sandwich. The meatballs were still steaming, and the bread was soft, with a good crust—in other words, a perfect meatball sandwich. Theo opened a White Rascal, took a bite of sandwich, gulped beer, and sighed.

"Orlando's fine with water," Auggie said, reaching for the fridge door, "but a beer sounds pretty good to me."

"I will stab the peanut-butter knife through your hand," Theo informed him.

"You know what? Water sounds good too."

The kids sat at the table with their water while Theo ate. Between sips of beer, he tried to figure out how bad it was going to be. Pretty bad, he guessed. Auggie normally would have stayed away for a while and then come back when he knew Theo had cooled off—or when an emergency made it impossible to avoid him any longer. The thought made the meatballs sink to the bottom of Theo's stomach. Maybe that's what this was. Another emergency driving Auggie to his door.

"Spit it out," Theo said as he balled up the butcher paper.

Auggie winced and looked at Orlando.

"Um," Orlando said, looking first at Auggie and then at Theo. "So, my parents."

Auggie nodded encouragingly.

"They want to hire you."

"No," Theo said.

"You haven't even heard him out," Auggie said.

"Fine. What do they want to hire me to do?"

"Us," Auggie said. "They want to hire us."

"The police are saying Cal's death is drug related. There's no way."

"Orlando," Theo said, trying to gentle his voice, "we saw the drugs. You and Auggie found them in his apartment. You knew he was using when you asked Auggie to help you find him."

"I know," Orlando said. He shot out of his seat and began pacing the kitchen. "I know, ok? I know. But there's no way someone killed him because of drugs. No way."

"A lot of deals happen at that rest stop. That's why we went to Maniacs. I asked around, and people I know, people who didn't have any reason to lie to me, they told me Cal used to go there sometimes to buy."

"Why? There are plenty of people who sell drugs in Wahredua. Why would Cal drive all the way out to that rest stop?"

"Better prices," Theo said. "Or a personal connection."

"Someone he trusted," Auggie said. "Or the opposite, someone he thought he could take advantage of."

Orlando shot a hurt look at Auggie.

"I'm just saying he could have had a reason," Auggie said.

"And this is a police investigation now," Theo said. "They'll figure out what happened."

"Like last year?" Orlando said.

"I think—"

"I don't care what you think." Orlando paused, as though shocked by his own words, but then he said, "All my family cares about is . . . is making this look better. I want you to find the truth. If it was drugs, fine. If that's the truth, then fine. But the police are going to sweep this under the rug. They don't care what happened because they think they already know. They think Cal was just some stupid user who got himself killed because he tried to steal from his dealer or because he couldn't pay up. My parents will pay you a lot more than two thousand dollars to come up with something better. I want the truth; you get paid. Everybody wins."

"What you're talking about, sweeping Cal's death under the rug, that's not how the police work."

"Don't do that!" Orlando's voice broke. "Don't pretend that last year didn't happen!"

Theo scratched his beard and looked at Auggie.

"Orlando, will you give us a minute?" Auggie said.

Wiping his cheeks, Orlando nodded and made his way out of the room. A moment later, the front door shut behind him.

"No," Theo said.

"Please."

"No, Auggie."

Auggie slid out of the chair onto his knees. He was faster than Theo, and he caught Theo's legs when Theo tried to back up. "Please, Theo. I'm begging you."

"This is ridiculous. Will you get up, please? And let go of me."

"Please. Please. I will literally do everything you tell me. I won't question you. I won't do stupid things like I did last night. I swear to God, Theo."

He was staring up at Theo, his dark eyes bright, lips parted, the hollow of his throat exposed. Theo couldn't help the thoughts. Theo couldn't even hate himself for thinking them, even though he knew they made him a very, very bad man.

"Why do you care?"

"I want to help Orlando."

"Don't you dare lie to me."

Auggie bit his lip. His fingers were warm and surprisingly firm at the back of Theo's thighs. "I need the money. I didn't take the two thousand; I couldn't take money from them, not after we found Cal dead. But—but I can take money for this, for helping them find the truth. And I do want to help Orlando. He's a total nutjob, but he's—he's actually kind of sweet once he's not a psycho stalker, and you saw how his family treats him."

"You can get a job at Dairy Queen. Hell, you can get a job doing jerkoff videos." And where in the world had that idea come from? "You can make money a million ways, Auggie. I don't want you involved in this."

"I can't do it without you. They won't hire just me; I already asked."

Theo opened his mouth to tell Auggie no.

Auggie's eyes were very soft and very brown.

"Not until I talk to Cart."

"Thank you."

"I'm not saying yes."

"Oh my God, thank you, Theo. Thank you." Auggie was trying to hug him around the legs, and Theo had his hand on Auggie's head, pushing him away, because he was pretty sure he was heartbeats away from popping a life-ending boner.

When Theo finally broke free of Auggie's grip, he said, "And you don't do anything until I tell you what I learned from Cart."

"Of course."

"Swear it, Auggie."

"I swear."

"And you do exactly what I say. When I say it. No arguments."

"Obviously. Of course. Exactly what you tell me to do."

He was giving Theo crazily big, innocent eyes.

"Auggie."

"What? I said I'll do it. Whatever you say."

"Stop looking at me like that."

"This is just me. It's just my normal way of looking."

If anything, his eyes got bigger.

"I hate undergrads. I hate them. You and the rest of them. You all think you're so goddamn funny."

Auggie fell back on the floor, laughing.

"Go away," Theo said. "I need more beer to deal with this shit."

15

Thursday morning, Auggie woke up early. He wasn't sure why he'd woken up early—it certainly hadn't been the plan—but he couldn't fall back asleep either. He lay in bed, watching the digital clock advance towards 7:00am, and checked his social media accounts. He didn't post or reply because it was too early and he had a certain kind of image to maintain, but he scrolled through the feeds.

One platform that he'd never really managed to get traction on was Vine. It featured short, looping video clips that were no longer than six or seven seconds. Auggie had been noodling some ideas for the platform, but his best videos—until now—had been significantly longer than six seconds. In general, his most successful work relied on clear characterization that was established quickly, escalation, and a twist at the end. Six seconds just wasn't enough time to do that. He lay in bed, thinking about that for a while, trying to figure out how he could condense his usual format. Then he tried scrapping his usual format and brainstorming something new. Then he thought about a guy with a bro flow of strawberry-blond hair and a phenomenal beard who was definitely, certainly, positively not Theo.

The thing about this guy who absolutely, completely, totally was not Theo, was that you needed like a million snapshots of him to really understand him. You needed a picture of that instant right when he was teetering on the edge between laughing and getting angry. You needed a picture of how his eyebrows drew together when he was reading Shakespeare—or something equally boring. You needed a picture of how he hooked one heel around his other calf to scratch his leg. You needed a whole series of pictures of him blushing. You could fill a museum with them. The very first hint of color beneath the beard, the crisp pattern of red as the blush solidified, the way he scratched his cheek or shook his head or pushed his hair behind his ears when he got flustered. The end of the blush, when he'd forgotten about being flustered, and his eyes were like watercolors.

Auggie pulled a pillow over his face, told himself no, and then proceeded to jerk off.

When he'd finished, he went to the bathroom, showered, and began getting ready for the day. He was staring in the mirror, toothbrush hanging out of his mouth, trying to get the right amount of gel to get the right amount of texture to get the right amount of lift in his crew cut, when the idea hit him.

"Oh shit," he said to the mirror.

Brock Spafford, who was squeezing zits at the sink next to Auggie, glanced over.

"Oh shit," Auggie told him and then sprinted back to his room.

He grabbed his phone and opened up an app he'd been trying to figure out how to use. Snapchat was still relatively new, but Auggie's gut told him it had a lot of promise. The idea of messages, videos, and images that self-destructed had a degree of intrinsic appeal, but more importantly, there was something about the built-in scarcity, the get-it-while-you-can nature of the app, that he thought was going to make it huge. And, of course, it never hurt to have people hanging on your next video because they knew it would be gone soon.

He messed up his hair so that it looked like bedhead, and then he set up his lights and climbed back in bed. He pulled the sheet to his waist, so that his abs and a hint of dark hair below his navel was visible. Nips out. Until now, he'd been safe, sweet, boy-next-door Auggie—no nips. But that had also been straight-boy, ultracloseted Auggie. And fuck that Auggie.

The first snap in his story was of himself in bed. The next was him just after the shower—water gleaming on his chest, wet hair hanging over his forehead. The next was brushing his teeth, making a ridiculous face. The next was trying to get his hair right. The next was picking out an outfit. The next was nominally picking out shoes, but he angled the camera to get his bare leg and a hint of underwear. The next was his backpack. The next was the front of the Sigma Sigma house. The next was Wroxall's gothic silhouette behind him—he slapped on the geofilter for this last one, because he was still trying things, and geofilter was new. Most of the guys in the frat didn't pay any attention; they knew who he was, and they knew what he did. Auggie did see a couple of them check their phones, and one guy—a junior named Tripp—did some pretty vigorous adjustments while staring at the screen.

Then Auggie saw the time and, swearing under his breath, sprinted to class.

He got to Tether-Marfitt two minutes after nine. He got to the fourth-floor classroom three minutes later. When he slipped into the classroom, Dr. Wagner was already droning on about something—it sounded like the publication history of *Romeo and Juliet*—and Auggie tried to sneak to the back of the class.

"Mr. Lopez," Dr. Wagner said in his dry, nasally voice. "I'm so glad you could come to class."

"Sorry," Auggie said, creeping toward the aisle that would take him to the back of the room. "I'm sorry I'm late."

"Please sit down, Mr. Lopez."

"Right. Yes, sir."

"Now, Mr. Lopez."

Auggie threw a frantic look at the front row, which was totally empty except, of course, for Theo. Auggie shot across the room and dropped into the seat next to him. Dr. Wagner watched the whole thing, waiting in silence while Auggie unpacked his laptop, a piece of chalk suspended in one hand. Auggie's face was hot as he opened the laptop and woke it up. He stared at the screen.

"If you're ready, Mr. Lopez?"

"I'm really sorry."

"I suppose you've decided you don't need to bother bringing your textbook to class."

Auggie stared at his backpack. "I forgot it. I'm sorry. It won't happen again."

"There's no point in you staying if you don't have your textbook, Mr. Lopez. Kindly remove yourself from the room."

"He can share with me," Theo said, sliding his copy of the Riverside Shakespeare to a spot between him and Auggie. When Dr. Wagner opened his mouth, Theo said, "Just for today."

Wagner chewed on this for a minute. Then he said, "You're very lucky you have such a good friend, Mr. Lopez."

Auggie tried to melt into his seat.

"Not everyone gets that kind of special treatment," Wagner said before turning back to the board, where he began scribbling dates again.

"Oh my God," Auggie whispered, his eyes screwed shut.

"Forget that old fuck," Theo whispered, "and open your eyes and take some notes."

After that, Auggie assumed class couldn't get any worse. But Wagner had clearly marked Auggie for punishment, and his retribution took the form of questions.

"When was the first, unauthorized quarto version published? Anyone? Mr. Lopez?"

Auggie's mind went blank. "I don't know. I'm sorry."

A few minutes later: "And, of course, the authorized quarto was published, yes, anyone? Mr. Lopez?"

"I'm—I'm sorry."

"I thought maybe you were late because you were doing the reading," Wagner said with a kind of ghoulish glee. "I see that I was wrong."

Auggie sank down in his seat.

"1609," Theo whispered.

"What?"

"The third quarto was printed in 1609, and it's the version the editors of the First Folio used in 1623."

Auggie shook his head.

"He's going to ask you," Theo said; Wagner was still droning on about the authorized quarto.

"I did the reading. I did it, Theo. I swear to God."

"I know."

It was the way he said it, so matter of fact, that helped more than the words themselves.

"And of course," Wagner said, "the third quarto emerged in, yes, Mr. Lopez, I'm sure you can help us with this one."

"1609."

Wagner stared at him for a long, silent moment. Then his gaze slid to Theo. "Well, we can't all have the TA sitting next to us, can we?" Then he began to talk about the textual variations of the third quarto.

Auggie started to pack up his laptop.

Theo's hand was warm when it closed around his wrist. The calluses were always a surprise; somehow Auggie forgot, again and again, how rough Theo's hands could be.

"Don't give him the satisfaction," Theo said.

"I'm getting you in trouble," Auggie said.

Theo rolled his eyes. "Wagner couldn't get me in trouble even if he wanted to. He's a thug and a drunk, and he's taking out his complete failure at life on you."

Auggie grabbed his backpack.

"Don't you dare put the laptop away," Theo said, squeezing Auggie's wrist. "Your ass is staying in that seat, and you're going to take notes and get an A in this class."

"What the hell kind of teaching assistant are you?"

"The kind that specializes in bullying smart but annoying undergraduates into reaching their full potential. Laptop open, Auggie. You're missing stuff that will be on the test."

The class got better after that. Not much, but better. Theo didn't stick around to talk; he was out the door before Auggie had finished

GREGORY ASHE

packing up his stuff. Auggie thought he might find him downstairs, where they could talk without Wagner listening to them, but Theo was gone.

Auggie dug out his phone and checked Snapchat. He was surprised to see he'd gained over a thousand followers in the last hour. And he was even more surprised to see a snap from dylan_j199. It was clearly an answer to Auggie's first snap: it showed Dylan in bed, his blond curls tousled, his eyes sleepily half open, a tiny smile tugging at the corner of his mouth.

He'd scrawled across the bottom of the snap, *nice way to wake up.*

Auggie hesitated. Then he took a snap of himself grinning and giving a goofy thumbs up and scribbled *very nice* and sent it back.

16

After the debacle in Wagner's class, the rest of Theo's day had been smooth sailing. He went to Downing, saw Lana, and made it back in time for class. He was taking a class on Renaissance lyric poetry and another class on the Victorian novel; the Victorian class was a required one, which meant reading a lot of 'greatest hits' along with a generous helping of Matthew Arnold. When classes were over, Theo held his office hour—nobody came, which he assumed was partly because it was the first week and partly because he was only a teaching assistant—and then biked home a little before five.

Cart's truck was in the driveway, and Theo did some mental juggling as he coasted to a stop. The day was hot, the air thick with humidity, and the chickweed and dandelions in Theo's front lawn were growing rampant in what was for them perfect conditions. The summer perfume of charcoal and searing meat floated to him from the back of the house. Theo wiped sweat from his face, dismounted, and adjusted his satchel. He walked the bike down the driveway and locked it up in the (now mostly empty and clean) garage.

Cart was standing at the grill. He was wearing a Cardinals shirt and jersey shorts and slides, which meant he'd had time to go home and change after his shift, and he was swearing under his breath and rubbing his head as he bent over the grill, considering something.

"You're going to burn your eyebrows off," Theo said. "I'd say you'll burn your hair off too, but you don't have enough for that."

"I'll still be better looking than a sorry-ass motherfucker who gets the fifteen-dollar wash and set at the Beauty Barn. How do you like your steak?"

"Medium-rare," Theo said, leaning against the deck's railing. "And I don't get the wash and set. I just cut the ends off with some kitchen scissors every couple of months."

"You're not getting medium-rare. Sorry."

Theo pushed his hair behind his ears.

"You can't stare at the steaks forever, Cart. You're going to have to look at me sometime."

"No, I brought sunglasses. I'm going to put them on and just stare at the wallpaper. You won't even be able to tell."

A robin fluttered onto the branch of an oak tree at the edge of the property. It checked itself with its beak, and then its little head swiveled before it burst into flight again.

"I cannot believe I burned these fucking steaks. I can't even goddamn believe it. I am one miserable, sorry, dumbass country motherfucker if I can't even grill up a decent steak. I brought some of that cabernet you like, and I brought real plates and real silver, and I even brought a tablecloth."

"What is a redneck son of a bitch like you doing with a tablecloth?"

"Fuck if I know," Cart said, still bent over the grill and poking one of the steaks with a pair of tongs.

"Cart?"

"I didn't burn the green beans. That's something, right? They're in the oven with bacon and those little almond slivers." Cart almost looked up then, catching himself at the last minute, as he mumbled, "I bought them at the Piggly Wiggly."

"Cart."

"And I got you some of that fudge cake from the Family Bakery. I think you like that, right?"

"Ok," Theo said. "Apparently we're doing this the hard way. Stand your ass up straight and look at me."

It took a minute, but Cart complied. His eyes kept darting away, and he must have forgotten he was holding the tongs because he tried to shove his hands in his pockets and then started swearing under his breath and scrubbing at the smear of char they left on his shorts.

"Full attention, please."

"I'm listening."

"Eyes and ears, Cart."

It took another full minute.

"I'm sorry I got so upset when you didn't text me," Theo said. "And I'm sorry I made a comment about how much of your personal life you share with your coworkers. Just so you know, it's really upsetting when you don't communicate with me. I understand that you get busy, but I need the occasional check-in. I feel really uncertain about things with you because, frankly, I'm scared shitless and sometimes I feel really, really guilty. About Ian. When you don't respond to my messages, my brain goes into overdrive with that kind of stuff."

"Yeah, well, I'm sorry too."

"You've got to do better than that."

"Well, I'm sorry, motherfucker. What do you want me to say?" That huge shit-eating grin broke out on Cart's face for an instant. "That didn't really sound like an apology, did it?"

"Not even close."

"Look, I know I'm a dumb son of a bitch. I know I'm lucky a guy like you would even consider, you know, a guy like me. I know I fuck things up every time I turn around." He rubbed his buzzed head. "I don't know what to tell you. I'm a miserable, stupid, fucked-up hoosier motherfucker, and I wish I treated you better. My brain is fucked every way from Sunday. I don't know what I'm doing anymore."

The robin had settled on a sweetgum tree farther down the line. The sun was huge and low in the sky, not quite sunset yet, but the shadows were long. Cart's gaze dropped to the deck, and then he looked up for a moment, an uncertain smile playing across his face.

"So what are we going to do differently?" Theo said.

"I can't promise I'm not going to get mad. I'm stupid as fuck, and I've got a temper."

"You're not stupid. Quit saying stuff like that."

"Well, I know I'm not as smart as you."

"I said quit it."

"I won't ignore you. I can't promise I won't get mad, but I promise I won't ignore you again."

"Ok. And I won't make comments about things that aren't my business."

Cart gave another of those uncertain smiles.

"But I have to say one thing," Theo said. "You know that whatever this is, Cart, if it's going to keep growing, it can't be a secret forever."

He scuffed one of the slides across the deck. "I know."

"I won't live like that."

"I said I know. Christ, is all that hair messing with your hearing? I ought to chop it off right now. Get me a knife and get over here."

"You are a fucking barbarian. You realize that?"

"Course."

"And you're shit at the grill. From now on, I'm grilling."

"Course."

"Then get the fuck inside and take your shorts off."

Cart blasted him with that crazy-ass grin and ran inside.

After, when they were curled up together on the floor, Theo grunted and squirmed, trying to find a position where the boards weren't quite as painful on his back, resting his head on Cart's chest.

"Do you have even an ounce of body fat? Jesus, you're almost as uncomfortable as the floor."

One of Cart's hands came up to stroke lazily through Theo's hair. He was making a quiet, rumbling noise in his chest. "I've never been so happy as I am with you."

Theo found Cart's arm, rubbed it lightly.

"Don't even know what the fuck I've been doing the rest of my life. Like you're the first thing that come into it that made any sense." He took a deep breath, his chest heaving under Theo's head, and his voice was tight when he said, "And Jesus fucking Christ, I feel like you're a million times too good for me and you're going to wake up one day and figure it out."

Rolling onto his stomach, his chin on Cart's ribs, Theo just stared at him.

"I'm going to, you know, tell people," Cart whispered. His fingers were still running through Theo's hair. "I ain't so fucking stupid I'll let you get off the hook. Not if I can help it."

"You're stupid enough to say ain't."

"That's cause I'm a goddamn redneck. Come here and kiss me."

Theo swatted his belly and said, "Let me brush my teeth."

"No, just—" Cart swallowed, his Adam's apple bobbing. "Just kiss me."

So Theo kissed him.

"I can taste it," Cart said.

"And what about me, dumbass?"

"I didn't say it was bad, I just said—aww, fuck." And then he pulled Theo down and kissed him again. "Maybe next time, I could . . ." He cupped Theo's dick.

"If you want," Theo said. "But only if you want." Then he swatted his belly again. "Now let's eat those charcoal bricks you call steaks."

The steaks weren't actually that bad, and the green beans from the Piggly Wiggly were surprisingly good. They talked about their days, and they talked about the demonstrations, and Cart explained the cut scabbing on his shoulder where someone had caught him with a sharp-edged rock. They both relaxed with the wine and the food, but the best part of the meal, by far, was the fudge cake from the Wahredua Family Bakery. Theo had a second slice, flipping Cart the bird when Cart started to laugh.

"So what's going on with Cal's death?" Theo asked as he scraped his spoon across the plate, gathering the last of the fudge. "If you want to talk about it."

Cart hesitated. "I don't know if I should say anything."

"Ok."

"Because you and that kid found him."

"You know his name."

"I just don't think I should say anything."

"I said ok."

"I'm not trying to pick a fight. It's just cause they might want to talk to you and that kid again."

"If you don't feel like you can talk about it, that's fine. We're not going to fight about that. But if you keep pretending you don't know Auggie's name, we're going to have a fight. A real one. Do you understand me?"

Cart made a face.

"Well?"

"I heard you."

Then Theo did something, and he didn't like himself for doing it. Picking up both their plates, he carried them to the sink and ran the water. "Has Upchurch talked any more about retirement?"

"No."

"I still think you should go up for detective when he does."

"He's not retiring anytime soon."

"He's got to be close to twenty years," Theo said. "You never know. Guys get their pension and then they take another job. He could go anytime."

"Maybe."

Theo grabbed a sponge and ran it over the plates; the dishwasher was on the fritz, so for the time being, he was washing everything by hand.

"It's just so fucking frustrating," Cart said. "You wouldn't believe the kind of sloppy work they're doing on this investigation. I mean, he's been dead for over a week. Blunt force trauma to the head. He's lying in the grass at the rest stop, but his car's not there. He's supposed to be there to buy drugs, but why the hell he has to drive all the way out there, nobody can say. Tell me how that adds up to a drug deal gone bad."

"That's what Lender's saying?"

Cart grunted.

"What about Swinney?" Theo asked.

"She doesn't like it, but she's not going to contradict him in front of the patrol officers." Theo heard more wine being poured, and when he looked over his shoulder, Cart was taking big drinks. He wiped his mouth when he finished and said, "I mean, do some fucking policework. He was wearing mismatched socks, for Christ's sake. His car's thirty miles away. Someone killed him, dressed him, and dragged him out there."

"Maybe he just put on the wrong socks."

"Nope. We talked to a woman—the chief sent me and Peterson out there, to the apartment. She said she'd seen him standing outside, waiting for someone. She was sure he was barefoot. She said she thought he was going to burn his feet on account of the day was so hot."

Theo thought about Vicki Miller, who had told him about Cal waiting outside, and he decided he'd call her and see if she was the same woman who remembered seeing Cal barefoot.

"That's what I'm talking about," Theo said. "You'd make a great detective. You're already doing better work than Lender and Swinney."

Cart made a disgusted noise.

"You are."

"You've got to have a degree to be a detective."

"So get a degree."

Cart made the same noise again.

"Why not? If you're right about Upchurch and he's not going to retire anytime soon, you've got time. You're plenty smart. If you need help, I'll do my best unless it's math."

"I'm not going back to school."

"Why not?"

Cart threw back the rest of the glass of wine. That crazy grin broke out across his face again. "Come here," he said, "and let me show you what I do to pretty long-haired boys with too much book learning."

17

By the end of the first week, Auggie was exhausted. On top of homework, creating content for his platform, managing his accounts, actually going to class, and hanging out with friends, he'd been spending two hours every day with Dylan at the gym. The workouts were ferocious. Dylan was relentless. And Auggie was aware that the way Dylan treated him—like an adult, demanding the best from Auggie and not settling for anything less, forcing him to try new things like meditation and tai chi in search of spiritual balance—was something he'd never had before, something he'd craved. He was also aware, at the back of his mind, that he was spending too much money; the blender bottles, protein shakes, and recovery drinks had set him back another two hundred dollars. Set Fer back, to be accurate.

On Friday, he dragged himself out of his last class and considered going back to the house for a nap. Instead, though, he forced himself to cross campus, heading for Liversedge and Theo's office. And after a few minutes outside, he started to feel better. The heat had broken, and the air was cool enough to make Auggie think of fall. People filled the quad: a circle of long-haired guys and girls with piercings and ripped jeans playing hacky sack; a shirtless guy—Auggie had to tear his gaze away—walking a rope he'd tied between two trees; a pair of freshman girls still wearing their orientation t-shirts and fighting an impromptu battle with branches as swords; a girl with full tattoo sleeves and a mane of curly brown hair reading poetry to the girl whose head was resting in her lap.

Inside Liversedge, of course, the energy dwindled. Auggie rode up the elevator with a pasty-faced guy who smelled like toothpaste and kept picking at the back of his hand. On the third floor, he had a quick look into the English Department's main office, where a pair of matronly women were stapling things and talking about *Jane the Virgin*. They both vehemently agreed that Jane was better off with Michael, but Rafael had what one of the women called 'SA,' which

Auggie mentally decoded to sex appeal. The other woman just made vrooming noises after she said his name. Rafael, vroom. Auggie couldn't figure out what that was supposed to mean.

But when he got to Theo's office and found the door ajar, he pushed inside. Theo was sitting at his desk, gaze focused on the computer, scratching his beard. His sleeves were cuffed above the elbow. He was filling out those chinos. Theo, vroom. And then Auggie got it. Vroom. Fucking vroom.

"Oh. Hey. How long have you been standing there?"

"Honestly? I don't know."

Theo rolled his eyes. "Shut the door. I was going to text you."

Auggie shut the door and pulled a chair over to Theo's desk.

"I talked to Cart," Theo said.

"And?"

"And I don't enjoy feeling like I'm sneaking information out of my boyfriend."

"He's your boyfriend?"

"Auggie."

"I just didn't know it was official."

Theo crossed his arms.

"Because usually people, you know, go out to dinner with their boyfriends, and they introduce their boyfriends to other people, and they take them to work events, and they double date. Hey, that's an idea. We can double date."

The computer fan whirred.

"There's this really cute upperclassman," Auggie said. "He's been flirting with me hardcore."

"How old?"

"He's been sending these adorable snaps from when he went to a friend's house and played with a puppy."

"You don't want to tell me," Theo said, "so either you don't know, or he's too old for you."

"I think we'd have a ton of fun on a double date."

Through the window came the clack of sticks, then a burst of laughter, and then a mock scream.

"I mean, did you guys actually say those words?" Auggie asked. "Like you both said, 'Ok, we're boyfriends now.'"

Theo scrubbed his face. "Ok," he said. "Here's what we're going to do: let's start over." He dropped his hands. "Hi, Auggie. How was your day?"

"Great. Great day. So good. Do you want to see a picture of Dylan? He's the upperclassman I was telling you about."

"Sure. Then I'll be able to recognize him when he shows up on *To Catch a Predator*."

"I'm nineteen."

"I remember." Theo held up a hand to stop Auggie from speaking again. "Cart thinks this was more than just a drug deal gone wrong."

"Cart's not a detective."

"Auggie, cut it out. I'm not going to do this with you."

"Ok, ok. I'm sorry."

"He says it wasn't even staged very well to look like a drug deal gone wrong. He's pretty sure someone killed Cal at his home, dressed him, and drove him out to that truck stop because they knew Cal had bought out there before." Theo ran through the rest of his conversation, including the detail of the mismatched socks. "I called the neighbor, the one I talked to, and she said she remembered that Cal was barefoot when she saw him. I asked her why she didn't say anything about it when I talked to her the first time, and she said, 'You didn't ask me.'"

"So helpful."

"Right. So this is the part of the conversation where I tell you that the only responsible thing to do—the only safe thing to do—is communicate these inconsistencies to the detectives in charge of the case and let them pursue the investigation."

"No."

"Auggie, please."

"You said you'd help me. You agreed. I said I'd do whatever you told me, and you said you'd help me."

"I said I wanted to talk to Cart first. Now I've talked to him, and I want you to drop this."

Auggie shook his head. "I'm not trying to be stubborn. Honestly. I know you think I'm—I'm immature, and maybe I am. But here are the facts: Cal was murdered, and the police aren't handling the investigation right, and Orlando and his family need help. And you and I both know it's not as simple as passing along information. Lender is dirty. And dangerous. And if he's not following up on something as simple as mismatched socks, then it's probably because there's a reason."

Theo leaned back in his seat. "I'm sorry, let me get something straight: you're going to get involved in this investigation because you're afraid a dirty cop is helping to cover up a murder?"

"Well, I don't like it when you say it."

"I'm going to call Fer. I'm sorry, Auggie, but I think I have to."

Auggie's first instinct was to cry. His second was to shout. He clamped down on both of them and kept his voice as steady as he could. "You can call him."

"He's not going to let you do this."

"He doesn't get to decide that. And neither do you. I do. Me, Theo. You might not like it, but I'm an adult."

"Adults don't rush into murder investigations. Adults don't take stupid risks."

Standing, Auggie nodded. He scooped up his backpack and slung it over a shoulder. He wanted to say something profound and mature, but his eyes were stinging, and he had to blink frantically to keep from crying. He made his way to the door.

"They won't pay you," Theo said. "You told me they won't pay you unless we both do this."

"I'm not doing it to get paid. Not anymore."

Theo made a frustrated noise. "At least tell me you're not doing this because Orlando's manipulating you, because you think you're in love with him or something."

"Please. Orlando couldn't manipulate a marshmallow. And you know I'm not in love with him."

"Are you doing this to prove something to me? Is that what this is about?"

"No, but it's adorable that you thought it was a possibility." Auggie took a deep breath. The air tasted like cumin and chai and cheap weed. He put his hand on the doorknob. "Thanks, Theo. For, you know, helping find him."

"Oh, for fuck's sake," Theo said, kicking the empty chair and then standing. He grabbed his satchel and dragged the strap over his head. "You're going to do whatever I tell you."

Auggie bit his lip, but the smile slipped out anyway. He nodded.

"And we're not taking any stupid risks."

"Definitely not."

"And I'm not going to manipulate Cart for information. I'm not going down that road."

"That's really ethical of you. Especially since he recently became your boyfriend."

Theo stabbed a finger at Auggie. "Keep it up. Keep pressing your luck." Then he let out a wild growl, grabbed Auggie, and maneuvered him out the door. "Come on. We're going to talk to Orlando."

"Great," Auggie said. "And Theo?"

Theo stared straight ahead, still manhandling Auggie toward the elevators.

"You can just get back to me about that double date whenever you want."

18

They crossed campus, heading south toward the Sigma Sigma house. Kids filled the quad, laughing, shouting, a group of them playing with bubble wands. Theo barely noticed any of it. He was still replaying the conversation in the office. He was still trying to figure out what had happened.

He'd had it all clear in his head. After the conversation with Cart, he'd scripted the whole thing out: what he was going to say to Auggie, how he was going to respond. He knew Auggie well enough to predict some of the moves, and he knew himself well enough to plan so that his outright fury at the thought of Auggie risking his life didn't overwhelm him. It had all been going well until—until what?

Until Auggie had refused, fucking refused, to listen to reason.

And then the whole thing had come crumbling down. Christ, Theo thought, Jesus fucking Christ, if he'd cried, if he'd even shed a tear, you probably would have offered to dance the cha-cha naked with Dr. Wagner. That's how much power you're letting him have over you. One kid, a sophomore who can't even grow chest hair. That's how much control he has over your life.

Auggie's laugh made Theo glance over, and he saw Auggie looking at his phone, where a short video was playing. In the video, a guy with blond curls was lying on his side, letting a puppy climb on him. The puppy got about to his shoulder when he tumbled off, and then the blond guy swore, fumbled, and caught the puppy at the last second. The video ended with the guy getting puppy kisses all over his face, his eyes squeezed shut.

Theo had taken some art classes, drawing and watercolors, at the encouragement of his therapist. After coming out, after his family's reaction to it, he'd needed something. He'd needed anything. And although Theo didn't consider himself an artist in any real sense of the word, he enjoyed sketching and drawing and painting, and he'd learned a little bit about how to look at the world. If he were going to draw Auggie, for example, it all came down to his mouth. Auggie was very handsome—a little too handsome, in fact, and growing into it in a way that made Theo's chest tight—but it was his mouth that made him, well, Auggie. His huge, goofy smile when he was completely unselfconscious about something. The showstopper smile he used in his selfies. The way he worried his lip when he was reading intently. The flickers of expression—lines, tightness, compression—that made his mouth a barometer.

After Auggie had watched the video again, he pocketed his phone.

"A friend?" Theo asked.

"Yeah." Too casual. Too cool.

So, Theo figured, that was the guy. The upperclassman. Blond curls. Muscular—a big guy without any fat on him. And a sense of humor. Theo wondered if the upperclassman would think getting hit in the side of the head with a wrench was funny.

"Is your leg hurting you?" Auggie asked. "You're making a face."

"Not my leg," Theo said.

"What?"

"I said I'm fine."

They found Orlando in his room. His roommate, who had dark brown skin and huge eyes, was lying on his bed, listening to something on a pair of Beats. He waved once at Auggie and then turned his attention back to his phone. Orlando followed them over to Auggie's. While Auggie unlocked the door, a pair of guys staggered past them. They reeked of weed and booze, and one of them was shouting that they were the pussy patrol.

"Nice crew," Theo said as Auggie opened the door.

Auggie flushed and shrugged.

"You like it here?" Theo said, looking up and down the hall. "I forgot these places always smell like feet. Jesus, is that a communal bathroom?"

"It's an experience, ok?" Auggie said. "Not everybody starts college when they're thirty."

"Wow. I was just asking."

"Yeah, I like it."

"Ok."

"Ok."

"Ok."

"Ok!" Auggie snapped.

"Ok," Orlando said. "Maybe we should go in the room?"

"That's what I wanted to do, but Auggie had to throw a temper tantrum."

Auggie threw the door open hard enough that it bounced back from the wall. He caught it and threw it open again as he marched into the room. Orlando sighed, catching the door on its second rebound, and Theo followed him into the room.

"I don't have a roommate," Auggie said when the door shut. "Is that ok with you?"

"Ok, I'll keep my mouth shut."

"And I haven't washed my sheets this week. I know that's a problem, so I'll wash them tomorrow."

Theo shook his head and stared out the window.

"Anything else I missed? Oh, I didn't pick up my shoes. Sorry, Dad."

"Augs, just chill," Orlando said.

"I am chill," Auggie said. "I'm perfectly fucking chill."

"Let's do this and get it over with before I catch a fungal infection," Theo said. The room looked out on the south edge of Wroxall's campus, and he was watching a guy with a hula hoop try to impress a girl. That's how it was supposed to be. You did stupid, dumb shit, and somebody else found it cute, and that was the end of it. You weren't supposed to innocently ask one question and get your head chewed off.

"Do you hear that?" Auggie said to Orlando.

"Oh my God," Orlando said. "Look, what do you guys want?"

"We're taking the case," Auggie said.

"You are? That's amazing. Ok, I'll tell my parents."

Auggie explained the information that Cart had relayed, and he managed to leave Cart's name out of it. When he'd finished, he said, "Does anything come to mind? Anything about Cal? Anything about who he might have been waiting for, what he might have been doing that night?"

"I knew he was murdered," Orlando said. He was crying, wiping his cheeks without seeming to realize it. "I knew it. Nobody else thought he was in trouble, but I knew."

"The next step is to find who did it, Orlando. Come on, think."

He shook his head. "I don't know. I mean, sometimes he was barefoot. I can imagine him running to the mailbox barefoot, especially on a warm day. Or if he was waiting outside but he wasn't planning on going anywhere, sure."

"Who would he have been waiting for?" Auggie said.

"I don't know. His guy. Like, his dealer."

"But who else could it have been?" Auggie said.

"You're running him into the ground," Theo said. "Ask the right question."

Theo went back to looking out the window, watching hula-hoop guy, but he didn't miss the way Auggie flushed, and he didn't miss the way Auggie had to pull himself together the instant before he lost control.

"I don't know what the right question is," Auggie said. "If I knew, I'd ask."

"The right question is who had a reason to want Cal dead."

In the silence that followed, Theo could hear the pussy patrol making their rounds again. It sounded like they'd gotten some new recruits. Somebody was laughing uncontrollably. Acid, maybe. Tripping.

"Nobody," Orlando said.

"You know that can't be true," Auggie said. "Theo's right, even though he's being a dick about it. That's what we have to think about: who would have wanted him dead?"

"But honestly, nobody. Cal was the sweetest. He was—" Orlando's face threatened to crumple. "He was nice, ok? You saw how the rest of them are. Cal was never like that. Everybody loved him." Then his resolve broke, and he started to cry in earnest.

Auggie put an arm around him, and after a moment, he pulled Orlando against his shoulder. Orlando sobbed for a couple of minutes while Auggie hugged him. Auggie's gaze came up to Theo's, and then Auggie flushed. But he didn't look away, and Theo was the one who broke first.

"What about money, Orlando?" Theo asked.

"I don't know. Maybe. We can go look through his papers. I don't know if we can get current bank statements, but maybe my parents can help."

"You don't know if he owed anybody money?"

"I know he borrowed money from Dad to start the business. He and Wayne borrowed it together. But they paid it back pretty quickly. They've done really well."

"Something with training?"

"Yeah. Private lessons, private coaching, private training. People call it different things, but that's what they do. Basketball, tennis, football, softball, soccer. It's still catching on; they're pretty much the only ones in town who do it, and they're doing well because everything's so competitive these days."

"They're good at all those sports?" Auggie asked. He had pulled Orlando onto the bed, and he sat with his arm around the other boy still.

"Pretty much. Cal played tennis, Division I, and Wayne played football. He was DI too. Everybody in the family's played at that level.

100

Well, you know. Except me. Sometimes they get the girls to help out with pointers, because Chris played softball and Pam played basketball and Billie played soccer, but that's the exception. Most of the stuff they do themselves. They're making really good money, I think."

Theo glanced at Auggie, and Auggie gave a tiny shake of his head.

"What about personal reasons? I know you said everybody loved Cal, but sometimes people carry a grudge, something that might seem insignificant to anyone else."

Orlando hesitated. Then he said. "Maybe Genesis."

"Who's Genesis?"

"My ex-girlfriend."

"Girlfriend?" Theo said.

"Cool it," Auggie said.

"I'm bi," Orlando said, blushing. "She and my brothers had some sort of argument about breaking a contract. I don't really know. I mean, my dad told me it was all fine, and she and I . . . we weren't dating anymore by then."

"That sounds like a money problem," Theo said.

"Ok, well, I didn't really think about it that way."

"How are we supposed to help you if you don't tell us important details like that?"

"He's going through a lot of shit," Auggie said. "Will you back off?"

"What about his girlfriend?"

"Jessie? She's not really his girlfriend."

"She seemed pretty mad when she thought he was cheating on her."

"What?"

"Never mind," Auggie said. "I'll tell you later. Anyway, she's out of the picture. I stalked her on social media; unless Aunt Marissa's sixtieth birthday party was an elaborate, deepfake hoax with three hundred collaborators, Jessie was out of town the whole weekend when Cal was killed."

"Come on, Orlando. What else? Bullies growing up. Or people that Cal bullied. Or his crazy exes. Or a player he hurt in college. Or a private coach he ran out of business."

Orlando just shook his head. "You don't get it. He wasn't like that, and he didn't do anything like that. He was a great guy. Um, except for, you know. The drugs."

Theo tried a few more times, but he couldn't get anything else out of Orlando. Auggie walked Orlando back to his room, and then he came back and shut the door.

"If they're making that much money," Theo said, "the brother has a motive."

"Are you kidding?"

"You met him. He's an asshole."

"You've been an asshole since we got here. Does that make you a murderer?"

"He has a motive, Auggie."

"Ok, fine."

"And the Volunteers."

"Who?"

"The Ozark Volunteers. The white trash, neo-Nazi dicktuggers who stomp around and pretend they're serious shit. They control most of the drug trade in this part of the state."

"I thought Cart said it didn't look like a drug deal gone bad."

"He did. But Cal was into drugs, and that can go wrong a lot of ways. Maybe he and a friend were using, they fought, and it was an accident. Or maybe someone killed him for his stash, but they missed that baggie you found. I'm just saying we can't close it down."

After a moment, Auggie nodded. "Is there anything else we need to talk about? Because if not, I'm going to text Dylan." He looked like he tried to resist, but then he said, "He's the one with the puppy."

"Just one thing," Theo said. "I'm sorry I said something dumb. I feel like I keep stepping on your toes, and I don't mean to do that. You did a great job taking care of Orlando when he needed it, and you knew how to get him to open up and keep talking. Besides, you're a good friend."

The effect was instantaneous: Auggie's shoulders dropped back, his chest came up, and he glowed. And his mouth. The smile was there, threatening to break out against his best efforts, lighting him up from the inside.

"I, um. I'm sorry I said you were thirty."

"I'm almost thirty, so you're not that far off."

"And sorry I called you Dad."

Theo laughed. "Honestly, that was pretty amazing."

"You're a good friend too, Theo."

"Not really," Theo said with a smile. "You'd better text Dylan. Have a good night. And I'm going to say this while I'm walking out the door so you can't throw anything at me, but be safe, don't do drugs, let a friend know where you are, don't let him pressure you into exploring your body, and if for some reason you do, use protection—"

Groaning, Auggie threw his weight into the door, forcing it shut.

Theo's smile dropped away as he headed for the stairs.

19

Auggie woke to his phone buzzing and a raging hangover. The night before, he'd made the mistake of accepting Dylan's invitation to a party. He'd driven the Civic over to Dylan's apartment, where forty people were crammed into the two-bedroom unit. He'd stuck to beer, and although a couple of guys had cornered Auggie, and one boy had tried to give him a hand job on the fire escape, Auggie had spent most of his time circling Dylan, checking out his bedroom—incense, a macrame mandala, dirty clothes everywhere—and watching the upperclassman, seeing if Dylan would make the first move to take their relationship from friends to something else. Dylan had hardly looked at Auggie, though, and Auggie had felt frustrated but also surprisingly intrigued by Dylan's indifference. Now, he was paying for the beer and the late night. He pulled the pillow over his face while consciousness reassembled, and then he lifted it long enough to peek at the message.

Theo: *Are you awake?*

Auggie let the pillow fall. He was halfway back to a doze when the phone buzzed again.

Theo: *I want to talk to Wayne today.*

After a moment, Auggie managed to unlock the screen and tap out a reply. *Can't.*

And then, because it was Theo, everything got out of sync.

Theo: *Don't tell Orlando.*

And then, almost immediately, another text: *Why?*

Ok, Auggie sent back.

What's ok?

Auggie was still trying to type a reply when another message came through: *Why can't you come? Why did you say ok to that?*

It was too early for this. Auggie abandoned his phone and burrowed under the pillow again. The phone buzzed a few more times, but Auggie ignored it, drifting deeper into sleep. When he woke again, he felt better. Not great. But better. And he figured it was time to keep developing the new Auggie. He set up his lights, got back under the covers, and sent a snap of himself in bed, crazy bedhead, the words *just kill me* at the bottom. A little bit of nipple showing. Then, almost immediately, another snap with the pillow over his head and the words *this is ur fault dylan_j199.*

He got a snap back almost immediately. Dylan had copied his pose, the pillow over his face, although Dylan had massive biceps and the pose showed them off to good advantage. *come over and ill make it better.*

Auggie grinned and headed into the bathroom. He snapped his way through a post-hangover routine, and judging by the snaps back, it was good material. He was thinking maybe this could be a thing, his morning routine snapped out. The same, but different. That's what people wanted—he'd figured that out pretty early.

He was in his room, trying to pick out which tank to wear over to Dylan's—he wasn't going to pass up the invitation—when a knock came at his door.

"Come in," Auggie called.

Theo opened the door and then pulled it almost shut again. "Put on a shirt."

"Grow up, Theo."

"And pants. Put on pants."

"You're making a big deal out of nothing."

"If you put on clothes, I'll give you breakfast from Big Biscuit."

Auggie could smell it now: bacon and egg and cheese, and definitely some delicious form of carbs. He pulled on his *I Do It Online for Money* tank, which featured a television tuned to a rainbow channel, and hopped into a pair of jersey shorts. When he opened the door, he held out his hand.

Theo smiled when he saw the tank, and he placed a paper bag in Auggie's hand.

"I can't go," Auggie said. "And I'm not giving you back this—what is it?"

"A breakfast croissant."

"I'm sorry, Theo. Can we talk to him later?"

Theo shook his head. "I just wanted to drop that off because I figured, first weekend, frat house, you probably needed some food in your stomach. Did you take something for your head?"

"I'm all right."

"Did you drink water?"

"I'm totally fine."

"You really need to drink water. When you're drinking, and when you're hungover."

"I'm not hungover," Auggie said around a mouthful of bacon, egg, and cheese goodness.

"Right," Theo said. "Ok, I've got to get over to Wayne's. Hope you feel better."

"Wait."

Theo stopped in the doorway.

"I mean, shouldn't I talk to him too?"

"You can't go."

"We could go later. Maybe tomorrow."

"It's a murder, Auggie. Every day, it's going to get harder to solve. Anyway, I was thinking about it on the way over, and I actually think it's better this way."

Auggie swallowed another huge bite. "Better what way?'

"You do your thing. Stay safe. Take care of yourself. I'll figure this out."

"Oh, fuck no."

"I'm not cutting you out. I'll still tell you what I learn. We'll work on it together, but this way, we can do it without putting you in danger."

Auggie tore off two savage bites and spoke through the mass of half-masticated food. "Oh. Fuck. No. Daniel. Theophilus. Stratford."

"If it's about the money, you'll still get your half. The Reeses never have to know."

"Get my slides," Auggie said, pointing at the closet.

"Excuse me?"

"You heard me."

"And the magic word is . . ."

"Now, motherfucker."

It had been a gamble, and Auggie let out a silent breath when a tiny grin crossed Theo's face. Theo opened the closet, found the Adidas slides, and tossed them onto Auggie's bed. Auggie polished off the sandwich, snapped an angry face to Dylan, and shoved his feet in the slides. "Let's go."

"No, remember? You can't."

"God, I hate you sometimes."

Theo had biked over, so they took the Civic. They were at a stop light when Auggie turned, grabbed Theo's elbow, and started punching him in the shoulder as fast as he could. Not hard. But over and over again. And not soft either.

"Jesus," Theo said, laughing and trying to twist free. "What the hell, Auggie?"

105

"You know what," Auggie said, releasing Theo's elbow to point a finger at him.

"Jesus," Theo said again. He was still laughing.

"Mother. Fucker." Auggie said, punctuating each word with another punch.

"I'm not going to be able to use this arm tomorrow," Theo said.

"Good. That's the least you deserve."

"What'd I do?"

"Don't do it again, Theo. Do you hear me? Your ass is toast if you do that again."

"What the hell happened to your language? You sound like you've been hanging out with Cart."

"The last thing you want to do, trust me, is bring up your boyfriend right now."

"Touchy," Theo said, but he was still smiling as he massaged his arm.

Then the light turned green, and a horn blared behind them. Something inside the Civic shrieked as they accelerated.

"And quit looking so goddamn pleased with yourself," Auggie snapped.

"Part of it's that it's just so easy," Theo said, a smirk growing, "but it wouldn't be so fun if you weren't smart enough to figure it out."

At the next stop light, Auggie punched his arm another twenty or thirty times. Just to make his point. Theo, the son of a bitch, just laughed and tried to fend him off.

When they knocked on Wayne's door, it opened almost immediately. Wayne was standing there, a sandwich in one hand; behind him, an open bottle of Miller High Life was sweating on the table.

"I guess you can come in," Wayne said. "I've got to leave in a few minutes."

"You said you didn't mind talking," Theo said. "That's why I called ahead."

"Yeah, well, you dicked around, and I had a client ask for an extra session. Come in if you're going to come in."

They followed him into the apartment. Mark McGwire was staring down at them from his frame. On the TV, a pair of talking heads rehashed a Cardinals game from the night before. Auggie had seen the show, but he couldn't remember what it was called. He caught a whiff of the beer when Wayne picked up the Miller High Life, and as Theo closed the door, Auggie pretended to stretch so that he could look over his shoulder into the kitchen. The recycling was full of brown glass bottles.

"Ok," Wayne said. "So how are you going to find this guy?"

"Who's that?" Theo said.

"The guy who killed my brother." Wayne waved the sandwich at them. Bologna, Auggie guessed. "Are you fucking kidding me right now? Peepee said you guys were smart."

"Don't call him that," Auggie said.

"He's my brother. I'll call him whatever the fuck I want. He might have popped your little cherry, but that doesn't give you the right to get involved in family business."

"Let it go," Theo murmured.

Auggie swallowed, but his face was hot.

"You said guy," Theo said. "Did you use that word for a reason? Do you have an idea of who killed Cal? Or is that just a general term?"

After another moment of silent contemplation, Wayne said, "What the fuck are we paying you for?"

"I guess that means it was general," Auggie said.

"I guess so," Theo said. "We were hoping you could tell us a little bit about your business."

"What?" Wayne said. "Why?"

"Because money can be a powerful motive."

"Hold up. Are you talking about me? Fuck that. Fuck both of you."

"We're talking about anybody who would have a financial reason to want Cal gone."

"What's my financial reason? We owned the business fifty-fifty. We'd repaid the original loan. We rent a practice facility, but we were talking to the bank about a bigger loan so we could buy our own place. That's dead in the water, by the way. They won't even talk to me now that Cal is out of the picture. We were making good money when Cal was alive. Now I've got two options: either I lose half my clients, or I hire somebody who's going to do a shit job at what Cal did for twice the money. Tell me how I benefit."

"You're the sole owner of the business," Auggie said.

"Dumbshit, use your brain. His half belongs to his estate. It'll go to Mom and Dad or whoever gets it after probate. Yeah, I know my brother didn't have a will. That's just one more reason I wouldn't want him dead. Probate is going to fuck my business up beyond belief."

"Ok," Theo said, squeezing Auggie's arm when Auggie opened his mouth again. "You won't mind if we look at your finances, will you? Just to verify."

"No fucking way."

"Really?"

"Not a fucking chance."

107

"Mind telling us why? It could help us figure out what happened."

"Sure. Here's why: mind your own fucking business." Wayne devoured the last bite of sandwich and chugged the beer. "That all?"

"What about angry clients?"

"We don't have angry clients."

"Orlando said Genesis, his ex, had some sort of disagreement with you guys."

The transformation in Wayne's face was immediate. "Don't get me started on that cunt. I'm not even going to talk about that."

Auggie didn't cut his eyes to Theo, but he could feel how Theo responded to the words, feel the same shocked curiosity.

"What—"

"I said I'm not going to talk about it. I've got to go."

"Anybody you guys have had money problems with?"

"No. I told you. I feel like I'm just talking to the air here. What's going on with you two? Don't you listen?"

"Ok, just one more thing," Theo said. "Where did you say you were that weekend?"

"Midwest Boys' Basketball Expo. It's an off-season expo. They get some recruiters."

"You deal with recruiters?"

"We train top athletes. You can't do that without at least one recruiter trying to crawl up your butt." Wayne stood and shot the Miller High Life at the recycling can. It went in perfectly, with the sound of glass breaking. "That's time, boys."

They followed him down to the parking lot, and Auggie guided the Civic out onto the street. He went around the block and parked until they saw Wayne leave in the BMW. Then they pulled back into the lot, went upstairs, and retrieved the spare from under the doormat.

"I should probably go in by myself," Theo said. "You'd better stay—ow, ow, ow, Auggie, all right, stop."

The dumb son of a bitch laughed like it had been the funniest joke in the world. And, Auggie had to admit, he smiled a little bit himself once Theo's back was turned.

20

They split up, with Theo heading for Wayne's room and Auggie going into Cal's. Wayne's room could have been the mirror of Cal's: a 2015 Cardinals poster, featuring the full lineup; a Lucite display case holding a baseball autographed by Ozzie Smith; a Rams jersey; a football autographed by Kurt Warner; a pair of battered football cleats mounted on a plaque, next to an award for Missouri All-State Football 2001. The floor was covered in clothes, mostly mesh shorts and t-shirts, and a mixture of mentholated foot powder and funk made Theo stand in the doorway, swinging the door back and forth to clear the air.

The lucky part was that Wayne had piled all his important documents in one place: on top of his dresser and underneath a plate that looked like it had held a grilled cheese sandwich at some point. Even his Social Security card was in the mix, which Theo learned when he picked up the pile and the card slid out. He also suspected that he could do anything he wanted with the papers except organize them, and Wayne would never know. The foot funk and mentholated smell made it hard to focus, so Theo carried the pages out to the living room and left them on the couch.

He went back to the room to do a few more sweeps. On the first pass, he examined the clothes—those on the floor and those in the closet and dresser—for any sign of blood. Cart had said Cal had died from a blow to the head, but he hadn't said anything about defensive wounds or other injuries. Without that knowledge, Theo didn't know how likely it was that the killer might have some sort of biological material on his or her clothes, but he didn't want to miss the chance to inspect Wayne's garments. He considered setting aside all the clothes that had dirt and grass stains, with the theory that the killer might have soiled his clothes in the tall prairie grass at the truck stop. But so many of Wayne's clothes had grass and dirt stains that Theo eventually gave up—and, when he thought about it, a guy who trained kids out on fields all day was bound to have those kinds of stains.

On the second pass, Theo did his standard search for contraband. His youngest brother, Luke, had been a master at hiding things—usually drugs—and Theo had learned most of the tricks from raiding Luke's bedroom. Theo went slowly: furniture, baseboards, the hollow-core door, outlets, light switches, even the light fixture on the ceiling. He found nothing. If Wayne was into drugs or anything else illicit, he was doing a better job hiding it than Cal. Or, Theo thought, he had simply transferred it into Cal's room after Cal had died.

"Find anything?" Auggie asked from the doorway.

Theo shook his head. "Just papers."

"Me too." Auggie held up a sheaf of pages. "Oh, and a few rails of cocaine, but don't get excited because I already did them."

"Funny."

"I thought you'd appreciate it because you've got all the jokes today. Come on, let's take a look at this stuff. We can have some beers and relax."

Theo crossed his arms.

"Kidding," Auggie said with that huge, goofy smile, the one that had nothing to do with Instagram or Facebook or whatever he was spending his time on.

"So funny."

They sat on the couch and pored over the paperwork. By some miracle, Auggie actually seemed to focus, which was a good thing because Theo struggled to make sense of the documents. He was very good at reading things closely—that was his job, after all—but numbers were difficult. He did all right with something straightforward, but all the credits and debits and dates swam together on the page.

"Interesting, right?" Auggie said.

"Yeah."

"Are you seeing what I'm seeing?"

"Let's hear what you're seeing."

"No, you first."

"Um, they're making a lot of money."

"Really? Let me see. No, that's from last October. Theo—wait, why are these out of order?"

Outside, someone was calling sooie, sooie, and then bursting into guffaws.

"Ok," Theo said, "so Ian always balanced the checkbook."

"Oh my God."

"Go ahead, you can laugh. I just—it doesn't make sense sometimes."

But Auggie didn't laugh. He was very still, his eyes not even focused on Theo. Then his gaze shifted. "When was the last time you had a good idea of how much money you had, what's coming in, where it's going, that kind of thing?"

Theo's face was on fire. He stared at the carpet.

"Never mind," Auggie said. "Sorry, it's not any of my business. I can't even believe I said that."

"No, it's—I mean, Ian died over a year ago."

Another of those long silences. The man was still calling sooie, and now a truck was beeping as it backed up.

"Doesn't that stress you out?" Auggie said.

"God, you have no idea."

"Can I—" Auggie smoothed the pages on his lap. "Would you let me help?"

"You really know how to do this?"

"Um, yeah. Fer is super good with it, of course, and he pretty much handles all the money now. But I don't think Chuy even knows how many pennies are in a dollar, and my mom is the same way. For a while, when Fer wasn't living at home, I had to, you know, figure some of this stuff out. And I do a lot of goals, projections, interaction numbers, that kind of thing with my social media accounts."

"I've tried, Auggie. I've really tried."

"Hey, I get it. Like I said, Chuy and my mom can't do it either."

"This is unbelievable."

"It's not as bad as when I had to see your bruised nipples."

Theo put his face in his hands.

"Just in case, you know, that comparison helps."

"It doesn't."

"Well, it's the thought that counts."

"No, it's not."

"Maybe I could help you with some of this stuff sometime."

"Yes. Perfect. That will perfectly wrap up how much my life has fallen apart. Oh shit, Auggie, I didn't mean it that way. This is so fucking embarrassing. Let's pretend we didn't talk about this."

"Ok," Auggie said slowly. "But it's just one thing. Everybody needs help with something. I won't bring it up again, though. Just— the offer is on the table." He smoothed out the pages again, the paper crinkling, and said, "Let me scan through Wayne's stuff and see if it looks similar."

"Great. I'm going to go put my head in the garbage disposal. Come get me when you're done."

Instead, somehow Theo ended up with Auggie's legs across his lap while Auggie stretched out and flipped through the paperwork. He had a tiny furrow between his eyebrows, and his mouth—that oh-so-expressive mouth—kept shifting. He'd bite his lip. Then his mouth would thin out. Then he'd chew the corner of his mouth. Then he'd bite his lip again. Why, Theo wanted to know, would anybody read *Cosmo* or buy paperbacks or watch porn when they could look at Auggie Lopez's mouth all day?

"So, it looks like Wayne was telling the truth. Kind of."

"Kind of?"

"Well, they were taking in between ten and twelve thousand dollars a month."

"Wait, what?"

"Each."

"Holy shit. Do you think anybody wants private Shakespeare lessons?"

"Sure, definitely, all those kids that smell like glue and wear black. Anyway, Cal and Wayne also had a lot of expenses. The facility they rented wasn't cheap, and it looks like they pay installments on a lot of their equipment. I guess it wasn't technically a loan, so Wayne wasn't lying, but he definitely made it sound like they were clearing a lot of income every month. From what I see, they were definitely splitting the money fifty-fifty. It went into Wayne's account first, and then he wrote checks to Cal, so there's no way Cal could have manipulated those numbers. Last year, after expenses and taxes, they both made about fifty thousand dollars."

"That's actually pretty good for a single guy without any debts," Theo said. "So why are they sharing a mid-range apartment?"

"I bet if you asked Wayne, he'd tell you they were saving money, something they could use for part of the purchase of their own facility."

"What do you think?"

"I think Cal had habits that meant he always needed more cash."

"Even making fifty thousand dollars?"

"Well, look. He took out regular cash withdrawals. A thousand here. Five hundred here. And it's cash, so once it's out of the account, who knows where it goes?"

"Drugs," Theo said.

"Definitely drugs. Or sex. Or booze. Or parties. Or clubs."

"What about Wayne?"

"I mean, he's socking money away in a savings account. It's not exactly a genius financial move, but he's not hurting for money." Then Auggie frowned.

"What?"

"Well, if Wayne did have a motive, it would revolve around their business. Cal was blowing through his cash. Maybe he'd gotten to the point where he needed more than he was making legitimately. He might have been stealing stuff from their training facility. He might have been doing private lessons off the books. There are a lot of ways Cal might have been threatening the business he and Wayne had built, and Wayne might have decided the only way to save things was to get rid of Cal."

"Shit. I guess we should talk to him again, see if we can pressure him into talking about the business side of things."

"Eventually."

Theo narrowed his eyes.

"There's no point in letting him know what we're thinking. Not yet. Let's wait and see."

"God, you're devious."

Auggie rolled his eyes. "Oh, and I checked Instagram and Facebook. Wayne's private accounts are locked down, but their company has accounts. SportsPeak."

Theo made a face. "It sounds like a douchey orgasm."

Auggie laughed so hard he had to bury his face in the couch. Theo didn't mind. His hand had come to rest on Auggie's calf, and he was surprised at how good it felt. And, of course, nothing was going to happen because of Cart, so it was safe. This was just friend stuff. They could just be friends.

"Anyway," Auggie said, smiling that huge smile, and Theo wondered if anybody else ever saw it, or if all they ever saw was the showstopper grin he put on for the camera. "There are a ton of pictures of Wayne at that basketball expo, and they were posted Friday, Saturday, and Sunday of that weekend. He was definitely there."

"I guess that's something."

"He could have hired someone," Auggie said. "For the murder, I mean."

"I thought you didn't like Wayne being a suspect."

"I don't."

Theo nodded. He was suddenly aware of the light dusting of hair on Auggie's shin, the firm muscle, the heat of his skin.

Then the door opened, and Theo surged to his feet.

"Jesus Christ!" Orlando shouted. He had on a backpack, dark shades, and the guiltiest expression Theo had ever seen on an adult male.

"What the hell are you doing here?" Theo said.

"Me? I'm—I was just going to check on Wayne."

"God," Auggie said. "You are such a bad liar."

21

One minute, Auggie had been enjoying the weight of Theo's hand on his leg, surprised—always surprised, again and again—by the calluses there. Theo smelled the way he always smelled: something he put in his hair and beard, something that made Auggie think of blue cedar needles and moss. When Auggie had been thirteen, spending the night at Logan's house, Logan's dad had taken out a Buck knife and sharpened the blade with a whetstone. That was what part of Auggie's brain recalled as he lay on the sofa, Theo's hand on his leg: the rasp of steel against stone.

Then the door opened, and Theo shot to his feet, red darkening his face. Orlando stepped into the apartment, and the dumbass immediately started lying.

"Check his bag," Auggie said when Orlando tried to lie again.

"You can't," Orlando said, stepping back and spreading his arms like he meant to block Theo.

"Why not?" Theo said. "What's in the bag?"

"Nothing."

"Great. I love nothing. Let me see nothing."

"Augs," Orlando pled.

"Quit lying and tell us what's going on," Auggie said. "You've got zero constitutional rights inside this apartment. You hired us to find out what happened to Cal; no secrets."

The indecision in Orlando's face was painful. "Fine," he said. "Fine. I wasn't coming to talk to Wayne."

"Why were you coming?"

"I can't tell you. I promised somebody I wouldn't."

"Who?"

Orlando shook his head. His thick eyebrows drew together; he looked close to crying. "Please, Augs. I swear it's nothing bad."

"Backpack," Auggie said.

Sighing, Orlando slung it from his back and passed it to Theo. Theo opened it, shook his head, and took out a bottle of charcoal lighter fluid and a lighter.

"Start talking," Theo said.

Orlando shook his head.

"Were you trying to burn down their apartment?"

"No!"

"Were you going to destroy evidence?"

"Of course not."

"Were you going to kill someone and cremate them?" Auggie said.

"Augs! That's not funny."

"I wasn't joking. I mean, not entirely. This is really sketchy, Orlando. What's going on?"

He folded his arms and shook his head again.

"Fine," Auggie said. "But we're not leaving you alone here."

"Wait," Orlando said, "what are you guys doing here? And where's Wayne?"

"Wayne's at work," Theo said, "and you're going to forget you saw us. Otherwise we're going to tell Mommy and Daddy Reese and all your siblings that we caught you sneaking in here."

"Why are you so mean to me? Why can't you be nice like Auggie?"

"I used up all my patience last year," Theo said. Glancing at Auggie, he said, "Anything else?"

"Just the cleanup."

"Right. Take care of that, would you? I'm going to keep an eye on balls-for-brains here."

Auggie saluted as he rolled off the couch. He grabbed the stack of papers he'd brought from Cal's room and returned them. Following Theo's directions, he returned the stack of Wayne's papers to the top of the dresser. By the time he returned to the living room, Orlando's face was white, and he was clutching the backpack to his chest and refusing to look at Theo.

"What happened?"

"Nothing," Theo said, but he looked way too self-satisfied.

"Orlando?"

"Nothing," Orlando mumbled.

Auggie looked at Theo, but Theo just shrugged again.

"Let's go," Theo said.

They moved outside, and Orlando watched as they locked up, shifting from foot to foot. When Theo turned to the stairs, Orlando said, "Aren't you going to put the spare back?"

"No, because if I do, you're going to sneak back here and use it."

"But Wayne will know!"

"Not immediately. It's a spare, right?"

"Augs, tell him to put it back."

"Come on," Auggie said gently, guiding Orlando toward the stairs. "If you'd just tell us what you need in there—and why you're going to destroy it—this would be a lot easier."

Orlando let himself be herded, but he shook his head. "I promised. And it doesn't have anything to do with Cal's death. I swear."

"That sounds exactly like what someone would say in a novel when something was secretly the key to the whole mystery."

"You've read a novel?" Theo murmured.

Auggie looked around for something to throw.

"So, um, what are you going to do now?" Orlando said when they got to the parking lot.

"Drive around the block," Theo said, "and wait for you to do something stupid like try to break into the apartment."

The shock on Orlando's face almost made Auggie lose it; he had to bite the inside of his cheek to keep from slipping. After a moment, Orlando managed to say, "I'm not even going to do that."

"Ok," Theo said. "But we'll stick around just in case anybody else has any crazy ideas."

"Augs." Orlando paused as though not sure how to finish, and he settled for repeating in a slightly more pathetic voice, "Augs."

"Go back to the house," Auggie said, patting his shoulder. "Relax. Take your mind off things."

Orlando took a few steps toward his slate-gray BMW. Then he looked over his shoulder.

Theo held up his flip phone and waved it. "Just so you know, the tracker I planted on you pings me every time you come near this place. I like to get a full eight hours, so don't wake me up in the middle of the night."

"You can't do that!"

"Oh my God," Auggie muttered. "Go home, Orlando."

Orlando marched to the BMW with wounded dignity. He refused to look at them as he pulled out and drove away. When the sound of the car had faded, Auggie shook his head.

"How long before he decides to risk it?" Theo asked.

"A day or two." Auggie shook his head. "You decided to pretend you have a GPS tracker synced to your flip phone?"

"He didn't even blink."

"Yeah, but Theo, that's not the point."

"What's the point?"

"It's so lame."

Theo blinked. "Sometimes I honestly forget you're eighteen."

"Nineteen."

"Right. Nineteen."

"Come here. Let me see that other arm."

Theo grinned and angled his body away from Auggie. "What's that dumbass up to?"

"Orlando? God, who knows? Whatever it is, he wouldn't be doing it if he thought it would hurt his family. Or—or us."

"Or you. Orlando would push me into a thresher if he thought he could get away with it."

"No, he wouldn't." Auggie cocked his head. "Ok, he might."

"Did you believe him when he said it had nothing to do with the murder?"

"I believed him. I'm not sure that's the same thing as it being true, though. I think the right person could convince him to do something, make him believe it was totally unconnected to Cal's death, even if it was actually very important."

"Yeah," Theo said, "that's what I was afraid of. Come on. Maybe Orlando's ex can help us figure out what goes on inside his head."

"I wouldn't count on it," Auggie muttered.

22

Genesis Evans lived with her parents in a suburb that looked like it had been built in the late 1950s, on the southwest side of Wahredua. Most of the houses had two stories, and they either featured Tudor-style timber and stucco or a mixture of fieldstone and wood siding. Her home was one of the latter, and the fieldstones were small and round and reminded Theo of going to the dentist as a child and seeing models of human teeth. The home sat at the end of a long blacktop driveway; the yard had a pair of willows in front that acted as a screen. A sporty black BMW was parked at the end of the drive, a sticker in the rear window proclaiming WROXALL TENNIS.

Auggie parked on the street, and they headed up to the house together. Theo knocked. A moment later, the door opened, and a young woman looked out at them. She was black, her hair done in neat braids, and she was wearing shorts and a t-shirt that said *Black Nerds Unite.*

"Genesis?" Theo said.

She nodded. "May I help you?"

"I hope so," Theo said. "We wanted to talk to you about Wayne and Cal Reese."

Her expression flattened, and she shook her head as she began to close the door.

"Please," Theo said. "We have reason to believe Cal Reese was murdered, and the family has asked us to look into his death."

She hesitated, the door still open a crack. "Orlando sent you."

"He mentioned you," Auggie said. "He told us there was a difference of agreement about a contract."

"Oh my God." Genesis shook her head. "He's still the baby, huh?"

"What do you mean?" Theo said.

"Genesis," a man shouted from inside. "Who's at the door?"

"Nobody," Genesis said over her shoulder. "I said nobody."

"I heard you," the man said. "So who are you talking to?" The door opened wider, and the man standing there was tall and big, wearing a button-down shirt and suit pants. He had his graying hair in a tight flattop. "May I help you?"

"We just needed to talk to Genesis," Auggie said.

"Regarding what?"

"Dad, leave them alone," Genesis said.

"We're just asking a few questions," Theo said.

"I understand that," the man said. "And I asked you what those questions are regarding."

Genesis shook her head.

"The Reese family," Auggie began.

"No," the man said. "You can speak to our lawyer."

He shut the door. On the other side, Genesis said something, her tone familiar to Theo: the disenfranchised late adolescent. Her father said something back. Then the deadbolt went home, and Theo looked at Auggie.

"So much for that," Auggie said.

"We'll try again later. Is she a student? Do you think we could catch her after class?"

Auggie shrugged. "I'll see what I can find."

They were halfway down the drive when an angry shout came from behind them. Mr. Evans, Genesis's father, was coming toward them in a pair of fuzzy moccasins, and next to him was a younger man who was even bigger—possibly Genesis's older brother, to judge by how he resembled Mr. Evans.

"Hey," Mr. Evans shouted again. "Stop right there."

"Jesus," Theo said. "Keep going. Get in the car."

"What?" Auggie said. "Are you kidding?"

"You promised, Auggie. You promised to do what I tell you."

"Theo, please don't do this. Please."

"Auggie—"

"Please. I'm not trying to go back on my promise. I'll do it if you say, but please don't make me."

"If one of them throws a punch, you run for the car."

Auggie was silent.

"Auggie?"

"Yes. Yeah. You're in charge."

Theo glanced over. "Why am I troubled that this was so easy?"

"Because it's a good plan. I'll get to the car, and then I'll run them over."

"Jesus Christ," Theo whispered.

"Young man," Mr. Evans said as he got closer, "I want you to listen very carefully to me. You go back to those scorpions, and you tell them that if they think they can intimidate my daughter, they've got another thing coming. I've already called the police, and you can expect me to file a full report. I have your descriptions, and this will be added to part of the lawsuit. You boys have stepped in it. You've really stepped in it. If you weren't in it before, you are now."

"Mr. Evans," Theo said.

"If I want you to talk, I'll tell you to talk. Do you understand? Get in your car, turn around, and go straight back to them. We don't scare. And I won't stand to have my children threatened in my own home. Is that clear?"

"Mr. Evans—"

"Yes or no."

"I understand that you're upset, but—"

"Yes or no."

Theo looked at Auggie.

"Yes," Auggie said.

"Now take a good look at this." Mr. Evans reached into the pocket of his suit pants and pulled out a revolver. A .38, Theo guessed. "Do you have any questions about this?"

"We wanted to talk to Genesis about—"

"Yes or no."

"No," Theo said.

"This is what you're getting if you come back. I don't care if they put me away for it. You, or anyone like you, show your face around here again, and I'll put all six bullets in you. I don't want you to have any doubt about that. Wise, make sure they understand."

The younger man, Wise, glanced at each of them. Theo recognized the look. This guy was young, inexperienced, frightened, and trying to be tough. Theo had seen the look on his own face growing up when he'd gotten dragged into fights that Jacob and Abel started. He'd seen it on Luke's face when Luke had gone drinking with Theo and some of the guys he logged with. He'd seen it when Luke got in too deep over and over again. He'd seen it on Auggie's face when Auggie had faced down the girl who held Theo at knifepoint. He'd seen it too many times.

"If my dad doesn't kill you," Wise said. "I will. Stay away from my sister. Stay away from our family." He touched the hem of the polo he was wearing, and the fabric tightened over the outline of the gun holstered underneath. "Understand?"

"Yes," Theo said. "I just want to be clear: we're not trying to cause trouble. We're looking into Cal's murder—"

120

"Oh no," Mr. Evans said. "You're not pinning that on any of us. If I'd met that man in the street, I would have shot him dead. You can put a Bible under my hand, and I'll swear to it. I'd have killed him with my bare hands if you gave me half a chance. But I own my actions. That's how we're different from the Reese family. We're not the kind to drag a man off and leave his body in the weeds; if I'd killed him, I'd be telling the whole world. We're not the kind who trap girls in dark rooms."

"What does that mean?" Theo said. "Why—"

"Get off my property," Evans said, gesturing with the .38. The movements were erratic and unsteady, and Theo could see the cartridges in the cylinder. Evans looked agitated enough that his finger might slip—accidentally or, for a man in his state, not quite so accidentally.

"We're going," Theo said, catching Auggie's arm. He moved in front of Auggie, and they shuffled backward together. "We're leaving right now."

"Don't come back," Evans said. "You come back, and I won't bother telling you again."

"We won't come back," Theo said. He still held Auggie's arm. Auggie was shaking. Theo was shaking too, he realized. The .38, which had looked small when it came out of Evans's pocket, seemed very big right then.

Evans and Wise watched them go.

A soft bump and then, "Car," from Auggie made Theo stop moving. "Ok," Auggie whispered after another moment. "Theo, you've got to let go of me now."

"I know."

But he didn't let go. He was watching the .38. He was seeing Luke in the hayloft, flies crawling on his eyes.

"Theo, it's ok. We're going to get in the car and drive away now."

"Yes," Theo said. Then he took a shuddering breath and released Auggie. The younger man sprinted around the car, and Theo eased into the passenger seat. Auggie started the engine, pulled around sharply, and sped back up the street.

At the end of the next block, when the Evans house was out of sight, Theo said, "Stop. Stop the car."

Auggie hit the brakes, and the Civic squeaked to a stop.

Theo grabbed Auggie and pulled him close, one hand in Auggie's short crew cut, one hand around his back, the smell of Auggie's hair in his nose, the feel of his face against his shoulder.

"We're ok, Theo. It's ok."

121

Theo released him and dropped back into his seat. He covered his face. He could still hear the flies. He managed to say, "Ok. You're ok."

"We're ok. We're both ok."

"Right." Theo took a deep breath, but he had to keep his hands over his eyes because it wouldn't help if Auggie saw him like this. "Right. We're ok."

23

Auggie drove back to the Sigma Sigma house at Theo's insistence.

"I really don't think you should bike home," he said when he pulled into the lot.

Theo's face was the color of that white, goopy cheese Fer liked. His mouth pulled into something that was supposed to be a smile, and he said, "I'm fine. Just need some fresh air."

"Theo, please let me drive you home. We'll put your bike in the trunk."

Elbowing open the door, Theo just gave that awful smile again and shook his head.

It didn't matter how hard Auggie argued; Theo wouldn't budge. Auggie stayed outside, squinting into the September sun, as Theo shrank to a black smudge. Then Theo swung around a corner and was gone, and Auggie went inside.

The Sigma Sigma house, by this hour, was busy. Auggie had been making an effort to learn names, so he recognized Kyle Whitney, blond, freckles, chasing Digs—Auggie didn't know the kid's real name—down the hall, snapping a towel at Digs's bare ass. Igor was in the kitchen making a club sandwich; he offered to make Auggie one, but Auggie just got water from the tap and shook his head. The kitchen had a pass-through that connected to a serving area, and the serving area had both doors open to the dining hall, and Auggie found himself watching the guys who had set up a board game—something really complicated, something with a million tiny painted figurines—and were laughing and shoving each other. Auggie only recognized Tayyib, who was trying to grow a goatee; the sophomore rolled dice and then howled with dismay, dropping out of his chair while the other guys jeered.

Auggie dumped out the rest of his water and went upstairs. His thoughts kept pace with him. Other guys played board games. Other guys chased each other with towels. Other guys didn't worry about keeping up Facebook and Instagram and Twitter and, now, Snapchat. Other guys didn't spend fifteen minutes getting the lighting perfect for one selfie before they even went to take a leak in the morning. Other guys didn't think about murders.

Did other guys think, if I could hold his hand, if I could kiss him, if I could make things better for him somehow, if he didn't think of me as such a kid, if I were smarter, braver, stronger older, maybe he'd finally see me, see me the way I see him (everywhere, every time I turn around)? If they did, they didn't talk about it. If they did, it was probably somebody their own age, somebody they actually had a chance with.

In his room, Auggie locked the door, crawled into bed, and pulled the pillow over his face. After a while, he got out his phone and texted Theo: *Are you ok? I'm worried about you.*

He fell asleep waiting for an answer.

When he woke, the thud of a bass line reverberated through the house, and the smell of weed filtered under the door. Guys were laughing, shouting, running through the halls. A voice that sounded like Miller Benitez crowed, "Dude, she is going to suck the fucking root tonight, I swear to God." Auggie groaned into the pillow, now sticky with drool, and pulled it away from his face.

He'd forgotten about the Sigma Sigma back-to-school party. It was a tradition—everything was a tradition—and since this was his first year as a full brother, it was his first chance to attend. Auggie scrubbed his eyes clear and made his way to the showers. Someone was in the stall next to Auggie, making outrageously loud fapping noises and moaning intermittently. Then somebody else picked up on it, and then another guy, and then somebody let out a sharp cry and everything was silent. Whether it was real or not, Auggie had no idea, but a chorus of laughter followed. Auggie laughed along with the rest of them until he remembered Theo, the expression on his face, his tone as he asked, *You like it here?* He rinsed off and left the showers; the other guys were screaming fake orgasms, but it wasn't funny anymore.

Snapping his way through the process, Auggie picked out clothes for the party—a tank that said *I'M THE COOL KIND OF BRO* and his skinniest jeans, paired with the ridiculously expensive Jordans that Fer had bought him last Christmas. He was pulling on his pants when he got a snap back from dylan_j199. It was a picture of Dylan's face, his eyes huge; judging from the background, Auggie thought Dylan was already downstairs at the party. Dylan had scribbled something—a drawing that might have been a dog. A second snap immediately followed, this time only half of Dylan's face, and he was covering his eyes. The text said, *thats a fox. ur a fox. dont judge me, i immediately regretted it.*

Grinning, Auggie finished dressing and headed downstairs. The party was going full force, guys and girls wandering the halls with red plastic cups in their hands, someone in the kitchen asking if they were going to order pizza, another guy selling drink bracelets. Auggie paid and put on the bracelet, and then he got himself a shot, which he did first, and a beer, which he carried with him.

Then he wandered the party. He wasn't looking for Dylan. He was just wandering. He just wanted to get a feel for the night. That's what he told himself every time he disengaged from a conversation, broke away from a group, pretended not to see someone flagging him down. The nice thing about the main-floor layout was that most of the rooms had multiple entrances: he could cut through the kitchen, wave at somebody in the serving area, pretend to spot someone in the dining room, and loop back through the mud room and into the gallery. He cut across the foyer, with its seating area that was only ever used by parents, the upholstery finely patterned with the Sigma Sigma emblem. He worked his way through the massive living room, where a grand piano and an enormous river-stone hearth competed with clusters of seating and flatscreen TVs. When he left through the other side of the living room, he passed the public restrooms.

No Dylan.

Not that it mattered. Not that he was looking.

He made his way downstairs. The frat had invested in a speaker system for the public areas, and a steady selection of recent music accompanied Auggie: Macklemore, Ciara, Pharrell. He could still taste some of the Milagro, even through the beer, and a stripe of heat licked its way from his collarbone to his navel. A blond girl passed him, leading her friend by the hand, and when Auggie looked over his shoulder at her, they were whispering and staring at him. The girls burst out laughing when they realized they'd been caught, and both of them blushed bright red. They ran up the stairs.

In the lower lounge, people crowded the sofas, the coffee tables, even the corners of the room. Some were small groups of guys and girls, laughing and drinking. Some were couples—swaying, dancing, kissing. Theo's beard, when he and Auggie had kissed, had been scratchy, but in a wonderful way, rasping against Auggie's skin until he was about to burst into flames. Auggie drank some more of the beer. He was sweating.

The basement wasn't as easy to loop through; he had to check the rooms one by one. The study—a threesome, two girls and a guy, were making out on the table. The gym—the door locked, empty and dark on the other side of the glass. The mechanical room—the door locked, the strip under the door dark. He skipped the bathrooms, went back to the lounge, and tried the multipurpose room. A blacklight had been set up, making Auggie's Jordans shine as a mob danced and grinded on each other. If Dylan was in there—not that it mattered—Auggie didn't have much of a chance of finding him. He kept going.

In the game room, people were sitting around card tables, heads close together as they shouted over the music. A group of guys was playing pool. Dylan had on a white t-shirt that was so tight Auggie could see his nipples, and he was wearing blue polka-dot shorts that only came to the middle of his thighs. Seeing him in person like this was always so different than the snaps. His hair was darker in the pictures, and tonight, the curls had been given more shape and definition with some sort of product. His face seemed less perfect, although familiar because of the smirk he wore without seeming to realize it. But mostly it was his size that shocked Auggie: he was just so damn big, something that Auggie had internalized from all the hours in the gym but that still managed to surprise him. Auggie, always sensitive about his own height, felt like a kid next to Dylan, but it was more than that. Dylan was built with muscle. He was huge. And he had an adult's definition to his body, not the rangy, stripling growth that many guys carried through most of college. He was chalking a cue, laughing, when his eyes cut to Auggie. He kept laughing, but now the smirk was there again, and he raised one eyebrow.

Auggie sat on the arm of a couch, sipped his beer, and pretended to watch the game.

It wasn't going well for the other guys. Auggie didn't know much about pool—in fact, he wasn't entirely sure that this wasn't some other game that also used a pool table—but he knew a little bit about people. Six guys were playing, split across two teams, and every time Dylan or one of his friends took a shot, the other guys muttered and growled and traded looks. Dylan's little smirk kept getting bigger. Then Auggie saw the cash neatly stacked on the edge of the table.

Auggie wasn't looking when it happened.

"Foul," one of the guys shouted. Auggie recognized him; his name was Trevor, and he played lacrosse with Dylan. He was the same guy who had made the comment about Auggie's jerkoff videos at tryouts.

Dylan looked relaxed; he was almost slouching, the cue tucked up against his shoulder. But his eyes were hard. "That wasn't a foul."

"Fuckface, you hit the cue ball twice."

Dylan shook his head.

"I saw you," Trevor said. "Joe saw you too."

Another guy, presumably Joe, nodded.

"I hit it once," Dylan said. "Now let's finish the game."

"No way. No way. You're a fucking cheater."

"What'd you say?"

The atmosphere in the room shifted abruptly. Music still pounded from the speakers—Imagine Dragons shouting about something radioactive—but everyone had turned their attention to the men around the pool table. One girl stood up, cradling a drink, and left.

"You're a fucking cheater," Trevor repeated. "We're done. And we're taking our money back."

"Seriously?" Dylan said. He glanced at his friends; neither of them made a move, and he shook his head. "Fine. Take your money. Fucking bad losers, that's what you are."

Trevor was counting out cash, and he waved it at Dylan. "Fuck you."

"No, fuck you," Auggie called from across the room. Then, before he could stop himself, he added, "Pussy."

Trevor turned. "What the fuck did you just say, dickhole?"

"I said you're a pussy. Fuck you."

Dylan was watching. He was wearing that little smirk again.

"What a fucking joke," Trevor said, shaking his head at his friends. "He's got a million boys playing with their tits for him, so he thinks he's tough shit."

"Say that to my face," Auggie said.

Trevor looked at him. "You're a fucking joke, and you're not good for anything except taking videos where you tweeze your cunt hairs."

Auggie shot up from the couch and hurled his beer. The beer hit Trevor's shoulder, spraying across him and his friends.

"What the fucking hell?" Trevor shouted as beer soaked into his Vineyard Vines shirt. "You're fucking dead."

Auggie straightened, clenched his fists, and waited. He was painfully conscious of Dylan's eyes on him, but he kept his gaze fixed on Trevor.

Trevor came around the pool table. Amber drops were still falling from the hem of his shirt. The first punch was fast, but Auggie pulled back. He never saw the second one, and it clocked him on the side of the head.

The world seemed to rise up for a moment, and then Auggie was on the ground, blinking, trying to put the pieces of his brain back into place. Everyone was shouting. Sneakers moved in and out of his field of vision. He got himself up onto an elbow, vaguely aware that if this was a fight, he needed to be on his feet. Then Dylan's face swam into view.

"He's ok," Dylan said over his shoulder; everything sounded underwater, even the pounding music. Then Dylan turned back to Auggie and said, "Are you ok?"

"Yeah," Auggie managed to say.

Dylan's eyes narrowed. "You sure?"

"Oh yeah."

"So you can, like, stand up?"

"Uh huh," Auggie said, and then he closed his eyes and lay down.

He wasn't sure if he lost consciousness, but when the world made more sense, he was bouncing up and down, smelling something like sandalwood, and aware of dense muscle underneath him and a hand on his ass. He opened his eyes and saw that Dylan was carrying him upstairs. He patted Dylan's shoulder.

"I'm ok. You can put me down."

"Sure thing."

Dylan kept carrying him.

"No, really."

"Gotcha."

"Ok," Auggie said, and then he slumped down again, resting his face in Dylan's neck.

"Little bro," Dylan said a few minutes later, "you want to tell me which room is yours?"

"Just put me down the trash chute," Auggie said. "Do they still incinerate the trash? That would be ideal."

Dylan laughed and swatted his ass. "Room?"

Auggie groaned.

"Come on. You need to lie down."

"Just put me on the couch. There's a lounge over there."

"Maybe you want a little privacy," Dylan said. His hand had settled on Auggie's ass again, not stroking or caressing, but heavy and solid.

"I'll be fine," Auggie said, most of his attention now shifting to a desperate battle not to throw wood at that exact moment.

"Ok," Dylan said, "either you're really subtly telling me to fuck off, or you're completely oblivious to the fact that I want to hang out with you. Alone. Can you tell me which one? Because you're not as light as I thought."

The words might as well have been a second punch. "Uhh."

"Room?" Dylan said.

"That one," Auggie said. "End of the hall."

When they got there, Dylan lowered Auggie to his feet, steadied him, and smiled. Auggie's hands were shaking a little as he unlocked the door. He flicked on the light, immediately saw the spread of clothes and shoes, and scrambled to pick up the mess.

"Slow down," Dylan said. He caught Auggie around the waist and lifted him again, this time settling him on the bed.

"I just need to—"

"Dude, they're clothes." Dylan kicked the door shut. "You should see my room."

"I saw it. When I went to that party at your place."

Dylan gave him that little smirk. He walked a circuit of the room, his head moving as he examined the walls, Auggie's photography equipment, the stack of textbooks.

"Shakespeare?"

"Yeah."

"Fuck. And you actually understand that stuff?"

"Not, you know, not really." And then, Auggie wasn't sure why, "I hate that boring old shit."

"I hear you." Dylan completed his short trip around the room and stood in front of Auggie. His hands came to rest on Auggie's knees, and he leaned in. His breath smelled like alcohol. "Didn't know you were my own personal bodyguard."

"That guy was a dickwad." Then Auggie felt his face heat. "I mean, I know you could have handled it."

Making a soft noise in his throat, Dylan ran his hands up Auggie's thighs. "Fuck, it was hot, watching you get all riled up."

Auggie grunted when Dylan's hand ran over his erection.

"Is that ok?" Dylan said.

Auggie nodded.

"Oh man, your face. Fuck, sorry. I forgot—I mean, never mind. You just got me all hot, and I wasn't thinking."

"No," Auggie said, catching his wrist. "I liked it."

"This isn't a good idea," Dylan said. "You got hit in the head, and you're, like, eighteen."

"Nineteen," Auggie said, and another wave of humiliation washed over him. He pulled Dylan's hand over his dick and humped it lightly. "And I know what I like."

"Yeah?" Dylan said.

"Definitely."

Dylan hesitated. "Sorry, this is just—"

"Get up here," Auggie said, "and let me touch your dick."

Dylan's little smirk was back as he climbed up onto the bed, straddling Auggie. Auggie touched him through the polka-dot shorts, grinned at the noise Dylan made.

"You're huge," Auggie whispered.

"Fuck yeah, little bro."

Auggie heard the whimper in his throat.

"You like that?" Dylan whispered, his thumb tracing the outline of Auggie's dick. "You want me to call you little bro while I'm pounding your pussy?"

Auggie swallowed. His face was burning. His whole body was on fire.

Dylan didn't wait for an answer. He kissed Auggie. It wasn't a great kiss—Auggie could feel that his own mouth was too tight, and it didn't meet Dylan's properly. Their teeth kept scraping. He bit Dylan's lip, and Dylan swore.

"Ok," Dylan said. "You're shaking, and I'm bleeding. There is no way—"

"I'm just—I'm just really into you."

Dylan's eyes were flat as he considered the statement. Then he reached into his back pocket and pulled out a stainless-steel flask. "You need to relax." He unscrewed the cap, took a drink, and held it out. Then his hand retreated an inch. "Never mind, you're only—"

Auggie grabbed the flask and took a slug. It hit worse than the tequila, burning as it went down his throat, and it reminded him of the Pine-Sol his mom used to clean the kitchen floors. Coughing, he pushed the flask back and said, "What is that?"

"You've never had gin before?"

"No, I have." But it hadn't tasted anything like the floor polish he'd just drunk. "I have, honestly. I just—I mean, I wasn't expecting it."

Dylan shook his head.

"I like gin," Auggie said. "Let me have some more."

"You've probably had enough."

Auggie took the flask and drank again, eyes open and watching Dylan. The heat of the alcohol ran through him. The ache along the side of his face faded a little.

Grinning, Dylan took the flask back. He had a long drink and wiped his mouth with the back of his hand. Then he crawled closer, grinding his erection against Auggie's, and whispered, "You're my little man, huh? Is that it?"

"I'm a man."

"Yeah, you are. You fight hard. You drink hard." Dylan's mouth quirked. "Do you fuck hard?"

"If you're lucky," Auggie said, his mouth dry, "you're going to find out."

That made Dylan laugh. When they kissed again, it was better, and Dylan's hand was confident and rhythmic as he jerked Auggie through the denim. Auggie thought of the last time he'd been in this situation, with Theo, the orgasm coming through him like it was jet powered. Tonight, he could feel it building again, although it wasn't the same. His head hurt. His mouth was sticky. The kissing was going on for too long.

"Hold on," Dylan whispered. He pulled a small plastic case from his back pocket, opened it, and took out a pill. Placing it under his tongue, he watched Auggie carefully. He was very still for a few moments. Then he held out another.

"What is it?"

"Molly."

"Oh. Cool. Molly."

Dylan burst out laughing. "Oh my God. You're such a fucking kid, it's adorable."

"It's just, I don't do, um, harder stuff."

Eyes half closed, Dylan rubbed against Auggie again, his movements slow and languid. "Oh yeah? My little bro doesn't do drugs?"

"Maybe, you know, some weed. I guess."

Dylan made a noise that could have meant anything.

"I just, um—it's just not really my thing."

"It's molly, bro. It's not like I'm doing cocaine. People who do this, they do it because it opens up your mind. It's therapeutic. And it's a spiritual experience, ok?"

"Right. That's really cool. I just don't—I don't know."

Dylan stopped moving. Then he slid off Auggie's lap, landed on the floor, and returned the pill to the plastic case. Auggie watched him.

"Look," Dylan said, "you're a sweet kid. It was cool how you thought you had to stand up for me. But I'm looking for someone who's at the same stage of life, you know? I'm too old for games, and I'm too old for one-night stands. I mean, you're adorable, but you've never even had gin before. Tell you what: let's find you a nice kid who'll blow you tonight. I'll be your wingman."

"No," Auggie said.

Dylan rolled his eyes.

"I know who I am," Auggie said. "I know what I want."

"No, you don't."

"Just because I haven't had as many experiences as you, that doesn't make me immature. And it doesn't mean we're at different stages. People mature at different rates. I really feel like we connected." He had planned out a million different versions of this speech, and it was coming out now, words that he thought he'd use another night, another place, another man. "The fact that you're older just means you get to share things with me that I haven't tried yet."

"I really think—"

"I want to suck your cock," Auggie said. "And then I want you to fuck me."

"Ok, fine, but it's weird if only one of us is having a spiritual experience. That's what sex is about for me, Auggie. It's about connecting as souls. I don't just want to ride your pussy and put you away. This is about you and me becoming one."

"That's what I want too," Auggie said. "That's exactly what I want." Then, working his jaw, he hesitated. "I'd really like it if you could, you know, help me through it on molly."

"I don't want to pressure you."

"You're not pressuring me."

"I don't want you to do something you're not comfortable with."

"I'm not uncomfortable. I can feel how strongly we're connecting. I want you to guide me through this." And he couldn't say, my first time, through my first time, I want you to keep me safe because it's my first time.

Dylan hesitated. Then he breathed, "God, you are fucking gorgeous. Do you know that?"

"Come over here and tell me again."

Producing the plastic case again, Dylan climbed onto the bed. He held out the pill.

Auggie's phone rang.

"Sorry," Auggie said with a nervous laugh, pulling out his phone to silence it. Theo's name was flashing on the screen.

Dylan sat back.

Auggie thought of Theo's face, the horrible attempt at a smile.

Dylan shifted his weight. His hand slid up to Auggie's dick again.

"I'm sorry," Auggie said. "I'm really, really sorry, but I'm worried about this friend. Can you just give me a minute?"

"Yeah," Dylan said, kissing Auggie's neck. "Of course, little bro."

"Theo?" Auggie asked. His voice was too high, on the edge of cracking, and he struggled to bring it back down. "What's up?"

"Can't."

His voice was wrong. Too thick. The single syllable was almost unintelligible.

"Theo—" Auggie pushed Dylan away. "What's wrong? What's going on?"

"Can't stop spinning."

"What can't stop spinning? Where are you?" Auggie slid off the bed, grateful he still had on his high-tops, and cast about for his wallet and keys. "Theo, I need you to tell me where you are."

"What's up?" Dylan said. "Something wrong?"

"Are you in a car?" Auggie said. "Did you get in a car, Theo?"

"In the car," Theo said in that drowned voice. "Can't stop spinning."

Then the line disconnected.

24

When Theo got home from the Sigma Sigma house, his clothes were soaked with sweat. He stripped in the kitchen, the lukewarm air from the window A/C like sandpaper against bare skin. Then he stumbled into the shower. His knee wasn't hurting, but he had trouble walking, as though his joints had locked up. He ran the water cold and stood under it, letting the spray needle his back.

The gun. And Auggie. His mind came back to those two things again and again. He tried to build out from them: Evans had pulled a gun on Auggie; Auggie could have been killed. But his thoughts kept collapsing into those two irreducible facts. The gun. And Auggie. Auggie. And the gun.

He left the shower, the water still running, and went back to the kitchen. He got a White Rascal from the fridge and drank it over the sink, water puddling around him. The house felt cold now, and a part of his mind recognized that it was because he was naked and wet, but even that barely registered. When he'd finished the first can, he crushed it against the counter and got another. Through the glass set in the back door, he could see the line of oaks at the edge of the property, the gnarled limbs, the still-green leaves, the network of branches and twigs. Behind it all was the blue of the September sky. Yes, he thought. Think about that. Twig, branch, tree. Blue sky. He crushed the beer and went back to the shower.

Warming the water by degrees, he felt better. The beer was already rounding off the edges. He could look at the whole thing from a few steps back. He ran the bar of soap across his chest, noticed the way it glided until it got to the chest hair. And then he thought about those little hairs sprouting on Auggie, which was a reminder that Auggie was, when you got to the bottom of it, still a kid. And maybe that was why Theo had come unmoored. Auggie was young. Auggie was just so damn young. And he still loved life, still didn't understand all the ways it came at you, again and again, until it broke you. He still smiled without even thinking about it. He said what he thought, without layers of self-protection, without the extra decade of social conditioning that would make him rethink, reword, rephrase. He still saw the future like the Serengeti, wide and untrammeled, pick your path, when really it was a rut in the ground that just got deeper, year after year, until you were shooting down a ravine and couldn't turn back.

Theo hammered the water off. He dried himself with a towel. He had a third beer.

And—he was realizing now, with the help of that third beer— Luke. He mustn't forget about Luke. That explained why Theo had reacted so strongly today. He had seen Auggie in danger, and he had spent so much of his life trying to keep Luke safe, and Luke had died. So it made sense that Theo would react. It made sense that he would feel a terror so vast that he was close to shitting himself.

Except, a little voice said. Except you've seen Auggie in danger before. And it scared you—when the guy tried to kidnap him at the Frozen King, and it felt like someone had knocked the wind out of you. When Jessica slashed at him with a knife, and you knew it was better to die than to let him get hurt. You've seen him in danger, you've seen him hurt, you've seen it all already, and you didn't react like this.

Still drying himself with the towel, Theo made his way upstairs, a fourth beer in one hand. His nipples were hard. His balls ached. His face felt too warm, and he let the towel drop and finished the stairs naked.

Who could explain why the brain did anything, he wanted to know. In the mirror over the dresser he had shared with Ian, he asked himself: who can explain one fucking thing about how the brain works? Can somebody tell you why you wake up every day next to the same man, year after year, and then he's dead and you keep waking up and for an instant, you don't remember that he's gone? You roll over to bitch at him about stealing the covers, or to tell him it's his turn to get up with Lana, or just to see his face, and then you remember.

Dropping onto the bed, Theo stared up at the ceiling, the cracked plaster, the nail pops, the signs that the house was shifting, that everything was shifting.

Who could tell you why you woke up one morning, one totally normal morning, just another day, and you're already reaching for your phone to text him, because he makes you laugh, because you saw something that reminded you of one of his goofy videos, because you can hear his voice in the words? Who could tell you anything about yourself? And if nobody could tell you something like that, if nobody could tell you anything about why you sit differently on the couch to leave room for him, or why you stock Doritos, or why some nights you think crazy things like where you could go on vacation, that cabin at the lake maybe, and what it would be like to sit on the porch, just let him talk until he ran out of things to say—he could talk all night if he wanted, and you wouldn't mind—if nobody could tell you anything like that, Theo wondered, why should I have any idea why I'm freaking the fuck out?

His breath was coming faster. The room wobbled. He got out of bed, pounded back the beer, and made his way downstairs, almost tripping on the towel. The fifth beer he drank at the table; his naked ass peeled away from the wood when he stood and tossed the empty at the recycling. Miss.

When Theo opened the fridge, the White Rascals were gone. He made his way up to the bedroom. This time he did trip on the towel, and he started laughing as he lay on the stairs, laughing until he couldn't breathe. His knee hurt, though, and he had to drag himself the rest of the way to his bedroom. Sitting on the floor, he unscrewed the outlet plate. Then he pulled the outlet out of the box. Then he pulled the box out of the wall.

Once, and only once, Cart had searched the house. Just so we can trust each other, Cart said, and Theo had smiled and nodded. He knew firsthand that if you had to search, everything else was bullshit. And Cart had been thorough. Cart was smart, even if he didn't give himself credit, and he was a cop and good at his job. But Cart hadn't lived with Luke Stratford.

Theo peeled the strip of tape from the back of the box. He liberated one of the pills—Percocet, plenty of refills, so Cart could take the bottle and Theo could smile and nod—and swallowed it dry. Then he closed his eyes and waited for the room to stop spinning.

But it didn't stop. It got worse, the whole structure tilting like Theo was on the deck of the ship. He was sliding on the floorboards. Another pill might stop it, so he tried that, and then he jammed the box and outlet back into the wall and left the plate for another time. He crawled into bed. The spinning got worse. For a long time, it seemed, Theo couldn't understand why it was getting worse.

And then it all made sense: he was still in the car. Still in the car with Ian and Lana. Still spinning. This wasn't the bad part, not really. One bad part had happened—when the semi struck the car—and a lot of bad parts were still coming. But this, the spinning, it was an in-between. It really wasn't bad.

Except it wouldn't stop. And somehow Theo got his phone. Then the spinning got worse, and the only thing left in his world was spin and drift.

He came back to a warm hand between his shoulder blades and someone saying, "Get it all up. Good. That's good, you've got to get it all up. Jesus, how much did you drink?"

"Auggie?"

"It's me."

Theo thought about this. Then he managed to say, "'m sick."

"I know. Just aim for the bucket, please."

When the next wave of puke came, Theo did. He thought he did a pretty good job, all things considered. Then he slept, and when he woke, the house was dark. His head was resting on a ribcage, and he could hear a heartbeat like the secret clock of the universe. He groaned.

"Any more puking," Auggie said, "and we're going to the hospital."

Theo weakly shook his head.

Auggie's hand settled on the side of his face. "Do you think you can keep down some water? I'm worried you're dehydrated."

Theo licked his lips, but his voice wouldn't come. He nodded.

"Stay right here. Don't get up."

Footsteps moved away. The stairs creaked. The boards on the main floor creaked. Old pipes groaned. Then everything in reverse until the mattress dipped.

"Do you want me to hold it for you?"

Theo shook his head. He opened his eyes. Auggie was Auggie, except for a purple bruise like a storm cloud on the side of his face. Something like foam had buried Theo, insulating him, but underneath, embers flickered to life. Hand trembling, Theo took the glass and managed to get a few gulps.

"That's probably enough for right now," Auggie said as he took the glass. It clinked against the nightstand. Then Auggie stretched out on the bed, head propped on his hand. "Want to tell me what you did?"

"Drank too much," Theo said, his voice so rough it was almost unrecognizable.

Auggie didn't believe him; it was in his face, because he was too young to have learned how to tell all the lies people learned to tell without ever opening their mouths. But he didn't argue about it either. The silence lasted a minute, then two, a familiar crack coming from downstairs as the house settled, the whine of the window A/C trying to keep up with the muggy Midwestern heat.

"I think I should stay the rest of the night," Auggie said.

Theo closed his eyes and nodded. After a moment, he felt Auggie against him, one hand pulling Theo to his chest. Theo wanted to fight it because it felt so good. What an insane reason, part of him said. Fighting this feeling every day, every time they were together—it was exhausting. Why not just stop? Why not just let things be easy for once?

Just for tonight, Theo told himself. Just because I'm so tired.

He rested his head on Auggie's chest. Auggie's fingers combed his hair back, tickled his neck, traced his shoulder.

"I ruined your night," Theo mumbled into Auggie's tank top.

The hesitation confirmed it, but Auggie said, "It's ok."

"I'm sorry. I'm sorry I ruined your night."

"Theo, it's ok. You're my friend. I want you to be ok." Another of those pauses. "I want to know how I can help you be ok so you don't . . . so you don't drink too much again."

Theo rocked his head back and forth, squeezing his eyes shut.

"It's ok," Auggie said, carding his hair again. "You don't have to say anything."

A while later, Theo could breathe normally again, and he said, "Your face."

Auggie laughed quietly. "Turns out I'm not as tough as I thought. It's just a bruise; I'll be fine."

"Auggie?"

Auggie held his breath. Theo could feel it, the way his chest stopped moving. The moment was like one of those secret doors in old movies, the wall that spun around. You stayed in place, but the whole world changed. But only if you did it right. Move a book. Pull a candlestick. Say the magic words.

And then a cat yowled outside, and thunder cracked in the distance.

"Thank you," Theo whispered.

This was the longest of the pauses.

"You're welcome," Auggie said.

Then Theo slept, and in the morning, Auggie was gone.

25

Dylan didn't answer any of Auggie's snaps the next day. Or the next. Or the next.

Theo didn't answer any of Auggie's texts the next day. Or the next. Or the next. He wasn't in class either. Auggie thought about driving out to the little brick house on the edge of the city. He even left the Sigma Sigma house a few times. Once he got as far as the Civic. Then he remembered Theo trashed on whatever cocktail he'd mixed of booze and pills, and he got so angry that he made himself go back to his room so he wouldn't do something he regretted.

By the next Saturday, Auggie had stopped trying to contact them. He worked on a few skits. Every idea was crap. He put together the numbers for August, looking at which videos and tweets and snaps had been most successful, trying to make a plan for how to build similar content and capitalize on his success. He barely got through the initial setup for his spreadsheet. Then he just slumped over in bed and lay there, staring at the wall.

Eventually, someone knocked on the door.

Auggie closed his laptop and pulled his pillow over his head.

Sometime later, another knock came. And then more knocking. And then more.

"Go away," Auggie shouted from under the pillow.

"Open up, Augs."

Auggie squashed the pillow against his ears.

The door rattled in the frame. "Augs, open this door right now!"

"Fuck off!"

"I'm not going away. I'll get somebody to unlock your door if I have to."

Auggie allowed himself to scream into the mattress for a few seconds. Then he made his way to the door and opened it.

Orlando was standing there, his thick eyebrows drawn together. He was wearing a Wroxall Wrestling tee and knit shorts. He smelled like Axe and Dove shampoo. When Auggie met his eyes, Orlando smiled uncertainly.

"Hey, man. How's it going?"

"Great," Auggie said and tried to shut the door.

Orlando was too fast, though, and he got his foot in the way. After a few moments of trying to crush Orlando's bones, Auggie gave up and retreated to his bed. He pulled the pillow back into place and breathed the smell of his own hair and the All detergent from the house laundry facilities. When the mattress dipped under Orlando's weight, he rolled to face the wall, taking the pillow with him.

"So," Orlando said. "How are classes?"

"Really, really good."

"Awesome. I have this bitchin' class on the history of rock."

"Oh my God, did you just say bitchin'?"

"How's your family?"

"They're really, really good."

"How are you, um, feeling?"

"Really, really good."

"Augs, come on."

Auggie lifted the pillow from his face. Orlando was studying him.

"What's going on?" Orlando said. "You've been totally shut down this week. Everybody's noticed. And—and, people saw you with Dylan."

"It's just a bad week."

"I know we have this weird history, and I've tried really hard to make things right. I mean, I know I can't make them right totally. But I want to make them better. I hope you think I'm your friend."

"What? Yeah, obviously. I mean—" Auggie fumbled for a way to say it. "Yeah."

"So you'd, you know, tell me. If something happened to you."

"Huh?"

"With Dylan."

Auggie shook his head. "What?"

"Like, when he was in here with you."

"Oh my God," Auggie said.

"If he raped you, Augs."

"Yeah, I figured it out."

"Well, you were staring at me like you had no idea what I was talking about."

"He didn't rape me. Jesus Christ. Wait. Has he done that to other guys?"

"I don't think so."

140

"So why in the hell would you say something like that?" Auggie scrambled to sit upright. "Why would you even think something like that?"

"I don't know. We were just talking about how different you were acting, and somebody said maybe, you know. I mean, he's older than you, and he's got a reputation, and you've seemed so upset this week, and it just kind of made sense." Orlando flushed and stood. "I'm so stupid. I'm sorry. I just—I know you think I'm, like, super pathetic and hung up on you, but I care about you, and it makes me sad that you're sad, and I wanted to make things better."

He was halfway to the door before Auggie said, "You're not stupid."

Orlando stopped. He rucked up his shirt absently, scratching his belly and the thick, dark hair there. The pinkish white of the scar was barely visible.

"It might help," Auggie said, and then he stopped. "I mean, if I could just talk about it."

This time, the smile was full and bright. "I'm pretty good at listening."

So Auggie told him all of it, everything with Dylan, even the stuff about Theo. While he talked, Orlando sat on the bed, and then he pulled his legs up, hugging his knees to his chest. The smell of Axe and Dove shampoo was oddly comforting—sometimes Chuy used Dove, and it reminded Auggie of home and high school—and Orlando really was a good listener.

When Auggie finished, Orlando said, "I don't get it. What is it about him?"

"Theo is—"

"Not him. You guys are crazy in love, you're both just seriously fucked up."

"I don't know if I'd say—I mean, I think I might feel something really strong, but—"

"I'm talking about Dylan. What's the deal? I mean, I get it: he's hot. But there are a lot of hot guys, and you don't go on dates, you ignore it when dudes try to pick you up. What's the deal with Dylan? Why are you hung up on him? He won't text you back; big deal. Go find some other hot fuckboy."

"He's not a fuckboy. That's the whole point. He's mature."

In the hall, somebody turned on Beyonce, and then two voices competed to sing "Single Ladies" at the top of their lungs.

"He is," Auggie insisted, catching Orlando's doubtful look. "He wants a real relationship, and he doesn't want to play games. He's smart. He's funny."

"He's funny?"

"Yeah. He's really funny."

"How is he funny? Give me an example."

"I don't know, he just is. And he's not doing stupid, teenage stuff that I don't care about."

"Augs," Orlando said gently, "you're a teenager. For another year, at least. You don't need to be ready for a real relationship. You don't need to be past playing games. You get to do all that stuff because that's what people are supposed to do at this age. If you don't want to do it, that's ok too. But you can also just have fun and hook up and figure out what you like and who you want to be with. That's kind of the whole point."

"Yeah, but—you know what? Never mind."

"No, no, no. I'm sorry. I'll try to help. You know the drugs thing is a little scary, right? I mean, you saw what happened to Cal."

"It's not like that. It's spiritual. And it's part of this experience of being together, really being together. Our souls, I mean."

Making a face, Orlando said, "You're sure about this guy? I mean, there's definitely something about Dylan?"

"We have this connection. I don't know how to explain it. I felt it when we met, and it's like—it's like we're connected."

Orlando got a huge grin that vanished almost immediately.

"What?" Auggie said. "You've never felt it, so you don't get to talk."

"I was just thinking of my English paper. 'The symbolism of black is death.'"

Auggie threw the pillow at him.

Laughing, Orlando batted it away. He was still sitting with his knees to his chest, arms wrapped around his shins, his dark eyes wide with amusement. Even after his injury, he was still so big—so much muscle, on a large frame. How could someone so big make himself so small, Auggie wondered. And then he thought about being called Peepee, and how Wayne sent him to the kitchen for a beer, and how Billie acted like he didn't even exist, and Auggie realized maybe it wasn't that much of a surprise after all.

"You're a really good friend," Auggie said.

Orlando shrugged. "You know, a lot of guys would love to hang out with you. Just friends, hook ups, whatever you want. If things don't work out with Dylan, I mean. I know you and Theo—no, I guess I don't know." He turned the end of it into a question.

"I don't either. I thought I did. At the end of last year, I said a lot of things to him. And then he turned around and started dating Cart, and—and I don't know, I feel like everything's different, and I get mad at him all the time, and I don't know why things have to be so awful."

"Fuck 'em," Orlando said. "Fuck both of them."

"I guess so."

"You deserve a great guy, Augs. We'll find one for you."

"Thanks. You do too, you know. Guy or girl."

Orlando just shrugged again. "Come down to dinner with me? The guys want to know you're ok."

"Yeah, just give me a few minutes to clean up."

After Orlando left, Auggie pulled his laptop onto his chest, opened it, and pulled up Facebook. Then he opened tabs for Twitter, Craigslist, and Google. He logged out of his social media accounts and created dummy profiles. Then he started trawling white supremacist forums, posting brief requests. He wanted drugs. He wanted to know who sold drugs. He did what he'd learned to do with his own social media platforms: he scanned the traffic, learned the lingo, and made it his own.

Orlando deserved answers about his brother's death. Every other road had led to a dead end, so now Auggie was going to do what he should have done at the beginning: he was going to follow the drugs. And according to Theo, that meant the Ozark Volunteers.

26

After his bad trip on Percocet and White Rascal, Theo only spoke to Auggie once before Thanksgiving break. He took a week off from life—Dr. Wagner didn't even reply to Theo's vague email about a personal emergency—and convinced Cart to call in sick for a day. They spent that day at a winery in the Ozarks, got a cheap hotel, and fucked and drank until they both passed out. Twice on the drive home, Cart asked if everything was ok. The second time, Theo gave him road head just to get him to stop asking.

The next Tuesday, in class, Theo sat near the blackboard, marking out a clear division between himself and the rest of the class.

Auggie, as usual, ignored the nonverbal warning.

He was wearing a button-up, pinstripe shorts, and dock shoes. He kept shifting his backpack, staring at Theo's feet, and then blurted, "Are you ok?"

"I'm fine, Auggie."

"Why didn't you text me back?"

"I had a lot going on."

"I was worried about you."

Dr. Wagner came into the room, set his briefcase on the desk, and opened the locks with two identical snicks. He pulled out papers and began assembling his lecture notes. Even from where he sat, Theo could smell the booze.

"I needed to do some thinking," Theo said.

"Thinking about what?"

"About what we've been doing. I'm done. And I hope you'll stop too."

Auggie shook his head. "Orlando needs someone to help him. The murder investigation by the police isn't going anywhere—"

"You don't know that."

"—and I think I could help him get some answers. I'm starting to think that if I can find the right person in the Volunteers, they might be able to tell me who was dealing to Cal—"

"Jesus Christ," Theo whispered harshly. He shot up from the seat, grabbed Auggie's arm, and forced him toward the hallway. Several students stared, and one boy even shifted nervously to the edge of his chair.

Wagner didn't seem to notice. He was already talking. "Today we will be discussing Friar John's role in act five of *Romeo and Juliet*. Although I believe I can safely assume that either you have not done the reading or you did not understand it, I will take a risk: can anyone tell us who Friar John is?"

A pretty girl, her hair in a loose chignon—Leah, Theo thought—raised her hand. "He's the messenger sent by Friar Lawrence. He's supposed to tell Romeo that Juliet isn't really dead. He's unable to deliver the message because he's forced to quarantine, and that miscommunication is what sets in motion the end of the play."

Wagner's sneer faltered and then returned. "An adequate summary, but to call it a miscommunication is erroneous. It is more accurately a failure of communication."

Then the door swung shut behind Theo. Out in the hall, he shoved Auggie up against the wall. "What the fuck are you talking about?"

"I know there's good reason to believe the murder wasn't a drug deal gone wrong, but—"

"I don't care about that. I don't care about any of that. The Ozark Volunteers? The goddamn Volunteers? Are you out of your mind?"

"I'm not going to get involved with them. I just want to know—"

Theo shoved him against the wall again. "That's involved, Auggie. That's exactly the definition of involved."

"Stop pushing me."

"No." Theo shoved him again. In his mind, he was seeing Evans with the gun. He was seeing Luke in the hayloft, the flies crawling over his open eyes. "No." He grabbed Auggie's shirt and wrangled him as Auggie tried to slip away. "No. No. I'm telling you no. We're done."

It took him a moment to realize that Auggie wasn't moving. A girl in a pink tulle skirt had stopped at the end of the hall to watch them.

"Fuck off," Theo shouted at her.

She sprinted away.

"Let go of me, please." Auggie's voice was calm, but the tiniest tremor underlay it.

Theo released him. The button-up was wrinkled where he had grabbed it.

145

"You're right," Auggie said. "We're done. I'm not going to do this. I'm not going to keep doing this."

"Great. I'm glad you're finally seeing reason."

"No, Theo. You and me. I'm done. I'm not going to watch you kill yourself because you're afraid of getting better."

Footsteps were ringing off Tether-Marfitt's stone floors. The echoes got inside Theo's head, bouncing around with the buzzing of flies.

"Is there anything else you want to say?" Auggie said.

"You don't want to be seen as a little kid? You're tired of it? Isn't that what you're always telling me?"

Auggie raised his chin but didn't answer.

"Then don't give fucking ultimatums like a fucking toddler."

He couldn't hear the footsteps anymore. *Toddler, toddler, toddler* ran up and down the halls.

"I'm going back into class," Auggie said, his dark eyes soft and very sad.

When the door clicked shut behind him, Theo marched to the end of the hall, kicked over a trash can, and then chased after the mixture of Starbucks cups and paper food wrappers that had spilled across the floor. He followed one of the cups all the way to the stairwell, chuffing uncontrollably, until he sent it spinning off the landing with one final kick. Then, after a minute to bring himself down, he picked up the rest of the garbage, washed his hands, and went back to class.

Days rolled into weeks. Weeks rolled into months. Late summer turned into fall, and by the end of November, fall teetered on the edge of winter. It wasn't that nothing happened during those months. Theo spent them working on his thesis, grading papers for Dr. Wagner, continuing his physical therapy exercises, visiting Lana, and building something—he wasn't sure what to call it—with Cart.

Many times with his brothers, Theo had gone cliff jumping. He had particularly liked a flooded limestone quarry only a few miles from their home. On a perfect day, the sun was hot, the air was humid and thick, and the water, when you plunged into it, crisply cold. The trick was knowing where the water was deep enough—and, therefore safe—versus those spots that looked deep but in actuality concealed rocks that could break your leg or your back or your skull.

With Cart, Theo didn't know what he was jumping into. They'd go out for burgers at the Mighty Street Taproom, and they'd drink beers and watch the Cardinals, and they'd shout over each other telling Miller to learn how to throw a fucking curveball. But that was buddy stuff, strictly straight-guy stuff, until they got behind a closed door and Cart was on his knees like he'd just finished a cocksucker correspondence course.

The Tuesday before Thanksgiving, Theo said, "I want you to know what I'm about to ask you isn't meant to be a big deal. I'm just asking you because I think it'd be fun. Do you want to go out to my parents' place on Friday and do some shooting? That's what my brothers and I do every year."

They were on the couch in Theo's living room. Cart was in sweats, flipping channels, his legs across Theo's knees while Theo tried to read. They'd just murdered two trays of take-out nachos. Cart's finger hovered over the Channel Up button.

"I think my parents have stuff that day," he said and clicked up to QVC.

"Ok," Theo said. He placed both hands face down on the book and said, "What about sometime around Christmas? A weekend? It would be fun to get away."

"Maybe."

"Ok," Theo said more slowly.

This time, Cart jabbed the button several times in a row.

"Is this too early for you?" Theo said. "Do you feel like I'm rushing you?"

"That's not what I said."

"You didn't say anything."

"The holidays are busy. Jesus, you ought to know that, Ian being a cop and all."

"Take it down a little. I'm just asking—"

"I know what you're asking. Don't get your pecker in a twist. I said maybe."

Leave it, a little voice in Theo's head told him. You'd better just leave it.

Instead, though, he said, "What about Friday the 12th. That weekend. That's right between Thanksgiving and Christmas. School will be out. Things will be quiet."

Cart muttered something under his breath and pulled out his phone.

"What was that?"

"I said I'm checking, you dumb hoosier." Cart scrolled on his phone, tossed it on the coffee table, and said, "Can't. Department Christmas party that night."

Leave it, that voice said again.

Instead, Theo said, "Good thing you told me. I'll put it on my calendar. I've got just enough time to get a new dress and heels."

Swinging his legs off Theo's lap, Cart sat up. He had patches of red in his cheeks, and he kept jerking on the collar of his sweatshirt, trying to get it back into place. Then he stood.

"What?" Theo said.

"You think you're so goddamn smart."

"Come on, Cart. What? It was a joke."

"Fuck you, you peckerbrained redneck jerkoff rag." Cart stomped his feet into his shoes.

"Sorry," Theo said, tossing the book onto the pile next to him. "I'm really sorry. I'm so fucking sorry I thought you might want to take your boyfriend to the department Christmas party."

Cart flipped him the bird, threw open the door, and left.

For ten minutes, Theo pretended to read. Then he turned off the TV, set the deadbolt, and locked the back door too. Just in case. He turned off the lights. He went upstairs. And he started unscrewing the plate over the outlet.

27

For Thanksgiving, Auggie flew home. The airports were a madhouse, his flights delayed, and the planes fully booked. By the time he got home, it was after one in the morning. Fer was smoking when he pulled up in the Escalade. He was in shorts and a Ramones tee, and his eyes were bloodshot and half closed.

"Are you stoned?" Auggie asked as he got in the SUV.

"I'm fucking exhausted is what I am," Fer said.

"I could have taken an Uber."

"Great. Great fucking idea. I'll go home, and you take an Uber."

"Jesus, Fer. I'm sorry."

They didn't talk the rest of the ride home, but the next day, Fer thawed. Things felt normal. Only they weren't normal. Everything was different, and everything was worse.

On Wednesday, Auggie got together with Devin and Logan, and they did a reunion video. Auggie had thought it'd be fun to redo one of their early videos with a twist. They agreed, and they shot a version of the too-small shirt gag, only this time, they used their college t-shirts. It was a lot of fun until the end, when Logan threw a fit because, according to him, Auggie always got the best parts, and Devin just made a face like they'd already talked about this a hundred times. Auggie tried to point out all the times he'd written parts just for Devin and Logan. Then, when he got angry, he pointed out that he was the one doing all the creative work. The fight got so bad that Auggie finally left without any of it being resolved, and instead of going to a party with more of his high school friends, he went to bed early. In the middle of the night, he woke up and stared at the ceiling for over an hour. Then he rolled onto his side and deleted the video without posting it.

Thanksgiving started off all right. Chuy was in his room all day, sleeping off whatever shit he'd done the night before. Their mom was in the living room with her boy toy. Auggie and Fer picked up the premade meal, and they worked together in the kitchen to make the dishes that they hadn't purchased: mashed potatoes and green bean casserole. Fer smoked a joint while they worked, and he looked more tired than ever, but at least he was talking and laughing and giving Auggie the usual amount of shit.

"I don't get it, Augustus. Why this boner bro who's like ten years older than you?"

"Dylan isn't ten years older than me. He's a senior. That's, like, three years. Tops."

"So what do you like about him? Does he have a huge dick or something?"

Auggie flicked mashed potatoes at him.

Laughing, Fer wiped his cheek clean. "Or is he your pussy boy? Auggie," he moaned, "Auggie, yeah, pull my hair, Auggie!" He ended with a shrill scream.

In the other room, the sound of conversation cut off for a moment, then their mom started speaking again. This week's flavor was named Carlos. When he laughed at something their mom said, Auggie made a face.

"If that's what you sound like in bed," Auggie told Fer, "no wonder you can't keep a girlfriend."

"Ha ha," Fer said, which was so unlike him that Auggie looked up and was surprised to see the hurt in Fer's face.

"Hey, wait, I was joking."

"Fuck it. I know; just a little too close to home." He gave the green bean gloop a giant stir. When Carlos laughed again, Fer stabbed the spoon into the mixture with vicious jabs.

"So, um," Auggie said. "How are you?"

Instead of answering immediately, Fer picked up the stub of his joint and lit it. "I'm fine, Augustus. Tell me about this boy you like. You sound serious about him."

"No, I want to hear—"

"Right this goddamn minute," Fer said, "so I know whether or not I have to buy you a chastity cage."

Auggie rolled his eyes, but he found himself telling Fer everything, even the things he hadn't known how to put into words with Orlando: how he'd felt something right away when he met Dylan, and how he very rarely felt anything that strong, especially with guys his age; how that feeling had magnified every time they got close; how Dylan pushed him to be better, forced him to grow, challenged him; how he'd watched Dylan at parties, laughing when Dylan was goofy, but mostly just observing because Dylan was cool, Dylan was reserved, Dylan moved through crowds and stood out because he had that indefinable quality that made him seem like an adult in a room full of children; how he worried that something was wrong with him because he didn't want to go on dates with guys his age.

"There's nothing wrong with you," Fer said. "Well, you're a total fuckup and probably nothing more than a frat house cum bucket, but there's nothing wrong with liking older guys. Jesus, Augustus, think about it. Who in their right mind would want to date most eighteen- and nineteen-year-olds? They're kids; you're light years ahead of them. Besides, you've obviously got a major daddy kink."

"Jesus Christ, Fer! I don't—you can't—what the hell is wrong with you?"

Fer grinned, but it didn't really make it to his eyes. "Just be careful, ok? It's not just getting pressured into doing something you're not ready for, although I'm worried about that too. A lot of guys, the ones interested in someone younger, they do it because they like the control it gives them."

"Dylan's not like that."

Fer mimed jerking off.

"He's not!"

"Whatever. Tell me again when he's got his whole hand up your chute and you're thanking him."

"I honestly think you need to see a shrink. You are the weirdest person I have ever met."

This time, Fer's smile looked a little closer to real.

For a moment, Auggie wanted to tell him everything about Theo too. About watching the back of Theo's neck in class and knowing the exact instant Wagner said something that Theo disagreed with. About the times he'd walked outside and headed toward Theo's house without even realizing it. About the weirdest things that would remind him of Theo: the weave of the upholstery on the couches in the third-floor lounge; peanut butter toast; the sound of a page being turned in a quiet room. Mostly he wanted to tell Fer that he didn't know what to do to stop hurting all the time.

Carlos's laughter, loud and honking, broke the stillness. Fer made that face again.

"Fer," Auggie said, "are you ok?"

"Yeah."

"I mean, really ok? Because I don't think you are."

Fer shrugged and spooned the green bean mixture into a casserole dish.

"Do you want to talk about it?"

"What's there to talk about, Augustus?"

"Why you're smoking so much weed. Why you're so tired. Why I think you're really sad and maybe feeling helpless or scared or something. I don't know. But it's freaking me out a little."

"The night before you got here," Fer said, leaning on the counter with both hands, head down, "I had to drive to a rave and pick up Chuy because he'd OD'd again. Again. I make him carry that Narcan shit because if I didn't, he'd be dead. And the week before that, he stole some fucking Gucci purse that Carlos gave Mom, and I had to track it down in Costa Mesa and haggle, fucking haggle, to buy it back because she was so sad she wouldn't get out of bed. And if it's not Chuy doing something messed up, it's her, because she's buying Carlos jewelry or she's taking him on a cruise, or it's Owen or Hayden or whoever it is that week, or she's out of Xanax, or she's just had a breakup and needs to go to a spa in Sedona. And if it's not Mom—"

He cut himself off.

"It's me."

"No."

"It's ok. I know I'm—I know I'm a lot for you to handle. I know I really annoy you, and I know you're paying for everything, and I'm not responsible, and—"

"August Paul Lopez," Fer said, looking up, then considering him, then pulling him into a hug. "You have donkey shit for brains."

"Fer, why didn't you tell me?"

Fer hadn't let him go; he was holding on to Auggie with the kind of desperation that made Auggie think of a drowning man. "What was I going to say? Things have gone to shit since you left? They were already shit, but now Mom doesn't even have to pretend to be responsible anymore, and Chuy—I mean, we both knew the way he was going. And I am apparently the most dislikable ass crumb ever to fall out of God's pucker, because I can't get a fucking second date to save my life."

"Maybe it's not you. Maybe it's bad luck. It's a numbers game, and you've got to keep trying."

Fer just let out a slow breath.

"Although," Auggie said, "you might want to ease up on the ass crumbs and puckers and chutes and cum guzzlers. On the first date, I mean."

Fer hugged him tighter.

"Fer, I can't breathe."

Fer hugged him even tighter.

"Jesus, dummy, put me down."

"You're a good kid," Fer said, squeezing even harder. "You deserve better than this fucktastrophe of a family. I hope you get boned like crazy by that way-too-old-for-you big-dicked bro you're crushing on. I hope he lets you scarf down his ball hairs."

For some reason, that made Auggie laugh so hard he started to cry, and then Fer was laughing too, and then both of them ended up lying on the tile, laughing until their mom came to see what was wrong. That just made them laugh harder.

After dinner, Chuy disappeared, and Auggie's mom and Carlos left not much later. Fer and Auggie watched TV, both of them in sweats, Auggie with a blanket. Fer rolled a new joint, and when Auggie asked, he shrugged and passed it over. It must have been pretty strong because it hit Auggie quickly. They passed the joint back and forth until they had smoked it down to a roach and Auggie was stoned out of his mind. The TV was still on, but he was having a hard time tracking what he was seeing. Mostly, he just enjoyed the lights and colors, and then he was past even that, and he woke up in the middle of the night, in bed, and realized Fer had carried him there.

"Because I want to have a fucking life too, you fucking sperm-bank reject," Fer shouted in the front room. "I'm sick as fuck of pulling your ass out of the fire."

Chuy answered in a low voice, the words lost to Auggie.

"Get the fuck out of my sight," Fer said. "I can't even look at you right now."

Quiet steps moved along the hall, past Auggie's room, and then the next door closed.

It took a long time for Auggie to fall asleep after that.

When he woke, he checked his phone. For months now, he'd been trying to find someone in the Ozark Volunteers who could give him a lead on Cal's dealer. To Auggie, it seemed like simple logic: the Volunteers controlled all the drug trade, and therefore, they ought to be able to identify who was selling to Cal. Even if the dealer hadn't had anything to do with Cal's death, he might still be able to fill in some of the holes in the days and weeks before the murder. If nothing else, he could give Auggie a more accurate sense of how deeply Cal was involved in drugs, and why the killer had tried to stage it to look like a deal gone bad.

Unfortunately, no matter how many usernames Auggie tried, no matter how well he parroted the language on the forums and social media groups that he visited, no one had taken the bait. Either they sensed the trap, or Auggie was simply targeting the wrong sectors.

Today wasn't any different: no responses to his requests. Nothing that might point him in the right direction.

After snapping a quick wake-up selfie, Auggie rolled out of bed and made his way to the next room. The house was silent. Fer didn't have work, so he was either still asleep or had already left for some other reason. Their mom—well, who the hell knew anymore.

Auggie didn't bother knocking. He let himself into the room, which had a faint smell like burnt electrical components and, of course, weed. Chuy was bundled up in a blanket. His dad—they all had different dads—had been white, and he was much lighter skinned than either Auggie or Fer. He looked awful, his skin greasy, muscle and fat wasted away until he was skeletal. But his face was still Chuy's face, although his lank brown hair was longer than Auggie remembered.

"Chuy," Auggie said, sitting on the mattress and shaking his brother.

Chuy groaned.

"Wake up," Auggie said.

After some more groaning, Chuy opened one eye. "Hey, Gus-Gus. What's up?"

"I need you to teach me how to buy drugs."

"Cool," Chuy said and closed his eye again.

28

The text came when Theo was driving home from his parents the Saturday of Thanksgiving break.

Found Cal's dealer.

Theo pulled over, stared at the phone, and then swore until his voice gave out. He was still staring at the phone when another text from Auggie came through.

Did u die from a rage stroke?

Theo texted back: *What are you talking about?* Then, because he knew Auggie too well, he immediately started composing again: *And don't explain what a rage stroke is.*

Too slow. Auggie's reply came as Theo was hitting send: *A rage stroke is when you get so angry your brain pops.*

Theo glared at the phone.

I'm giving u five seconds to catch up, Auggie wrote.

Explain to me very clearly what you did.

In person.

No, Auggie. Right now.

But Theo was still typing those words when, *Tomorrow. When I get back to Wahredua,* came through.

Theo hit send.

Five second catch-up, Auggie sent.

Theo took those five seconds to breathe deeply. Then he texted, *I'm incredibly upset right now. I'll talk to you tomorrow. Text me when the shuttle is getting to Wahredua.*

And so, after a sleepless night and an unproductive morning—Theo tried to work on his thesis and ended up, instead, pacing and occasionally throwing things—he was sitting on the low stone wall outside the Sigma Sigma house when the Silver Bullet Airport Charters bus pulled up to the curb. A handful of guys got down from the bus. Auggie was the last one. He smiled and waved at Theo as he waited to retrieve his luggage. Then, towing two huge bags, he headed for the Sigma Sigma house.

"Excuse me," Theo said.

"Hi, Theo. Just going to drop these off."

"You have ten minutes, starting right now."

Auggie laughed.

"We'll see if you're still laughing in ten minutes and one second," Theo said.

Something in his face must have communicated what he was feeling because Auggie offered a sickly smile and hurried toward the Sigma Sigma house. By the third step, he was running.

It was the last day of November, and it was practically balmy, unnaturally warm for that time of year. Theo had decided against a coat before the ride over, and now he unbuttoned his flannel work shirt, grateful he had chosen to wear a tee underneath. The bus pulled away, the engine rumbling up, the whine before shifting gears, and then the street was silent. Behind Theo, the door to the Sigma Sigma house opened. He checked his watch.

"Eight minutes, sixteen seconds," he said without looking over his shoulder.

"I had to pee," Auggie said, his voice drawing closer. "And some people actually like me. They wanted to say hi."

"No," Theo said when he saw Auggie. "Go back inside and put on appropriate clothes."

Auggie pulled at the tank that said *Slutbreaker* and glanced down at the shorts that were barely long enough to cover his crotch. The little shit had changed clothes in the eight minutes and sixteen seconds he'd been out of sight. And he'd done it on purpose, the way he did everything on purpose, to fuck with Theo.

"What?" Auggie said, pulling up the tank to chew on the collar. In the process, he exposed the faintly defined muscles of his stomach. "It's a nice day. It's in the seventies. It's beautiful, especially for November."

"Do not test me, Auggie."

More chewing. A thoughtfully arched eyebrow. Considering noises. "I mean, if it makes you uncomfortable . . ."

"Get your ass back inside and put on clothes."

"I have clothes on."

"Real clothes."

"These are real."

"Auggie!"

He didn't smile. He didn't even look remotely close to pleased. If anything, he looked slightly hurt, and he plucked at his tank as though seeing it for the first time. But Theo knew Auggie better than he knew just about anyone, and he knew that inside, Auggie was gloating.

When Auggie came back, he was in his Jordans, jeans, and a long-sleeved tee.

"Talk," Theo said.

"We might have to talk as we drive," Auggie said. "I want to catch Sadie before she leaves her apartment."

"Is Sadie the dealer?"

"I mean, she's a person, Theo. I don't think she identifies primarily as a drug dealer."

Theo stood up from the wall. Auggie took a step back.

"Cut it out," Theo said. "You're mad at me. Fine. You want to punish me. Fine. I'll take all the shit you want to dump on me because I know I treated you badly, and I'm sorry. But what you're playing around with, it's the real thing, so don't act like we're talking about scoring weed from a kid after gym class. If you aren't taking this seriously, you're putting both of us in danger."

The color under Auggie's light brown skin was a dark, dusky red. His chin came up. "I'm taking this seriously."

"Then act like it."

He bit his lip, and for a moment, his eyes were shiny. Then he blinked and said, "She's the dealer."

"How do you know she's Cal's dealer?"

"I'll tell you in the car if you want to go with me. If you don't want to, then I'm going by myself."

"I'm here, aren't I?" Theo said.

In the Civic, they were both silent for the first five minutes of the drive. The car provided its own soundtrack: the screech of brakes, an ominous gasping noise on even the slightest hills, and a rhythmic whumping that kicked on and off to no pattern that Theo could discern.

"We'll have to be fast," Auggie said. "There's a party tonight at the house. Everybody's going to be there."

Theo rolled down the window.

"Dylan will probably be there."

Theo put his hand out to catch the breeze. The air felt good between his fingers.

"Maybe I'll see if Sadie's got any good weed."

"You made your point, Auggie."

"I'm not making a point."

"You just wanted to casually remind me that you do drugs."

"Not everything is about you, Theo. I didn't change my clothes to make you mad. And I'm just making conversation."

Shaking his head, Theo tried to concentrate on the portion of Wahredua they were passing through. It was mostly a blur. An aluminum mailbox with stick-on numbers. A newspaper still in its plastic, although it had obviously been left out in the rain. How long, Theo wondered. A week? Two? A month? A Pepsi two-liter caught in a storm drain.

Then he was talking even though he didn't want to. "So now you're a frat boy."

"What?"

"Last year, you started off as the tough guy with the cigarettes rolled in your sleeve. Then, for a while, you actually seemed like a human being. Now you're a frat boy. Next thing, you'll be talking about all that pussy you're getting. You'll be a straight boy in a rugby shirt. Send me an invite when you get that tribal tattoo. I want to make sure I'm keeping up."

Auggie's hands tightened on the wheel. When he spoke, his voice was thick. "Fuck you. Why are you so mean to me?"

"Because you're trying to make me mad with this bullshit. And I am mad. And I'm scared. And I look at you, and I think about Luke, and I can't even see straight. My brother died, Auggie. He died caught up in this kind of shit. And now you're doing it too. I can't even breathe. I thought maybe you'd started thinking clearly when you didn't talk about this for months, and now, out of the blue, I find out you've been looking for drug dealers this whole time. My heart just about jumped out of my chest. Jesus, Auggie, how the fuck am I not supposed to be terrified that something's going to happen to you?"

They drove for another mile, start-and-stop traffic, a long red light, someone's car thumping with bass, the smell of fried chicken from the KFC on the next block.

"I'm sorry," Theo said. He risked a look; Auggie's jaw was still set. "That was a lot to unload on you. I've been carrying it around, and I didn't know how to say it. I definitely didn't want to say it like that."

"No, it's—" His voice was strained. "It makes sense. I knew about Luke. I just didn't put it together. And I wish you had told me that's why you were acting so weird. I thought you just hated me because I saw you, you know, when you weren't having a good night. And it's been really hard because you're my friend and I've really missed you."

"I've missed you too."

The street they were on was residential, with small frame houses and untended yards. On the closest lot, a pair of pink flamingos had been nail-gunned into a plastic swimming pool—on the off chance they might decide to take flight, Theo guessed. Auggie nosed the car up to the curb, parallel with the flamingos. Then he wiped his eyes. Then he put his hand over his face, and his shoulders shook.

"I'm sorry, Auggie. I shouldn't have said those things." He touched Auggie's arm, and Auggie turned into him, sobbing, and buried his face in Theo's shoulder. Theo held himself stiffly at first, and then his arms closed around Auggie, pulling him tight, and he strummed his fingers up and down Auggie's ribs and made quieting noises.

"It's not that," Auggie finally said when he pulled away. His eyes were red, and he wiped his face again. "I had this horrible Thanksgiving break, and things are so bad at home, and Fer won't say it but I know I'm just making his life harder, and Chuy is a mess like Luke, and he's going to die, and Dylan won't even acknowledge I'm alive, and you wouldn't talk to me, and—and I thought I'd wear that dumb outfit and you'd laugh or smile or something, but you were just mad, and things got worse when I tried to sound cool, and then I ended up crying like a huge baby, and I'm tired of being the baby. I'm always the baby."

In spite of his best efforts, Theo started to laugh.

"Stop it," Auggie said, jabbing him in the ribs.

Theo laughed harder.

"God, you're the worst," Auggie said. He smiled, though. "I haven't heard you laugh in a long time."

"I don't think I've laughed in a long time. Let's do this one by one, shall we?"

"Do what?"

"First, you're not a baby for crying. My parents fucked me up in a million ways, but that's not one of them. If you want to cry, cry. If you don't, don't."

"You don't cry."

"I'm not exactly a model for how to deal with your problems, Auggie. Second, I'm going to apologize again for being a jerk. I'm sorry, Auggie. I just can't seem to say anything right around you anymore, but I know I shouldn't have treated you that way. Will you forgive me?"

"Yeah, duh. And I'm sorry that I'm—you know, I guess I take things the wrong way or too seriously or whatever."

"Are we ok?"

"Definitely."

"Ok, number three, Dylan—"

Auggie made the sound of screeching brakes. "Nope."

"Why not?"

GREGORY ASHE

"Umm, gee, well, I don't know, maybe because I'd rather be hit by a truck and then be chopped up for circus-animal food."

"You helped me with Cart," Theo said.

"Please let's jump over Dylan. I don't want to talk about him with you."

"Ok. If you change your mind, I promise I will try to be less of a prick than normal."

"Wow."

"I know. It'll be hard." Theo grinned, and it felt like a foreign expression after all those months. Then the grin dropped away. "Tell me about Chuy and Fer."

And Auggie told him—about break, about how things had been getting worse.

"It's not your fault," Theo said, "and you can't carry it. I know you're going to think it's easy for me to say, but you've got to let it go."

"Let it go? Theo, he's my brother, and he's going to OD one time and nobody will have Narcan, and then he'll be dead."

"I'm not saying you can't love him or care about him or worry about him. But the thing you've got to understand about addicts is that they'll always be addicts, and they're the only ones who can make the choice to get clean. Fer can bail him out as many times as he wants. You guys can send him to rehab. You could lock him up in a box. I did all of it with Luke. I'm not lying, Auggie. I locked him in the cellar at the end. I thought he was going to have a come-to-Jesus moment. I mean, I'm not a monster—he was comfortable, he had everything he needed. We got through the detox and all the puking. He looked and sounded like Luke again. God, I really thought I'd figured it out. He cried. We both cried. My parents cried. My brothers came by, and they cried. And Luke knew all the right things to say. I opened the door, and he went upstairs, and it was like I had a brother again. That night, he went to bed, and he was still there in the morning. And the next day. And then the third day, I found him in the loft. The dumbshit hadn't used in weeks, and his tolerance had dropped."

Auggie was crying again. "That'll kill Fer. You don't know him. It'll kill him."

"It just about killed me."

"But I don't know what to do."

"That's what I'm trying to tell you: you can't do anything. That's hard to hear, but it's the truth, and I wish I could tell you something else."

"Ok," Auggie said. "Ok, but that doesn't mean I have to stop trying."

160

His cheeks were red. His nose was a little snotty. But his eyes were bright, and there was a hardness in his face, a determination in the way he compressed his lips, that Theo had noticed once or twice before.

"No," Theo said. "But you're going to get hurt. That's probably all you'll get."

"If it were Jacob or Abel or Meshie, would you just shrug and say, 'Eh, I learned my lesson with Luke, I'm going to stay out of this one'?"

Theo shook his head. "But I'm a dumbass hoosier, as Cart likes to point out."

"You're not," Auggie said. "You're the smartest man I know."

"Not smart enough," Theo said with a smile, "to handle my own shit, apparently. Do you want to talk about Fer?"

"There's nothing to talk about. I'm this huge drain on him: his money, his time, his energy. It's not fair to him. He's never gotten to have his own life because he's spent it taking care of me, and that's not right, but I'm still making him do it. I'm a fucking adult, but I swipe his credit card when I go out to eat, I send the tuition bills to his house, I drive a car he paid for."

Something kicked on in the car, and a belt in the Civic whined in agreement.

"You know, there are a lot of ways to do college on your own," Theo said carefully. "I'm trying really hard not to dad out on you, but there are scholarships, student loans." Then, testing the ice, "You could get a job."

Auggie flopped back in the seat, arms and legs akimbo, and groaned. "Oh my God, you're going to make me work at Frozen King, and I'll have to wear one of those paper crowns."

"That's not the worst option."

"I'd honestly rather be dead."

Theo caught himself before responding to that. The whumping sound in the Civic had gotten louder, even though they were still parked, and the smell of something burning was filling the car.

"Auggie, I think you might need a mechanic to look at this. Don't be mad."

Sitting up, Auggie grinned and shifted into drive. "You don't have to say, 'Don't be mad,' after everything. And it's fine; the car always makes the smell."

"Ok, but in my experience, dealing with anything like this early on is better than waiting until it's too late—"

"Dad," Auggie coughed into his fist.

161

Sighing, Theo sat back and raised his hands, silent. Then he glanced at his watch. "Shit, when was Sadie supposed to leave her house? I know you said we had to hurry."

"Oh, um. I kind of made that up."

Theo let the tires thrum for a moment.

"Just the part about her leaving her house," Auggie said in a rush. "Because you were so mad at me, and I thought if we could start working together again, maybe you'd forget about being mad." Hesitating, Auggie offered a weak smile. "Don't be mad."

After the Civic had limped another mile, Theo trusted his voice enough to say, "Why don't you tell me how you found her and why you think she's Cal's dealer?"

"Oh, that was easy once Chuy explained how it works. It's all about knowing the right person, which I kind of knew, but I didn't realize you had to, um, know them. Like, I thought it'd be the way I do stuff, where you can connect online, but I guess drug dealing is still stuck back with the dinosaurs."

"God," Theo said, "how awful."

"Right? Anyway, I did get Orlando to talk to his parents, and they let me sign into Cal's account on Facebook—they have access to his account now. I just worked my way through his pictures, checked it against his friends, made a list of everyone who I could see partying in the pictures or who bragged about partying in their feed. Then I took that list and ran it through Missouri's online court records. Lots of them had some sort of criminal record, but Sadie was the only one who'd been busted for possession with intent to distribute, so I decided to start with her."

When Theo had digested this, he said, "That's amazing."

Auggie's shoulders relaxed, his chest came up, and he smiled.

"So she doesn't know we're coming?"

Shaking his head, Auggie said, "I thought it'd be best if we took her by surprise."

"And what were you going to do if I refused to go with you?"

"I'm going to spare you the embarrassment of pretending that was a real question."

When they got to the house, it looked like yet another of the 1950s-era homes that had weathered the intervening decades without much assistance. The asphalt shingles were hairy and green with algae, and in many places the shingles were missing, and the tarpaper underneath looked waterlogged and saggy. More of the same green algae stained the siding, which had once been white. Several tall trees shaded the house, and the grass had killed the lawn and left bare earth and patches of moss. When Auggie stopped the Civic, the breeze that rushed into the car through the open window was cold and smelled like half-frozen soil. Theo buttoned his flannel shirt again, then stopped when he saw Auggie shivering and tugging on his tee.

"Here," Theo said, shrugging out of the flannel.

"No, I'm fine. I just—it was a lot warmer at home, and then it felt like a nice day at the Sigma Sigma house. I should have—"

"Auggie, for the love of Christ, take it. I'm fine. I didn't just fly in from the land of milk and honey and board shorts."

Murmuring something, Auggie pulled on the flannel. It was too big for him, and he cuffed the sleeves, but as usual, somehow he made it look good.

"What was that?" Theo said.

"Nothing," Auggie said with a sugary smile. "Just remembering your deep, unrequited love for California."

Theo grunted and opened the door.

"Theo?"

When he looked back, he was unsurprised to see Auggie's eyes were wet again. "Just, thanks." Auggie plucked at the flannel and added, "For everything."

"Will you please stay in the car until I tell you to come up to the house?" Theo raised his hands. "I'm not going to cut you out of this. You found her. But I want to check something first."

Auggie nodded. Apparently being the single most difficult part of Theo's life more than a dozen times in one day was exhausting; he slumped back in the seat, chewing the placket of the flannel shirt, face already lost in thought.

Instead of approaching the house directly, Theo followed the sidewalk to one end of the lot, and then he doubled back and followed it in the other direction. A few cars passed him, but the yards and sidewalks were empty; it was mid-afternoon, and most people were either at work or school. The sun moved behind clouds as Theo turned back for his third trip along the sidewalk, and goosebumps tightened the flesh on his arms when that wet, frozen-moss breeze picked up again.

On his three passes, Theo got good, long looks inside Sadie's house. The windows didn't have blinds or curtains, and he could see into a bedroom and the living room. A girl with short, dark hair sat on the couch watching TV. She was eating something out of a bowl, and she was wearing pajama pants and a tank top. Maybe she could borrow *Slutbreaker*, Theo thought, and he grinned at the indignation he imagined on Auggie's face.

At the end of the lot, Theo turned and followed the property line, which was marked by a four-foot section of chain fence, the rest having either been ripped out at some point or never been installed. He passed a massive linden tree. Its berries carpeted the ground, most of them black and withered, some of them squishing under Theo's boots with a slight whiff of rotten fruit. A tiny window marked this side of the house—the bathroom, Theo thought. The glass was frosted, so he couldn't see inside, but it was dark. He assumed that meant it was unoccupied. The backyard was even worse than the front—big branches had fallen in several places, and a stake and a rusting chain marked where some poor animal had been kept at one point. Theo stretched up to peer into the kitchen on the other side of the glass. Nobody there either. He made his way back to the car and rapped on the trunk. When Auggie opened it, he took out the tire iron and carried it to the passenger window.

Auggie was chewing on the collar now; Theo was starting to think he'd need to buy puppy spray.

"I think she's alone," Theo said. "I want you to play nice at the front door. Be newspaper-subscription Auggie or door-to-door-vacuum-sales Auggie."

"Gross. That sounds like work."

"You just need to keep her occupied."

"Yeah, but newspapers? It's not the 90s, Theo. I might as well offer to sell her a *Jurassic Park* t-shirt and a *Fraggle Rock* nightlight." Auggie's eyes widened when Theo pointed the tire iron at him, and he hurried to say, "You know what? Newspaper subscription was a great idea. You're so smart."

"Too late."

"And strong. Look at those guns you're flexing."

"Just keep her talking, please."

"And wise," Auggie called after him. "You're so wise, Theo. Because of your years of life experience."

Theo walked faster. At the back of the house, he grabbed a rock. Then he went up the three rotted-out steps to the back door and slid the end of the tire iron between the door and the jamb, right where the latch was set. When he heard Auggie's voice at the front of the house, he hammered on the end of the iron with the rock, forcing the door a fraction of an inch to the side. The latch popped free of the jamb, and the door swung inwards. Discarding the rock, Theo went inside and adjusted his grip on the tire iron.

"Bitch, I told you," Sadie was saying, her voice deeper than Theo had expected, "I don't care if your car died. Walk to a fucking gas station."

"My brother will pay you," Auggie said. "Come on, I don't want to walk. I just got these Jordans."

"Fuck off," Sadie said.

Theo took the last two yards at a sprint, crossing the spearmint-colored shag carpeting as Sadie reached for the door. He was as quiet as possible, but she must have heard something because she started to turn. He got the end of the tire iron between two ribs and said, "Uh uh."

She froze.

"Hands up. This is long enough to go all the way to your heart."

Sadie raised her hands, and her tank top slid up.

"Come inside," Theo said to Auggie. "Shut the door. Then go get a chair from the kitchen and put it in the middle of the living room."

Sadie smelled like milk and body odor, and her hair was lank, barely longer than Auggie's but looking greasy and unwashed. The tank top revealed a scattering of acne on her back and shoulders.

"You guys are fucked," she said with a tight laugh. "You guys have no idea who you're fucking with."

"When I want you to talk, I'll tell you."

"You think you can bust my stash and walk away from it? You motherfuckers are dead. Dead. When—"

Theo caught a handful of her hair and smashed her face against the door. The movement took her by surprise, and she never had a chance to resist. He was pretty sure he heard her nose break.

"I got a chair," Auggie said, "what do I—Jesus, what happened?"

Still steering her by the hair, Theo propelled Sadie toward the straight-backed chair that Auggie had set in the middle of the room. "Go find something to tie her with," Theo said.

"I don't—"

"Now," Theo shouted.

Auggie ran into the bedroom.

Staring up at Theo, her nose flattened and misshapen, blood covering her mouth and chin, Sadie said, "You are a fucking dead man."

"I've heard it before," Theo said. "Be quiet."

"It's not me. It's my boss. And his boss. And his boss."

"Yeah, the Ozark Volunteers, every goddamn one of them jerking off with his sister. I know. Shut up."

Auggie came back with a belt and a bedsheet.

"She doesn't have anything—"

"The belt is fine. Pull her arms back, put it above the elbows, and get it as tight as you can."

"I thought we were just going to talk to her."

"I know what you thought. I tried to tell you, this is serious shit. Tie her up."

"They're going to cut off your fucking face," Sadie said, blood bubbling at her nose. "I'm going to watch them, and then I'm going to take a shit on you." She looked like she was thinking about struggling, but that stopped when Theo put the tire iron's tip to her throat. Auggie secured the belt, and then he stepped back, his hands out to the side like they were dirty and he didn't want to touch anything.

"Go outside now," Theo said.

"No."

Theo's gaze shifted to his face: the soft, dark brown eyes, the worried crinkles around his mouth. "Please go wait outside."

"I can do this."

After a moment, Theo nodded. "Watch her." He made his way into the kitchen and did a quick search, throwing open cabinets, the oven, the warming drawer. He found the first stash when he lifted the range cover: dozens of baggies, already filled with crystal and ready for sale. He found kilo bags taped to the back of the sink. A box of Wheaties had more of the baggies.

"Stay the fuck out of my shit!" Sadie screamed from the other room.

When Theo went back to the living room, Auggie was pale and sweating, hands tucked under his arms. Theo touched his back lightly, and Auggie flinched. Then Theo sat on the couch facing Sadie.

"Every time you refuse to answer one of my questions," Theo said, "I'm going to take one of your baggies. Do you understand?"

"Fuck you."

"Go get one of the little ones," he said to Auggie.

Auggie's steps squeaked when he reached the linoleum.

"You fucking pieces of shit," Sadie screamed, thrashing in the chair, kicking wildly. Theo was just out of reach, but she kept trying. "I will fucking kill you!"

"Do you understand?"

"My boss is going to spend days on you. Days. He's going to take you apart."

"Take one of the medium ones," Theo said. Then, to Sadie, he added, "Next time, it's a kilo because you're pissing me off. Do you understand?"

Sadie stared at him. When Theo opened his mouth, she screamed, "Yes, God damn it!" She was taking huge, uncontrolled breaths, and a blood bubble at her nostril inflated and shrank wildly. "Yes, I fucking understand!"

"Here's the thing about drug dealers: you're all so fucking suspicious of each other." Theo let a silent moment expand. "That's because you're all pieces of shit, of course. About the foulest, most disgusting shit on the planet. So in case you're having a hard time understanding how everything is going to play out—drug dealers are also notoriously fucking stupid, which I'm assuming is true for you too—I'll explain it. You're already short because I took some of your stash. That means you're going to have to make up the difference yourself when the middleman shows up to collect. If you're lucky, you either paid in advance or you've got some money saved up, but I don't think that's the case here. So you'll have to cover the money from selling the rest of this shit. If you're careful, I think you'll be fine. But if I take a kilo, boy, that's going to be really hard to cover. And even harder to explain. What are you going to tell him? You got robbed? Maybe he believes you. Maybe not. Either way, you're no fucking use to him." Theo took another breath. "We're going to have a talk. Then we're going to leave with—God, for your sake—I really hope no more than two baggies. And you're not going to tell anyone, and that'll be the end of it. Am I clear?"

She jerked her head once in a nod.

"Tell me about Cal."

"I don't know what you're talking about."

"All right," Theo said with a sigh. "That's a kilo."

"No, fuck, no. I just don't know what you mean."

"Specificity," Auggie said from the kitchen opening. "Take a breath."

It was a moment before Theo realized Auggie was talking to him, and then, as though he were seeing himself from the outside, he was aware of the haze of rage and fear that was making it difficult to think, that was forcing him to breathe in rapid, gulping swallows. He took a few deep breaths and met Sadie's gaze again.

"Did you sell to Cal?"

"Cal Reese? The sports guy?"

"That's the one."

Another of those jerky nods.

"When was the last time you saw him?"

"I don't know, man. He's been dead forever. It was a long time ago."

"Did you kill him?"

"What? Fuck no. I heard they found him out at the rest stop."

"Was he out there buying drugs?"

"Damn, man. I don't know. He could get whatever he wanted from me. He was fun to party with. If he was out there to buy, nobody's talking about it."

Theo tried to gauge her sincerity. "So you don't know who killed him? You don't have any idea?"

"No. Who the fuck do you think I am? I sell crystal. I party. This isn't some *Breaking Bad*-style shit."

"Think really hard," Theo said. "How long was it between when you sold to Cal and you found out he was dead? A long time? A short time?"

"You broke my nose, fucker. Holy shit. That's really starting to hurt."

"You want me to take another bag?"

"I don't know! I told you, I don't know. I don't remember. Sometimes he scored every week. Sometimes more. Sometimes less. It was months ago, man."

Theo glanced at Auggie.

"Who might have wanted to hurt Cal?" Auggie asked. "Did he ever talk about what was going on in his life? Problems he might be having?"

"Oh, sure. We braided each other's hair and I told him how Missy's mom had gotten fake titties and he told me he kissed Polly under the swing set." To Theo, she added, "You probably shouldn't bring your baby out to play with the big kids. Not until his balls drop, anyway."

For a moment, the rage that twisted Auggie's face made Theo forget everything else. It was a degree of anger that was totally out of proportion to the comment. Then it was gone, but Auggie's cheeks were flushed, his dark eyes wide and the pupils huge.

"Just for that," Theo said, "you can get that belt off yourself. Come on."

Still carrying the baggies, Auggie followed him out of the house.

They drove a zigzag of blocks until Theo said, "Stop here."

Auggie stopped the car and glanced over his shoulder. "Do you think she's—"

"Give me those."

"What?"

"Give me those baggies."

The hesitation was worse than the words. "Theo, I'm trying to tread really lightly here, but you've got a history of—"

"I'm not going to keep them, dummy. But I don't want you keeping them either. I'm going to dump them down the storm drain."

"Great," Auggie said. "We can do it together." He shifted the car into park, got out, and walked to the storm drain.

Theo swore. Then, yanking on the handle, he opened the door and got out. When he got to the storm drain, Auggie displayed the two baggies and emptied them both down the drain. Then he displayed the empty bags.

"Those too."

Auggie tossed them.

"Relieved?" Theo said. "I barely managed to resist the urge to light up a pipe and smoke them right here."

"You can be mad at me if you want," Auggie said. "I'm used to it by now."

"I'm not an addict, Auggie. I made a mistake. I took a pill for my knee and thought I could handle a beer on top of it. I learned my lesson." He blew out a breath. "And I don't even think I thanked you for, you know, helping me."

"You puked a ton."

Theo winced.

"And you scared me."

"I'm sorry. That was months ago, though. I'm fine."

"Yeah," Auggie said, and for some reason he looked tired. "Let's just go."

They drove through the rundown neighborhood, taking different streets this time, looping back toward campus by a route that took almost twice the time it should have. The Civic's whining had taken on a new intensity, and something heavy was clunking rhythmically under the hood. The burned smell was worse than ever. Theo fought the need to say something; whatever peace they had established was tenuous, and he didn't need Auggie biting his head off again for an innocent observation about preventative maintenance.

Instead of heading for the Sigma Sigma house, though, Auggie kept going west to the little street at the edge of the city limits. They pulled up in front of Theo's garage—now that it was relatively empty, Theo had moved the Malibu inside. As they rolled up onto the driveway, the Civic released a shrieking hiss, and something—steam or smoke—boiled up from under the hood.

"Shit," Auggie said, stomping on the brakes. "Shit, shit, shit."

The car coasted to a stop and died.

"Shit," Auggie moaned, dropping his head onto the steering wheel. "There is no way this is happening."

Fanning the air, Theo said, "Let's get out and take a look. I'll call Cart; he's good with cars."

"No, it's fine, I'll get a tow truck out here."

Theo elbowed open the door. "It's your choice, but Cart's great at this kind of stuff, and—"

A brown Ford sedan was pulling up at the end of the driveway, blocking them in. Behind the wheel, Theo recognized a familiar face, complete with huge glasses and bristly mustache.

Theo slapped his keys into Auggie's hands. "Go inside. Right now."

Auggie was staring at him.

"Run!"

But it was too late. Albert Lender, detective for the Wahredua PD, was already out of his car. He wore a cheap suit that was the exact same color as his sedan. The glasses, with their enormous plastic frames, conspired with the mustache to hide most of his face. At first glance, he probably made most people think of a dentist or a tax accountant: short and squirrelly, harmless. In reality, though, the opposite was true. He was corrupt, he was ruthless, and he was perhaps the most dangerous man Theo knew.

"Hello, Theo," Lender said. "Is that August in there with you? Wonderful. I had a feeling I'd catch the two of you together. Let's go inside and have a talk."

My boss, Sadie had said. And his boss. And his boss. Theo had made a mistake. Theo had assumed she'd be too afraid to report their theft. But her fear of the men she worked for had trumped the other fear, it seemed.

"Auggie was just about to walk home," Theo said. He was still sitting in the car, the passenger door propped open. He wouldn't be able to put any force behind a blow. He wouldn't be able to surprise Lender with speed. "Car trouble."

"Walk home?" Lender clucked his tongue. "I don't think so, young man. No sidewalks out here. Something nasty could happen. Something really nasty. Walking on the shoulder of the road like that, he could get clipped by a car." Smiling, Lender put his hands on his hips, pushing back the jacket just enough to display his holstered gun. "You know, once, I saw this fellow run over a rabbit. Did it on purpose, out of plain meanness, I guess. He was driving a nice little sedan like mine. But he didn't stop there. He backed up and did it again. Went back and forth over that thing until it looked like he'd painted it on the asphalt with a roller brush. What do you think about that?"

"Theo?" Auggie whispered.

"It'll be ok," Theo said. His hand slid across the Civic's console, found Auggie's, and squeezed. He kept his gaze fixed on Lender. "Maybe he should wait here, then. He can wait for a tow truck."

"I don't think that's a good idea," Lender said. "Car jackings, you know. Sometimes they walk right up to the glass. Shoot you before you even know they're there." He tapped on the rear window with one chewed nail. Tap. Tap. Tap. "Hell of a mess."

Theo nodded. "Come on," he said to Auggie.

Auggie clutched his hand fiercely for a final instant before they got out of the car. They made their way up to the porch, with Lender following a safe distance behind, and Auggie tried to unlock the door. He dropped the keys twice because his hands were shaking. On the third try, Theo put his hand at the small of Auggie's back.

"You're going to be ok," Theo whispered. "You're smart and strong and brave, and you're going to get through this."

After a deep breath, Auggie nodded. He slid the key into the lock, and they went inside.

Lender kicked the door shut behind him. He looked around. "Well, Theo, you've really done a number getting this place looking so good. I expect that's thanks to Officer Cartwright as well. He's really a man of many talents, isn't he? I understand the two of you have become very close friends."

"What do you want?" Theo said.

"Well, Theo, August, I have a problem. And the problem is, I am what you might call an investor. And for the most part, I like to be a silent partner in this little business. It's something extra that I set aside for retirement, you understand, and I don't have time for the day-to-day operations. But every once in a while, I get a call, and I have to handle something. That's ok. I understand. That's what being a partner is all about. You've got to do some of the unpleasant stuff." A smile lifted his mustache. "Paperwork, for example. God, I hate paperwork."

"Paperwork," Auggie said, and then he laughed shrilly.

Theo found his wrist blindly and clamped down, and Auggie's laughter cut off with a wet noise that sounded suspiciously like a sob.

"And today, boy, I've got a hell of a mess of paperwork to sort out. Somebody assaulted an employee. A low-level employee, but you know, we're something of a family. And somebody stole some merchandise."

"We can pay—"

"The money isn't really the thing, Theo. You're missing the point. The point is paperwork. The point is that certain things need to be communicated. Now, I happen to know the little devils who caused all this mischief. When my partners called and told me that these rascals were asking questions, told me about two young men causing a world of trouble, I knew immediately who they were. And I offered to take care of things. Because, you know, I've got a bit of affection for these young men. Not paternal. What's the word? More like an uncle."

"Avuncular," Auggie said. He cleared his throat. "You mean avuncular."

"That's right, August. Very good." Lender fished a pair of handcuffs from his belt and tossed them to Theo. Theo caught them by reflex. "Put those on, Theo."

"No," Auggie said.

"August, be quiet. Today, you're going to sit and watch while Theo and I fill out some paperwork. Next time—if there is a next time—Theo will sit and watch, and you and I will work on the forms together. Theo, the handcuffs, please."

"No," Auggie said. "No, Theo, don't. Mr. Lender, we didn't know you were involved in this. We wouldn't have messed up your business if we'd known. It's a big misunderstanding. Please, we'll—"

"August, August, goodness. Calm down, please. There's nothing personal here; this is business. And the sooner done, the better."

The first cuff snicked shut around Theo's wrist.

"Behind your back, Theo."

He clicked the second cuff shut, his arms now pinioned. "Auggie, go sit on the couch. He's going to sit down; you said this is just about you and me."

But Auggie didn't budge.

"Very well, August," Lender said. "You can stay there if you like. But if you interfere, well—" Lender tapped the holster. Without any apparent concern, he turned his back on Theo and Auggie and walked to the coat rack near the door. He seemed to consider something for a moment. Then he snagged the cane Theo had used after the accident. It was solid hickory, and it could do a lot of damage. Theo knew because he'd been beaten with it before.

"Please don't hurt him," Auggie was saying, his voice choked with tears. Theo couldn't bring himself to look at Auggie's face; whatever was there would undo him. "Please. Please don't do this."

"Now, Theo," Lender said, swishing the cane through the air. It whistled. The sound raised the hair on the back of Theo's neck. "Remind me: which knee did you injure in your accident?"

Theo's throat locked up. He thought of the surgeries. The weeks and months of PT. The agony in simple things like hobbling to the fridge, struggling to keep his balance while he took a leak.

"This one," Lender pointed with the cane. "Correct?"

"No," Auggie said.

"I have to admit it's been a long time since I took an English class, but using your cane to cripple you—that's a kind of irony, right?"

"No," Auggie said, louder.

Theo managed to say, "Situational irony."

"Ah, that's it. You're so clever. And I am very sorry about this. I'll make it as fast as I can."

Lender brought the cane up and to the side.

Auggie jumped in front of Theo.

For the first time, annoyance flashed on Lender's face. "August, get out of the way."

"Move," Theo said. "Auggie, for the love of Christ, move."

"Not his knee," Auggie said. "Please. You don't know how hard that was for him."

"I'm losing patience, August."

"You can break my knee instead."

"No," Theo shouted. With his hands cuffed behind his back, he couldn't do what he needed to do: grab Auggie, shield him, get him away from all of this. All he could do was try to force his way forward. Auggie didn't even let him do that; with one hand, Auggie reached back and shoved Theo onto his ass, and Theo sat there, stunned, staring up at him.

"It doesn't matter which one," Auggie said. Theo was sitting slightly to the side, and he could see the weak smile that came onto Auggie's face. "Dealer's choice."

"Well, August, this is really very touching. I hope Theo realizes how lucky he is to have a friend like you."

"No," Theo screamed, his heels scraping across the floor as he tried to get up. "Lender, you motherfucker, don't you dare do this."

"And," Lender added with a wink, "I hope Officer Cartwright knows he has some stiff competition."

"Let me just—" Auggie said.

The first blow came so quickly and suddenly that Theo's warning scream cut off. The cane caught Auggie just below the shoulder, and Auggie shouted, the sound a mixture of pain and surprise. The next blow was almost as fast, landing just a few inches lower. Then another. The flurry of blows created a kind of humming noise, the pitch rising and falling, punctuated only by Auggie's shouts, then his screams. Somewhere between the fourth and fifth blow, Auggie fell. He tried to crawl, and Lender came after him, whipping him with the cane.

That was when Theo charged. He'd gotten to his feet; he wasn't sure how. He only knew he was going to kill Albert Lender, even if it meant tearing out his throat with his teeth. Lender heard him coming, straightened, turned, wiped sweat from his forehead. He jabbed Theo in the throat with the cane, and Theo went down, puking and gagging, almost aspirating some of the vomit and coughing even harder. For a while, that was all Theo could focus on: trying to clear his lungs and get air. His face was hot and wet, the taste of bile in his mouth, when he realized the sounds had stopped. Almost. Lender's labored breathing seemed to fill the room.

Then the cane fell, clattering against the floorboards. Lender's steps moved toward Theo.

"I'm going to kill you," Theo said, trying to rise from the puddle of his own sick.

"Just so we're clear, my partners and I had nothing to do with Calvin Reese's death. My suggestion is that this should be a natural endpoint to your investigation."

Theo tried to rise, but Lender kicked him once in the side of the head, and the world scrambled. When Theo came back, his wrists were free, and Lender was speaking.

"—boys have a wonderful Christmas. I know we're supposed to say holidays, but I'm old fashioned that way. And August, make sure you study. I expect you to get those straight A's again."

Then the door clicked shut, and Theo slid through his own vomit toward Auggie.

SPRING SEMESTER

JANUARY 2015

1

Auggie got back to Wahredua at almost midnight on the last Sunday in January, having put off his return as long as he could. The cold was eye stinging and started a minor headache. Under the crescent moon, the slush glowed so whitely that it verged on purple. With a pop of brakes, the shuttle pulled away from the curb behind him.

Maneuvering his bags one-handed, Auggie trudged toward the Sigma Sigma house, his high-tops sliding on the ice and old snow. The bags kept falling; his wrist was still healing, and he couldn't keep the smaller bag balanced on top of the larger one. Thank God the cast was about to come off.

At the side door, Auggie punched in the code, dragged his bags inside, and was greeted with the familiar post-party bouquet of spilled beer, body odor, and overdone perfume. A couple was passed out in the hall, the girl with her hand possessively on the guy's ass, and ahead, in the gallery, someone was asleep with a lampshade on their head. Ironic? Or just a genuine love for indoor lighting paraphernalia?

Auggie didn't even bother trying to make things easy for the partygoers. He dragged his luggage down the hall, ignoring the grunts and half-formed protests when he bumped into someone. He stopped in the kitchen, raided the fridge, and loaded half of a Blimpie's sub and a can of PBR on top of the luggage. Getting everything upstairs required two trips, and by the time he'd finished, his wrist was throbbing, and he was covered in a thin layer of sweat. His room was a disaster and, worse, had a serious, locker-room funk—apparently he'd forgotten to do laundry before leaving. After cracking the window, Auggie ate the sub sandwich in the dark. He finished the beer. He thought about brushing his teeth and gave up.

Giving up had slipped into his life after that day at Theo's. For the first few days, the combination of painkillers and aftershock had numbed Auggie to what had happened. He'd been comfortable. Hell, he'd been bouncing off the walls. Theo had spent the night with him at the hospital, and then he'd made sure Auggie got back to the Sigma Sigma house safely the next day. They'd worked up a story about a mugging, leaving Theo out of it, which was good because when Detective Somerset and Detective Upchurch came to take a statement from Auggie, Auggie thought Somerset in particular didn't look convinced. But Theo had obviously known how things would go, and he'd coached Auggie on which details to invent and which details he could claim to have forgotten; eventually, the detectives had left him alone.

After that, for a while, things had gotten even better. The mugging—and the fact that Auggie still had his phone and wallet—had given him a new level of street cred among the Sigma Sigma brothers. The guys who picked fights in bars and bragged about crushing the other team on the lacrosse field, the guys who hit the gym every day and who would get up in a stranger's face, screaming, they were the same guys who had grown up in six-hundred-thousand-dollar homes, driven Porsches and Beamers and Mercedes and Audis and Infinitis, had gone to prep schools and reform schools where the closest they'd ever come to real danger was if they were required to take wood shop. When they talked to Auggie, they seemed aware of the fact that the testosterone-fueled violence they manufactured in their day-to-day lives was the equivalent of shadow boxing. They hung on his every word.

And, of course, so did Auggie's online following. His idea to snap his way through his morning routine had solidified his place on Snapchat, and he'd kept up a solid stream of new, funny content on Instagram, Facebook, and Twitter. But the assault changed everything. Auggie was human in a way he'd never been for his followers. He snapped everything. He scripted and filmed a satire of frat boys getting mugged with Ethan and Orlando and a handful of friends he liked to rotate through his content; the video almost hit a million views. An agent who had dropped Auggie two years before called. "I fucked up, Auggie," were the opening words. "Tell me how much shit you want me to eat so I can make this right, and by the end of next year, I can have you making six figures."

Starting at the hospital, and every day after that, Dylan was there. He'd show up for a few minutes, bringing tea, a book of Zen meditations, a leather bracelet he had tooled by hand for Auggie. He snapped Auggie constantly, silly stuff that made Auggie smile: one raised eyebrow, with a lecture hall in the background; those huge, muscled legs stretched out on the sofa, ostensibly showing Auggie a new pair of red socks stitched with green Christmas elves; a sunrise after he had finished tai chi. Neither of them mentioned the night in Auggie's room. It was as though it had never happened.

Even finals went well. Four of Auggie's professors exempted him—he had solid A's in every class—and although Wagner begrudgingly gave extra time for Auggie to finish writing his essay, Auggie didn't really need it. He had already written most of it in his head before that day at Theo's, and he finished it with a battered paperback copy of *Romeo and Juliet* that Theo had provided without any sort of explanation. After Auggie submitted the paper, Wagner had written back a single line in an email: *A. Extenuating circumstances.* Theo had sworn a blue streak when Auggie told him; Auggie found the whole thing funny.

Theo was the problem. One of the problems. Theo was with Auggie for as much time as Auggie would allow. At first, it was comforting. Then, by degrees, less so. Theo didn't eat, as far as Auggie could tell. After a week, his face was hollow, his eyes marked with dark patches. He'd go home and shower and change his clothes, but when he'd come back, he'd be worse in some ways: his attention wandering, his pupils dilated, his words trailing off in the middle of conversations. When Auggie permitted it, Theo slept on the spare bed. Theo tried to laugh. Theo tried to make conversation. Theo tried to be Theo. But by the end of finals week, Auggie felt like he was being haunted by Theo's ghost, and it was a relief to get on the shuttle and pretend he didn't see Theo standing there, watching as he drove away.

Another problem, although in a different way, were the four weeks at home. Fer alternated between overly busy and having nothing to do. Chuy slept away the days and disappeared at night. Auggie's mom had spent the first forty-five minutes after he got home cooing over him, calling him her baby, making an ice pack for his bruises—"It happened weeks ago, Mom. I don't need an ice pack."—and then Birch called, and she left, giving air kisses as she backed out the door.

"He's twenty-two fucking years old," Fer said after he and Auggie had burned through half a joint together. "If I have to pay for that fucker to have braces, I'm going to fucking kill myself."

When they were well on their way with the second joint, Fer came back from his room with a gun.

"What the hell?" Auggie said.

"Who did that to you?"

"What?"

"I'm going to kill whoever did that to you."

"Fer, Jesus, I told you: I got mugged. I don't know who did it. Wait, when did you get a gun?"

"When our shit-bucket brother decided to become a junkie." Fer set the gun on the coffee table and hit the joint hard, staring at the weapon's dull metal plating. Passing back the joint, he exhaled and wiped his eyes. "I want to kill them, Augustus. I want to do to them everything they did to you and then perforate their anal cavity with this fucking gun, and I'm not talking about using bullets."

That was the first night of the dreams, although dreams might have been too strong of a word. There was nothing visual to them, only the sense of being trapped, the memory of the blows that wouldn't stop, the helplessness of it. He jolted out of sleep, crying so hard that he had to bite the blanket because he was afraid he'd wake someone up. That's why he was awake when Chuy got home. That's why he was awake when he heard the sound of gagging in the next room. He found Chuy passed out on his back, trying to breathe through his own vomit. Auggie screamed for Fer, flipped Chuy onto his stomach, and pounded on his back. By the time Fer got there, the gun in one hand, Chuy was breathing somewhat normally again.

"What are we supposed to do?" Auggie said.

"Nothing. It's his mess; let him clean it up."

"Fer—"

"And I'm not just talking about the puke."

Fer went to bed without saying another word. After that, Auggie woke up at night to check that Chuy was home and breathing. He slept fitfully in the day. He smoked more weed with Fer on the days Fer seemed at a breaking point. The day, for example, the medical bills from Missouri started coming in. Fer had smoked down three joints that night, shuffling papers at the kitchen table long after Auggie tried to go to bed. When Auggie did sleep, and when he woke screaming, he was somehow unsurprised when the door opened and Fer was there, the way Fer was always there. He stretched out on the bed next to Auggie, smelling skunky, his voice distant and dopey as he told Auggie to go back to sleep.

"You did this when I was a kid," Auggie said as the black tide rolled in, the memory startling in its reappearance, something he hadn't thought about in years. Men coming over. Strange men. Frightening men. His mother's friends, who were loud and laughed too much and played music when they closed the door to his mother's room. And Auggie remembered the creak of the bunk beds when Fer climbed up to make sure Auggie could sleep.

"Go to sleep, Augustus," Fer mumbled, his voice like a kite pulling away.

Now, in the darkness of the Sigma Sigma house, with winter blowing in through the window, Auggie felt relief again, the relief of having escaped. He slept. He dreamed. He woke shivering and crying, and he stumbled to the window to shut it. The world outside was quietly luminous: the snow, the streetlights, the moon, a lone pair of headlights adrift on the black current of asphalt. This was the world, he thought with half-waking clarity. Shiny and dead.

2

The Sunday night before spring semester began, Theo finished the Percocet with the last of the Christmas ale. It wasn't anything serious. It wasn't anything like an attempt. It was more like what Theo remembered with his brothers growing up. Jacob, the oldest, had been a carbon copy of their father: a lover of rules, a drawer of lines. At eleven, Jacob had been literal about the lines, once chalking a boundary down the middle of the room he had briefly shared with Theo. And although Theo couldn't put it into words—wouldn't be able to put it into words until he was in therapy—he had resented Jacob, resented his father, hated how easily they seemed to fit into the world they had outlined, and how Theo sensed but couldn't name all the ways he fell outside their lines. So Theo had made a game of it, edging up to that skinny chalk stripe while Jacob read Leviticus, his big toe threatening to cross over. It always ended in a fight, usually with Theo's ear puffy and aching, maybe his jaw throbbing, maybe a bloody nose. With the Percocet, it was like that: getting right up to the line, waiting for somebody to come along and clock him so he'd get back in place.

For the time being, Cart seemed the most likely candidate to do the clocking. The first few weeks after that day, Theo and Cart had seen each other only once, the night after Auggie was home from the hospital. They had fought—Theo wasn't clear about what because he'd been exceptionally drunk—and after that, they had avoided each other, with Cart sending brittle messages asking if Theo was ok, and with Theo answering only when his guilt about Cart briefly overwhelmed his guilt about Auggie.

Then Auggie had left, not even glancing back from the shuttle, on an overexposed December day. The sun rode on the shuttle's panels, gleaming so brightly that the afterimage lingered in Theo's vision, and he had to bike home with the purple ghost of the shuttle floating ahead of him. That night had been another big fight, another one that Theo didn't remember.

He remembered that day with Lender very clearly, but he took great pains not to remember anything after the hospital. Everything up to the hospital—the ambulance ride with Auggie, squeezing Auggie's ankle, biting his own lip so hard that one of the paramedics made him tilt his head back and pinched his lip with gauze to check if it needed stitches—was clear. And then the emergency room, the tiny examination cubicle, the papery texture of the privacy curtain, the smell of disinfectant. Even the semi-private room where Auggie lay, stoned, in a hospital gown and sporting a woody that defied whatever narcotics the doctor had given him. Then Theo had decided he couldn't do this anymore, not and keep himself straight at the same time, and after that the days and weeks became a blur.

After Auggie left, though, Cart came over more often. They traded blowjobs. Cart made dinner. Or he brought pizza. Or he brought booze, and he drank as much as Theo, and they fucked until both of them blacked out. One night, Cart made Theo sit on the floor between his legs, trying to work the tension from Theo's shoulders, and Theo had blacked out with his head against Cart's knee. He had woken up in bed, unsure of how he had gotten there—Cart couldn't have carried him, so Theo must have walked—with Cart in the middle of a conversation that Theo belatedly realized he was part of.

"—why won't you tell me what's wrong?" Cart was saying. "Why won't you just tell me?"

"I don't know," Theo said muzzily. "Nothing's wrong."

"Well fuck, you peckerbrained motherfucker. I can't fix nothing!"

Theo skipped Christmas with his parents that year. He couldn't stand the thought of dealing with them. He couldn't stand the possibility of anything that might bring Luke or Auggie to the foreground. He spent all of Christmas with Lana—in the weeks since that day, Lana had been the only bright spot in his life, but a reminder, too, because he'd been supposed to keep her safe as well— and helped her open the toys that the OTs had recommended. He didn't go home until she fell asleep. Cart was sitting in his truck at the curb when Theo walked down the street.

"Where were you?" Cart said in the kitchen while Theo opened a Christmas ale.

Theo took a long drink before answering, "Seeing Lana."

"You walked?"

"I had to walk back."

"On your fucking knee?"

"The buses had stopped."

"And what the fuck am I? I can't give you a fucking ride?"

Theo drained the beer. He rinsed it in the sink and pitched it into the recycling. "Seems like a lot." Then he brushed past Cart toward the living room.

"No," Cart said, grabbing his shoulder. "No goddamn way. What does that mean?"

"You don't want to meet my family. You don't want to go to my department holiday party. You don't want me to meet your family. You don't want me to go to your department holiday party. But now you want to pick me up after I visit my daughter, the one I had with my dead husband, my little girl who's probably got permanent disabilities. Just seems like a lot."

Swallowing, Cart released Theo. "You sure know how to cut up a guy, don't you?"

"Sorry. That's not how I meant it."

"Sure."

Cart rode his dick that night, Theo struggling to stay hard and, more importantly, conscious. It was the first time Cart had let him anywhere near his ass, and after Cart came, gasping, on Theo's chest and belly, he bent forward, his flushed and sweaty face against Theo's shoulder, his body so still that Theo drifted away again.

"—be my boyfriend," his voice pulled Theo back, "or be boyfriends or however the fucking hell I'm supposed to say it. And I'll—I'll do whatever you want. I just need to take it slow. I'm scared shitless, but I'm even more scared I'll lose you if I just stand around jerking off."

"No," Theo said softly, walking his fingers up Cart's shoulder, feeling the wiry, country-boy strength there. The erection that had been so difficult to maintain a few minutes ago was suddenly there, and Theo nudged Cart with his knee, rolling Cart onto his back, Cart's eyes widening. Theo slid into him, shushing him as Cart whimpered. "Neither of us is going anywhere. Now let me show you how good this can be."

After that, Cart slept over more often. He was there the night before spring semester, flat on his back, one arm under the pillow. Theo's hand was on his belly, the brown hairs over Cart's country-boy abs tickling his palm. The Percocet was doing something different tonight. Theo hadn't been able to get hard, but he'd asked Cart to fuck him anyway, and a white noise, like a train's steam whistle, built in his head through the sex. It was still there now, a silent scream inside his head, making everything foggy. Tomorrow: pick up the copies of the syllabi, make sure the projector works, grab the interlibrary loan that just came in. Go back, start over: shower, make Cart oatmeal and bacon and eggs, pump up the bike's rear tire. Go back, from the top: put an extra bar of soap in the shower for Cart, then shower, then make Cart oatmeal and bacon and eggs. He could do another year of this. On the outside, Theo thought as he slid his hand along Cart's belly, he could do five.

3

The message appeared in Message Requests, which meant it had come from someone Auggie wasn't friends with. It also meant he almost missed it—he checked the requests regularly, but he mostly skimmed because too many were from fans who assumed that Auggie's cheerful, happy-go-lucky, and adorable virtual persona meant they would be automatic best friends.

Genesis Evans: *I need to talk to you and your friend.*

Auggie considered the message. Then he went back to the comments on his latest video: a goofy montage of Ethan dragging Auggie out of bed for class. Even though he no longer tried to respond to all of the comments—even if he'd wanted to, it would have taken too much time—he still made sure to stay in touch with his fans. He always hit the three S's: sad, sweet, and silly. For sad, he thanked *tommyin_da_house* for asking about his injuries and explained that a full recovery would take a long time; for sweet, he answered *aplolsgirlo3*'s post where she asked to marry him with a quick spin on how talented and funny she was, and how she'd find a straight guy soon; for silly, he found *gayfratbro*'s comment about climbing into bed with Auggie instead of dragging him out and informed him that he'd have to provide his own footsie pajamas.

Throughout all of this, Genesis's message was in the back of his head. His thumb paused in the middle of scrolling, and he remembered the cane catching him on the shoulder. He was typing out his joke about footsie pajamas, and he remembered the weeks after the attack, Theo's glassy eyes and the way his head rolled on his neck. When he'd finished answering the comments, he closed his social media apps and started getting ready for class. This semester, he had a relatively late start—nothing until eleven.

But his phone buzzed again almost immediately. It was a snap from Dylan. He was lying on his stomach in bed, one hand playing with his curls in way that accentuated the muscles in his arm. The message said, *Rambo, let me see them guns.*

Since the attack—and the story Auggie and Theo had concocted about Auggie defending himself from a mugger—Dylan had dropped "little bro." Now it was thug, beast, monster, stud, and the one that seemed to be Dylan's personal favorite: Rambo. Auggie took a picture of a corner of his face, his eye squinting in mock anger, and wrote, *Creep.*

Dylan's next snap was of him on his back, shirtless, his lower lip caught by his teeth, his fingers playing with one nipple. *Please?*

Auggie immediately screenshotted the image. Then, after a moment of hesitation, he sent Dylan a picture of his coat.

The snap that came back was of Dylan's abs, his thumb hooking the waistband of a jockstrap. *I keep thinking about how you fucked up those muggers. I know violence shouldn't turn me on . . .* The next snap came almost immediately: Dylan's fingers inching down the elastic to expose matted blond pubic hair, the bulge of his dick outlined where the jock's fabric pulled tight. *. . . . but you're just such a fucking man.*

The heat that started between Auggie's legs pooled in his belly, ran up his chest, and sent a flush into his throat. He wriggled out of his tank, adjusted the lighting in the room, and did a few pushups. Then, after checking himself in the mirror—his arms were tiny next to Dylan's or Theo's—he perched on the desk, fist under his chin, elbow on his knee. He sent the selfie before he could reconsider.

Dylan's response: his hand squeezing his junk, the words *fuck yeah.* Then, almost immediately, another: his face, the curls a messy tangle over his eyes. *Been missing you and that killer body. Gym?*

Part of Auggie thought about the vast silences that opened up in their messages, all the times Dylan didn't answer, even times when Auggie really needed someone. The usual flood of excuses followed. Dylan was busy. Dylan had made it clear he wanted to build something real, which meant moving slow. Dylan hadn't known that Auggie needed someone because Auggie hadn't told him. And so Auggie walled away the tiny voice that said Dylan ought to have known, at least for the big stuff, without Auggie telling him.

Another snap came from Dylan. This one was a checklist: *1. Gym 2. Yoga 3. Meditate 4. Smoothies 5. Chill and catch up.*

Auggie snapped a picture of himself rolling his eyes.

Dylan's snap back was cockier than usual, on his back again, arm behind his head, exposing the blond fur of one pit. *Fuck yeah, slayer.*

Auggie went to the shower and jacked off. He got ready for the day, snapping his way through the process, and then, dressed in

Sperry's, khakis, and a Vineyard Vines sweatshirt, he sat on his bed. He kept thinking about the interaction with Dylan, about being called Rambo, about the way Dylan got hot just for a picture of Auggie. Dylan didn't worry about Auggie getting home safely. Dylan didn't nag about Auggie finishing his homework. Dylan didn't give humiliating lectures about condoms or about how most people couldn't separate sex from the emotions that came with it. Dylan didn't even seem to think about that stuff, probably because Dylan saw Auggie as an adult, as his equal, instead of as a kid.

Auggie tapped out his message to Genesis before he could reconsider: *Where and when?*

Almost immediately, the composition bubbles appeared by her name.

While she was still replying, he opened a separate message to Theo and typed, *I'm meeting with Genesis today, if you want to come.* As soon as he sent it, he regretted opening the message that way. *Oh, and happy New Year, Merry Christmas. I got back to Wahredua last night.*

Because Theo still used an ancient flip phone, Auggie had no idea if he was replying.

Genesis's message came through: *Library? 1:30?*

2? Class.

2.

Auggie sent her a thumbs up. Theo still hadn't responded, so Auggie sent him the time and place and headed for class.

4

Theo was assisting Wagner again—another section of the same class that Auggie had been in the semester before—when the texts came through. The classroom smelled like wet wool and what might have been rust, which he associated with the massive radiators that were used to heat the building. Wagner was at the front of the room, droning through the syllabus. Half the kids were already asleep, and the other half were barely on this side of consciousness. Staring at his phone, at the messages from Auggie, Theo managed not to scream.

The rest of class was a blur. He went to his office. He turned on the computer. He left the door open, hoping the smell of vanilla-and-chai tea, which Grace must have left on her desk over the break, would dissipate. Then, at his desk, he stared at the document he had pulled up on the screen. His thesis. The *Romeo and Juliet* chapter. And for the life of him, he had no idea what it said.

Over the course of the next few hours, he typed a handful of words. He ate the peanut-butter sandwich he'd brought from home. When he needed to break up the monotony of staring at the screen, he shuffled the printouts of scholarly articles. At quarter to two, he packed his satchel, locked the office, and headed across campus to the library.

In the lobby, which had been redone a few years ago in the blond woods and glass and chrome that made it look like a Scandinavian spaceship, he found Auggie.

"Hey," Auggie said, a huge smile spreading across his face. He stepped forward and hesitated.

"Just give me a hug," Theo said, "so we can get it over with."

Auggie squeezed him hard, his face against Theo's shoulder, the cast on his wrist bumping Theo's back. The hug lasted a long time, and Theo felt the tremors working their way through Auggie. He ran his hand down Auggie's spine, counting the bumps of vertebrae, until Auggie pulled away. The younger man's face was blotchy, and the smile was twitchy, slipping away every time Auggie seemed to forget to keep it in place.

"I didn't know—" Auggie stopped. "It's really good to see you."

"How are you?"

"Me? I'm great." The smile twitched some more. "How are you?"

"Really? You're great?"

"Yeah. I had a great break. I had such a great time being home. What about you?"

"Yeah," Theo said. "Me too. Are you sure you're ok?"

"Um, yeah. Just kind of overwhelmed. I thought maybe—I don't know, I was having this great morning, Dylan and I were—" He faltered, then rushed ahead. "And then you never texted back, and I thought maybe you hated me and didn't want to see me anymore. So I'm just really happy. You know. Happy to see you."

But he didn't look happy. That first smile, the huge one, had looked like Auggie. But the person in front of Theo had dark circles under his eyes, and he held himself awkwardly, as though keeping a very specific pose to avoid aggravating his injuries any further. Whatever he said about being worried that Theo might not show—and Theo didn't doubt that was true; he was irritated he hadn't forced himself to answer Auggie's texts—something else was at the heart of Auggie's distress. Something that had been torturing him for a lot longer.

"How are you?" Auggie asked.

"How do I look?"

Auggie bit his lip, and Theo couldn't tell if he was on the brink of smiling or crying. He wasn't sure Auggie knew either. "Pretty awful."

"There you go," Theo said.

Before Auggie could respond, Genesis stepped into the lobby. She still had her hair in braids, but she was wearing a parka and snow boots—a far change from the t-shirt and shorts when they had seen her months ago. Theo could glimpse a t-shirt under her parka: *Cowboy Bebop.*

"Hi," she said. "Sorry I'm late."

"You're not late," Auggie said. "I booked us a study room. Is that ok? Or do you want to talk down here?"

"No, a study room would be better." She glanced around. "Can we go up?"

They headed through the security gates, up two flights of stairs, and past a row of carrels. The study rooms lined the back of this floor, with soundproofed windows and a thick door so that groups could collaborate without disturbing other library patrons. Auggie directed them toward one at the end, where windows overlooked a portion of the quad: a few patches of pristine snow, but mostly slush and a muddy crisscross of tracks. A banner on the side of the arts facility said JUSTICE FOR DEJA – RALLY FOR JUSTICE FRIDAY. Two boys were playing catch in tank tops and shorts, obviously hoping to impress passersby with their total disregard for the cold. Theo hoped their sense of self-satisfaction endured having their dicks de-tipped after they got frostbite.

When Auggie shut the door, Genesis let out a huge breath. She laid both hands flat on the table, as though steadying herself, and said, "I'm sorry about last time."

"There's nothing to apologize for," Auggie said. "Your dad and brother were being protective."

Genesis shook her head, but she didn't respond. Overhead, the fluorescents buzzed, and the vent in the wall gave a little cough as something in the HVAC system shifted. Then Genesis shook her head again, this time squeezing her eyes shut, her fingers curling on the table.

"Genesis?" Theo said.

"I'm sorry." She grabbed her bag. "I'm sorry, I can't do this."

"Let's see if we can help you," Auggie said. "You don't have to do it on your own."

Lowering her bag, she sank back into the seat.

"Something happened with you and Cal," Auggie said. "Is that what you wanted to talk about?"

Genesis nodded.

"And you think it has something to do with his murder?"

Another nod.

"What happened?" Auggie asked.

Covering her eyes, Genesis shook her head.

"You know what happened," Theo said to Auggie. "Or you can guess. They were in a room, just the two of them. The door was shut. Maybe it was late, after everybody else had gone home. And then Cal assaulted her."

The whining static of the fluorescents was the only answer.

When Genesis spoke, her voice was perfectly controlled, but she kept a hand over her eyes. "They have a massage table; they're both trained physical therapists. I'd been back there plenty of times. My elbow, my shoulder, my thigh. Tennis is hard on your body, and it's even harder if you want to be good. We'd gotten back from a singles tournament. My parents and my brother miscommunicated; nobody came to pick me up. It's not like we live in New York City. I could have walked home. But I'd had a bad fall in the last match, and my leg was hurting. Cal offered to take another look and then drive me home. I walked back to the massage table. He closed the door. He turned off all the lights except one on the opposite side of the room. To help me relax, he said. He told me to lie down on my stomach. Then he went out of the room for something."

She stopped, took a shuddering breath, and uncovered her eyes. They were red and puffy, but she wasn't crying. If anything, she looked closer to anger than tears.

"If you don't—" Auggie began.

Theo touched his shoulder and shook his head.

"When he came back, he grabbed my neck, like this, hard." She demonstrated, grabbing the back of her own neck. "He was holding me down. I said something, I don't know what, and then his hand was up my skirt. He got a finger—" She stopped, exhaling slowly. "He kept saying, 'You're such a dirty girl. This is what dirty girls need, isn't it?' Weird, sick stuff like that. I just lay there. I was scared. And he was hurting me. But mostly I was just so surprised. You never met Cal?"

Theo and Auggie shook their heads.

"Then you can't understand why it was such a surprise. In a million years, the Cal I thought I knew never would have done something like that. So I just lay there."

"You can't blame yourself," Auggie said. "I just—I just got attacked, and I didn't do anything either. Sometimes surprise makes it hard to act."

"Oh, I did something. As soon as I processed what was happening, I screamed. He flinched, and it was enough for me to sit up and push him off me. Then I hit him. I kept hitting him until he got out of my way. He was shouting at me, telling me I'd misunderstood. How the hell am I supposed to misunderstand him sticking a finger in me? As soon as he was out of my way, I ran for the door. I ran all the way home."

"But you didn't tell your parents," Theo said quietly.

Wiping dry eyes, she studied him. "No. I didn't. Not for a while, anyway. How'd you know?"

"No assault charges. No rape kit. No physical evidence collected from both of you. What you described, the way he touched you, the way you hit him—it would have left plenty of proof to confirm your story."

"I took a shower," Genesis said. She laughed softly, playing with her braids. "God, I just felt dirty. And I didn't tell my parents because everyone loved Cal. They loved Cal. I loved Cal. And I kept thinking he was right—that somehow I'd misunderstood. But I couldn't go to practice anymore. I tried, once, and had a panic attack. He was just standing there, talking to the girls, laughing, all of them in love with him the way I'd been a few days before. I skipped. I lied. Eventually it caught up to me, and my parents wanted to know where I'd been. I told them. I didn't even mean to—it just came out."

"But by then," Theo said, "Cal's bruises were gone."

She nodded. "If I even left any on him. I couldn't tell very well from a distance, but he didn't look like he had bruises. I mostly hit him in the arms, the chest, trying to get him away from me. I asked some of the other girls if they'd seen anything, marks on him, anything that looked like he'd been in a fight. They all said no."

"Did you file charges?"

"It had been months. We talked to the police, but nobody could confirm my story. Nobody remembered me staying late with Cal. Nobody could prove that I'd been alone with him. Nobody believed me. That's not what they said, but I knew what they meant. My parents want to go ahead with the civil lawsuit, but apparently that's pending too because the county attorney's office is still trying to decide if they'll charge Cal, and the lawyer told us to keep it quiet until we see what they do. It's been unreal; everybody talking about him, not knowing what he really was. I mean, he's dead, so I guess they'll never know. I don't know. It's been this nightmare that just won't end."

"Until Cal died."

Swallowing, she nodded.

"Where's Orlando in all of this?"

"I met him through Cal and Wayne. He'd come by the training facility in the summer to do odd jobs. He's sweet, you know? A little . . . a little intense, I guess is the right word. He comes on really strong. And he can be clingy."

"Obsessive, I'd say," Theo muttered, but he ducked his head when Auggie shot him a look.

"He really liked me. And I liked that—that he'd do whatever I asked him to do, put up with me being at practice for long hours, put up with me not bringing him over to my house, put up with me never having a weekend free. Wayne gave him so much crap about being whipped." Her expression softened. "You ever see how his family treats him?"

"Yes," Auggie said.

She nodded, as though that explained everything. "After what happened with Cal, though, I couldn't be around him. The whole family, they all look the same, and every time I even thought about Orlando, I would see Cal, feel him touching me. I didn't even break up with Orlando. I just stopped talking to him. I couldn't—I couldn't be around him."

"Shit," Auggie said. "And Orlando did what pre-therapy Orlando always did: he kicked it into overdrive."

"My parents thought he was this crazy psycho stalker."

"They weren't wrong," Theo said.

Auggie shot him another look.

"I tried telling them," Genesis spread her hands, "he was sweet, he was just intense, he wouldn't hurt anyone. But my brother and Orlando got into it one time. Wise is just as strongheaded as my dad, and when he ran into Orlando, they started fighting." She snorted. "Wise hasn't ever thrown a punch in his life. He's a big guy, though, and Orlando can be scary when he gets intense—he's a wrestler, you know, and he knows how to hurt people. My parents separated them before they really did any damage, but I told Orlando I never wanted to see him again. I still don't. It's not his fault; I know he's a good guy. But I can't ever be around him again. I can't."

Theo opened his mouth, but Auggie spoke first. "You messaged me for a reason," he said quietly. "And I don't think it was just to tell us this story."

After giving her braids a tug, Genesis shook her head. She pulled out her phone, tapped the screen, and a recording began to play.

"—and I said I don't care. Fifteen thousand dollars—"

"Fifteen thousand dollars is a lot of money, Dad!"

"Not enough for what he did to your sister. That man deserved to die. I don't have any regrets."

Then a door slammed in the background, and the recording ended.

"My dad," she whispered, "and Wise."

5

"Fuck, Rambo," Dylan said, spotting the barbell as Auggie lowered it. "You're getting some legit guns."

Auggie exhaled sharply, lifting the weights, ignoring how his arm screamed at him.

"Fuck yeah, Rambo." Dylan held the other end of the bar, enabling Auggie to lift it one-handed without using his broken wrist. "Fucking get it."

He made it through six reps before he grunted, and Dylan helped him rack the barbell.

"Ten more pounds this time," Dylan said.

Groaning, Auggie wiped his face.

"Come on, Rambo. Don't wimp out on me."

"Let's switch."

"Not yet. Ten more. Last set." Dylan straightened from where he had bent to pick up two five-pound weights, grinned, and said, "Let me see those weapons of mass destruction."

Auggie flipped him off.

Dylan waited.

Grinning, Auggie flexed his arm.

"Fuck yeah."

When Auggie flipped him off again, Dylan laughed and added the weights to the bar.

By the third rep, Auggie's arms were shaking, and he was releasing tiny bursts of breath as he struggled to keep the barbell steady.

"Do it," Dylan shouted down into his face. "Do it! Get that fucking bar up or quit wasting my fucking time!"

Somehow, Auggie did it.

"Fuck yes," Dylan said. "You are a fucking stud!"

Workouts with Dylan were always intense—had been, even before Lender had broken Auggie's wrist. Dylan knew exactly how far he could push Auggie. He knew how much he could ask of him. And Auggie gave it to him because of the way Dylan grinned at him, slapped him five, wrapped an arm around his neck, called him Rambo.

They mixed protein shakes in blender bottles, sitting at a table in the gym's tiny recovery area. Auggie fumbled with the cap a few times; he was shaky, but the good kind of shaky, like he'd pushed himself just past where he thought his limits were. Dylan was sweaty and had gotten a good pump, but he hadn't worked nearly as hard. He didn't need to. He was already layered in muscle.

"How many grams of protein are you getting every day?" Dylan asked.

"This has sixty grams."

"I'm talking total."

Auggie shrugged.

"I told you to count your macros."

"Right, I know. Sorry."

"Your body is a temple, Auggie."

"I know, I know. I just—I kind of fell off the wagon after I got hurt."

Dylan grunted and looked away, watching other guys in the gym.

"I'm going to try that app you recommended," Auggie said.

"Sure," Dylan said. He was studying a twinkie blond who was standing in front of a mirrored wall, doing hammer curls with fifteen-pound dumbbells.

"And I did a lot of research," Auggie said, rattling the blender ball in his bottle. "This is the best protein on the market. It's whey, and it's a protein isolate, so way less fat and stuff. They even blend in some creatine." He didn't add that the tub of powder had cost almost two hundred dollars.

"You're probably not drinking enough water."

"No, I'm going to start doing what you told me, about taking a gallon jug to class with me."

"You're going to start?"

"I mean," Auggie said, "I was doing it, but—"

Dylan pushed back from the table, pounded the rest of his shake, and stood. He looked at Auggie, looked at Auggie's blender bottle, and said, "I guess I just think you shouldn't be violating your body with animal products. Sorry. That's just me. I only do plant-based protein powders."

"But I thought you told me—" He stopped because Dylan had already left, headed for the locker room. When he caught up, Dylan had stripped down to his compression shorts. His body was chiseled—he was a big guy without a trace of fat, every muscle crisply defined. A hint of stubble showed on his chest, and it was obvious Dylan had manscaped everywhere he could reach. The first few times they had worked out, Auggie had tried not to stare. Now he enjoyed looking, but only because it was just the two of them in the locker room.

"If you start doing what I tell you," Dylan said, his gaze fixed on his shirt as he turned it right-side out. "And I'm saying if because you apparently think I'm full of crap—"

"No, I don't. I must have missed when you told me—"

"—then I think you're going to be a fucking beast by the time lacrosse season rolls around."

Auggie was too surprised to say anything. Then he finally managed: "Really?"

With a tiny grin, Dylan looked up. "I know I'm intense. But I want what's best for you, and I care about you because I know you're special. I know you've got potential."

"It's ok," Auggie said. Heat ran through him, and his heart hammered in his ears. He turned himself out of his shirt, the movement awkward because of his cast. "I can handle intense."

"Holy shit," Dylan said. He was staring at Auggie.

"I don't really think I've gotten much bigger—"

"Auggie, I had no fucking idea." He was staring at the bruises, mostly green and yellow now, some almost completely faded. "I thought—I mean, I knew you hurt your wrist, but I had no idea. Why didn't you tell me?"

Auggie shrugged.

Coming closer, Dylan brought up a hand. His touch was light, slick with sweat, gliding along Auggie's scapula, following the curve of his ribs, tightening around the swell of his bicep. They were alone, and Auggie's dick hardened, his nipples hardened. Dylan's erection was visible through the thin nylon of his shorts.

"Who the fuck did this?" he mumbled, seemingly to himself.

Covering one nipple with his hand, Auggie said, "I don't know, I just—"

Dylan locked both hands around Auggie's waist and steered him backward, guiding him down the length of the locker room. The showers were private here, individual rooms with long curtains. The air was humid and smelled like Zest soap. When Auggie pushed through the curtain, the wet vinyl clung to him, cold enough to make him shiver, and then it fell shut behind Dylan.

"Dylan," Auggie said.

"Be quiet." He shoved his shorts down. His dick was huge, bobbing out in front of him, and next he grabbed Auggie's gym shorts and the compression shorts underneath, forcing them down past Auggie's knees. Auggie was painfully hard, and he whimpered when Dylan grabbed him. He kissed Auggie once, their teeth clicking together, and then he forced Auggie's head to the side, sucking hard on his neck. He moved down, bit Auggie's collarbone, and whispered, "You are such a fucking man." His hand tugged, and Auggie groaned. "You are my fucking man, aren't you?"

"Yes," Auggie whispered.

"You're so goddamn special. You're real." His head came up, and he locked eyes with Auggie. "You're real, and everybody else is so fucking fake. You've got an old soul, and God, you are so fucking beautiful." He licked his lips. "Touch my dick."

Auggie did. He was surprised, his mind already making comparisons, like mine, not like mine, gratified when Dylan moaned and thrust into his hand. He'd come close to this with Theo, once or twice, but that was all. And now it was happening, happening with someone who turned Auggie on, turned every light on and left it blazing.

Dylan pinched Auggie's nipple using his nail, and Auggie let out a sharp noise. The pain was intense, but so was the electricity arcing to his dick.

"Be quiet," Dylan growled again. He hoisted Auggie up, lifting him as though he weighed nothing. Auggie lost contact with Dylan's dick, and for a moment, he wasn't sure what was happening. Then his butt settled on the chrome safety bar, and Dylan hooked Auggie's leg over his shoulder. The bar was wet and cold. The tile behind Auggie was wet and cold. Dylan was sweaty and hot, panting, his breath like steam on Auggie's chest and shoulder. This new position made Auggie's heartbeat accelerate. He was open. He was exposed.

"Dylan, I'm not sure I'm ready—"

"Relax; we'll be safe."

Then Dylan's finger was there, prodding, pressing, and his other hand encircled Auggie's dick again. Sweat eased some of the friction, but when his finger popped through, it burned.

"Ow," Auggie said. He tried to reach for Dylan's wrist, but Dylan's other arm was in the way, still pumping. And Auggie was shaking, his muscles worn out from exercise, the rush of hormones making him drunk. He was nineteen, and in spite of the discomfort, he had another guy's hand on him, and he was on the brink of orgasm.

Dylan worked his finger in and out. In and out.

"Ow, Dylan, hold on." His tone changed. "Oh fuck. Oh fuck. Oh fuck."

"I want your load all over me," Dylan said. His eyes locked with Auggie's, refusing to release him, and Dylan said, "Come for me."

Auggie came. He was vaguely aware of gritting his teeth, trying not to make any noise, his head cracking once against the tile. Then the crest of the orgasm passed, and Auggie was shaking harder, his hip aching from having his leg forced up over Dylan's shoulder. Dylan was staring at him, his gaze still holding Auggie's as he jerked himself off. A moment later, hot wetness streaked across Auggie's leg.

Outside, a couple of guys were talking—from their voices, older men, probably staff or faculty using the campus gym around their work schedule. Laughing. One of them talking about a bike ride from the weekend before. Auggie's hip was on fire, and he slowly worked it down from Dylan's shoulder. Dylan leaned against Auggie, the damp curls on Auggie's chest, his hands tight on Auggie's waist again. Tight enough to hurt. Auggie played with his curls.

Dylan lifted his head, kissed Auggie, and helped him down. Picking up Auggie's compression shorts, he said, "Go grab my soap and towel, would you? You really hosed me down, and I want to get cleaned up."

That night, washing his face, Auggie still felt the pain between his legs, still had one nipple throbbing. He looked in the glass. Dylan's fingers had left faint purple marks on his hips. Water ran down to his jawline, beaded, dripped off. I guess it's going to hurt, he thought. I guess it's really going to hurt the first time.

The next day, when he tried to copy Dylan's advances in the locker room, Dylan shook him off.

"Are you kidding me?"

"It was fun. I thought—"

"It was fun. Great. That was a transformational moment for me, Auggie. That was something special and serious when everything changed between us. But for you, it was fun. That's great. I'm not interested in playing jerkoff games; sorry."

He had to spend the rest of the day apologizing over text before Dylan forgave him.

The next day, he didn't try anything. He just did what Dylan told him. He showed him the app where he was tracking macros. He asked about plant-based protein powders and ordered some while Dylan watched his phone screen. He displayed the gallon jug he was using to stay hydrated. And that day, everything went smoothly.

On Friday, though, he messed up again. It was the Sigma Sigma back-to-school party (the spring semester edition), and Auggie had gotten his cast off that morning. He snapped Dylan a picture of two outfits and the message, *What should I wear to the party?*

The snap back was just a black screen and the words, *Whatever you want, I guess.*

A snap of Auggie's face, eyebrows raised—hopeful and curious was the expression he was going for. *What time are you coming over?*

The next message wasn't a snap; it was a normal message. *I can't even believe you'd ask that.*

I'm sorry. I did something wrong, and I don't know what I did wrong. Will you please tell me so I can make it right?

I really expected better of you, Auggie. As a person, and also as someone I'm trying to build something unique with. How is this going to work between us if you don't listen to me?

What did I forget? I'm sorry. I'm really sorry, D.

The demonstration for Deja.

But Auggie didn't remember Dylan telling him anything about the demonstration. He composed a message saying that, and then he stood there, sweat prickling under his arms, and deleted it. Instead, he typed, *I am so, so sorry. I didn't realize that was tonight.*

The composition bubble appeared, disappeared, appeared, disappeared. The message didn't come through for five minutes, five minutes that Auggie spent perched on the edge of his bed, sick to his stomach, the smell of flop sweat building in the room.

I can't even believe I have to say this, but I expect that the person I make my life with is going to care about social justice. Sorry if that's not something you're interested in. Have a great time at your party.

Auggie had to call three times before Dylan picked up.

"I was planning on going," Auggie said. "I just got the days mixed up."

Dylan's breathing was slow and assured. "I feel like you're telling me what I want to hear."

"No. Dylan, you know that's not who I am."

"I've tried really hard to communicate with you. I'm worried that you're too distracted with those people you call your friends. And all you care about is your social media stuff. You're not listening to me, and I know it's because you don't have room in your life for anything else. You don't have any place for stillness, inner peace, harmony. Those things are really important to me."

"They're important to me too," Auggie said. "I want to have those things in my life. I want to have you in my life."

Outside, Peter, a junior who lived a few rooms down, was singing Kesha, "Tik Tok." Music thumped in the background.

"There's room for you," Auggie said. "In my life, I mean. I can—I can think about ways to spend less time on social media."

"If you want to come with me," Dylan said, "you need to be at my apartment in fifteen minutes. If you're not here, I'll know why."

Auggie pulled on clothes. The Civic was still at the mechanic's, so he sprinted out into the cold and snow and ran.

6

Since winter break, when things had turned a corner with Cart, Theo had decided life was getting better. When he went to Downing in the morning, Lana seemed more alert, although her physical needs meant she still had to have a full-time caretaker. At school, assisting Wagner had turned into a cushy job once Auggie was no longer in the picture. Theo still drew his full stipend, but he spent most of class reading articles for his thesis, and the grading was minimal. Cart hadn't moved in, but he was at Theo's almost every night. He'd started framing the basement, even though Theo had told him that he didn't have money to pay for materials. Cart bought them himself, ignoring Theo's protests.

The fights had stopped too. They had both adapted. They were both making compromises. And compromises, Theo reminded himself, were part of mature relationships. He and Ian, for example, had made plenty of compromises: they bought the beers Ian liked, but Theo usually picked their movies. That's what a relationship was all about: compromise.

So Theo made compromises. He parked the Malibu on the street, where it was buried in snow, so that Cart could get his truck into the garage.

"Why does it matter if someone sees your truck?"

"It doesn't matter. I just don't like it sitting out in front of your house every night."

And Theo had let it go; that was a compromise.

On Friday night, at the end of a long week, Cart was stretched out on the couch, shouting at the Blues as they gave up the first goal. Cart was in sweats, his preferred winter loungewear, with huge, fuzzy wool socks. Theo was in a hoodie and shorts, a blanket over his legs, flipping back and forth in his Riverside to reference the right lines from *Romeo and Juliet*. The television was on a lot more these days, and Theo had to concentrate extra hard.

Cart nudged him with one fuzzy sock.

"I'm working," Theo said, slapping his ankle. "Jesus Christ, will you watch it with those fucking hooves? I'm going to have a bruise."

"For the eighth time, do you want to order pizza?"

"Yes, fine. Just get whatever you want; you know I'll eat it."

A car commercial came on. Jerry Reese looked heavier on TV, in a suit that had probably cost a lot of money but didn't seem to fit him. "Our New Year's sale has been extended! Get in while you can. I'm practically giving these cars away!"

"Change the channel," Theo said.

Cart didn't. He just said, "So, about that pizza?"

"Oh," Theo said. "Right." He got out his phone, called in an order for an extra-large supreme, and at the last minute added garlic knots. Another compromise: Theo always ordered the takeout and delivery. Cart didn't mind paying, but he wouldn't make the call.

For the next half hour, Theo worked, and Cart got them each another beer, and on the return trip he lay down with his head in Theo's lap, and Theo rubbed the short, bristly hair while he read. When the knock came at the door, Cart got up without a word, tossed cash to Theo, and went to the bathroom.

As Theo answered the door, he told himself it wasn't worth a fight. What would he say, anyway? I've noticed you have to pee every time someone knocks on the door. You bought me flowers, and you forgot to hide the receipt, and I saw you drove all the way to St. Elizabeth to buy them at the CVS instead of from the Piggly Wiggly just up the street. When neighbor kids were having a snowball fight and they got too close to the house, you closed the blinds. And Theo knew that if he said any of those things or all of them, Cart would pretend he didn't understand. He might even pretend they hadn't happened.

Theo gave the pizza girl an extra-large tip courtesy of Cart.

Cart came back from the bathroom. They ate pizza, the cheese and sauce still hot, the sausage spicy, the peppers and mushrooms just exactly the right degree of crisp. When they finished eating, Cart cleaned up, and when he came back, he sat next to Theo, put his arm around his shoulders, and kissed his neck.

"I've got to finish these articles," Theo said.

"I didn't even say anything, you cocky son of a bitch. Mind your own fucking business."

Theo flipped the page.

Cart bit his earlobe. His hand landed on Theo's knee, knocked the blanket aside, and slid up under his shirts.

"Howard Cartwright," Theo said.

"Just keep doing your work. I'm fine over here."

When Cart groped him through the boxers, Theo's highlighter skidded off course, leaving a long yellow slash across the page.

"Oops," Cart whispered, his breath hot on the side of Theo's face. "You get distracted?"

Theo shifted in his seat, but Cart had an arm around him and wouldn't let him slip away. His fingers wormed under the elastic. His thumb brushed the side of Theo's dick.

"Shit," Theo whispered. "Why are you so much fucking trouble?"

"Because I'm a fucking redneck who's hungry for pecker," Cart said. "Why else?" He kissed Theo's cheek, and the gesture was surprisingly hesitant. "Who made you so goddamn cute?"

Theo rolled his eyes, turning to face Cart, letting out a sound of appreciation as Cart stroked his thumb lightly against Theo again. "Cute?"

"Beautiful," Cart said quietly. "You're just the god-fucking-damnedest most beautiful thing I've ever seen."

Theo's throat was tight. He blinked a few times.

"Who made you so goddamn smart too? I wish I was half as smart as you."

"You're plenty smart," Theo said. "You're a lot smarter than you give yourself credit for."

Shaking his head solemnly, Cart said, "No, sir. But I am the luckiest son of a bitch on God's green earth. I want to show you how lucky I am." He squeezed once, making Theo gasp, and then he pulled away, tugging off his sweatshirt.

An alarm sounded on Theo's phone.

"Shit," Theo said.

Cart groaned. "No way. Whatever it is, it can wait." He gave another tug.

Squirming free, Theo got to his feet and said, "Deja's demonstration is tonight."

"What?" Cart asked.

"The demonstration. I can't believe I forgot."

Theo jogged upstairs. Behind him, he could hear Cart grumbling.

He grabbed jeans and thick socks because the temperature had continued to drop over the course of the day; tonight, it would be well below freezing. Then he went downstairs.

Cart was staring at the TV.

As Theo pulled on his socks and a pair of boots, he said, "What? You're mad at me? I'll be back in a couple of hours." He tried to smile. "I still want you to show me how lucky you think you are."

Clutching the remote so tightly that his knuckles were white, Cart said, "I think I might spend the night at my place."

"You're joking, right? You've got a case of blue balls, so now you're mad at me?"

"I'm mad at you," Cart said, punching the power button to turn off the TV, "because you're going out there to support people who hate the police. I don't have any fucking idea why you need to do that. This is more of your ivory tower fucking nose-in-the-air bullshit."

Standing, Theo put his hands on his hips. "Do you want to run that by me again?

"I said," Cart threw down the remote, "you are going out there to support people who want to fucking kill the police." Cart's gaze came up, challenging, to fix Theo. "Did I stutter?"

"OK," Theo said. "OK. Yeah, maybe you should spend the night at your place."

Cart made a disgusted noise in his throat.

"If you've got something to say," Theo said, "then you'd better goddamn say it. Because I'm not going to pretend I understand what that noise means."

Outside, brakes squealed, and a car passed the house. Then the only sound was the wind battering the glass.

Cart rubbed his face. "Yeah, I guess I do have something to say." He stood. He pulled on his sweatshirt, making a face when his head popped through the neck. Then he said, "I'm sorry."

Theo stared at him.

"Well," Cart said, "what the hell is the matter, you fucking redneck?"

In spite of himself, Theo grinned. "You are the absolute worst," he covered his mouth to hide the smile that was still growing, "at apologies. Worse than anyone I have ever met. You're terrible."

"Yeah," Cart said, "but when you only fuck up once a year like I do, you don't need to get very good at it."

"Do you really think I'm going there because I don't support the police?"

Cart's silence was longer than Theo would have liked. Then Cart said, "No. I know you support the police. Or at least you support me. But the thing is, not everybody's like you. Just a couple of weeks ago, somebody shot a cop in the back of the head while he was filling up his car. That's what you're getting yourself tangled in. You might not think that's what it is, but that's what it is."

Theo grimaced. "OK, I can see how you would make that connection. But I don't think that's what this is. This is a way to show support for a girl who got killed and for her family. They still have to deal with that. She got killed by a cop, Cart. That's a fact."

Hands on his hips, Cart said, "I know it's a fucking fact. I know how that girl died. And that son of a bitch is going to pay for it. But that doesn't mean people have a right to go around shooting cops in the back of the head."

"That's not what these people are saying. And that's not what any of us want. Not anybody I would be around, would ever support. Do you believe that?"

"Of course I fucking believe it."

"Are you going to leave if I go to the demonstration?"

Scratching his belly to expose the dark hairs scattered over his country-boy abs, Cart smirked and said, "Am I gonna get lucky when you come back?"

Theo rolled his eyes. "You have a one-track mind."

Tugging at his crotch, Cart said, "Do you blame me? I like what I see. Turn around."

"Hoosier."

"I just want to make sure I remember that fine ass."

"You, you magnificent dumbshit redneck, think with your dick instead of your brain."

"Course," said Cart. Settling back onto the couch, he flipped on the TV. "Pick up some of that ice cream on your way back?"

"I thought you were focused on a different treat," Theo said.

Cart smirked and tugged at his crotch again. "I can have two treats."

After kissing him goodbye, Theo made his way to the door.

"Theo," Cart said, "be careful."

"It's a peaceful demonstration."

"I've heard that one before."

7

"Oh shit," Auggie said. "No, no, no."

"What?" Dylan asked.

People crowded Wroxall College's South Quad. Many of them were young, probably college students. Two girls with matching lime-green watch caps hugged each other near Auggie. A guy with a wispy goatee was carrying a guitar on his back. A couple of Dylan's friends had come with them, with the improbable names of Burger and Smash, whom Auggie knew from the times he'd interrupted hacky-sack games. Burger was picking his nose.

The night was crisp and clear, the cold so intense that Auggie's eyes watered, and his feet were already numb in the Jordans. Dylan was holding him close, both arms wrapped around Auggie, carrying the faint smell of weed. The warmth was nice, but Auggie found himself struggling with the urge to pull away. That urge doubled when he spotted Theo moving through the crowd. Theo didn't seem to have seen them yet, but it was only a matter of time. In spite of the crowd, Theo was heading directly toward them, his gaze scanning back and forth.

Auggie tried to drop down, acting out of instinct more than anything else, but Dylan's arms were too tight. Dylan leaned in, the weed smell overpowering now, and whispered, "Hey, you ok?"

"Yes," Auggie said, "can we just move a little over—"

"Auggie?" Theo said. "Auggie!"

Auggie groaned. "Hi, Theo."

Dylan was glaring.

"Hey, hi." Theo glanced around, taking in Dylan, taking in Dylan's arms around Auggie, taking in Burger and Smash. Auggie could hear his thoughts, even if Theo had the decency—this time—not to say them out loud. *These are your friends? This is who you want to hang out with?*

"Who are you?" Dylan said his chest puffing out.

Auggie wondered if he could die just standing there. "Dylan, this is Theo. Theo, this is Dylan."

They shook hands. Theo grimaced, and although the expression was faint, Auggie noticed. He also noticed Dylan's chest puffing up again.

One of the girls with the lime-green hats stomped her feet. Holding the guitar at a strange angle over his shoulder, the kid with the goatee strummed a cord. This, Auggie was sure, was approximately the same experience as the world ending.

"So," Theo said. "You're Dylan."

"You know what?" Auggie said. "We were just about to try to move locations and get up near the front."

"Great," Theo said. "Let's go."

They made their way to the front of the crowd, with Dylan doing a lot of the elbowing and muscling. In order to do so, he had to release Auggie, and Auggie found himself hanging back with Theo.

"He seems nice," Theo said.

"Do not." Auggie stopped himself. "Just do not do this right now."

Theo raised one eyebrow. He had his long, strawberry-blond hair tucked under a hat, and he smelled like cedar. Over the murmur of the crowd, he said, "I'm sorry, I guess I misread things. Do you want me to go?"

Auggie picked at his lip. Then, shaking his head, he said, "No. I'm sorry. I'm just—I'm just nervous. I want you guys to get along." Then, unable to stop himself, he added, "He really is a great guy."

"Well, if he's a great guy, we're going to get along."

It took Auggie a few more minutes to recognize the weight that Theo had placed on that if.

It looked like most of the college had turned out for the demonstration. Since coming to Wahredua, this was the most racial diversity in one place that Auggie had seen. It reminded him—in good ways—of California. Although there were still plenty of white faces in the crowd, the majority of the audience seemed to be black, with heavy pockets of people who looked like they were of Asian descent, or Latino, or Pacific Islander. A young woman with her dark hair chopped short was carrying a poster that said *I am the Cheyenne Nation. Justice for Deja is Justice for Everyone.* She smiled when she met Auggie's gaze and then her eyes slid back toward the podium.

The stand that had been erected had obviously been done quickly and without any regard for longevity. The wood was particleboard painted black, and judging by the dust, the scuffs, the sticky residue, and the strip of old green tape, Auggie guessed that this had come from somewhere in the theater department. Wires and cables snaked through the snow, connecting the microphone on the stand with speakers placed at various locations throughout the crowd. Auggie wasn't sure how long this event had been in the planning, but it definitely showed an attention to detail and a care in execution that made him realize the people behind it were more than angry kids. There were brains at work here. Serious brains.

As though summoned by the thought, a group of young black men and women emerged from the crowd and mounted the stand. All of them were wearing long-sleeved black shirts with white letters that said *Justice for Deja*. They had sacrificed their coats in spite of the cold so that the shirts could be seen. Several of them were shivering and chafing their arms as they huddled together on the stand in a last-minute conversation.

"I didn't know you were going to come to this," Theo said. "I wish I had. We could've come together."

"Yeah," Auggie said. "Social justice is really important to me."

"Is that how you met Dylan?"

Auggie shook his head. Before he had to explain how he had met Dylan—he could imagine the look on Theo's face if he ever learned that they'd met at the Sigma Sigma move-in—a young woman approached the microphone.

She was tall and muscular, her skin very dark and her hair in a tight fade. In that moment, Auggie thought she might be a lesbian. He couldn't have said why, but the thought came to him, and it wouldn't go.

"My name is Nia," the girl said. "Deja was my sister. Thank you for coming." She stopped. When she spoke again, her voice was thick with emotion. "It's hard for me to believe that if things had been different, my sister would be here right now. She was an excellent student. She was an amazing athlete. She had committed to come to Wroxall," at this point, she waved a piece of paper as evidence, "and I was looking forward to being her teammate as well as her sister and her best friend." She paused again, this time to wipe her eyes. "I want you to know how much tonight means to me and my family. Deja would be so proud to know that each and every one of you is not willing to look the other way in the face of injustice. I know that together we can—"

The crack of a gun interrupted.

Nia stumbled back, one hand to her chest. Then she fell.

The crowd dissolved into chaos. More shots followed. Snow puffed up from the quad only a few feet from where Auggie stood. Screaming, pushing, shoving, fighting. Everyone surged toward the exits. Someone must have hit the podium because it toppled off the stand, and feedback from the mic exploded over the speakers. A young guy in an enormous, puffy jacket crashed into Auggie. Auggie stumbled, and he would have gone down except Theo caught his arm.

Auggie!"

The shout came from Dylan, somewhere behind Auggie. He glanced around, darting aside when a mother carrying a small child almost checked him with her shoulder. Then he saw movement along the balcony of a building at the far end of the quad. Tall, narrow windows were full of light, and framed by them, the shooter carried a rifle as he ran.

"There!"

Theo was still holding his arm.

"Auggie!"

"Dylan's trying to get to you," Theo said. "I think we should—"

Auggie broke away from Theo, racing toward the far end of the quad where he'd seen movement on the balcony.

8

For the first ten yards, Theo kept up with Auggie. Then the crowd was too thick, and Theo began to fall behind. Auggie, with his slim frame, slid between clumps of frantic people. Theo tried to copy him, but a massive guy in a Cardinals hat got in his way. Something must have triggered the guy's fight mode because he threw an elbow at Theo and almost caught him in the throat. Theo dodged, but the elbow still connected with the side of his head, and he stumbled. A woman leading two girls by the hands circled past him; one of the girls had wet herself, and the smell of urine followed her.

"Auggie!" Theo shouted, righting himself and taking a staggering step. "Slow down!"

A hand grabbed Theo's shoulder. He spun, already trying to shake off the hold, when a voice stopped him.

"Where the fuck is he?" Dylan's face was red with cold and exertion. He shook Theo and said again, "Where is he?"

Turning back, Theo scanned the dissolving crowd. Auggie had disappeared. "I don't know." Then, pointing at one of the quad's exits, he said, "You go that way. I'll go this way."

"What the hell was he thinking?" Dylan shouted over the cries of panic and distress. "He was running into the worst of it."

Less than ten yards away, a man howled, hands over his face, and stumbled back. A girl in a biker's jacket held a can of pepper gel. Even from a distance, Theo could see her hand shaking, but she got enough of the gel on the man's face to make him scream and stagger away.

"Fuck this," Dylan said. "I'm out of here."

"Auggie needs us—"

Shaking his head, Dylan turned and ran for the closest exit. Burger and Smash—Theo did a mental headshake at the names— followed, and then Theo was on his own, facing down a crazed, broken rabble that was desperate to get out of the packed quad.

Theo had never been in a riot before, had never been in a panicked mass of people like this one. But he had been in plenty of bar fights, and he applied some of the same principles here: move purposefully, put a wall at your back, and hit the other guy first. Rather than trying again to duplicate Auggie's weaving through the crowd, Theo cut across the stream of people at an angle. He wasn't huge like Dylan, but he was big enough, and plenty of people did last-second calculations and decided to go around him rather than trying to knock him down. Cardinals-hat guy appeared in Theo's path again, looking like he'd gotten turned around, and he took an angry step toward Theo. This time, Theo didn't hesitate; he popped the guy once in the face. The Cardinals hat flew off to be trampled by a pair of bros in sweatbands and trucker's jackets, and the big guy sat on his ass in the mud and snow.

After that, Theo had pretty smooth sailing. He stuck close to the buildings that lined the quad, moving around the perimeter instead of plunging into the milling chaos. The last thing Auggie had done before breaking away was point at Eveleigh, the robotics building. Eveleigh was one of the oldest structures on campus. It had the same faux Gothic details as the other original buildings: the stonework, the leaded glass, and the tall, swooping frame with vestigial buttresses. It also had a large balcony that faced the quad. Whatever Auggie had seen, Theo guessed that it involved the balcony.

To clear the quad, Theo had to merge with the press of bodies funneling out of the exit. For a handful of heartbeats, he was carried along by the current. Bodies jostled him. Fingernails clawed at his sleeve. He caught a whiff of cotton-candy perfume, and then a stronger whiff of coffee. When someone checked him at the hip, he stumbled, envisioned himself going down, the flood of bodies flattening him against the pavement. Instead, though, he stumbled free, caught a breath of the jaggedly cold air—clean air—and realized he was out.

He found Auggie running in the opposite direction, coming toward him from the far side of Eveleigh. Even in the dark, even at a distance, even with the panicked voices and the shouts and cries for help making Theo's adrenaline surge, even through the layers of clothing, he knew Auggie the moment he saw him.

"He hasn't come out," Auggie shouted. "I saw him go into the building from the balcony, but he hasn't come out."

"Great," Theo said, grabbing his arm. Auggie was still moving pretty fast, and his momentum swung them both in a circle, but Theo held on. "Now we're leaving. We'll call the police—"

"I already called. I couldn't even get through to dispatch." He pried at Theo's hand. "They're overwhelmed, Theo. My phone wouldn't even work on a second try. Everybody's calling the police right now." He grabbed Theo's hand again, but this time, he didn't pull. Wrapping his fingers around Theo's, he looked up and said, "He's going to get away."

Theo thought of Luke, the flies, the spin of the whole world suddenly out of his control.

"My purse!" a woman shouted. "That kid took my purse!"

A couple of young guys with black armbands turned in response to her cries. One of them clotheslined a kid who was sprinting away. The collision sent all three of them tumbling to the ground, and a sick crunch made Theo think broken bones were involved, maybe worse.

"Not him!" the woman shouted. "That one over there."

"What a shitshow," Auggie said. "People are going crazy."

"Come on," Theo said, dragging Auggie away from a fight that had broken out between a white man in camo gear and a younger black man wearing one of the armbands.

"Theo, I saw the shooter. I'm not going to leave—"

"I know, God damn it. I know you won't. But I have an idea of what he's doing."

Auggie's mouth hung open for an instant. He let Theo pull him into a run. Maybe that was the secret, Theo thought. Just overload him with surprises so that he'll shut up and do what he's told for five minutes at a time.

Five minutes was optimistic. They were only halfway along the length of Eveleigh before Auggie twisted to look back and said, "Theo, the doors are back there. If he comes out—"

"Eveleigh used to be the Field House."

"What?"

"When they built the campus, it was the Eveleigh Field House." They were still running, and Theo's knee was starting to burn. The cold air crackled in his lungs, and pressure built behind his ears.

"The gym—"

"The gym is new." The ground sloped down, exposing more of Eveleigh's foundation. They followed the hill toward the east side of the building. Small windows looked into the basement—in some, yellow light painted the glass, while others were dark. A pair of fire doors were the only exit here. "Five years, maybe six. Until then, the athletics department—"

One of the fire doors opened. A wedge of yellow light cut the darkness. Someone burst out of Eveleigh, and Theo had just enough time to think: man, well built, still moves like he's young, camo, possibly one of the Ozark Volunteers. Then the door slammed shut, and Theo was blind, his night vision ruined.

Auggie swore, ripped free from Theo's hand, and raced down the steepest portion of the hill.

"Hey!" he shouted. "Stop!"

The shadow moving below them stopped. Turned.

A gun fired. The muzzle flash partially blinded Theo. Auggie's feet flew up from under him, and for a moment, he was a silhouette against the pale stone of Eveleigh. Then Auggie came down hard, the frozen crust of snow snapping under him, and he slid to the bottom of the hill.

"Shit," Theo shouted, running now. "Shit, shit, shit. Auggie?"

A groan answered him.

Taillights flooded the parking lot with red. An engine roared to life. Then, spinning up loose gravel, the car shot out of the lot onto one of the many service roads that webbed Wroxall's campus. And then the lights winked out, and the car was just thunder fading into the night.

Theo was having a hard time navigating the hill—fear of damaging his knee slowed him—so he dropped onto his ass and scooted, sliding the last few feet. He was soaking wet by the time he reached Auggie.

Blood, black in the weak light, covered Auggie's face. Theo ran his hands over Auggie. Everything was wet, which made the job more difficult, but he couldn't find a bullet hole. Just scrapes, but plenty of them. Auggie was already wiping snow from his face, shaking it out of his hair, trying to sit up.

"Slow down," Theo said.

"Damn it," Auggie said, collecting another palmful of slush from his hair and flinging it aside.

"Stop moving." Theo managed to rein in his voice. "I don't think you're shot, but you're banged up pretty bad. Hold still, please."

Auggie blinked up at him. "Hey, Theo. When did you get here?" He craned his neck, winced, and touched his shoulder. "Where's Dylan?"

Theo grimaced. "How hard did you hit your head? Let me look at your eyes." He caught Auggie's chin with one finger and turned his head. The pupils were dilated, but that could have been because of the darkness. "Damn it. We need to get you to the hospital."

"Do you think Dylan's mad because you came? I didn't even know you were coming."

"Dylan is a fucking—" Theo bit back the rest of it. "Dylan is fucking lucky to have you. Don't worry about Dylan."

"Man," Auggie said, laughing as he tried to stand. He would have fallen again if Theo hadn't caught him. "Did I have something to drink?"

"You better not have."

Shivering and hugging himself, looking something like a drowned rat, Auggie glanced around again. "Is he mad because I wouldn't take that pill?"

"What?"

"Dylan. Are you even paying attention? I'm talking about Dylan."

"What pill? What did he try to give you?"

Auggie pressed one hand to the side of his face, his eyes tightening. "My head—my head really hurts, Theo."

"Ok," Theo said. "It's ok. Can you walk? We just need to walk a little way."

Auggie nodded, and Theo helped him back up the hill.

9

The headache was bad, but whatever they had given Auggie was helping, and mostly he just wanted to sleep. That didn't seem to be an option; every time he tried to lie down on the floor, Theo got hold of him and pulled him back into the seat. Auggie's second best option seemed to be slumped against Theo, his head on Theo's shoulder. Sitting like this, he could feel when Theo breathed, smell the faint hint of pizza that clung to his hoodie, the cedar scent in his hair and beard. They were in a quiet stretch of a hospital hallway. Occasionally a doctor went by, white coat whipping around his or her legs, and once two nurses walked past with coffee, laughing quietly at something one of them had said. Auggie had the sense that other areas of the hospital were busy with the flood of injured people from the demonstration, but his head was too foggy to figure out why this section was quiet.

"You two look cozy. Nobody got you a complimentary bathrobe? Mint on your pillow?"

Auggie had heard the voice a handful of times, and like now, it was never really directed at him. He glanced up. Howard Cartwright was a police officer; he was wearing his uniform tonight. He had his dark hair buzzed at a zero, and he was wiry. Handsome in a rough, country kind of way. Theo's boyfriend was staring at Theo as though Auggie didn't exist.

"When I called," Theo said quietly, "I didn't mean you had to put on your uniform and come down here. I just wanted you to know where I was."

"All hands on deck for this shitstorm. I've only got a minute, and then I need to get back to the ER and make sure a riot doesn't start. How's your boy?"

"Not tonight, Cart."

Cart shifted his weight, thumbs in his belt, and after a minute he said, "Well?"

"He's all right. Mild concussion." Then Theo related the night's events. Some of the details, like the shooting, Auggie remembered clearly. Others, like the hill where he had fallen, were completely gone.

"What did he see?"

"I don't know. I'll ask him when he's feeling better."

"The gun," Auggie said. He thought about pushing himself up from Theo's shoulder, but he was too tired, and it felt too good to stay where he was. "I could see him on the balcony of that building. The light in the windows. He was carrying a big gun."

"Great. A big gun. I'll put that in the report."

"Ease up," Theo said. "I told you: not tonight."

Auggie could feel the words vibrate in his chest.

In a flat voice, Cart said, "They think they found the car. It's registered to one of those Ozark Volunteer, Klan-loving fuckbuckets in the county. Reported stolen a week ago, of course."

"They found the car?" Auggie said.

Cart didn't look at him; with his gaze still on Theo, he nodded. "The state boys are going to take a look. Techs will take it apart piece by piece if they have to."

"That's something," Theo said.

"I need to go." Cart shifted his weight. "Take good care of your boy."

"I'm not his—"

"Sit right here," Theo said, squeezing Auggie's arm. Then, standing, he caught Cart's shoulder and steered him to the end of the hall. As they went, Auggie heard Theo growl, "Are you a grown-ass man, Cart? Are you a fucking grownup?" Then they were too far away for Auggie to catch Cart's response, but he didn't miss how Cart jerked away from Theo's touch. The two men talked furiously at the end of the hall. It looked like it might have gone on forever, but then a CNA came around the corner with a stretcher, and they stepped to opposite sides of the corridor to clear a path. When the stretcher was past, Theo said something and took a step. Cart held up a hand, shook his head, and left. Hands on his hips, Theo stood there, staring at the linoleum.

Auggie got out his phone. He was surprised to see it was barely ten o'clock. He snapped a selfie, scribbled *frat life, rough life* at the bottom of the picture, made sure to include a glimpse of the hospital surroundings in the background, and blasted it out. Then he messaged Orlando: *need 2 talk*.

The phone's screen timed out.

217

Auggie called, and it went to Orlando's voicemail. "Call me back. This is serious."

"Let's get you home," Theo said. His touch was gentle as he took Auggie's arm and helped him to his feet. "Either my couch, where I can keep an eye on you, or—"

"Ethan can stay with me. He's in the next room."

Theo nodded. "Or Dylan."

"He's not answering; I tried him earlier."

Theo just nodded again.

"I mean, thanks," Auggie said. "I just don't want to make things worse for you with Cart."

"It's not your fault. I manage to make them plenty bad all by myself. Come on."

They had to catch an Uber; the distance from the hospital to the Sigma Sigma house was walkable, but Theo refused even to consider it. Their driver was a young Asian girl who played a staticky AM jazz station. The car smelled like piña colada air freshener. When they got to the Sigma Sigma house, Auggie unbuckled himself.

"Do you want me to come up?" Theo asked. "To make sure you get settled?"

"I want you to come up," Auggie said. The words were coming out of the headache, out of the feel of Theo's shoulder under his cheek, out of the seed of fear underneath whatever meds they had given him. They came out of seeing Theo standing at the end of the hall, hands on his hips, staring at the linoleum. "Do you want to come up?" Auggie asked, and he meant the question a dozen different ways.

Theo, because he was Theo, heard all of them. He shook his head, just a tiny fraction of a shake. Then he pulled Auggie into a hug. His beard tickled the side of Auggie's neck.

When they separated, Auggie managed to smile. "Thanks, Theo."

Then he slid out of the car. The wall of cold made his head ache twice as bad; the sedan's exhaust snaked around his ankles, warm and too sweet. Then the car pulled away, and at the next corner, the taillights turned and vanished, and Auggie was alone in the dark.

10

Theo slept in snatches, woke in fits, and read tweets and news blurbs about the shooting through bleary eyes. In the morning, he called Auggie.

"The shooting might be connected to Cal's death," Theo said. "Cal and Wayne used to coach Nia; I found a short article the *Courier* published when she signed to play for Wroxall."

Silence.

"And the shooter might have seen your face," Theo added.

Auggie groaned. "Hello?"

Theo paced his small bedroom, almost bumping his head several times on the low, sloping ceiling. "The shooter. I think he might've seen your face."

"Oh. Shit." Another groan. "God damn, my head."

"Are you ok?"

"Uh huh, yup, great. Morning, Theo."

In spite of everything that had happened in the last twenty-four hours, Theo smiled. "Good morning, Auggie."

"So, I guess we better solve this murder."

"You don't have to sound so happy about it."

"I'm not happy about it. I'm dying. I'm dying right now."

"I'll bring you one of those breakfast sandwiches you like."

"With bacon?" Auggie's voice was tentative. "And cheese?"

"Get dressed."

"And a Piggly Wiggly doughnut?"

"Real, adult clothes, Auggie. None of that frat-boy stuff, please."

Auggie was still swearing as Theo disconnected.

The January day was even colder than the night before; the sky was bluish white behind clouds that look like tissues rubbed too thin. Theo picked up the doughnut from the Piggly Wiggly, and he picked up two breakfast sandwiches at the Wahredua Family Bakery. By the time he got to the Sigma Sigma house, Auggie was waiting for him in the lobby. He had on jeans, a sweater, and a heavy coat. The scrapes on the side of his face looked much better.

"Doughnut?"

While Auggie opened the paper bag, Theo caught his chin and turned his head, examining him. "Did you take that prescription?"

Auggie's answer came through a mouthful of chocolate long john.

Because Auggie's Civic was still in the shop, and because they didn't have time to head back to Theo's house to get the Malibu, they took an Uber to the hospital. They tried to get in to see Nia, but they were rebuffed by a grim-faced woman at the visiting desk.

"Immediate family only."

"We are family," Auggie said.

Theo sighed, covered his eyes, and led Auggie back outside. The cold made Theo's nose run, and he sniffled as he said, "I am so sick of this weather."

"We'll get an Uber."

Theo shook his head. "No, I don't—"

"I'll pay for it." Before Theo could object, Auggie had his phone out and was tapping rapidly.

They took the Uber to Wayne's apartment. His BMW was parked in the assigned stall. In the intense brightness of the January sun, the building's freshly cleaned mortar glowed. They were getting out of the Uber as Wayne came down the stairs from his apartment, crossed the parking lot, and emptied a box into the dumpster.

"Now that's interesting," Theo said.

Auggie nodded.

Wayne was halfway across the lot when he saw them, stopped, and then resumed walking jerkily. "Hello," he said. "Looking for Orlando?"

"Looking for you," Theo said.

Wayne just grunted and climbed the stairs to the apartment again. Theo and Auggie followed. Inside, the apartment was clearly undergoing a massive cleanout. Cardboard boxes lined one wall, stacked as high as Theo's head, with flattened, empty boxes piled on the couch. Mounds of clothing covered the floor, divided into piles that had no clear organization to Theo. A black Hefty bag, the flaps pulled back, held shoes: sneakers, boots, cleats, even flip-flops. From where they stood, Theo could see into the kitchen; every cabinet door stood open, and the contents were spread on the counter, the table, and the floor.

Leaning down to speak into Auggie's ear, Theo said, "Go look in the dumpster."

Auggie nodded and left.

Wayne had disappeared into one of the bedrooms. When footsteps moved toward the living room, Theo was surprised to see Orlando. Orlando, on the other hand, did not look surprised to see him. Instead, Orlando looked guilty. His shoulders were hunched, and his head hung down, and he barely managed a wave and "Hello, Theo."

"Orlando, what are you doing here?"

"Just helping."

"Helping with what?"

"Oh, you know. Stuff." Orlando's thick eyebrows drew together. "Where's Augs?"

"He'll be up in a minute." Theo looked around the apartment again. "Is Wayne moving out?"

Heavy steps announced Wayne's return. He was carrying an enormous cardboard box, which he passed to Orlando, and he said, "Take this one down." Then, to Theo, he said, "We're cleaning out Cal's stuff. Orlando is probably going to move in."

"Really?" Theo said, trying to catch Orlando's eye. Orlando wouldn't look at him, and he shuffled past Theo, using the box to hide his face as he made his way out the door. "Seems pretty fast to be getting rid of Cal's stuff."

"Yeah, well, what am I supposed to do?" Wayne squatted, digging through a pile of clothes. "You gotta move on with your life."

"Where were you last night?"

It wasn't that the world went silent. Down the hall, a child was shrieking something about Barney. Through the wall, a TV was playing the *Jeopardy!* theme song. The bathroom fan whirred. But the way Wayne went suddenly and completely still made Theo think the world had pressed mute.

"What?"

"Last night. Where were you?"

Wayne straightened. He turned to face Theo. "What the fuck business is it of yours?"

"Just a question."

"Me and my family, we're sick of your questions. You and your twinkie buddy have been nothing but trouble for my family. For some reason, Orlando still thinks you guys are helping us, but the rest of us are sick of this shit."

"Pretty good speech."

"Ok, I'll try again: get the fuck out, and quit bothering my family." Wayne cleared his throat. "Got it?"

"So you can't tell me where you were last night?"

The door opened, and Auggie and Orlando entered the apartment. They were in the middle of their own conversation.

"—I'm just saying," Auggie said, "I was worried when you didn't answer your phone last night. That's all. And I was just curious where you were."

"It didn't sound like you were worried," Orlando said. He came to an abrupt stop, crossing his arms, studying Theo and Wayne as though he'd sensed the tension in the air. He shot a sidelong look at Auggie and said, "It sounded like you thought I had something to do with that girl getting shot."

"I don't know why you won't tell me where you were," Auggie said.

"Augs, just leave it—"

"We were together." Wayne's gaze locked with Theo's. "Out of town. Got back this morning. Right, Orlando?"

Orlando hesitated. Then he nodded. "Right."

"Where?" Auggie said.

"That's it, then?" Wayne looked from Theo to Auggie to Orlando. "That's what you came for? To accuse me and my brother?"

Orlando looked ready to cry. "Augs, did you really think—"

"And you got what you wanted," Wayne said, pointing at the door. "So it's time for you to go."

"Orlando," Auggie said, "if you're in trouble, I want to—"

Orlando pulled away. He took two trembling steps and sidled up to Wayne.

"Orlando?" Auggie said.

Theo touched Auggie's arm and nodded at the door. They left.

In the parking lot, Theo glanced at the dumpster. "Find anything?"

"That was such a nightmare." Auggie scrubbed one hand through his crew cut. "What? Oh. No, just junk. Old Wroxall College gear, a tennis racket, a bag of bathroom trash. And then some really foul stuff, you know, all the garbage that's collected over the week. It doesn't look like it's been picked up yet."

"What do you think that was all about?"

"They were lying."

"I agree, but why?"

Auggie shrugged. "Because they have something to hide."

Theo considered the apartment, and then he looked Auggie in the eye. "Whoever took that shot last night, he knew the inside of that building better than most people. It used to be the athletic facility, and that exit on the bottom floor is the one that the trainers used to use. And Wayne and Orlando just gave about the worst alibi for each other I've ever heard."

The breeze picked up, and leaves skittered across the asphalt. The air smelled cold and dry. Auggie was touching his temple.

"How is your—"

"I know what you're saying," Auggie said, "but why would Orlando or Wayne or both of them want Nia dead? I cornered Orlando at the dumpster and made him confess that he'd known about Genesis. What really happened, I mean. He said his family had tried to keep it a secret from him; that's why he lied. Maybe there's something there, a motive, although I can't imagine Orlando doing any of this." Frowning, Auggie shook his head. "I don't understand. I believe you that all this could be connected, but I don't know how."

"Let's see if we can figure it out."

It only took a few minutes for Auggie to find an address for Cedric and Tonya Corey, Deja and Nia's parents, on a white-page lookup. Over Theo's objections, Auggie paid for an Uber again, and this time they headed to a pleasant, middle-class neighborhood of homes that had been built in the 80s and 90s. It was near the center of town.

When they got to the Coreys' home, though, it was empty. Nobody answered the door, and by the time Auggie and Theo had given up knocking, the Uber was gone. Auggie requested another ride, and while they waited, Theo went around back. He checked the windows to make sure nobody was inside, refusing to answer the door. The curtains were open. He recognized the signs of a family trying to control an uncontrollable grief. The home looked neat at first glance, the furniture all relatively new, everything color coordinated. But patches of darker paint on the walls showed where pictures had been removed. Empty casserole dishes were stacked in the kitchen sink, and a pile of cards—our deepest sympathy, my sincere condolences—lay on the kitchen table. By the time Theo came back to the front of the house, he had made up his mind.

"What took you so long?" Auggie asked.

"Let's have a look inside."

Auggie canceled the ride request, and together they went around to the back of the house. A pair of French doors led into the living room, and they were easy for Theo to jimmy. As soon as they opened, though, an alarm sounded.

"Shit," Theo said. He closed the doors, wiped down the surfaces he had touched, and caught Auggie's look. "Well, how was I supposed to know?"

Auggie pointed at the sticker on the inside of the French door's glass. Brinks Home Security.

"You could've said something."

"I just noticed, but I'll have plenty to say later," Auggie said, with a tiny smirk. "In fact, I think I'm going to be talking about this for a long time. But right now we should probably skedaddle."

"Skedaddle," Theo grumbled. Then he ran.

They ran for half a mile before Theo thought it was safe to try for another ride request; he suggested a visit to Genesis. But Auggie hesitated. Then he said, "You said she's an athlete."

"Who? Genesis? Deja?"

"They are too, but I meant Nia. Tennis. Just like her sister. And you said she signed with Wroxall."

"Like Genesis too," Theo said.

Auggie frowned. He opened his mouth, seemed to consider what he had been about to say, and shook his head.

"What?"

"I don't know," Auggie said. "But you're right. It's a strange coincidence. I want to check a few things on campus."

So they went back to Wroxall instead of the Sigma Sigma house. When the Uber dropped them off, Auggie had his hand pressed to the side of his head.

"Let's call it a day," Theo said. "Your head must be killing you."

"It's not even noon. And I took my medicine. I'll be fine."

"I really think—"

"Brinks Home Security."

Theo gritted his teeth.

"Every time," Auggie said. "You're never going to live it down."

"God damn it."

They walked through Eveleigh, but since the old Field House had been transformed into the robotics facility, there wasn't anything they could link to Nia, Deja, or Genesis. For that matter, there was nothing they could connect to Cal or Wayne—or Orlando, although Theo wasn't willing to voice that particular suspicion yet.

It was Saturday, but the building still seemed half-full, young men and young women working in the labs, some of them fiddling with what, to Theo, looked like robots—which made sense—while others were busy on computers. In a lounge, several of them sat laughing, drawing equations on a whiteboard they had laid across the back of a sofa, laughing more whenever somebody got something wrong. It all seemed surprisingly good-natured, although Theo couldn't for the life of him understand what was so funny.

Next, they went to the new athletic center. They swiped in with their student IDs, but when Theo headed for the main area, Auggie jerked his head to the side, and said, "This way."

"Equipment and locker rooms are this way," Theo said. "Although how we're going to get into the girls' locker room—"

"The team locker rooms are downstairs; Orlando mentioned it last year. Over here. Come on."

He was right. They went down a long flight of stairs to the basement, which was lit with steadily humming fluorescents. The smell of a heavy-duty cleaner tried to cover up the stink of sweat, mildew, and what Theo imagined was a raging infestation of ringworm. They passed a young guy who was carrying a pair of football pads; he didn't give them a second look. In an alcove, two very tall girls were holding a volleyball between them, turning it back and forth. One of them explained something about spiking the ball. She was using her hand to demonstrate.

Auggie stopped at a sign that said Women's Tennis. He raised his eyebrows.

Elbowing open the door, Theo called inside, "Custodial."

"Creative," Auggie whispered.

"A little less feedback—"

"Brinks."

Theo snapped his jaw shut. Auggie just grinned.

When no one responded to a second call of "Custodial," they went inside. The locker-room funk was even worse—apparently girls were not an exception—and their steps echoed against the tile and the bare cement. A dogleg hallway connected them to the locker room proper, and Theo and Auggie took a few minutes orienting themselves.

"Here," Auggie called, tapping a locker. The metal rang out under his touch.

Theo joined him. A plaque with a piece of tape held Nia Corey's name written in Sharpie. A padlock secured the locker.

"Great," Auggie said. "So much for this."

"Find something small and hard," Theo said.

"What?"

"Small and hard. Preferably with a handle."

Theo moved off to begin his own search, and after a moment, he heard Auggie's steps moving across the tiles. The first place Theo checked was the locker room door, hoping for a doorstop, but he didn't have any luck. He backtracked and checked the other lockers, hoping to find one open. No luck there either. He tested the door to the team office, and the handle jiggled slightly, but then it held.

Behind him, Auggie's sneakers squeaked. "What about this?"

Theo turned around.

"It's a hammer, right?" Auggie said.

"It's a reflex hammer. It's perfect."

Theo accepted the hammer and move back to Nia's locker. He worked two fingers into the shackle on the padlock, pulling it tight, and then he turned it so the fixed end of the shackle was facing him. With the hammer, he delivered a series of sharp, quick strikes. The shackle popped open, and the lock turned in his hand.

"Holy shit," Auggie said. "Holy shit, that was amazing."

"Regular padlocks, you can knock the pins clear if you try long enough. And if you ever say Brinks again, I'm going to beat your ass with this hammer."

Auggie grinned and mimed zipping his lips.

Theo worked the lock loose and opened the locker. They did a quick search. There was the usual stuff of course: workout clothes, a racket, a spare racket, athletic tape, a water bottle that looked slightly moldy.

Auggie found the pills.

"What the hell are these?" He pointed to the bag.

Theo shook his head. "Take pictures of all of it. Document everything." He was about to say more when he saw the paper. He reached, remembered fingerprints, and stopped himself. Auggie had seen his movement, though, and spotted the paper too. He grabbed it before Theo could say anything.

"Stay away from me and my sister," Auggie read, "or I'll kill you."

11

From the hospital waiting room, Auggie sent a direct message to Nia's Instagram account. It was simple and to the point: *Saw the stuff in ur locker let's talk.*

Theo was pacing. The lobby was deserted, which seemed strange for a Saturday afternoon. Somehow the older man kept catching his foot on the tubular metal legs of the chairs, as though he were trying to navigate an unseen crowd. On the next pass, he came to a stop in front of Auggie's chair, put his hands on his hips, and said, "She's not going to do this. Not yet. We need more pressure."

"No, we have pressure. We just need to apply it in person. Why don't you sit down? You look like your knee is bothering you again."

Instead, Theo started pacing again.

A text from Fer came through a moment later: *Why the fuck are you taking so many Ubers? My credit card alerts are blowing up.*

Sorry emergency.

What kind of emergency?

It's all good now promise. Then, after a moment's consideration, he added, *I'm fine, everybody's safe, it's ok.*

Call me right fucking now.

Can't, Auggie messaged back. *Later.*

What's this $230 charge from FuelWorld?

Auggie dismissed the message.

As he was putting the phone in his pocket, another message buzzed. He glimpsed it: *Don't you dare put your fucking phone in your fucking pocket. Answer me.*

He shoved the phone out of sight and figured he could pretend he hadn't seen that one.

"Why is your face red?" Theo said.

"I'm hot." Auggie fanned his coat for emphasis.

"It's freezing in here."

"Why don't you go ask them to call up to her room again?"

Theo's eyes narrowed, but he left.

Auggie took advantage of the respite to close his eyes. The pounding in his head had intensified, and he blamed it on the smell: someone had puked into a potted plastic fern, and apparently nobody could be troubled to clean it up. They'd picked the seats in the opposite corner of the lobby, but it hadn't helped. If he could just get some fresh air—

"One to ten?" Theo said quietly. He dropped into the chair next to Auggie, the metal legs squeaking against the linoleum.

Ten, Auggie thought. "Six." He had both hands on his temples as though he were holding his skull together.

Theo's hands settled on Auggie's shoulders, turning him slightly.

"If you're going to strangle me," Auggie said as Theo's fingers moved to his neck, "remember that we're in a hospital and they'll be able to revive me."

"I've taken that into consideration."

Theo dug his thumbs into Auggie's shoulders, then into his neck, then his shoulders again. He used enough force that sometimes it hurt, but it was a different kind of pain, and Auggie's head didn't bother him quite as much.

"I'm such an idiot," Auggie mumbled. "I can't believe I did that last night."

"I might have thought something along those lines," Theo said. After a moment, he added, "But you're the only reason anyone has a description of the shooter. More importantly, you kept your head. You're brave, you're resourceful, you react thoughtfully and decisively in danger. You were amazing last night, Auggie." One hand caught Auggie's shirt, tightening the collar into a noose, and he said, "But if you'd gotten yourself shot, dummy, I would have brought you back to life and killed you myself."

Forest fires could start from a single spark, Auggie thought. They had wildfires every year in California. Miles and miles burning because an ember drifted into a dry patch of weeds. Auggie's face was hot. Sweat stung him under the arms, across the shoulders.

His phone buzzed.

A message from Dylan: *u ok?*

Auggie dismissed it.

His phone buzzed again. *I've been worrying about u all night things got crazy and I couldn't find u i went to the ER but they wouldn't tell me if u were admitted. If ur ok will u please tell me I don't know what to do.*

This time, Auggie's finger hovered over the screen.

"Is it Nia?"

"No." He tried to work moisture into his throat. "Dylan."

"Oh." Theo's hands fell away. "That's nice of him to check in."

"Yeah, well, it would have been nicer if it wasn't twenty hours after we got separated at the scene of an active shooter."

"He didn't—" Theo stopped. A middle-aged man with a mop and bucket shuffled into the room. The bucket was on casters, and one of them emitted a short shrieking noise at regular intervals. "I don't know what to do here, Auggie," Theo said. "I feel like I mess up every time I try to talk to you about stuff."

Squeezing his eyes shut, Auggie shook his head. The caster's squeals came closer.

"Maybe you should just ask him what happened," Theo said, "before you decide anything. Will it help if I tell you a story?"

"No," Auggie said. "But I'd wither away if I didn't get to enjoy the wisdom of your advanced age."

Even with his eyes closed, he could feel Theo smile.

"One time," Theo said, "really early on when Ian and I had started dating, I made a big deal out of our three-month anniversary. Ian was the first guy I'd dated seriously, and I felt old—wipe that look off your face, please—to be learning how to date. Everybody else had already done all this stuff, and I was ashamed that I'd waited so long to come out, ashamed I'd waited so long to start living my life. I decorated the apartment where I was living, candles, a tablecloth, all that stuff. And I didn't exactly make dinner, but I bought something nice and warmed it up. And then Ian was an hour late, and he hadn't even changed out of uniform."

In spite of his best efforts, Auggie opened his eyes. Theo was leaning back in the chair, his expression distant, alone with his ghosts for a few heartbeats.

"I bitched him out," Theo said. "Jesus, you wouldn't believe what that poor guy had to put up with from me for the first couple years. I was so insecure, and that was part of the problem, but I also loved him—already, so early it seems ridiculous now—and I was terrified he'd figure out I was the wrong one and take off."

"So the natural solution was to bitch him out."

"Obviously," Theo said, his grin bright and fast and gone. "He just stood there and took it. He apologized. We had dinner. He was Ian, which meant he was charming and funny and softened me up pretty fast. It ended up being a really nice night." Theo shook his head. "The next day, we ran into his partner at the time—this was before he and Cart were working together—and he asked about the flat tire, if Ian had made it to dinner all right, that kind of stuff. I spent the next six months apologizing."

229

"I guess he forgave you," Auggie said.

"I guess so."

Turning his phone in his hands, Auggie said, "I think something's wrong with me."

Theo cocked his head, but he didn't say anything.

Now the dam had broken, and the words rushed out. "I'm so messed up. I don't like boys my age. I . . . I don't feel that kind of stuff for a lot of people, I guess. I mean, I can tell when I think someone is hot."

"Robert Pattinson," Theo murmured.

Auggie slugged him. Then he had to blink to keep the tears from spilling. "And people ask me why I like Dylan and I don't know. I just feel something with him, and it feels good to feel something for someone else. Someone else who feels the same way. I'm tired of . . . tired of feeling alone, and I'm tired of people seeing me as, I don't know, not me. Coming out made it better, for sure, but it's still—I don't know. I feel like ninety-nine percent of the people I meet still see the cardboard kid from my videos. He's just a gay cardboard kid now." Auggie wiped his eyes. "God, see? I'm really, really screwed up."

In the corner with the potted plastic fern, the custodian was wheeling his bucket back and forth, casting an uninterested gaze around the area, occasionally stopping to swab a patch of linoleum. If the vomit in the fern bothered him, he didn't give any sign of it.

"So," Theo said, "a few things. First, you like who you like. You can't change that, and you shouldn't want to. It's a big mix of factors, and you only need to worry about it if you have a pattern of bad relationships. Then, yes, you definitely need to figure out how to break that pattern. If you like older guys, great. I mean—" Red flooded his face. "You know what I mean. And you might find in five or ten years that you like guys your own age. Or maybe not. Maybe you'll have some weird diaper fetish and you'll be dating a guy in a nursing home."

Auggie's eyes almost dropped out of his head. Then he punched Theo in the arm, counting the blows. By three, Theo was laughing. By seven, he was laughing and trying to pull away. Auggie caught his coat and landed the final punches.

"Ten," he said. "God, you are the worst."

Still laughing, Theo held up two fingers. "Number two is kind of an extension of number one: you like who you like, and you don't need to meet a quota. If it's one guy a year, that guy better realize how lucky he is. If it's ten guys, well, maybe you're the lucky one." Theo paused, held up a third finger, and said, "Number three is tricky, and you probably aren't going to like it."

"I know. I know you think I should break up with Dylan, but you don't really know him, and—"

"Auggie."

Auggie stopped.

"The hard part about loving someone, anyone, romantically or not, is that you'll never be able to explain why you love them. Not completely. You'll be able to say some of the reasons. And some people will claim they know exactly why they love another person. But the reality is that like any emotion, some of it's up here," Theo tapped his head, "and some of it's in here," he tapped his heart. "Or in the subconscious, if you want to think of it that way. Or at the level of hormones and biochemistry, if you want to think of it that way. Or in the soul. Don't feel bad if you can't explain why you like Dylan. I mean, he'd better have some redeeming features to make up for a pair of friends called Burger and Smash—"

"I knew you weren't going to let that go. I knew it."

"—but if you like him, you like him, and if he makes you happy, that's what matters."

After a moment, Auggie nodded.

"I don't know what to tell you about feeling like people don't know you," Theo said. "I mean, we all feel that to some extent. We want somebody who will see us, the good part of us. But you're in a tricky situation because you've made one facet of your life very public, and it's taken over. I know you're going to hate this next part, but please don't scream at me. Not in public, anyway. You're nineteen; you've got a lot of time to find people who will be your friends, people who will love you for the real you, including someone to have a relationship with."

Whistling "Go Tell Aunt Rhody," the custodian shuffled out of the lobby. The puke was unattended. Two shiny patches showed where he'd run the mop in lazy arcs. Auggie waited until he was gone.

"I guess that makes sense," he said. "Some of it."

"You're welcome."

"You're lucky you have the advantage of all those extra decades of experience."

"Ok."

"Even though time has robbed you of strength and speed and good looks—"

Theo sighed.

"—at least you have the small recompense of wisdom."

"When I get a job," Theo said, slumping back into his seat, talking to the empty waiting room. "If I get a job, I am going to refuse to teach underclassmen. Refuse. Categorically."

Auggie leaned against Theo. After a moment, Theo's hand came up, running over the crew cut. Then Auggie's phone buzzed.

"I guess I should ask Dylan what happened last night."

"I'm all out of free advice. Go try Orlando."

"Oh God, I can't even imagine." Auggie picked up his phone and then sat up straight, dislodging Theo's hand. "It's from Nia. She says she'll talk to us."

12

The hospital room was nominally shared, but a uniformed police officer—Patrick Foley—stood at the door, and Theo guessed that Nia would have the room to herself for the foreseeable future. A second bed stood cattycorner to Nia's, the privacy curtain pulled back to reveal that it was empty. The bathroom door was open, and although the light was off, Theo could see that the bathroom was empty as well.

"Do you want to check under the bed too?" Auggie whispered.

Instead, Theo studied the girl in the bed. Nia was long: long arms, long legs, a long torso. The hospital gown and the thick bandages around her chest did nothing to hide the compact muscle that padded her frame. Her skin was very dark, and her eyes were even darker. After a moment, her eyes slid to the window, and she touched her tight fade with one hand.

"Where are your parents?" Auggie asked.

"They had to go out." Her voice was flat and slightly nasal; judging from her eyes, Theo guessed she was high as a kite. "Dad won't say it, but he wants to get back to work. He's a chemical engineer at Tegula." She shook her head. "I don't know if that man has ever taken a day off. Even at home, he's always scribbling equations, ideas, you know. Mom gets crazy picking them up. She went home to shower."

"You waited until they were gone to tell us we could come up," Auggie said.

Nia nodded.

"Why?" Theo asked.

"I didn't want them to know." Her voice tightened, and she ran one hand along the bed rail. The metal chimed. "Please don't tell them. I don't have a lot of money. God, after this, I'm not going to have any money. But I'll figure something out."

"We're not here to—" Auggie began.

"Let's start with information," Theo said. "That's what we want first."

Nia nodded listlessly.

"How long has this been going on?"

Nia laughed. "A long time. A long, long time. Since high school. The summer before, actually."

"Who—" Auggie began.

Theo slashed the air with one hand, the gesture at waist level, and Auggie cut off.

"Do you know what it's like?" Nia asked dreamily, "having Deja as your sister? Having the tennis champ as your sister? I had to hear about it all the time. 'Why aren't you as fast as Deja? Why aren't you winning like Deja? Why's Deja still at practice and you're sitting on your butt in front of the TV?'" Nia fell silent, and then, choking on the words, she added, "For one minute, for one single minute, I was actually relieved when I heard she was shot. I thought she'd just been hurt. I thought that was the end; I wouldn't have to hear about tennis anymore. And then they told me she was dead, and ever since, I've been living in a shrine to Deja. And I'm part of it. I'm supposed to be part of all of it. I've got to be in every march. I've got to be in every picture." She shuddered, cried out quietly, and then sagged back against the bed. "Oh God, I can't even think clearly. What are we talking about? The pills. We're talking about the pills. You won't say anything?"

"That depends," Theo said. "Tell us about Cal."

"Just a fight," she said. "It was just a fight."

"Keep going."

"Someone told him. Deja. Probably Deja. She didn't like that I was getting stronger. Didn't like that I had a faster serve. Asked me why I looked different, sounded different . . ." Her voice trailed off, and her head nodded. Blinking herself awake, she said, "I don't know how she got into my locker. Must have taken my keys."

"And then?"

"Big fight. Mom and Dad crying, they didn't even know why. She left." Nia made a choking noise. It looked like she was trying to cry, but her eyes remained glassy. "Got killed because she was in a hoodie and because a scared man had a gun and a badge."

"And then?"

Muzzily, she said, "And then Mom and Dad knew why they were crying."

"What happened with Cal?" Theo asked.

"Is he here? I don't want to see him. What he did, messing with my head, I told him I was going to kill him." Pushing back the bedsheets, she mumbled, "Want to see a mirror. Want to see what I look like. Freak, that's what. Deja saw it. She ran out of the house."

"Hold on," Auggie said, running interference, trying to keep Nia in bed by filling up the space next to her. She ignored him, trying to extricate herself from the bedding, sliding one bare leg toward the edge of the mattress. Thick, dark hair covered her thigh. "Nia, just wait—"

"Sit your ass back in that bed," Theo barked.

Auggie stared at him. Nia shrank back.

"Put one foot on the floor, and the pictures go straight to the head of athletics. They don't need a warrant to open your locker, and they'll spot the pills, and that's the end for you. Do you understand?"

"Yeah," Nia said. She lay back. "I understand."

"Theo, maybe you should—"

"When was the last time you saw Cal?"

"I don't know."

"Bullshit. You killed him, and we know you killed him. If you tell us the truth, it's going to go a lot easier for you."

The door opened, and Foley stared in. "What's going on?"

"Nothing," Theo said. "Close the door, Patrick."

Foley stayed where he was, though, and his gaze shifted to Auggie. Auggie looked away. Then Foley looked at Nia.

"S'all right," Nia said. "Everybody's upset."

When the door closed, Nia said, "I killed Cal, huh? God, don't I wish." Her hand hovered over the mass of bandages on her chest and then flopped back onto the mattress. "Don't even know why someone shot me. If I were five years younger, Cal and Wayne would have lost their minds about this; I don't know if I'll play again, definitely not competitively."

"With physical therapy," Auggie said, "and a lot of hard work, you'll be able to play again."

Nia didn't grace that with a response, and Theo kept his opinion to himself.

The afternoon sunlight fanned across the linoleum, across the side of the bed, filling in the scratches on the chrome rail and exposing the metal's texture. Nia played her fingers through the light for a moment, watching the shadow they cast. Then she picked up her phone.

"What are you doing?" Theo said.

"I'm looking up the last time I called Cal."

Theo shot Auggie a look, and Auggie nodded. He inched closer to the bed to see the screen. After tapping and scrolling several times, Nia said, "August 22nd. See?"

The day Cal had disappeared.

"What did you talk about?"

"He wouldn't talk long on the phone." Closing her eyes, Nia settled back against the mattress. "He was so mad. I think Deja tattled. She was the star, so she got star treatment. The rest of us were dogs they ran into the ground."

"You fought with Cal about the steroids? On the 22nd?"

"He practically bought them and put them in my hands. I don't know why he got so worked up about them."

"What about Deja. That was the same day she got shot, the 22nd. Where does Deja fit in?"

"She wrote that note," Nia mumbled. "Stay away from my sister, or I'll kill you. She would have done it too. Would have killed him herself. I needed to warn him. If I drove, I'd be faster."

"Did you go to Cal's apartment that night?"

Her answer was rough, uneven breathing.

"Nia, did you go to Cal's place that night?"

Her eyes were glassy.

Theo felt it, the invisible connection they were on the edge of unearthing. It was like reading a play or a novel or a poem and sensing the outline of something, knowing you just had to excavate it. How could it be a coincidence that the same night Deja died, Cal Reese went missing? "You did. You were there. You were at Cal's place that night. Let me tell you how I think it happened: the night Deja died, you and Cal fought, and you killed him. You were arguing about a lot of things—the drugs, how he favored Deja. But mostly you hated him because you envied Deja. And now, the dealer who supplied you and Cal has decided you're a little too crazy to keep as a customer, and she's decided to get rid of you."

Nia's eyes were half-closed.

"Well?" Theo said.

"I don't even know her name," she mumbled. "I thought I saw her. Cal called her the White Rabbit. Don't know why Cal didn't see it coming. He was mad. I was mad. I wanted him to die; he deserved to die." She sucked in a deep breath, aspirated saliva, and coughed. Her whole body contorted with the effort, and pain from the gunshot wound made her eyes bright and wild. Auggie sat next to her, supporting her with one arm until the coughing eased. Then he helped her lie down again.

"Why did Cal deserve to die?" Auggie asked.

"He took Deja away from me. Turned us against each other. I was never as good as Deja. If I won, it was luck. If I lost, it was because I didn't work hard enough. But Deja—always doing things exactly right, just the way he wanted. When we talked on the phone, he was so mad. Wanted to know how I could ruin everything for him. Wanted to know how I could risk that. I wanted to say a few things myself. I wanted him to know he put those pills in my hand. The minute I knew I couldn't be what he wanted me to be, not without some help, he might as well have put those pills in my hand himself. The White Rabbit was always there, but all Cal was worried about was the money." She tried to sit up. "He didn't even congratulate me when I signed my letter of intent with Wroxall. Didn't even look at me when I told him. When Nicki got her letter from one of those Indiana schools, though, he threw her a party. All he cared about was the money." Her eyes shut to slits again.

"She's exhausted," Auggie whispered.

"What money?" Theo asked. "Auggie, wake her up."

"Theo, she's—"

"Right now."

Auggie shook Nia's arm and spoke into her ear. When her eyes came open, nobody was home.

"What money?" Theo asked. "Cal cared about the money, that's what you said. What money?"

"They got a new car," she said in that flat, droning voice. "Indiana temporary tag."

"Who's the White Rabbit?"

But her eyes shut again.

"Wake her up."

"No."

Scratching at his beard, Theo shifted his weight. "Wake her up, Auggie."

"No. She's exhausted. She's hurt. She can't think clearly."

"We don't have time to coddle her. I want to ask—"

"I said no." Auggie stood from where he perched on the mattress. "We're done for right now."

The sun painted half of his face. That expressive mouth was a tight, hard line. He looked older. Then, touching his temple, he winced, and he was just Auggie again.

Theo nodded, and they left.

13

On the Uber ride to the police station, neither of them spoke at first, which was a relief. The headache had turned into a thunderstorm, and Auggie struggled to think through it. Looking at his phone made him feel like he had shards of glass in his eyes, and requesting the ride had made his head hurt so badly that he'd almost gotten sick in the hospital lobby. Now he lay with his head against the seat, his eyes closed, smelling the faint hint of cigarette smoke on their driver, a skinny white boy with a Bob Marley tattoo on his nape.

"Do you really think it was the dealer?" Auggie asked over the instrumental music playing on the car's speakers. *Braveheart*, maybe? "I don't know if that makes sense. Nothing seems to make sense."

"I think Nia wasn't telling us everything. She can claim that Cal made her feel pressured to improve her performance, but she admitted that he didn't want her using. If someone had learned that Cal and Wayne's athletes were doping, that would have been the end of them professionally. And the sibling rivalry thing bothers me. Something really hinky was going on there."

"Like with Genesis."

"Yes, exactly. If Cal was also in a relationship like that with Deja or Nia or both, I could definitely see the sibling rivalry thing escalating to a jilted-lover murder."

The *Braveheart* soundtrack got louder, and the front seat squeaked. Apparently the white boy with the Bob Marley tattoo didn't want to be liable for anything he overheard.

"No," Auggie said, "I mean, Genesis's dad and brother were talking about money too. A lot of money."

"Fifteen thousand dollars isn't a lot of money."

"Says the guy who can't afford a new air conditioner." Wincing, Auggie pressed his face against the glass, grateful for the cool. "I could definitely use fifteen thousand dollars."

"The problem is that they stood to make a lot more from the civil suit. They wanted him alive, not dead. Nia on the other hand—"

"Nia couldn't have shot herself during the middle of her own speech."

"The White Rabbit could have shot her."

"Sadie? Why? To cover up the fact that she was selling steroids? That's piddly stuff, Theo. The shooter took a huge risk last night, and it required planning, timing, and a cool head. Do you really think that sounds like a tweaker who hangs around a private gym and sells roids? Besides, it's a weak motive. Whoever did this is capable, yes, but he's also got a serious motive." After a moment, Auggie added, "Or he's crazy."

The *Braveheart* music got even louder. This track had a lot of bagpipes, which felt to Auggie like the acoustical equivalent of a Phillip's head in the ear canal.

When Theo spoke again, his voice was thoughtful. "Kickbacks to trainers and coaches aren't exactly uncommon. Every few years, there's another scandal, and everybody has to act shocked and surprised that big universities and professional teams are offering financial incentives. Some of it goes to the athletes, but the smart teams understand that a coach or trainer usually has a lot of pull, and so they'll court the coach too: lavish vacations, generous donations to the local team's fundraising efforts, a cushy consulting job."

"A car with a temporary out-of-state tag."

"I wondered how Cal had been able to afford that Mustang. I figured any extra cash was going into his coke fund."

"Um, guys," the driver said. "Friendly reminder that I'm still up here, you know? So if you could be cool, please?"

"Head?" Theo asked quietly.

"It's ok."

"I can handle this part on my own."

"No, I want to be there."

The duty officer at the front desk was named Murray—at least, that's what his tag said—and he looked well past the age of retirement. Auggie pegged him at somewhere in his mid-seventies; he had a stray white nose hair that reached halfway to his lip. Theo seemed to know him; he walked right up to the officer and said hello.

Murray stared at him and said, "Yes, sir. May I help you?"

"We're here to see Detective Somerset," Theo said. "It's about the shooting last night."

"He's very busy, but I'll let him know. You gentlemen can have a seat."

"Is everything going ok, Jim? How have you been holding up?"

Phone in one hand, Murray blinked a few times, seeming to consider his options, and settled for, "That's Officer Murray, sir. Please have a seat."

"It's me, Theo."

"Yes, sir. Please sit down now."

When Auggie and Theo sat, Theo muttered, "Don't."

"I just think it's cute that you kept trying."

"I said don't."

The station smelled like burnt coffee, floor wax, and overheated bodies. Someone was running a hand dryer in the bathroom; voices competed, rose, and merged into a babble. Where the light came in through the double glass doors, it glowed against the white vinyl tiles. Auggie closed his eyes; a moment later, someone was saying his name softly, and he realized he had fallen asleep.

"Sorry." He wiped his mouth, spotted the drool patch on Theo's coat, and mumbled, "Oh God."

"It's fine," Theo said quietly.

"Are you ok?" The voice was familiar: friendly without being forced; warm without being cloying. Detective Somerset bent down to examine Auggie. "You're pretty pale."

"I'm fine," Auggie said.

"Are you—"

"He said he's fine," Theo said. "Thank you."

"Yeah, ok. Can we talk here, or do you want to come back?"

"Better go back."

So they followed Somerset to the bullpen, where desks had been pushed together in pairs. Somerset pulled two chairs up to one of the desks, sat, and took a long drink of coffee. "Sorry. It's been a long night."

By then, Auggie's head had cleared enough for him to study the detective. Somerset was gorgeous; there was no denying it. The golden tan that had survived the winter. The tropically blue eyes. The lean, muscular swimmer's build, nicely displayed by the trousers hugging his ass and the button-down with its sleeves cuffed. Tattoos. Those Auggie hadn't remembered. Just a hint of ink where the sleeves were rolled up, but Auggie guessed there was a lot more. Wedding ring, too. Not that it mattered. Somerset was pretty, but he had nothing on Theo. Today, the detective had dark circles under his eyes, and he kept yawning.

"What can I help you guys with? Not to be rude, but I've got a pretty full plate."

Theo told him about the connection between Nia, Deja, and Cal. He mentioned Genesis too, at Auggie's insistence.

"I'm not sure what you want me to do," Somerset said.

"We're just trying to figure out how this fits together," Theo said. "What about the White Rabbit? We think that's probably a girl named Sadie. Does that ring any bells?"

"Theo, it's good to see you again, and I appreciate you bringing this information to me. But this is a very high-profile investigation. A lot of people got hurt last night, and we're dotting every i on this one. I'm going to loop Detective Lender in, and I'll tell him what you—"

"No!"

Somerset froze.

"I mean," Theo said, "I don't want to be connected to this."

A pair of uniformed officers strolled past the bullpen, one of them laughing, the other shaking her head. From the lobby, where Murray worked the desk, came a querulous voice demanding that a full police turnout be ordered to keep children from sledding near the river. Somerset's eyes held Theo, and then they slid to Auggie.

"What's going on?"

"Nothing," Auggie said. "It's just messy, and we don't want to get involved in something like this again."

"Theo?"

"Like he said: nothing."

"It sounds like you're already involved in it. We've got a shooting incident that you claim is somehow connected to a murder that happened five months ago, but you can't explain why. You've got a story about performance-enhancing drugs and someone called the White Rabbit. When I mentioned Detective Lender, you both looked like I was holding a gun to your head. So I'm going to ask you again: what's going on?"

"We just wanted you to know what we found," Auggie said.

"What did you find? Help me unravel this, Auggie. Somebody killed Cal Reese. Maybe it's Genesis Evans's family, and they want revenge more than they want money. Fine. Why do they come back and shoot Nia five months later? Or it's drugs, which is what Detectives Lender and Swinney thought from the beginning, and you're here telling me about this White Rabbit character, but it just brings up the same question: why does she pop up now?"

"The drugs in Nia's locker, the story she told us," Theo said, ticking the items off on his fingers. "If you ask her, she won't have an alibi for the night Cal disappeared. She could have killed him. Now someone else wants revenge. Or wants to keep her quiet because she knows something."

Auggie could sense the change. It wasn't anything obvious—Somerset didn't make a face, didn't turn away, didn't laugh. Maybe a new distance in his gaze, that was all.

"Ok," Somerset said. "Thank you."

"I'm not insane," Theo said. "Ask her. She won't have an alibi."

"It was five months ago, Theo." Somerset's voice was gentle. "Nobody has an alibi for five months ago. I understand that the last year and a half has been very difficult—"

"Don't you fucking dare."

"Ok," Auggie said. He put his hand on Theo's arm; the muscles were tight and hard. "I think we should go."

Theo just stared at Somerset. They both might have been statues.

"My head is really hurting, Theo," Auggie said.

After a moment, Theo gave a jerky nod. He got out of his seat, and Auggie followed. Somerset accompanied them to the door, which Theo elbowed open. A blast of cold slapped Auggie.

Turning back, Auggie said, "Deja's shooting. Could it have been connected to all this?"

Somerset hesitated. Then he said, "I don't see how. Unofficially—and I'll deny I ever said this—there's absolutely no doubt about what happened. Deja was running. Eddie Barth told her to stop. She had earbuds in, music blasting, and her hood up. She didn't hear him. Eddie thought she had a weapon. If you believe Eddie, he told her to stop again. He believed his life was in imminent danger. He shot her."

"He could have been paid to kill her," Auggie said. "Maybe someone wanted her dead."

The distance in Somerset's gaze was greater now. "We'll keep an open mind."

14

"Let's get you home," Theo said. "You really don't look good."

It was late afternoon, close to sunset, and the light had turned reddish gold. It was the only thing putting color in Auggie's face. A patrol car passed them, heading halfway up the block to turn into the police-only lot. Across the street, a brick strip mall held, among other things, a small café, a Family Video, and a bail bondsman. The door to the Family Video swung open, a bell jingled, and a woman emerged, holding the hand of a child who couldn't have been more than four years old. The little boy was screaming at the top of his lungs about a *Bubble Guppies* DVD.

"I'm fine." Auggie was still pressing one hand to his temple. "I think we need to figure this out."

"Figure what out?"

"I—"

"There's nothing to figure out, Auggie. This is it. We hit the end. Anything else and we're asking them to put Lender on our trail."

"I—"

"And even if we wanted to," Theo said, waving one arm, "what could we do? We've got nothing. We've got a bunch of things that don't go anywhere. We've got a dozen different pieces of the puzzle that don't fit together. Hell, they might even be from different puzzles."

"I—"

"And I know you might be in danger. I know this is a big deal. I'm probably more afraid than you are. But we keep running into walls, and there's nowhere left for us to go."

"I really think I need to sit down," Auggie said, swaying.

"Oh my God." Theo took his arm. "How about—" Theo pointed at the café. Auggie nodded. They crossed the street. It was only two lanes of blacktop without any cars coming in either direction, but Theo still kept a tight grip on Auggie's arm. In spite of the cold, sweat glistened at Auggie's hairline. His face was waxy. They had barely made it to the curb when Auggie bent his knees and was sick.

Theo held him by the shoulders, bracing him until it was over.

"My shoes," Auggie whispered.

"Your shoes are fine. Come on, let's get inside so you can sit down."

The café smelled like freshly brewed coffee and cinnamon. A chalkboard menu listed the day's specials, which included a peanut-butter-and-onion sandwich, a tuna sandwich with crushed potato chips, and a cranberry-almond salad. Acoustic pop played over a pair of speakers set near a small stage. There was no one behind the counter.

Theo helped Auggie to a chair, touched the back of his hand Auggie's forehead, and said, "Did you bring your medicine?"

Auggie shook his head.

Theo made his way to the counter, spotted the bell, and rang it a few times. A girl with a crazy map of freckles and her hair in finger coils emerged from the batwing doors at the back of the room. Her smile faltered when she saw Theo's face.

"May I help you?"

"Would you call an ambulance?"

"No," Auggie protested from where he was sitting. "I'm fine. Theo, stop."

The girl patted her dark curls, her gaze moving from Theo to Auggie and back to Theo.

"Really," Auggie said. "It's just a headache. I'll be fine in a few minutes."

"I've got Midol," the girl said.

After a moment, Theo nodded, and the girl went back through the batwing doors. When she returned, she was carrying two pills, which she handed to Theo with another attempt at a smile.

"Two coffees," Theo said. "And water, and . . . maybe that brownie over there."

The girl rang up the food and drink, and Theo paid. He carried everything back the table were Auggie was sitting with his head in his hands. Auggie's leg was bouncing rapidly, and his fingertips were white where he was clutching his head.

"You at least have to take these pills," Theo said. "Or we're going to the hospital."

Auggie took the pills with some of the water.

"And now I'm realizing you haven't eaten today." Theo resisted the urge to swear. "I know you probably don't feel like it, but you should try to get a little something in your stomach. Do you want to try the coffee or the brownie?"

Auggie's knee bounced faster.

"I know you feel sick, but either you eat something, or we go to the hospital."

"The brownie."

Auggie barely managed three bites before he pushed the dessert away. Then he held his head in his hands again, his knee still bouncing like crazy. A little less than a quarter of an hour later, though, his leg stopped bouncing. His head came up. He finished the brownie, chasing it with a few swallows of coffee.

"Sandwich?"

Auggie nodded. Then, with a washed-out smile, he said, "Not the peanut-butter-and-onion, unless you're trying to punish me."

Theo ordered two of the tuna sandwiches, which came on croissants, and which were accompanied by kettle-cooked potato chips. By the time they'd finished eating, some of the color had come back into Auggie's face.

"Thanks," Auggie said.

Theo shrugged. "Headaches are tricky, and concussions only make things more complicated, but no food or drink will always make them worse."

Auggie stirred his coffee. He spoke without looking up, but his voice was firm. "What's the most likely reason someone took a shot at Nia? You told Detective Somerset several possible reasons, but I want to know what you think is the real one."

"I don't know about real, but the most likely is that she knew something."

Auggie nodded. "That's what I think too."

"But that doesn't mean—"

"It means I'm still a target, and so are you Theo. I'm not trying to be stubborn. I wish I could say I was doing this to help Orlando. I wish I could say I was doing it because I cared about justice, or because it was the right thing. But I think we have to keep going, or whoever did this is going to come after us."

Theo worked his jaw. His throat was dry. "I won't let anything happen to you again."

"That's exactly what I'm afraid of." Auggie offered a tiny, wry smile. "Let's go back to the beginning. Why would someone kill Cal Reese?"

"Drugs."

"Lender told us it wasn't drugs."

"And you believe that psycho?"

"He hasn't lied to us. Not . . . not really. He's always been clear about what he wanted. Even if he didn't tell us why he wanted it, we knew what his goals were. He didn't get upset when we started looking into Cal's death. He got upset when we messed with one of his dealers."

"So you do believe him."

"I think, as far as it matters, we should assume he was telling the truth. Honestly, if it was drugs, I don't even know where to start. The White Rabbit? Jesus. Let's leave that to one side for a moment."

"Ok." Theo drummed on the table. "The most common motive is money. Or jealousy."

"Jealousy?"

"I didn't want to say anything, but I guess we should talk about it. Hasn't Orlando's behavior seemed strange to you?"

Auggie dropped the coffee stirrer. His gaze came up, and he locked eyes with Theo. "Orlando did not do this."

Theo put both hands flat on the table. He studied the particleboard between his fingers.

"He didn't." Auggie's voice rose. "He did not, Theo."

"This is why I didn't want to talk about it."

"You're damn right we're not going to talk about it." He raked fingers through his hair. "Money. Fine, let's think about money. Who might have wanted money from Cal?"

"Ignoring the problem won't make it go away."

"Don't you dare do that. Don't you dare talk to me like I'm a fucking kid."

Theo let out a slow breath, but he couldn't stop himself from balling his fists.

"That's your strategy whenever you don't like what I think." Auggie was breathing rapidly, and the only color in his face came from red blotches. "You throw that in my face because you can't find a way to argue with me legitimately."

"When you act like a kid," Theo said deliberately, "I'm not going to pretend otherwise. But that's not what I was trying to say." He gritted his teeth, but the next part escaped him, and he looked up. "And you've got your own strategy too, Auggie. Whenever I say something you don't like, whenever my opinion is different from yours, whenever I skate within a mile of sounding like I'm passing judgement, you scream your head off about how I treat you like a kid. How the hell is that fair? It's not my fault we're different ages. It's not my fault I have different ways of thinking about things. Some of that's just personality, but some of it's the fact that I'm ten years older than you, and I've grown out of—"

"Fuck you." Auggie wiped his eyes. "And I'm not crying; my eyes are watering because my head hurts."

The girl was playing with the sound system, the music skipping from track to track. What was the right style of music for a public argument with a much younger man you had dirty dreams about? Probably a country-western cover of Bowie, Theo thought.

"Ok, I'm sorry," Theo said. "If you want to talk about immature, I think I just gave you a prime example. Also, I thought we talked about this. I thought we agreed crying is ok."

Auggie kept wiping his cheeks.

"If you don't want to talk about Orlando—"

"He's a good guy. He's my friend. And what would Orlando even be jealous of?"

"Cal sexually assaulted his girlfriend, and as a result, she broke up with him. It's not classic jealousy, but he might blame Cal for ending his relationship. And let's face it: Orlando isn't exactly stable."

"He's a lot better. He's getting therapy. He's on the right medication."

"He says."

"Stop it!"

The shout drowned out the cheery bubblegum pop that the barista had settled on. Auggie's voice echoed back from the high ceilings.

"Ok," Theo said. "Let's both try to act like adults—I'm including myself in that statement. Talking about Orlando isn't productive. You seemed like you thought money might be the issue; let's see where we can get with that."

The set of Auggie's jaw announced that he wanted to keep arguing, but after a moment, he managed to say, "If Nia was right and Cal and Wayne have been getting kickbacks, where's the money?"

"We saw Cal's car. The police have it now. Or his parents. Or somebody."

"I'm not talking about the car. I'm talking about the rest of it. If they were getting paid by check, it would have shown up in those bank statements. That's obviously a no because a major team or a university isn't going to leave a paper trail. We didn't see direct deposits from other employers, and I don't think Cal and Wayne would be stupid enough to use their company finances to launder the blackmail money. That's an easy way for the IRS to get interested fast. We've been to the apartment, Theo. We went through their finances. They weren't depositing extra money in any of the accounts we saw. So if they're getting kickbacks, where are they?"

Theo frowned. "They could be intangible. I mean—"

"I know what intangible means."

This time, Theo waited until the song changed. A guy with an impossibly deep voice came on.

Flushing, Auggie said, "Sorry."

"Maybe they've got some sort of honorary position. Maybe they're plugged into the old boys' network now. I could see something like that going a long way."

"But would Cal and Wayne have kept it a secret? No way; being able to brag about something like that is the whole point. And can you imagine Daddy Reese failing to mention that his boys are special coach's assistants at Missouri Douche State?"

"No, I can't. And please never say Daddy Reese again."

To Theo's surprise, Auggie grinned. "If Nia's right, and if they're getting some sort of kickback, then I think they're receiving tangible items."

"The car."

"Right. The coach goes to a major donor, explains the situation, and suddenly Cal Reese buys a muscle car with a high-end trim for pennies. Or maybe it's even simpler: maybe someone just shows up with an envelope full of cash."

"The old ones are the best." Over the speakers, the guy with the deep voice was singing about sex. He wasn't calling it that, but there was a lot of *you and me*, a lot of *playground* and *party* and *give you what you need*. Songs, Theo thought, unable to keep himself from tracing with his eyes the hollow of Auggie's throat, the cut of his jaw, that expressive mouth. Songs usually missed the whole point. He cleared his throat and said, "But we've been through that apartment, and we searched it pretty thoroughly."

"I thought about that," Auggie said. "I think there are two places Cal and Wayne might have been stashing their goods. Well, Wayne, anyway. Cal probably blew most of his on drugs."

"At their training facility," Theo said.

Nodding, Auggie said, "Or at their parents' house. Flip a coin?"

"No need. Jesus, you remember what those people are like. Ma and Pa Reese made museums out of those bedrooms. And Chris said something about the boys in the family, how they still liked to sneak up to their rooms." In a rush, Theo added, "She was talking about Orlando too, Auggie."

Auggie just nodded again. "Ok. Let's go burgle my friend's house."

15

Theo objected to every part of the plan.

At first, Auggie tried to explain to Theo that the food and the medicine had helped. His head was much better. Then, when it became clear that Theo wasn't listening, Auggie tried to explain that it was his decision, and Theo had no say in it. When that didn't work— Theo started shoving his hair behind his ears, the movement agitated and repetitive, and parroting back phrases from Auggie—Auggie settled for ignoring him. He requested an Uber, and they rode out to the Reeses' country-farm illusion of domestic bliss.

The January day was almost over. Behind a thick windbreak of cedars, the sun was fat and golden as it slipped behind the horizon. The light made the world look like it had been painted two-tone, with shadows and gold-leaf: the needles on the cedars, the fescue blades, a sagging split-rail fence, the culvert in the runoff ditch. More important things too: Theo's face in profile, his cheek, his nose, his eye, strawberry-blond hair catching fire. His shirt and coat hung askew, exposing inches of collarbone and a hint of one powerfully defined shoulder. With his gaze fixed somewhere outside the Uber, he looked relaxed. Sometimes, when he talked about Shakespeare, when he forgot all the rules he'd made for himself and doled out fragments of his life with Ian and Lana, he looked like this, suffused with light that had nothing to do with sunset. Then Theo turned, gold and shadow warping across his face, and he just looked tired.

When the Uber dropped them off, Theo said, "I think I should be the one to search. Before you tell me that I'm treating you like a child—"

"Ok."

"What? I mean—what?"

"Ok," Auggie said. Wind snapped the cedar branches and rustled the grass, and he hugged himself. "I'm more charming, and you're basically the equivalent of a professional home intruder. When it comes to searching, I mean."

Theo blinked. "I'm sorry, run that by me again."

"Hurry up; we look weird just standing out here."

On the porch, Auggie knocked. The wind kicked up again, howling through the trees, snaking between his legs. He rocked back and forth and knocked again. "How do people live here their whole lives without their feet freezing off?"

"We wear socks," Theo said. "For starters. Real socks. Not those paper-thin things you're wearing. And you could try a pair of boots."

Auggie made a face. "Next thing you're going to make me wear overalls."

Sighing, Theo leaned past him to pound on the door.

When a couple more minutes had passed and still no one had answered, Auggie looked at Theo and raised an eyebrow.

"Let's take a very careful look around outside first," Theo said.

"In case they have a home security system," Auggie said.

"Exactly."

"You're so smart."

Shaking his head, Theo went down the porch stairs.

"It's all that age," Auggie said, following. "The distilled essence of experience. Your vast expertise concentrated on this particular problem."

"Now would be a good time for quiet."

"Does Cart know about your criminal predilections?"

"Hit the brakes with the SAT words, Auggie."

"Does he have any idea that you're a nefarious older man initiating a tyro into the mysteries of felonious larceny?"

Theo stopped, put his hands on his hips, and looked up at the sky—a nice sky, Auggie thought, purple bleeding to black, a breath of cirrus clouds in the west. "I hate people," Theo announced. "All of them, more or less. But God, I really, really hate undergrads."

Auggie stumbled. "Oh shit, my head."

In less than a heartbeat, Theo was there, catching him. He had one arm around Auggie's waist. The other had caught Auggie by the shoulder. Their legs slotted together, and Theo bent at the waist to compensate for Auggie's weight.

"Oops," Auggie said. "Never mind."

But with the heat of Theo's thigh between his legs, the joke was too thin. Some of Theo's hair had swung in front of his face, and it hung there now, trembling when the wind picked up, flattened one moment against his high cheekbones and then whipped back when an eddy changed direction.

"Must have been a mini-stroke," Auggie whispered. He was painfully aware of his hand on Theo's arm, the corded muscle under the thick coat. "I'm fine now."

Theo held him a moment longer, pupils dilated, and then they disentangled themselves. Neither of them spoke again while they circled the house.

When they ended on the back porch, Auggie said, "Nobody's home, and I didn't see a security sticker. We might as well try."

Theo nodded. He squatted, rocked a planter onto its side, and then let it fall back into place.

"Can't you just pick the lock?" Auggie asked.

"Why bother? They've got six kids who lived here as teenagers. They've got a key hidden somewhere."

"They might have removed it after the kids grew up."

"They didn't."

Auggie glanced around the porch: Adirondack chairs, terracotta planters, a welcome mat.

"Are you just going to stand there thinking up your next way to make me look stupid?" Theo said as he kicked back the welcome mat. "Or do you want to help?"

"I wasn't trying to—"

Theo moved away, lifting one of the Adirondack chairs, shaking it, and then dropping it. It sounded like a gunshot when it hit the boards. He moved on to the next one.

Sighing, Auggie rubbed his temple—the headache really was coming back—and began to search along the porch in the opposite direction. He checked the planters, even digging into the frozen soil a few inches. He checked the Adirondack chairs in the same way as Theo, although less forcefully. Then he started on the window frames, dragging one of the chairs with him so he could reach. Theo, he noticed, could conduct his search simply by stretching up.

Auggie was climbing down when he spotted the key. A piece of molding stuck out at an angle from the base of one of the porch columns. Brass glinted. Auggie knelt, worked the molding back and forth until it came loose, and retrieved the key.

"Got it."

Theo just grunted. After unlocking the door, Auggie returned the key to its hiding place, and they went inside. The house smelled like rising bread, and Auggie guessed that Ma Reese was preparing something delicious for Sunday dinner. A few lights were on, scattered throughout the house, but the only noises were the slosh and whir of the dishwasher. A cuckoo clock broke the quiet.

"Holy shit," Auggie whispered, stumbling back. Theo caught him again, and a part of Auggie recognized the mirrored moment; it made him feel awful.

Theo didn't laugh. He didn't say anything. He just held Auggie until the initial shock passed, and then he squeezed Auggie's arm, and they moved forward again.

The door to Cal's childhood bedroom was still open, and it looked exactly how they had left it all those months before: the photos, the tennis whites, the trophies. A quick search yielded nothing. They went to the second door from the landing. Auggie opened it, saw the twin bed with the blue polyester comforter and the wrestling trophies, and shook his head.

"Orlando's."

Theo nodded.

The third door held a home office: an L-shaped desk, a computer, a scanner, a printer, a banker's lamp with a green shade. A cedar humidor stood on top of a mini-fridge-sized wine cooler. The room smelled like toner and freshly vacuumed carpet. Auggie looked over his shoulder at Theo, and Theo shrugged.

"Maybe there's something here."

"I didn't say no, Auggie. I shrugged because I don't know."

"Well, can you try to help instead of being mad at me?"

"Fine," Theo said, pushing past Auggie into the room. "Let's look."

They divided the room in half without speaking—Theo seemed like he might kill Auggie if Auggie got too close, and Auggie was too busy replaying those moments on the driveway—the heat of Theo's densely muscled thigh, inches from his crotch—to make sense of his own welter of emotions. The closet doors rattled open on their track, and the sound of hangers sliding on metal accompanied Theo's portion of the search. Auggie dedicated himself to the office furniture. The wine cooler and the humidor were easy to search and then dismiss. The desk, however, was more complicated. It had several drawers, and all but the top one was locked.

A quiet tapping made Auggie look up. Theo was pointing to something written on the back of the closet wall.

"He wrote his name. It says Wayne. Guess Ma and Pa Reese didn't leave everybody's bedrooms as shrines."

Nodding, Auggie returned his attention to the locked drawers. He rattled one, but the lock seemed solid.

"Check the bottom," Theo suggested. "Some of those desks have the same locking mechanism as a filing cabinet. If it does, you might be able to force the locking rod up, and the drawer will open."

Blind, dark minutes passed as Auggie felt along the underside of the desk. He even lay on his back, his phone as a flashlight, and still couldn't see anything. When he sat up, Theo was waiting, and Auggie shook his head.

"Does he have a letter opener?" Theo turned to pull down what looked like hat boxes from the closet shelf. "Usually those desk locks pop right open if you apply some force."

Crowing with triumph, Auggie grabbed a letter opener from the unlocked drawer. He knelt and inserted the blade between the top of the first locked drawer and the desk.

"Be careful not to—"

Auggie bore down on the blade, and with the sound of splintering wood, the drawer—lock and all—ripped free from the desk.

"Oh shit."

Theo froze in the act of returning a hat box.

"Oh fuck," Auggie whispered, staring at the broken drawer. "Oh fuck, oh fuck, oh fuck."

Theo came around the desk, hunkered down, and examined the scene.

Auggie's face was hot, flushed with pins and needles, and he wanted to squeeze his eyes shut. The humiliation was worse than the fear. He could already imagine what Theo would think if he cried. He fought against the knot in his throat.

Theo's hand was dry, the calluses rough, as he took the letter opener. With an easy movement, he forced open the remaining drawers, splintering the wood each time. When he spoke, his voice was calm. "Go downstairs and get some kitchen towels. Remember what you touch and wipe it down. Then come back up here."

"Theo, I'm sorry. Oh my God, I'm such a fuckup, I'm—"

"It's fine. Go get the towels, please."

Auggie sprinted downstairs. He opened drawers one by one, touching only the pulls, until he found the towels. Then he grabbed an armful and worked his way backward, wiping down every surface he had touched. When he got back to the office, he had to stop in the doorway to stare. The desk lay on its side. The computer monitor was trapped underneath and obviously broken. In one corner, the humidor was upside down, and cigars poked their way out of Theo's pockets. Somehow he'd ripped the door off the wine cooler—kicked it loose, a dryly observant part of Auggie's brain suggested.

"Wipe everything down in the closet," Theo said. "Drawers, hang rod, those damn hat boxes. We can't pretend nobody was in here, so we might as well make them think it was a burglary."

"You've done this before." Auggie tried to swallow, but whatever was in his throat was too tight. "You did this for Luke."

"Auggie, if you can't do this, that's ok. I'll handle it. But I need you to tell me the truth."

In the dishwasher, silverware clinked and rattled.

"I can do this," Auggie said.

"Then do it."

So Auggie wiped down surfaces. Theo accepted one of the towels and used it to search the documents in the drawers that they had forced open. They finished at roughly the same time, and Theo shook out the contents of the drawers, snowing them across the office floor to expand the illusion that the place had been pillaged.

"No cash," Theo said. "No safety-deposit box keys. Nothing even close to what we were looking for."

"Let's go," Auggie said, bouncing on his toes.

"Grab some of the wine. With the towel," Theo added when Auggie reached for a bottle. "We've got to do a few more rooms to make it look real. Even then, a good cop will know something isn't right, but it'll be the best we can do."

Without waiting for an answer, Theo left the room, and Auggie heard the next door open. Adjusting the towel so it covered his hand, Auggie considered the bottles. He grabbed four that he thought Theo might like, based on what he'd tried at parties and what Fer had taught him in bits and pieces. Then he left the bottles on the landing and went into Orlando's bedroom.

Theo was already busy in the closet, knocking things onto the floor, duplicating the appearance of a hasty search. Auggie went to the bed, got his fingers under the mattress, and flipped it. It crashed against the window; the aluminum blinds crinkled.

"Good idea," Theo said.

Auggie repeated the movement with the box spring. Then he said, "Theo?"

Dumping an armful of clothes onto the floor, Theo glanced over. "What?"

"Take a look at this."

When Theo joined him, he swore.

Some of it was athletic gear—team apparel from high-end brands. Some of it was jewelry, mostly watches, but a few rings and one necklace. At least one of the watches, Auggie knew from too many hours of listening to Fer talk about the doctors he worked with, was worth upwards of twenty thousand dollars. But what really made Auggie pause was the cash, all of it in bricks tightly wrapped with plastic. Enough cash to get him through college. Enough cash that he'd never have to ask Fer for money again. Enough for Theo, too. Enough that Theo could take care of Lana the way he wanted to.

Under Orlando's bed.

"Take pictures." The harshness of Theo's voice startled Auggie out of the fantasy. "Then we're leaving. We'll call the police, make an anonymous tip about a burglary in progress, and let them find things just like this."

Auggie tried to count the cash.

Theo shook him. "Now."

But as Auggie pulled out his phone, he heard a door open downstairs.

16

For one moment, Theo thought they could make it. He glanced at the window. He was still holding Auggie's arm, and he could visualize dragging him across the room, helping him out, lowering him until it was safe enough to drop.

But it was already too late.

The steps came up the stairs at an easy jog. Then they stopped.

"What the fuck?" Wayne said from the landing.

Then he moved into view, framed by Orlando's doorway, and stopped again. He stared at them, and then his gaze flitted past them to the overturned bed and the hidden cache. Color drained from his face, but his voice was still hard when he said, "What the fuck are you doing?"

"I think you're the one who needs to explain," Theo said. "What is this stuff? Where did it come from?"

"I don't know." He rocked back and forth, and then he glanced around. "Where's Peepee? What the hell is going on? Peepee? Get your sorry butt up here!"

"Don't call him that," Auggie said. Theo's fingers tightened on Auggie's arm until his knuckles ached, but Auggie either didn't understand the message or ignored it. "You're all terrible to him. Stop calling him that."

"Screw you. You two don't have any idea the kind of trouble you're in. Jeez, what you did to Dad's office—Peepee's going to be lucky if he's not sleeping in a gutter by the end of this. Peepee, where the hell are you?"

"I told you to stop it," Auggie said.

"Leave it," Theo ordered quietly.

"Peepee!"

"Stop!"

"Not now, Auggie!" Theo snapped.

The silence that followed was worse. Auggie refused to meet Theo's gaze. Wayne was still looking around the landing, hands on his hips. Theo half-expected him to check his watch. Rules of the house: when somebody yells Peepee's name, Peepee comes running. But the only sound was the rhythmic slosh and rattle of the dishwasher.

"Holy crap," Wayne said. "He's not here, is he?"

"You'd better tell us about the money," Theo said. "Start talking now, and you'll make your life easier down the road."

"Boy, you two really think you're the stuff, don't you? I get kids like you all the time. They're whizzes at Little League, but put them in front of a pitching machine and they swing like they're trying to knock down a piñata. I know Peepee thinks you're these grade-A detectives, but you're a joke. Like him. And I'm calling the police."

"This is yours. Yours and Cal's, the money and the watches and the gear," Theo said. "You took it as kickbacks for steering your best players to the right team, the right school, the right club. You pull the best players from several counties; you've always got talent you can peddle. Cal might have pissed his money away on drugs, but you've got a nice stash here. How long has it been going on?"

Wayne held his phone in one hand, thumb hovering over the screen, ready to place the call.

"I guess that part doesn't matter," Theo said. "What matters is that you and Cal reached a breaking point. He wanted more than his share. Maybe you just argued about it. Or maybe he showed up here and took some of yours. He couldn't bring himself to sell the Mustang; that was his baby. But he couldn't afford his next hit either. Good thing you had a piggy bank he could raid."

"You were angry," Auggie said, "when you found out. You'd worked so hard, and now your drug-addict brother was going to ruin everything. Drove you crazy. Trust me, I know a tiny bit what that feels like. And when he started stealing from you, well, you had to put a stop to that. You argued."

With a merry beeping noise, the dishwasher announced that it had completed the cycle. The shadows on the landing had deepened. They lay across Wayne's face, obscuring him so completely that when he tapped the phone to keep the screen unlocked, the renewed brightness of blue light only offered a weak outline.

"Maybe you can convince everyone that you didn't mean to kill him," Theo said. "Maybe you can make them believe that it was an accident. But it wasn't an accident, was it? Because you realized, later, that your ass was still hanging in the wind. Nia knew about the drugs. She knew the White Rabbit. She knew you and Cal had argued. And you were afraid she was going to tell someone. The night of the

GREGORY ASHE

demonstration was the perfect opportunity: everybody would assume it was the Volunteers. You made sure you looked the part. You wore the right gear. You planned the perfect escape."

"Yeah?" Wayne tapped the phone. The blue haze intensified again as the screen woke. "Let's talk about it when the police get here."

Auggie laughed. "You don't want the police here."

"We'll see who's laughing when—"

"Oh, it'll be us," Auggie said. "We'll be laughing. You've been a fucking joke your whole life."

"Shut up. Yes, I need officers at my parents' house. I caught two people trying to—"

"You're the punchline to a joke that this family has been telling for thirty years, right?

"Shut up," Wayne shouted.

"I didn't see it until right now, but it all makes sense: you're a joke. That's why you sit around your apartment drinking beer by yourself. That's why they turned your room into a fucking home office. That's why you're so hard on Orlando; you were so glad when Orlando came along. So relieved that someone else might get dumped on for a while. That's why you ride him harder than anyone."

"Shut the fuck up! Shut up!"

"You're the oldest boy, but you must be shit at everything you touch. Cal was the better athlete. Cal was the better businessman. Cal was even better at partying. I bet after all those pills you popped to get big, you've got balls the size of grapes and a dick as hard as a piece of licorice. No wonder Cal had a girl while you had to sit on the couch at home with a finger up your ass."

Wayne's hand with the phone dropped to his side, a tinny voice asking questions. His pulse fluttered in his temple. Everything human had been ground out of his face; he looked like he was wearing a Wayne mask. His fingers spasmed, and the phone hit the carpeted landing with a soft sound.

"He's a kid," Theo said, moving in front of Auggie. "He's just a kid. He's saying dumb shit to rile you up."

"Yeah," Auggie said. "That explains a lot. You're obsessed with Orlando's dick. That's why you call him Peepee. Did you catch a glimpse of it one time, and now you can't get it out of your head? Your baby brother with a big old swinging cock, when you couldn't jump start yours with anything less than a lightning bolt."

"Auggie, enough," Theo said. "Wayne, just walk it off. He's saying stupid, kiddy stuff, and you're going to do something really stupid because of it."

258

"I bet you stay home nights, playing with your dried-up Twizzler, thinking about Orlando's giant dick."

The sound Wayne made was somewhere between a scream and a roar. Theo was ready for him when he charged. There wasn't any finesse behind Wayne's attack, just rage and force. He clubbed at Theo's head, and Theo pulled back. The punch still clipped him, a low heat on the side of his head, and then he moved. Shifting his weight, he reached for Wayne's other arm, intending to swing him around and lock his arm behind his back.

Instead, Auggie shoved Theo out of the way, screaming, "Come on, motherfucker. Come on. I'll show you a fucking kid."

Theo stumbled. He landed on his ass, and his head cracked against the wall. For one crazy moment, he felt like he had front-row seats, right at the ropes.

Auggie took a swing. A total whiff. Wayne saw the opening; Theo saw it too, how Auggie overextended the punch, his whole body carried in a quarter circle by the force he had put behind the blow. It was a stupid, showoff way to try to hit a guy. The way, Theo thought in the bizarrely distanced clarity of the moment, kids fight in a high-school hall.

Wayne took the opening. His first punch was a jab that almost looked like a love tap. Auggie's head rocked back. Blood sprayed from his nose. The second was a hook, Wayne's knees and hips generating the power behind the blow. He caught Auggie on the side of the head, just above the ear. Auggie's eyes rolled up in his head. For a moment, he stayed on his feet, his body unconsciously attempting to keep its balance with a drunken sideways step. Then he went down.

Wayne loomed over the boy and hit him again.

Theo's world went white. He was vaguely aware of regaining his feet. He came up behind Wayne. He fought the way he'd learned logging, the way he'd learned in barrooms and in blacked-out alleys where the weapons were knives and broken bottles, and men meant to kill because their lives had narrowed to that single, pointed moment of hate and fury. Part of him was still there, still in one of a dozen shitty bars where he'd saved Luke's ass, still in one of a dozen filthy cribs he had to drag Luke out of, still in the flophouses and roadside motels where he'd had to stand up and keep standing up, no matter how many times he went down, because he was the only thing between them and Luke.

His first punch took Wayne in the kidney. Wayne tried to scream, but his whole body locked up with pain. Theo hit him again, adding more power this time. Before Wayne could recover, Theo caught him by the hair and dragged him backward. Wayne fell; some of the hair ripped free from his scalp, and his blood was hot against Theo's fingers, but he was still clutching enough of Wayne's hair to drag him toward the dresser. He smashed Wayne's face against the painted pine—once, twice, until he felt his nose break. He released him; his hand came away covered with dark curly hairs and blood.

Wayne's eyes were glassy, no longer tracking anything. Blood covered his face, dripped from his chin, spattered the Blues jersey he was wearing. He fell, but Theo grabbed his hand. He opened one of the drawers, lined up Wayne's fingers, and kicked. The force of the kick drove the drawer along its tracks. Wayne screamed as his fingers broke, and then he passed out. Theo repeated his move with the other hand. Then he kicked Wayne. Belly. Ribs. Ass. He moved up to Wayne's head, ready to finish things, but the sound of sirens snapped him out of the frenzy.

He knelt next to Auggie, checked his breathing, and then lay on the floor. He kept his hands behind his head and waited. He knew how the next scene would play out.

17

The first twenty-four hours, Auggie had a hard time staying awake. Some of that was the head injury. Some of that was the strangeness of the hospital: the antiseptic smell, the sound of footsteps at irregular intervals, a stranger's laughter, light when there should have been dark. Men and women kept coming in and asking him questions, and when they'd leave, he'd tumble into another fitful sleep. And some of it, he knew, was whatever they'd give him. And a small part was that he didn't want to deal with whatever was coming down the road.

He knew he didn't have an option when the lights came on and he heard a familiar voice.

"Get up, dickcheese. Right fucking now. I know you're faking."

Squinting against the sudden brightness in the room, Auggie said, "Hi, Fer."

Fer looked terrible. His eyes were so shadowed that it looked like he'd gotten punched. His hair was lank and greasy. He was wearing an old LA Ram's sweatshirt and an ancient pair of blue jeans, his comfort clothes.

"What the fuck is wrong with you?" Fer said.

That was the tip of the iceberg. Fer shouted for a solid forty-five minutes. A female nurse came and asked him to keep it down, and he shouted at her until she left, crying. A male nurse came. That poor guy was actually sobbing by the time Fer was done with him. In between bouts with the staff, Fer gave it to Auggie with both barrels, and Auggie got smaller and smaller in the bed.

"And if you weren't such an actual, living example of the stupidest cock-gobbling cunthole that any human being has ever been saddled with, if you weren't such a fuckup and facing criminal fucking charges, August, I would drag your ass out of this bed right now. You're done here. Do you understand me? You're done. If they throw your ass in jail, fine. But as soon as your asslips stop dripping your cellmate's cum, you're coming home." Fer drew himself up. He hesitated. And then his voice broke as he said, "I am so disappointed in you. I feel like I don't even know you anymore."

Auggie started to cry.

Fer shouted for another half an hour, which was strangely comforting, and then he sat on the hospital bed and hugged Auggie until Auggie's snot and tears had soaked through the sweatshirt. Fer scratched his scalp and neck, alternating between brisk and gentle.

"Tell me all of it, Augustus. And for the love of God, help me understand why."

So Auggie told him. Not all of it, although he tried. He kept to the clearest reasons: Orlando's plea for help last semester, and then Auggie's own involvement once he had raced after the shooter at Nia's demonstration. The fear that he and Theo were both targets, and the need to find the shooter before the shooter found them.

"Why the hell would you get involved in something like this?" Fer asked.

"It just happened."

"I know that line, Augustus. That's what you're going to tell me when you're squirting babies out of your little boy pussy. But nothing just happens. You let a guy put a dick up there, cause and effect."

Auggie shoved him off the bed and wiped his face. "You're such a homophobe."

"Christ knows I'm not going to put your little bastards in diapers and formula. They can suck on your tits until the milk runs dry."

"What happened to you when you were a kid? What messed you up so severely in the head?"

"You," Fer said, and his grin appeared and vanished like a card trick.

"Fer, please don't make me come home."

"What am I supposed to do? Less than a month ago—less than a month ago, Augustus—you called me and told me you'd gotten mugged. Then, yesterday, I got a call telling me you were unconscious in the hospital, beaten within an inch of your life. And if you open your mouth and tell me those things weren't connected, I'm going to flip you over and spank your ass raw. Those rent boys you keep hiring with my money are going to think they're plowing into a pair of traffic lights. Do you understand me?"

"Oh my God. This is actually worse than being dead. Do you understand that?"

"Augustus!"

"Ok, yes. I . . . I didn't want you to worry."

"Of course I worry! All I do is worry about you! Jesus fucking Christ, I worry about you getting your heart broken again, I worry about you getting gay bashed in this state that is the geographic equivalent of America's pucker, I worry about your grades, I worry about your major, I worry about you getting a job when you graduate, I worry about you making the right kind of friends, I worry that you aren't having enough fun, I worry that you're having too much fun, I worry about you finding a nice guy that'll get your tummy packed full of babies, I worry about you so much that I don't sleep sometimes. I love you, you stupid drip of cocksnot. How the fuck am I not going to worry about you?"

Auggie cried some more. Fer cooled down after round two. Things got better, and they split the Jell-o that came with Auggie's dinner and watched *Wheel of Fortune* on the CRT mounted in the corner.

"Fer," Auggie said when Fer was getting ready to leave for his hotel. "Please don't make me go home."

Fer grunted.

"Please. I promise things will be different."

"If," Fer said as he pulled on an old barn coat that Auggie hadn't even known he owned. "If you do not get sent to prison, where your asshole will be converted into a receptacle for toilet wine—if!" He held up a finger. "We can discuss maybe the possibility that you could be allowed provisionally to finish the semester."

"Thank you. Thank you, Fer. Thank you, thank you, thank you."

"Jesus Christ," Fer muttered as he left. "What the fuck did I do to deserve this?"

18

Theo spent two days in the county jail before a lawyer named Aniya Thompson bailed him out. The first day was bad. His hands hurt from the punches he'd landed, and the nurse wouldn't give him anything stronger than Tylenol. He kept seeing flashes of the fight: the punch connecting with Auggie's head; that drunken half-step; Auggie on the ground; the blizzard that had whited out his vision. Not since Luke, he would think to himself in sudden bursts of clarity. Not since Luke had he done anything like that, felt anything like that. And in other moments, with a vividness that made his guts twist, he would count all the pills he knew he still had stashed around the house. He would walk himself through each room: four behind that electrical outlet; one inside that burned-out lightbulb; a strip of Scotch tape with six where the jamb was loose. It was better than going to the movies.

The year before, Theo had visited an inmate at the Dore County Correctional Center with Auggie. Before coming into the building, as they'd sat in the Malibu, Theo had kissed Auggie. He'd done it for a lot of reasons: because he wanted to, because he'd been thinking about it for months, but mostly to make a point. Whatever the point had been, Theo had forgotten it, but he remembered the kiss. Remembered the softness of that expressive mouth under his own lips. Remembered Auggie's owlish eyes after.

Thompson was wide-hipped and generously built, her hair in beaded braids. In her suit, she looked so fresh she might have just snagged her diploma from the dean and hustled off to take her first case. She waited while Theo collected his belongings.

"Who hired you?"

"Sorry. Client confidentiality."

"It wasn't my parents," Theo said. "And it wasn't my brothers. So who was it?"

"Mr. Stratford, I've got other things to do. I want to get you home, talk about options, and move on."

"If it was Auggie, you can tell me. I won't let him know."

She put her hands on her hips. She looked like she was three seconds away from tapping her foot.

"Fine," Theo said as he pulled on his coat. "I'll figure it out."

On the drive back, she said, "The Reese family isn't pressing charges for the breaking and entering or the attempted burglary."

"Nice of them, since I wasn't attempting anything."

"Regardless of what Wayne Reese decides in terms of civil action, I'm pretty sure the County Attorney will be moving forward with assault charges. She'll start with second-degree, which is a felony, but if you'll keep your mouth shut and let me do my best, I think we can get it down to fourth-degree, which is a whisker over the line into misdemeanor. Your boyfriend had been attacked and rendered unconscious. Normally, it'd be a pretty clear case of self-defense, but the damage you did . . ." She shook her head. "The county's going to have a lot of fun with pictures of him in the hospital. People won't be able to tell it's Wayne Reese, that's how bad it is. Tell me what happened."

"I've already told everyone what happened."

"Get used to it. You're going to tell me a hundred times if I ask you to, so start talking."

Theo worked his jaw. "He's not my boyfriend."

"Well, you'd better tell me about that too."

Theo sketched out the events that had taken place from the moment Wayne walked into the house. Thompson asked questions. He ignored them. They drove the last ten minutes in silence.

"Think about what you want," Thompson said when she dropped him at his house. "But if you dig in your heels now and then decide you want my help after they've got you in county again, my rates are double."

Mumbling thanks, Theo got out of the car. He went inside, locked the door behind him, and went to the bathroom. He took down the shower curtain rod, held it at an angle, and rocked it back and forth until the plastic baggie slid free. He took two of the pills, replaced the bag, and returned the shower rod to its mounting. After dry swallowing, he leaned against the sink, his back to the mirror. He considered the floor, where he'd left a trail of muddy shoeprints and snowmelt. This isn't normal, a part of his brain told him. Normal people aren't in such a hurry that they can't take off their shoes, can't even wipe their feet before they get their fix. He pulled the towel from the rod and mopped up his trail, and then he toed off his boots near the door. He was vaguely aware that the furnace had turned on, the pills had kicked in, and he was flushed and sweating. Stripping out of his clothes, he stumbled to the couch, lay down, and fell asleep.

Knocking woke him.

Everything had balanced out by then, the slight cloudiness in his thinking just enough. Wrapping a blanket around his shoulders, he made his way to the door. Brown eyes, he thought. Mouth shifting nervously from grin to worry and back to grin. He'll be tangled in his scarf, and I'll have to help him out of it.

When he opened the door, Orlando was standing there. The January air—no, February, it was February now—stung Theo's bare chest and legs. He adjusted the blanket. Orlando was wearing a coat and heavy gloves. His hands opened and closed, and the boards squeaked as he shifted his weight.

"If you're going to deck me, deck me. If not, I'm freezing my balls off."

"Stay away from my family."

"Fine."

"And tell Augs too. I don't want to see either of you around my family ever again." Orlando's thick eyebrows drew together; he looked on the verge of crying. "Just stay the fuck away!"

"Is that all?"

"Wayne admitted to the kickbacks. His whole life is ruined, thanks a lot. And it's my fault."

"It's not your fault. It's his fault. Your family is just going to treat you like shit because it makes the rest of them feel better."

"I shouldn't have ever asked you and Augs to help. I never should have done that. I'm so fucking stupid."

The wind whistled through the open door. Theo's face was freezing by inches. He angled his body and said, "Why don't you come in?"

"No."

"I think you need to talk to someone."

"No!"

They stood there, Theo's skin pebbling, Orlando huffing. His breath was still steaming, whipping around him in the wind. On the other side of the road, something small and brown moved through the weeds. A vole, Theo thought. He had the sudden urge to find the .22 downstairs and shoot it.

"He didn't do anything to Cal. He turned over his cell phone records. He was at the basketball expo that whole weekend. He never left the hotel. Same with Nia getting shot. He was out of town. So it's over. I wanted you to know that: it's done."

266

"Ok. Like you said, it's done. But you're not the one who needs to carry this around, Orlando. You don't need to feel bad for what happened."

Orlando's face screwed up. He shook his head.

"Come on," Theo said, "just come inside for a minute."

When he touched Orlando's shoulder, Orlando punched him. It wasn't much of a punch, just enough to split Theo's lip. He caught the blood with the back of his hand.

"Fuck you," Orlando said. He ran down the stairs, climbed into a slate-gray BMW, and pulled away. The tires slewed at the turn. For a moment, it looked like he'd go off the road. Then, somehow, he recovered, and the car roared out of sight.

Theo was in the bathroom, trying to stop the bleeding with a gauze pad, when he heard the back door open. The sound of heavy boots came across the kitchen. In the mirror, Cart was a backwards version of himself. It was more noticeable with the uniform, the badge and gun, everything reversed.

"Good. Somebody already got things started. I was worried I was going to have to beat some fucking sense into your white-trash brain all by myself."

After a quick glance at the blood-soaked gauze, Theo tossed it in the trash and grabbed a clean pad.

"Give me that." Cart grabbed his hair, turning him, and snatched the gauze.

"Ow," Theo said mildly, tossing his head to try to loosen Cart's grip.

If anything, Cart pulled harder. His fingers clamped the gauze down around Theo's lip. "What the fuck do you know about getting hurt? What the fuck do you know about anything?" He yanked on Theo's hair again. "You stupid redneck motherfucker. I don't even know you. Do you realize that? I have no idea who you are. Are you just some pencil-dicked pillbilly so desperate for cash that you'll break into somebody's house to pay for your next fix?"

With the gauze in his mouth, Theo couldn't answer.

"Don't you dare lie to me," Cart said. "Don't spin me horseshit about how you're not using anymore. I am a stupid son of a bitch, but I am not that stupid, and I'm tired of you treating me like I am." On the last word, Cart released Theo's hair. He peeled the gauze away with surprising gentleness, and only a few red spots marked it.

"I wasn't there to steal anything."

"Jesus Christ, that's great fucking news. So you broke into that house for shits and giggles with your boy toy?"

"Don't call him that."

Cart's hand cracked against Theo's bare chest. The slap only stung for an instant, and then the sensation was of tremendous heat. Theo glanced down, unable to believe what had just happened. When he looked up, Cart was crying.

"What the fuck is wrong with you?" Cart said. "What the fuck is going on? Do you know what the last two days have been like for me? I couldn't see you, couldn't talk to you, couldn't think straight. Had no idea how bad things might be. Do you know the kind of hell that is?"

"You could have come seen me. You could have answered your phone. Instead, you hid behind a lawyer."

Cart's breathing deepened. His gaze moved to Theo's chest.

Theo followed his eyes. The handprint was red, its shape clear against Theo's pale skin.

"I'm sorry," Theo said, part of him wondering why he was the one who said it.

Cart undid his belt and holster, lowered the gear to the tiles, and unbuttoned his trousers. "Get on the floor."

Theo crossed his arms. In his boxers, though, it was impossible to hide that he was hard.

Grabbing a handful of Theo's hair, Cart half-pulled, half-shoved him down. "Was there something you didn't understand?" He released Theo long enough to force his trousers and boxers below his knees. Then he got behind Theo, bearing him down so that Theo knelt over the tub. Theo's heart beat so loudly that he couldn't hear anything. Cotton ripped, and his boxers fell away. He flinched when something cold and wet ran between his cheeks.

It was over for both of them before Theo really knew what was happening. He came against the side of the tub, Cart's hand hard and tight around him, and a few minutes later Cart grunted and finished. They stayed there, Cart draped over him, their breathing out of time. Then Theo felt something hot on the back of his neck. Tears. And Cart's mouth pressing a kiss there.

"I'm sorry," Cart whispered. "I'm sorry, I'm sorry, I'm sorry."

The aches in his hands, in his whole body, were awake again under the blanket of Percocet. Theo rested his head on his arms, the tub cold where his cheek touched it. At least I felt something, he thought. At least this time I felt something.

19

Weeks passed. And weeks turned into months. By March, winter had grudgingly given way to a wet, cold spring. When spring break came, Auggie was glad to go home. When break ended, he was even gladder to go back.

Nothing had changed at home. Nothing had changed at school. He was doing fine in his classes. He was building his presence on social media, strengthening his brand, experimenting with content. It didn't matter; after news leaked of his break-in at the Reeses' home, nobody would touch him. No more phone calls from prospective agents or managers. No more talk of deals. On bad days, he read about gay guys on social media who were getting huge marketing and advertising deals for makeup, hair products, diet supplements. Unless Auggie learned how to apply eyeliner and master contouring, though, it seemed he was out of luck. Nobody was interested in a gay boy who made silly videos and was a part-time criminal. Straight boys, on the other hand, were doing just fine. Devin and Logan, his buddies from home, had started their own account without even bothering to tell Auggie. They'd each gotten five figure deals— Auggie's ex, Chan, had been happy to share that information on his Facebook wall.

Nothing had changed with Dylan either. A week would go by when they spent every day together, with Auggie trying to navigate the microstorms that started up every time he made a mistake. Then three or four days with no contact. Dylan had finally allowed Auggie to jerk him off. Then to suck him. He never returned the favor; he wanted a real connection—that was the explanation every time—and he wasn't sure Auggie was even capable of it. They agreed, because Auggie had learned what happened when he didn't agree with everything, not to put any labels on what they were doing.

A real connection, a cynical part of Auggie realized, meant a dick up his ass. It was the only thing he held out on. Ever since Dylan had touched him in the gym bathroom, Auggie had felt a resistance he couldn't name or explain; he wasn't ready to take that step in their relationship. He gave up eating meat when Dylan gave up meat. He went back on meat when Dylan decided an ethical diet could include animal proteins. He meditated. He drank the stupid tea that Dylan wanted him to drink. Sometimes, if he agreed to take molly, Dylan would let Auggie jerk himself off after. When texts came late at night, usually no more than *u up?* Auggie would drag on sweats and drive across town—the Civic was back in working condition, although only by a stretch of the definition—to provide another hand job. The one time Auggie had said he was too tired, Dylan had gone radio silent for ten days, and Auggie had bought him a watch (on Fer's credit card) as an apology gift.

He stayed away from Theo. At first, it had been because Theo had claimed his lawyer had told him it was for the best. But as things went on with Dylan, Auggie found himself finding new reasons. When he spotted Theo on campus—or someone who looked like Theo—he changed course. When they bumped into each other, once, in Tether-Marfitt, Auggie had dragged out an unbelievably complicated lie and then run away. One night, after getting home from Dylan's, from another jerkoff session that had ended with Dylan rolling off the bed, pulling up his joggers, and telling Auggie he needed to call it an early night, Auggie had almost called. Then he had started crying so hard that he dropped the phone, and eventually he'd fallen asleep. When he woke in the morning, he wasn't even sure what he'd been going to say.

The phone call from Lender came like a thunderbolt.

"Get over to the hospital," the detective said. "Immediately, August. I want you to talk to someone."

The call disconnected. After fifteen minutes of panic, Auggie went to the hospital.

Lender was waiting in the lobby. He took Auggie's arm above the elbow, steered him into an elevator, and pressed a button.

"What—"

"Be quiet, August."

They rode up two floors in silence. Then Lender took his arm again and walked him down to a shared hospital room. The woman in one bed was older, her eyes closed, her breath rattling in her chest. The women in the other bed was Sadie, Cal's drug dealer, whom Theo and Auggie had tied up and interrogated. She had the same short, dark hair that Auggie remembered, but she was paler now, and thick bandages padded out her frame under the hospital gown. Her eyes were dopey and half-closed.

"Tell him," Lender said.

"Oh shit," Sadie said. "You're the kid from my house."

"She was shot," Lender said. "Twice. In the back. The same kind of bullets as that girl Nia."

Auggie glanced over. "Wait, what?"

"You heard me." To Sadie, Lender repeated, "Tell him about Cal's apartment."

"Oh shit." For a moment, Sadie struggled to sit up. Then she sagged back against the inclined mattress. "Went over there that night. He said he was going to have cash. I wouldn't give it on credit, but he said he was going to have cash."

"What night?" Auggie said.

"The night Cal Reese disappeared," Lender said.

"You said you didn't know when you saw him. You said you didn't remember."

"Lied."

"And? What the hell happened?"

"Didn't answer the door," Sadie mumbled. "Lights were on. Nobody home. Car was there. Mustang. I like Mustangs. And a BMW."

"What color? What color was the BMW?"

"Dark."

"The car was dark? Or it was too dark to see?"

"Black girl ran away. Too weird. Might be a setup, so I left."

"What did the girl look like?"

"Strong," Sadie said.

"What—"

"That's all," Lender said, grabbing Auggie's collar and forcing him toward the door. When they stood in the hallway, Lender added, "Now you've got your White Rabbit. That's because I want this wrapped up before anyone looks closer at the breadth of my investment portfolio. Do you understand?"

"If I could just ask her—"

"She's not even supposed to be awake, August. And that's all she remembers. Now. I did you a favor today; I expect you to return it."

When Lender left Auggie in the parking lot, Auggie got out his phone and called Nia.

"What?" she asked.

"Were you at Cal Reese's apartment the night Deja was shot?"

The call disconnected, and when Auggie tried again, it went immediately to voicemail.

Next, he sent a message to Genesis: *were u at Cal's apartment the night Deja Corey got shot?*

No answer.

I really need to know.

Nothing.

He called.

Nothing.

He thought about the three people he knew who drove dark BMWs: Wayne, Genesis, and Orlando. Three people who might have a motive to hurt Cal. He texted Theo—short, spare messages, just the facts. After ten minutes, when Theo still hadn't responded, he went home.

It was almost a week later when he was in the Sigma Sigma dining hall, eating scrambled eggs and fruit—Dylan was off processed carbs, so Auggie was off processed carbs—that he saw a two-day-old issue of the Wroxall *Rag*, the student newspaper. The cover featured a picture of a man with long, strawberry-blond hair. It had been taken from the back, probably to showcase the handcuffs he was wearing, but Auggie recognized Theo. He snatched the paper and read the article.

He went first to the county jail. Then he drove back across to town to the little brick house. Theo answered on the third knock. He was wearing gym shorts and a t-shirt with Shakespearean insults listed on it. He looked better than Auggie had expected, although still worn out. Not taking care of himself, as usual. And probably not even aware that he wasn't.

To Auggie's surprise, Theo wore a tiny smile, and he gave a half shrug. "You saw the paper."

"Holy shit, Theo! Why didn't you tell me?"

"Come on in. Shoes off, if you don't mind."

Auggie kicked his muddy Jordans off near the door. The house was spotless. Even Theo's stack of printed-out articles, monographs, and journals had been put away—although Auggie couldn't guess where.

"Wow," Auggie said.

"Cart and I have had some conversations. And I want him to feel comfortable here."

The watercolors were gone. In their place hung a few neutral pieces of department-store art: brightly colored flowers in an otherwise desaturated photo; giclee prints of abstract paintings; the St. Louis skyline at night.

"Theo."

"There needs to be space for him too," Theo said, crossing his arms. "I'm trying to meet him halfway. And I'm really happy to see you, so let's please not fight." That tiny smile came back. "Not this early, anyway. Want some Doritos?"

So they sat at the table in the kitchen, and Auggie murdered Cool Ranch Doritos while Theo drank tap water.

"I thought you were in jail."

"I was in jail. For about fifteen minutes. This time, I mean. I bailed out. It was all routine."

"Damn."

"If I try to go to Frozen King, though, I'll officially be a wanted fugitive."

"Damn," Auggie said again. "That's the real injustice."

Theo laughed. "I've got a good lawyer. Things are going to be fine."

"How's Lana?"

"She's doing well, thanks." He had that Theo glow, the one that changed him from handsome to heart stopping, as he tucked his hair behind his ears. "It's nice to be able to spend more time with her."

Auggie stopped mid-chomp.

"Never mind," Theo said. "I wasn't supposed to bring that up."

"They fired you."

"They didn't fire me. I'm a grad student. I'm basically forced labor."

"Theo, why the hell did they fire you?"

"I was asked to take a leave from my assistantship. That's all. Apparently, I'm distracting all the civically minded students from their work with my deviant, criminal behavior."

"And?"

"And nothing."

Auggie surprised himself—and, by the looks of it, Theo—by reaching across the table and tugging once on Theo's hair. "The rest of it."

"It's a formality, Auggie. There's going to be a disciplinary committee. I've got to stand up and tell them I'm sorry I set a bad example, please let me stay in your program, I'll be a good boy. It's nothing." He shrugged. "I haven't even told Cart."

"That's bullshit."

"He doesn't need to worry—"

"No, I mean, the disciplinary thing. What about innocent until proven guilty?"

"It's the English department, Auggie. Less like the Supreme Court, more like an ineffectual parliament made up of a bunch of petty dictators."

Auggie choked on a chip when he laughed. By the time he'd cleared his airway, with Theo pounding on his back, he had an idea. "Hold on."

"I don't like the sound of that."

"Just hold on." He grabbed his phone, pulled up a picture from last year—he'd taken it while Theo had his Shakespeare Glow on, chewing the eraser of a pencil as he sat on the couch, reading an article. His hair had been perfect that day. Well, everything about him had been perfect that day. And Auggie hadn't been able to resist taking the picture. He messed with a few filters, settled for only the most basic enhancements, and posted it. No comment. No explanation. Just a tag: #hotguysreadshakespeare. Questions began to pour in. *omg is he ur boyfriend?* And *he's so hawt* were among the most frequent.

"What did you just do?"

"Nothing."

"August Paul Lopez."

"Nothing!" Then Auggie grinned, "God, sometimes I think you and Fer would be best friends."

Theo grunted suspiciously.

"And sometimes I think you would run away screaming."

"If he's anything like his younger brother," Theo muttered.

Auggie kicked him under the table, and Theo glared and massaged his shin. Auggie popped a few more chips in his mouth, rolled the top of the bag closed, and said, "Well, since you're not in jail, I guess I shouldn't take up all your time. I just wanted to make sure you were ok."

"And eat my chips."

"And eat your chips."

"Not with your mouth full, please." Still rubbing the spot where Auggie had kicked him, Theo said, "Jail might be the least of my worries."

"What do you mean? What's going on?"

"Nothing."

"Oh boy."

"I'm being dramatic. It's nothing."

Auggie rested his head in his hand.

"Just, you know, hypothetically," Theo said, "what would you like to get on your birthday?"

"If I'm me, or if I'm a butch cop who buzzes his hair? Because if I'm me, my birthday was in February, and Dylan had a party, and we did shots of—"

Theo was making a noise.

274

"—um, ginger ale and watched *Little House on the Prairie*."

"God damn it. I'm sorry, Auggie. Things were crazy; I dropped the ball."

"It's fine. But I don't think you were asking about me. I think you were asking about Cart."

"Ok. Ok, maybe I am."

"Oh my God."

"Please don't do this."

"Oh my God, it's finally happening."

"No. Stop. I take it back."

"I wasted my first opportunity. Now I finally get a second chance."

"I regret this. I regret everything."

"You are asking me for boy advice. You." Auggie pointed at Theo. "Asking me." He pointed at himself.

"It's not boy advice, because I'm not fourteen and reading *Teen Vogue*. It's just advice in general. About birthdays. And I want to restate that I regret everything."

"Hold on, I've got to get in the right headspace. Ok, first, gotta do this." Auggie mimed pushing long hair behind his ears. "And then, gotta make my face super serious. How's this?"

"You're me? Is that what this is supposed to be?"

"And the voice gets deeper. Super serious."

"Goodbye, Auggie. You can take the chips, but just go."

"Something like this: 'Well, Theo, giving a present to someone is very serious. It's awakens all sorts of complicated, adult emotions. You really have to be sure you're ready before you jump into it.'"

Theo started to push his hair behind his ears. He caught himself mid-act and glared at Auggie.

"You can't just go around giving presents to everybody," Auggie continued. "You have to be thoughtful about it. Be an adult. Really think about what it means to give somebody a present."

"I hate you."

"If you're going to give someone a present, you have to be really careful. Your present always has to be wrapped, and make sure you don't get cheap paper. If your wrapping tears when you're giving them the present, you could be in a lot of trouble."

Groaning, Theo dropped his face into his hands.

"And when you give it to them, you have to give it to them gently at first. You can get rougher later on, but first you have to be a gentleman, show them how important they are to you, just delivering that package like uh, uh—"

"Ok," Theo said, sliding out of his chair. He grabbed Auggie under both arms, hauled him out of the seat, and manhandled him toward the back door. "Goodbye, Auggie."

"No, stop," Auggie said. "Please, I was just about to tell you about the end, when you open the present afterward."

Theo wasn't even really trying, but he did keep pretending to force Auggie toward the door.

"You need to have tissues. It can get messy."

"Please don't come back until you're forty."

"No!" Auggie mock-screamed. "I've got so much wisdom to impart."

It turned into wrestling after that, with Auggie laughing like crazy, part of him still unable to believe that Theo was willing to play along. Theo pretended to try to throw Auggie out; Auggie tried to force his way past Theo and deeper into the house. Eventually, somehow, they ended up on the couch in the living room, both of them breathing a little faster than normal, color bright in Theo's cheeks.

"You cheated," he said. "I don't know how, but you cheated."

It was the way the spring sunlight came through the window. It was the way his hair, which hung loose again, fanned shadows across his cheek. It was the way he was trying so hard to look grumpy. It was the fact that he looked happy in a million tiny ways—the creases around his eyes, the faint hint of a flush, the curve of his mouth— when Theo so rarely looked happy.

"Don't move," Auggie said. He got out his phone.

"Auggie."

"I said don't move!" He took a picture and posted it with the same hashtag. The previous one was already filling up with questions and comments.

"What am I going to regret now?" Theo asked.

"Nothing. You just look so happy. And it makes me happy."

And for some reason Auggie couldn't understand, that snuffed out whatever he was seeing in Theo's face.

"Hey, Theo?"

Theo raised an eyebrow.

It was there on the tip of Auggie's tongue, versions of the question he couldn't bring himself to ask: does Cart use the peanut butter knife, or did he make you wash it? Does he ever stretch out too far on the couch and knock over all your papers? Why didn't he understand what the watercolors meant to you? Does he know how far out you are, that you're swimming in deep waters, that you're so tired of struggling? If he does, why hasn't he made things better?

"I, um, asked Fer about giving somebody a present. Once. And he had pretty good advice. Although with Fer, it's hard to tell. There's so much swearing that it turns into static, and you have to kind of fill in the blanks."

Theo rested an arm on the back of the couch, his body angled toward Auggie, all his attention directed at him.

"The best present is one that shows the other person you know who they are, that you care about them, and that you like them."

"That's good advice."

"So, what's Cart's deal? I mean, what does he like? What does he enjoy?"

"He's been talking about a reciprocating saw—what?"

Auggie had turned his face into the cushions. "How do you find people who will put up with you? Honestly, I want to know."

"He likes that kind of stuff! And that's what you said, something that shows I know who he is."

Flopping onto his back, Auggie said, "Please tell me you never got Ian a reciprocating saw."

"Give me a little credit."

"Oh my God, it was worse."

Scratching his beard, Theo looked like he was trying not to smile. He failed. "Our first Christmas in this house, I bought him a space heater."

With a groan, Auggie tried to bury his head between the cushions.

"He was always talking about how his feet were cold."

"I can't handle you right now. Go write a sonnet or something." Then Auggie sat up. "Oh. Damn. Can I make a suggestion?"

"I swear to God, if you try to make one more joke about presents, I'm kicking you out."

"The wrapping paper can be textured. Double his pleasure with ribbed—"

"Auggie!"

"A birthday party."

Theo shook his head. "He's not very big into public displays of affection. He's—well, we're keeping things quiet for now."

"But it doesn't have to be big."

"I think it'd be weird if I—"

"Just listen: Cart loves hanging out with his friends. That's all he posts about on Instagram and Facebook, and he tweets about bro nights all the time."

"Wait a minute, you're following him on social media?"

"Yes, duh, I'm stalking him. Try to keep up. His friends are his whole life. Well, and you. So why not combine them? Throw a party, invite all his friends."

"Because he would freak the hell out."

"Why?"

Theo's mouth twisted. "Never mind. It's just not a good option. I appreciate the idea."

"You don't like his friends?"

"I don't know his friends, not unless they were also friends with Ian."

"Oh."

"Please don't do that. Please don't feel sorry for me."

"What if the party—hold on, hear me out—what if somebody else threw the party? You could plan it and prepare it, and afterward, you get all the credit, and he gives you good sex to show you how grateful he is, but it doesn't feel like . . . like you're overstepping?"

This time, Theo thought about the idea longer. "It can't be a Sigma Sigma rager."

"I'm going to make an exception because you're stressed. I'm going to let the fact that you just used the word 'rager' not ironically pass. I'm not talking about me; I'm talking about one of his friends. Doesn't he have any cop buddies who would do this for him? Or other friends? With his charming personality, I'm sure—"

"Thin ice."

Auggie grinned and zipped his lips.

"Maybe," Theo said, "maybe there is the tiniest possibility this is a good idea. Kind of like a steppingstone. I can meet some of his friends, but it's low key, non-threatening. It's not about us. It's about him. And I think he'd like, you know, feeling like he can connect these two parts of his life."

"Oh my God, I'm the shit at planning parties. Ok, how many kegs are we going to need? Do you think whoever hosts will already have a beer bong? How many glow-in-the-dark bracelets should I order? Two hundred? Three hundred? From one to ten, how powerful should the blacklights be?"

Theo's face was pure horror.

Auggie's façade cracked, and a grin slipped out.

"You are a monster," Theo informed him.

"Some wrapping paper is flavored—"

Auggie didn't get a chance to finish before Theo started trying to drag him out of the house again.

20

Theo moved one of the coolers full of beer. It had wheels, so it was easy to roll. Then the new spot looked even worse than the old one, so he moved it back. At which point, the drain plug came loose, and ice melt leaked out onto the floor.

"Shit," Theo said, glancing around. He grabbed a wad of napkins from a table loaded with appetizers and finger foods, and then he shoved the plug back into place and mopped up the water.

"Everything ok?" John-Henry Somerset asked from behind him.

John-Henry had been one of the few people Theo had considered calling when he had decided to go along with Auggie's plan. In theory, the idea that another of Cart's friends could host a surprise party was a solid one. And although Theo knew there were risks involved in forcing Cart to do something in public with him, he also felt like it might be the only way to get Cart to make the jump. The problem, of course, was that Ian's and Cart's shared friends all tended to come from the Wahredua PD, and while those men and women had been pleasant enough to Theo while Ian had been alive, they'd all vanished from his life after the accident. Cart was the exception, for obvious reasons. John-Henry, however, was everybody's friend; the proof was that he hadn't asked any questions when Theo had pitched his idea. He'd even offered his house before Theo could find a polite way to ask.

"Fine," Theo said. "Sorry. I think I messed up the floor."

A soft laugh announced Cora's entrance. John-Henry's wife was beautiful: tall, pale, her dark hair artfully curled. Slipping her arm through John-Henry's, she rested her cheek against his shoulder and said, "You can't mess up the floor, Theo. This house is tiny and ancient, but it's apparently indestructible."

"If you ask the guy learning how to mix cement and reinforce rotting joists," John-Henry said drily, pausing to take a drink of the Bud Lite he held, "you might get a different opinion."

"Do you want me to grab a towel?" Theo asked.

"It's fine," John-Henry said. "Relax. Take a breath. This is going to be fun."

And it would be fun, Theo reminded himself as he got to his feet. He glanced around the Somersets' small home. Cora had helped him hang the birthday banners, and John-Henry had moved the furniture to open up enough space for people to mingle. Most of the food and drink, Theo had brought himself, but the Somersets had contributed beer and tequila.

Over the course of the next half hour, guests began to arrive. Since John-Henry had been the one to organize things, they focused their attention on him and Cora. A few of the off-duty patrol officers stopped to talk to Theo, but their conversations were short and stilted. Theo wasn't sure what they saw when they looked at him. Ian, dead? Lana, disabled? A man with the broken pieces of his life lying at his feet?

When Auggie and Dylan arrived, Theo took a controlled breath. Things were going to be fine. Dylan got a beer. Auggie grabbed one too, but before Theo had to do anything, John-Henry had crossed the room and was talking to the younger men. Auggie nodded and smiled and chatted and put the beer back as discreetly as he could.

"This is going to be great," Auggie said when he and Dylan joined Theo.

Dylan, holding a brown-glass Goose Island, already looked bored out of his mind and was making no effort to hide it.

Before Theo had to answer, John-Henry called out, "Five minutes, people."

The lights went off. The party settled into an awkward stillness that made Theo's heart pound. A few people whispered. One man laughed too loudly.

"Don't you want to move up to the front of the room?" Auggie asked in a whisper.

Theo shook his head, then realized it was too dark for Auggie to see. "No."

He thought his voice had been under control, but after a moment, a hand found his in the darkness and squeezed once. To his own surprise, Theo squeezed back. Sweat soaked the back of his shirt. He was starting to realize he'd made a terrible mistake.

The knock at the door made Theo jump. John-Henry's footsteps crossed the room, and then the door swung open. Light from the porch spilled into the house, and Theo blinked as his vision adjusted. His stomach twisted and made a dangerous noise. Auggie squeezed his hand again.

"Cora's got a migraine," John-Henry was saying, "sorry about the lights. Come in. I'll grab those papers, and you can—"

When Cart stepped inside, the lights sprang on, and everyone shouted, "Surprise!"

And he was definitely surprised. His mouth made an O, and he scrubbed one hand over the bristles on his head, turning back and forth to gape at the people packing the house. Then everyone seemed to start talking at once: John-Henry clapping Cart on the shoulder, bending down to speak into his ear, friends surging forward to congratulate Cart, one of the younger officers, Moraes, shouting to ask what kind of beer Cart wanted. For a moment, Cart's eyes found Theo's in the crowd, and terror paralyzed Theo. Then, his face heating, Theo gave a tiny shrug.

Thank you, Cart mouthed.

After that, the party was perfect. People ate. People drank. At the beginning, Cart had to make the rounds, a beer in one hand as he thanked people for coming. Before too long, though, he had found his way to Theo's side. Theo kept things casual: no kissing, no holding hands, nothing that might take this beyond what Cart wanted. They settled for a one-armed hug; Cart's body was tight with tension, but when they separated, he just laughed and drank deeply from the Goose Island he was carrying. Pretty soon Auggie and Dylan were back—Auggie had a beer, which he immediately handed off to Dylan when John-Henry and Cora got near.

Groups formed and dissolved. Cart was there, and then he wasn't. This could work, Theo thought, something bright unfurling in his chest. Baby steps like this. Friends in public. And then, one day, when Cart was ready, more than friends.

"You're a good friend," John-Henry said, slinging an arm around Theo. His breath smelled like tequila, and Theo was mildly surprised to see that John-Henry was well on his way to being trashed. "You're a really good friend, you know that?"

Auggie and Dylan were standing in the corner. Dylan was frowning, shaking his head, and then he gestured once at the door with his beer. Auggie was trying to say something.

"We've got to find you a good guy," John-Henry said. "You know what? We've got to find you a great guy."

"Ok, honey," Cora said, touching John-Henry's arm. "Theo's doing just fine, I think."

"No, no, no. I'm serious." John-Henry steadied himself. "I'm serious, Cora. Theo's an awesome guy, and we—" He paused. "We've got to find him an awesome guy."

"I think I'm all right for now," Theo said.

"Not a cop this time, though." John-Henry leaned against Cora, bussing her cheek. "Right, Cora? Remind him what a pain being married to a cop is."

"Why don't you let me take that?" Cora said.

John-Henry moved the beer out of her reach.

"I think we're going to go," Auggie said. Dylan stood a few feet behind him, draining a bottle of Goose Island. "I hope you guys have fun."

In a quiet voice, Theo said, "Thanks for this. For the idea, I mean. You were right: it's perfect."

For a moment, Auggie was aglow, his whole face bright, a hint of a flush in his cheeks as he bit his lip. "Yeah," he said. "Cool. Night, Theo. Night, Detective Somerset."

"John-Henry, Auggie. Just John-Henry tonight."

"Umm, right. Night, John-Henry. Night, Cora. Thanks for the party."

A chorus of goodnights answered.

As Auggie turned to go, Cart emerged from the crowd. "Auggie." The word sounded a little too thick. "Auggie, don't go. Hold on." Grabbing Auggie by the shoulder, Cart added, "Come on, it's early." It came out 'searly.

"He's tired of hanging out with old people, Cart," Theo said. "He and Dylan want to go have fun with their friends."

"Or do something else," Cart said, wiggling his eyebrows. "Right?"

"Oh my God," Cora said. "Are you two dating? That's adorable."

"Yeah, well," Auggie said, a blush darkening his light brown skin. His eyes cut to Dylan. "It's, you know, we don't like to put labels on things."

"Way to go, guys," John-Henry said, stretching past Theo to fist-bump first Dylan and then Auggie. "Way to fucking go."

Dylan said, "Yeah, man. Fist bump. Sick. Surf's up."

More red blotched Auggie's cheeks. John-Henry frowned and then tried to recover with a smile. Someone had put on music, and "I'm a Barbie Girl" chirped away in the background.

"So," Cora said, "how long have you guys been dating?"

"Auggie told you," Dylan said. "We don't like to label things."

"God." Cart grinned over the bottle of Goose Island. "That's fucking adorable, but Dylan, word of advice, if he's dragging you to parties, you might as well own up to the fact that he's your boyfriend."

Dylan's only reply was to take Auggie's arm above the elbow; Auggie flinched but didn't pull away. Cart was still laughing at his own joke, but all the amusement—and much of the drunkenness—had evaporated from John-Henry's face, and both he and Cora were watching Dylan as though seeing him for the first time. Theo watched him too. In his mind, Theo kept seeing the drawers snapping shut on Wayne Reese's fingers.

"Aw, come on," Cart said. He must have caught the mood because he continued, "Don't be mad. You guys look like a good fit, that's all I'm saying."

"Cut it out," Theo said.

"You should have seen him last year." Cart wagged the bottle at Auggie. Something nasty shone in his eyes. "Little Auggie had the worst case of puppy love I've ever seen. Followed Theo around with his dick like a tentpole."

"Cart," John-Henry said, "let's get some food in you."

Auggie blinked rapidly and cleared his throat. "Yeah, well, Theo's a really great guy. I hope you know how lucky you are."

In the background, a synthesized record scratch cut off the music, and then "The Bitch is Back" came on. Patrick Foley, a redheaded officer Theo only knew in passing, shouted, "Fuck this, Billy Joel fucking sucks."

Cart's mouth hung open a fraction. His eyes were glazed.

"I didn't know you and Cart were—" Cora began. She fell silent when John-Henry touched her arm.

"Oh," Auggie said. "Shit. Oh shit."

It was the look on Cart's face, that look of having been stabbed, that roused Theo. "Not funny, Auggie. Not funny at all." He sounded mechanical even to himself. "You know Cart and I are just—"

Cart turned and stumbled into the press of bodies.

"Jesus Christ." Theo went after him.

John-Henry caught his arm. "Maybe he needs a minute."

"I'm sorry," Auggie was saying. "I didn't know. I'm sorry."

"I'll find him," John-Henry said, "give him a chance to cool down—"

"I'm sorry, Theo, I'm so sorry."

"Will you shut the fuck up?" Theo said, rounding on Auggie.

"Watch your fucking mouth!" Dylan pulled Auggie back, interposing himself between Auggie and Theo.

"Get the fuck out of here. Get the fuck out!"

"Everybody calm down." John-Henry put a hand on Dylan's chest; the frat boy was pretending to try to get to Theo. Theo ignored him. His gaze was fixed on Auggie, who looked like he was about to cry.

"I'm sorry," Auggie kept saying. "I didn't know, I thought—"

"Theo," Cora said, touching his shoulder, "maybe you should get some air."

Instead, he plunged into the midst of the party, trying to guess where Cart had gone.

21

The worst part was that Auggie wasn't even drunk. Hadn't had a single drop, so he was painfully sober in the car. They drove to Dylan's apartment in Dylan's Subaru. The light from the instrument panel illuminated the dust fuzzing the dash. The sitar music they'd listened to on the drive over was still playing, but now Dylan was ranting about Theo, about the party, about Cart. Distantly, Auggie was aware that Dylan's rage was primarily about not getting to punch out Theo and having Cart suggest he was an owned man. By the time they'd reached the end of the street, though, his voice had become an instrument track for the white noise inside Auggie's head.

I didn't know, Auggie wanted to tell someone. Wanted to tell Theo. I knew you weren't making a big production out of it. But I didn't know. Although, Auggie thought, a part of him had suspected. He had never seen Theo and Cart out on a date. He had never heard Theo talk about going out on dates. He had seen firsthand at the party how Theo displaced himself, just one more friend who had come to celebrate. He had seen the awkward hug when the two men greeted each other. And a part of him had been tallying that up. But was that the same as knowing? And had he known how badly things would turn out when he opened his mouth? He didn't know the answer to that either.

When they got to Dylan's apartment, they went upstairs. Dylan had a hand on the back of his neck. The gesture used to feel protective; now it felt possessive. Burger and Smash were on the couch playing Halo, and they called hellos over their shoulders. Dylan ignored them. He steered Auggie through the kitchen, where empty pizza boxes and cans of Pabst Blue Ribbon were stacked on the counters and overfull garbage bags made a maze out of the floor.

His bedroom was the same as ever: slightly stuffy, smelling of unwashed clothes and incense. The macramé mandala on the wall was askew, as always, and the ceramic Buddha watched gleefully from his perch on the chest of drawers. Dylan lit another stick of incense, tapped his phone, and a slow, thudding beat came out of a set of speakers.

"Get on the bed," he said, kicking off his shoes.

Auggie sat on the bed.

Dylan grabbed the hem of his shirt and then released it. "Do you have any idea how fucking humiliating that was for me?"

"I'm sorry."

"I'm tired of this, Auggie. I'm tired of living some sort of half-life because you're not willing to commit to a real relationship with me."

"Dylan, I'm sorry."

"I don't care if you're sorry. I had to stand there tonight and sound like a fucking high-schooler, talking about not putting labels on things, because you aren't willing to be an adult. I honestly think you like it. I think you like dragging me down to your level. I think you like humiliating me."

And a part of Auggie thought, that's what tonight was about for you? And a part of Auggie thought that Dylan had been the one to insist on no labels—hadn't those been Dylan's words from the beginning?

But he said, "I don't. I swear to God I don't. I hate how tonight went. I hate how I fucked everything up." His face was hot. His eyes wet. When he reached up, he found his cheeks already sticky where tear tracks had dried. "God, I ruined everything."

"I think you should go. I don't do drama, Auggie. I told you that from the very beginning. And you don't want to make this thing real."

You thought it was real enough when my hand was on your cock, Auggie thought. You thought it was real enough when you tried to face-fuck me and made me choke.

"No, Dylan, please. I'm just—I'm not ready."

"Yeah, well, you're never going to be ready. I guess I figured out why: you're still hung up on Theo."

"I'm not."

"Yes, you are. Go home, Auggie."

"Please don't make me go. I want this. I want to make this real."

Dylan shook his head.

Turning himself out of his shirt was awkward in a sitting position, but Auggie managed. Then he unbuttoned his jeans, arching his back to work them down to his knees. He touched himself through his Jockeys, scratched lightly at his chest.

With an irritated grunt, Dylan pulled off his own shirt. He kicked his pants loose and stepped over to the bed to stand between Auggie's knees. He kissed Auggie, pulling his hair hard enough that Auggie whimpered, clawing furrows into Auggie's thigh with his free hand. Then he climbed up, straddling Auggie, pinning him against the wall. The kisses were bruising. He bit Auggie's lip until Auggie cried out and tasted blood. His nails twisted Auggie's nipples. Auggie recognized that this was punishment; it wasn't nearly enough.

When he felt the capsule pressed to his lips, he opened without thinking. Dylan's thumb rested on his throat until he swallowed.

After that, things got hazy. His skin was like fire, but it was also like light. Dylan's mouth, wherever it touched Auggie, left a shimmering trail. Auggie was vaguely aware that his shoes and jeans were gone, and he moaned at the sensation of cotton dragging over his erection as Dylan removed his underwear. When cold air touched his skin, he reached down.

"Don't you fucking dare," Dylan said, moving Auggie's hands back up over his head. Auggie was on his back. He was staring up at the macramé mandala. *This is a place of peace,* Dylan had told him once. *This is where I come to be centered.* The cheap incense stunk, but Auggie could smell himself too. Something cold touched him between his legs. *This is a place of peace.* He flinched at the sensation of pressure, and his head thumped the wall. The mandala trembled.

"Hold on," Auggie said in woolen voice.

Pain.

"Ow, Dylan, I said hold on. Hold the fuck on!"

He pushed with his feet, only to find that his feet were in the air, over Dylan's shoulders.

"Calm down," Dylan said, twisting the finger inside him.

"No, stop. Hey! Dylan, stop!"

"You're going to like this."

Auggie kicked him in the face. Dylan sat back, his face blank with shock, and then fell backward off the bed. Auggie slid up the mattress until his shoulders touched the wall. He tried to sit up, and the whole room tilted.

"What the fuck is wrong with you?" Dylan shouted.

"Um, Dylan, bro," Smash called from the kitchen. "Everything all right?"

"Fuck off," Dylan screamed. He kept touching his nose, but as far as Auggie could tell, he wasn't bleeding. Getting to his feet, Dylan said, "Are you out of your fucking mind?"

"I don't—" The room twisted, as though the walls were made of putty, folding together and then stretching apart. "I don't want to do that. Not yet."

"I can't believe I wasted so much fucking time on you. You owe me. You owe me this. Do you realize that? I've wasted months, wasted an entire fucking year on you."

"I need to go. I want to go."

"Then get the fuck out."

Somehow, Auggie got to his feet. He had to hold on to the bed to keep himself from falling. His vision was blurred, and he couldn't tell which clothes on the floor were his and which were Dylan's. The incense made him want to gag.

"Do you know what you are?" Dylan said. Something soft hit Auggie in the face, and he caught it, mostly by chance. Underwear, he thought, and tried to pull them on. "You're nothing. You've got nothing inside you. You're fake."

"Need my . . . need my pants."

"I thought maybe you were just a kid, but you know what, Auggie? It's even worse. You're not just a kid. You're going to be a kid for your whole life. You're going to play with your stupid videos, do your stupid jokes, and the whole world is going to pass you by. Do you even know how fucked up you are? You're a joke to everybody in the frat. People laugh when you walk by. You can't get a boyfriend. You can't get a hookup. You can't even get anyone to take you seriously. And that's all you're ever going to be. You're as real as one of your fucking videos. I can't believe I wasted my time on you."

Denim hit Auggie in the face. He caught the jeans, and somehow, he stepped into them. That was enough. He didn't care about the rest. He wasn't even sure he could stay on his feet, but he made it to the door and stumbled out into the kitchen. The light. The smell of old garbage. The rasp and rub of the denim against his skin. His senses were in overdrive.

Burger was standing. Smash was sitting. Both were still holding their Xbox controllers, and both were staring as Auggie stumbled past them.

Dylan came after him. "Nobody is going to put up with your kiddie shit, Auggie. You have no idea how lucky you were with me. You have no idea how patient I've tried to be. And then you pull this shit on me again and again. You are going to come crawling back— turn around and look at me!"

Auggie kept going.

"If you walk out that door, I'm not taking you back. Good luck finding someone else to deal with your fuckups. Nobody is going to want you. Nobody is going to want a kid who hides behind a screen, who doesn't have a single real thing in his whole life. You are going to fucking regret this!" The last was delivered in a choked scream.

The cement of the steps was cold and pitted under Auggie's bare feet. In the parking lot, broken pieces of asphalt made him stumble. He slumped against the Civic, tried keys blindly until he managed to get the door open, and dropped inside. He shouldn't drive. He shouldn't drive.

But this had been his whole life, thinking someone cared about him, turning around to find that there wasn't anything inside him for them to care about. People liked the cardboard cut-out. It wasn't even that they disliked the real him; the problem was that there wasn't anything but the cardboard.

He buckled the seatbelt. Then, patches of blackness, the sensation of speed. A dark highway. Trees. Humidity hanging in the branches, sparkling like gemstones when the headlights swung across them. The Missouri air, thick and damp, whipping through the window. The smell of hot electronics. The smell of mud, animal dung. An open field. A wide turn.

Space. The sensation of flying, and then a shuddering series of thuds and scrapes. Something was cutting into his shoulder. I'm upside down, he thought, and he turned off the car.

At first, the Civic's door wouldn't budge. Auggie had to unbelt himself and stand on the ceiling, bracing himself to force it open. For the first inch, the door scraped away a layer of grass and soil, and then it was clear of the ground and opened easily. Auggie stumbled out into the field. His foot came down in something soft. The stink of shit came up to him.

He walked.

He stood on the porch of a small brick house, leaning against the bell.

When the door flew open, Theo was in boxers and a tee, his face white. "Cart, I—" He stopped. "Holy shit. What happened to you?"

In his mind, Auggie said, *Theo, I'm really sorry for troubling you like this, especially after I ruined your whole life, but I'm on a really bad trip, and I think I'm going to fall down now.*

What came out of his mouth was a lot of drool and a moan.

Theo caught him before he hit the floor, and then he helped Auggie stagger inside. "What the fuck—" Then Theo's breath came in sharply. "What did he do to you?"

Auggie couldn't string words together. He tried to get to the couch, but Theo steered him toward the back of the house. "Um, not quite yet. You're covered in shit—sorry, but it's the truth—and that couch is new. Well, new to me, anyway. Let's clean you up. Then we'll get you to bed."

In the bathroom, Theo helped him out of the jeans, and then he used a washcloth. The rough warmth felt good. Theo's hands were rough and warm too. He touched Auggie's face, and that didn't feel good. Auggie tried to pull away.

"No, you've got glass here. I don't even want to know how that happened. For that matter, I don't want to know where the Civic is. Hold still." Auggie tried to pull away again. "August Paul Lopez, hold still. Ok, I've got it. Good job. You did really well. The rest of these are just little cuts, but I'm going to clean them up." When he'd finished, he repeated, "Good job. You were great. Let's get you to bed."

It had been a long time since someone had told Auggie he was good—someone who wasn't talking about a video or a skit or his cheekbones. He started to cry.

"Ok, we can do some crying too," Theo said, grunting as he got an arm around Auggie and helped him up. "Jesus God, how much muscle have you put on in the last few months? You've got to help me out here a little, Auggie. Ok. Yep, keep going, just like that."

The steps were a challenge; in the end, Theo hoisted him over one shoulder in a fireman's carry. The sheets were cool and crisp and smelled like Gain. Theo sat on the bed next to him, massaging his shoulder, and then he stood and tucked Auggie in.

Auggie tried to say, *Don't go.* He wasn't sure how much of it Theo understood, but it must have been enough because Theo sighed and walked around the bed and stretched out on the other side. He turned off the lamp, and then the room was dark.

It wasn't quite sleep. It wasn't quite waking. Whatever else had been in the molly—it could have been cut with anything from strychnine to drain cleaner—it fucked Auggie up. Flashes of the macramé mandala. A whiff of incense. The cold pressure between his legs.

When Theo moved, Auggie didn't realize what was happening until he was tucked under one of Theo's arms.

Then it was sleep, and the dream was one dream: the way Theo held his head when he laughed, and what his hair looked like when the sun was behind him, and happiness carrying Auggie up like someone had dialed back gravity. He came awake as it was happening.

"So help me God," Theo muttered, "if you just peed my bed—oh."

Auggie managed to blink his eyes open. He was surprised to see Theo's face was red as he peeled back the bedding. Then Theo sighed.

"'thappened?"

If anything, Theo's face got redder. "Nothing. Don't worry about it. I'll clean us both up, and you go back to sleep."

"Made a mess."

"You surely fucking did."

He sighed again and left. When he came back with a towel and another washcloth, he helped Auggie out of the sticky underwear, ran the washcloth briskly up and down and then between his legs, and laid the towel over the wet bedding. Auggie was cold and shivering. When Theo pulled the bedding back over both of them, Auggie wrapped himself around the older man. His t-shirt smelled clean; the muscles of his thigh felt good between Auggie's legs.

"Sorry," Auggie mumbled into his chest.

From a long way off, Theo laughed. "I'm not going to lie." He stroked Auggie's hair. "It's a nice ego boost."

Auggie woke again, briefly, near dawn. Theo was dressing in the dark.

"Theo?"

"I'll be back in half an hour. I just need to take care of one thing." He straightened; Auggie could feel the weight of his gaze through the shadows. "Will you be ok?"

"Yeah."

"Half an hour."

When Auggie woke again, Theo was next to him in bed. Sun came in through the windows. On top of the quilt, Theo's hands were visible, his knuckles freshly split and scabbing in the morning light. He ran his hand down Theo's arm and laced their fingers together.

22

Theo was sitting on the couch, papers spread around him, when Auggie came downstairs. He was wrapped in the sheet. Late morning sun climbed the far wall. Through the cracked windows came the smell of dew-soaked earth and grass.

"Morning," Theo said. He was aware again of his hands aching pleasantly; on one split knuckle, he'd resorted to a butterfly bandage, which was already coming loose.

Auggie groaned.

"I put a new toothbrush on the kitchen table."

Another groan, this one with an underlying note of gratitude, as Auggie staggered toward the bathroom. The sound of running water came, and Auggie spat several times. Then the shower came on. Theo flipped pages and continued to work. Eventually the shower turned off. Clothing rustled. The sound of bare footsteps moved over the floorboards.

Auggie dropped onto the couch face first, knocking over one of the piles of papers. He was wearing the Van Halen t-shirt and mesh shorts that Theo had left in the bathroom for him. He smelled like soap.

"How's your stomach? I think you need to eat, but I don't want to make you feel worse."

The cushion muffled Auggie's groan but didn't hide it completely.

"Ok. We'll wait a while."

For the next twenty minutes or so, Theo actually managed to get some words on the page—a feat that had become less and less common during this school year. This chapter of his thesis was about *Romeo and Juliet*. It should have been easy. He'd had plenty of time in Wagner's class to think about the text, to re-read the criticism, to assemble his own argument and contextualize it. Theo even had necessity on his side: if he wanted to finish the PhD in a reasonable timeframe, he needed to submit his thesis over the summer and transition to working on his PhD-level coursework and his dissertation. But he came home to an empty house. Or he came home to Cart. And either way, whatever he typed was shit. He took advantage of this rare burst of clarity and typed like mad.

In those twenty minutes, he got more done than he had in the last three months. He checked his notes, made sure he'd included the references he wanted, and added the header for the next section.

"You type very aggressively," Auggie croaked.

"I'm excited. I'm finally making some progress."

"That's great."

"How are you feeling?"

"I've got the perfect description. And I was going to share it with you. But lying here, I've realized the only good option left for me is to sneak out the back door and run away and join a circus traveling through South America. So I think I'm going to do that. 'K, bye."

Theo caught his leg as Auggie tried to worm his way off the couch.

"What do you think about this part?" Theo asked. "When Capulet tells Paris, 'My child is yet a stranger in the world,' his point to Paris seems simple: Juliet is too young to decide about marriage, and so Paris must wait two years before she can consider his offer. But estrangement is at the heart of the play, along with the misunderstandings that accompany it. So many deaths in the play result from misunderstanding—or an incomplete understanding. Tybalt and Mercutio, Romeo and Tybalt, Romeo and Paris, and Romeo's suicide. Perhaps the only character to see clearly is, ironically, Juliet, who wakes and immediately and correctly understands the sequence of events that have preceded her death. While an argument may be made for dramatic exigency, it is nevertheless significant that Juliet, the character marked most clearly as a child-stranger, is the one who sees and understands. Such an accounting of Juliet opens up larger questions about the play's thematic interest in estrangement. To what extent, the play demands, are we all strangers to the world? To each other? Perhaps, even to ourselves? Friar John's missed message provides an opportunity to examine the praxis of estrangement within the world of the play, as I shall show in the next section."

Auggie flopped onto his back. He put an arm over his forehead and looked out at Theo from under it. "That's really good."

"Thanks."

"Except you plagiarized my essay."

Grinning, Theo slapped Auggie's leg. "I didn't plagiarize, dummy. Look." He turned the laptop to show Auggie. "The footnote."

Auggie propped himself up on an elbow and read, "I am indebted to August Lopez, a rising Shakespeare scholar, for this reading of estrangement in his unpublished paper blah blah blah." His eyes came up to meet Theo's. "I'm not a rising Shakespeare scholar."

"You are if I have anything to say about it. Plus it was an awesome analysis, and I want to steal it, and in order to steal it, I have to give you credit. So, boom."

"Oh my God, did you just say boom?"

Theo smiled. "Let's get you something to eat. Big Biscuit, on me."

Arm across his eyes again, Auggie shook his head. His voice was thick when he said, "I don't deserve Big Biscuit."

"Well, it's more a question of—"

"Theo, I am so, so sorry. I hate myself. I hate myself for what I did last night. I never meant to out Cart. I mean, someone did that to me, kind of, and it was horrible, and then I did it to him. I thought—I was just trying to say something so Dylan and I could leave, and, I don't know. I knew he didn't want things to be very public, but I didn't know he was totally closeted. And then I showed up here, and I was a mess, and oh my God, if we ever have to talk about what happened last night, the other thing, I mean, I'll probably never be able to have sex again. So, um . . ."

Water dripped in the bathroom. Outside, a cardinal streaked past the window, a red comet that interrupted a chickadee's fee-bee, fee-bee. Then the cardinal was gone, and the chickadee picked up its song again.

"Do you know what he gave you?"

Auggie cleared his throat. "He said it was molly. Well, he didn't say that, but we've done it before. Molly is—"

"I know what molly is." The tightness in Theo's chest made it difficult to speak. He tried to keep his voice even. "So you took something and you didn't even know what it was? That was really stupid."

"I know."

"If you know—"

"Please don't do this," Auggie whispered. "You can be mad and hate me, and I'll never bother you again, but please don't do this."

Theo leaned back against the couch. He ran his hand up Auggie's leg. In his mind, he was in the loft again, looking down at Luke's face, the flies crawling on his eyes. After everything Theo had done, after the brawls, the knife fights, the nights of searching, the days of making sure he didn't choke to death on his own vomit.

"I don't know how," Auggie said, "but I'm going to make things right. I'm going to talk to Cart. I'm going to—God, I don't know. I'm going to figure it out."

"Good luck. He's not answering his phone. He wasn't at his apartment last night, and he wasn't there this morning. I knocked loud enough to wake up his whole building. Both times, actually."

Auggie moved his arm away from his face. His eyes were wet. "Is that how you hurt your hands?"

Theo shook his head.

Then Auggie saw the Jordans he'd left at Dylan's sitting by the front door. "Did you—"

"Don't ask me," Theo said. "And I won't have to lie to you. Your clothes are in the dryer."

"God, I've ruined your whole life. I'm sorry, Theo. I'll just go. You can burn my clothes. I'll wash these and mail them back to you."

"You haven't ruined my life. Cart's problems are Cart's. I guess I knew—I guess I knew I was pushing him farther than he was comfortable. I knew the party was a bad idea, but I thought I could show him that we could take small steps. Anyway, it is what it is. If he still wants me, well, I'll help him through it. And if he doesn't, well, I'll figure that out too."

"He's an idiot if he doesn't want you."

"It's nice to know somebody thinks so. Right now, I'm guessing Cart wishes he'd never met me. Anyway, that's enough of that. Let's go get something to eat. You'll feel better."

Auggie shook his head. "I'll go home. I think I need to go home. I'll crawl into my room and never see a human being again. And—oh my God." He groaned. "My car."

"Did you crash it into City Hall?"

"No, but I flipped it, and it's in a field somewhere."

"I know, Auggie. I was the one getting your cow-shit-covered clothes off of you. I was making a joke."

"Oh."

"A bad one. There's nothing you need to do about it right now. Let's see if you still remember how to mix Krusteaz."

So they went to the kitchen, and Auggie got down the blue bag of pancake mix, and Theo was surprised to learn that he had a carton of eggs in the fridge. The kitchen wasn't really big enough for both of them to work at the same time, but they did it anyway, with a few *excuse me*'s, but mostly working without talking: Theo putting his hand between Auggie's shoulder blades to keep him from stepping back at the wrong moment, Auggie accidentally elbowing him in the ribs when Theo stretched to toss eggshells in the trash.

They ate. It turned out that Auggie did still remember how to mix Krusteaz, and Theo still couldn't figure out why the pancakes tasted so much better when Auggie made them. Then they went back to the couch. Theo worked on his thesis; Auggie did a lot of tapping and swiping, which Theo assumed meant he was busy handling his online platforms. Then Auggie made a sad noise.

When Theo glanced over, Auggie said, "There's another demonstration for Deja tonight. Their likes and comments are way down; I think they're losing momentum, which is a horrible thing to say because momentum shouldn't matter in something important like this."

"People have short memories," Theo said. "And the world has new tragedies every day."

Auggie sat up, studying his phone. A video was playing on loop, and by the third time, Theo gave it his full attention: footage recorded by a bystander of the shooting that had taken Deja Corey's life. Deja was already on the ground. The officer who had murdered her was shouting something unintelligible.

"What is that?" Auggie murmured to himself.

"Why are you watching that?"

"Because I don't understand it. He shot this girl for no reason."

"Not quite. For a bad reason. He thought she was carrying a weapon."

"But what was it? Something that looked like a gun? This is the best angle, but I can't figure out what it is."

"It was a piece of paper," Theo said absently, already turning back to his computer.

"What?"

"Paper. She was carrying a letter or something. The officer claimed he thought it was a knife."

"How can you tell? It's just a shape."

"It was in some of the in-depth reporting that came out the first day or two after the shooting. You probably weren't even back in Wahredua by then."

And then Theo froze, his hands locked on the keyboard. Fragmented images came together: Genesis on the massage table in a dark room, Nia and Deja arguing, the dark BMW parked at Wayne and Cal's apartment, Wayne at a basketball expo, the cash hidden under Orlando's bed. Friar John's undelivered message.

"Holy shit," Theo said. "I know who killed Cal."

23

First, they went to Genesis Evans's home. It was the middle of the day, and the house looked empty. They searched the yard and the tree line at the edge of the property. Then they searched around the outside of the house. Auggie found the rifle; it was covered by a tarp, buried under pale, round stones that lined one side of the house. A corner of the tarp was sticking out.

"Sloppy," Auggie said.

"It's a Savage 110," Theo said. "That's got to be the gun." Looking up at the house, he asked, "Whose bedroom window do you think that is?"

"Genesis or Wise."

"Wise," Theo said. "No question."

They took pictures and covered the gun up again.

Auggie made a burner email account, sent a message, and then had to wait almost a week. He heard nothing from Dylan. Once, looking out from his bedroom window on the third floor of the Sigma Sigma house, he thought he saw him on the sidewalk: a guy with his nose taped, one arm in a sling. Auggie pulled up Theo's contact information and sat there, finger hovering over the call icon, watching the guy who might be Dylan talk to a couple of other bros. Then maybe-Dylan left, and when Auggie stopped shaking, he had to take a shower to get rid of the smell of flop sweat.

When Orlando slipped up, though, Auggie was ready.

From where he sat on his bed, studying for finals, Auggie had a perfect view out into the hallway. The noise wasn't ideal—Chad and Tanner, down the hall, had resurrected an original Xbox from somewhere and were playing (ironically, Auggie thought) Guitar Hero at full volume. But when Orlando emerged from his room in a black t-shirt, black cargo pants, and black sneakers, with a black backpack over his shoulders, Auggie spotted him right away.

Everybody spotted him, Auggie was pretty sure. The only thing Orlando was missing was the *Pink Panther* music and a knit cap.

he's doing it, Auggie texted Theo.

They'd agreed to park the Malibu at the Sigma Sigma house. The Civic had been totaled in the wreck, and once Fer had finished screaming, he had told Auggie that he had lost car privileges. It didn't mean much, since Auggie didn't have a car anymore, but it still stung.

It was late, and although the days were getting longer, the sun had slid below the horizon by the time Auggie picked up Theo. They raced back across town, and Auggie released his breath slowly when he saw Orlando's BMW still parked in the lot of Wayne's apartment building; Wayne's car was gone. Sodium lights buzzed overhead. Moths swooped and spun, battering themselves against the glass.

"Texting him now," Auggie said.

He sent a message to Wayne: *at your apartment.*

Auggie's phone buzzed again almost immediately, but Auggie pocketed it. The response, whatever it was, was meaningless at this point. He nodded, and he and Theo got out of the car.

A faint hint of exhaust lingered in the air. Auggie's second step flattened a Whopper wrapper next to the curb. In the apartment building, a window was open—the day had been perfect—and the theme song for a TV show played. Auggie hummed along until he saw Theo staring at him.

"*It's Always Sunny in Philadelphia*," he whispered.

"I don't care," Theo whispered back. "Could you be quiet, please?"

And while there had probably been a nicer way to communicate the sentiment, Auggie took his point and stopped humming. They climbed the stairs, and Auggie didn't protest when Theo caught his arm and took the lead. Theo tested the handle. It turned, and they pushed into Wayne's apartment.

All the lights were blazing. The smell of a cleaner with an artificial lavender scent hung in the air. Boxes and piles of clothes had covered the floor on Auggie's last visit, but now the apartment was back to normal—a few dirty socks next to the couch, a can of Budweiser on the coffee table, the remote for the TV wedged between two cushions. In the back of the apartment, a drawer slammed shut.

Auggie shut the door and followed Theo toward the noises.

They found Orlando in the room that had belonged to Cal. The mattress and box spring were turned on their sides, exposing the metal brackets of the frame. Drawers stood open and empty. The closet door was ajar, exposing the bare shelf and hang rod. Orlando slammed a drawer shut and swore.

"Can't find it?" Theo asked.

Orlando spun around. For a moment, the relief in his face was so comical that Auggie wanted to smile. Then Orlando said, "Shit, Augs. Theo. What the hell? You about gave me a heart attack. Hey, what are you guys doing here?"

"We could ask you the same thing," Theo said. "Time to fess up, Orlando."

He tried for a smile, but he only got the corner of his mouth. Sweat glistened on his forehead. "You know, trying to find something I lent Cal."

"Oh yeah?" Theo said, moving deeper into the room. Orlando took a step back. "What?"

"Some stuff."

"Bullshit," Theo said and took another step.

When Orlando stepped back this time, his shoulders hit the wall. "Augs?"

"Don't talk to him," Theo said. "I'm talking to you. Talk to me. What are you doing here?"

"I'm—"

"Don't fucking lie to me, Orlando," Theo shouted.

Auggie touched his arm, and Theo fell back a step. "Orlando, we know. You and Genesis planned the whole thing pretty well, but we still figured it out."

Orlando shook his head.

"I should have known the first time you showed up here," Auggie said. "When you had lighter fluid. When you wouldn't tell us what you were doing. She sent you to destroy evidence, didn't she? And that's why you're here again. She's worried she left something behind, something that will link her to the murder, and she sent you to get rid of it. She's using you."

"No," Orlando said. He looked side to side. His eyes were huge. "No, she didn't—we didn't—"

"We found the rifle," Theo said. "We found it. Your prints are all over it, Orlando, and you don't have an alibi for the night Nia was shot. You're a murderer, and you're a fucking coward, and I can't wait to see you in court. You're going to be a fucking laughingstock, Peepee."

"Don't call me that," Orlando said.

"Why not, Peepee? Are you going to cry? Do you think that's going to help you when you're taking the heat for this? Because you'd better fucking believe Genesis isn't going to admit she was part of it. She's going to let you shoulder the whole thing, Peepee."

"Stop it."

"Peepee, Peepee, Peepee. You are one stupid son of a bitch. Did you know that?"

"Stop!" Orlando shouted.

"No, I'm not going to stop, I'm going to—"

Auggie caught Theo's shirt. "Give us a minute."

"Not a fucking chance."

"Give us a couple of minutes. You're upsetting him."

"He ought to be upset. He's a fucking murderer."

"Theo, get out."

Face twisted with rage, Theo lunged at Orlando. Auggie got between them, and after a few moments of tussling, forced Theo out into the hall. Theo stomped toward the next bedroom. A door slammed shut, and the crash shattered the silence.

When Auggie turned around, his back to the hallway, Orlando was crying. The tears shone in his thick scruff. "Augs, I did not do this. I didn't! I swear to God."

"Last chance, Orlando. You can get out in front of this and make it better."

Orlando was silent for at least five minutes; Auggie let him have the time, let it work on him. Auggie heard the front door open and felt a thrill run through him. After that, the only noises were stray sounds: the squeak of a floorboard, a click that came from the kitchen. Theo grunted in the hallway, probably annoyed by the wait.

"We've got the rifle with your prints, Orlando. It's open and shut. You're going down for murder and attempted murder."

Something steadied in Orlando's visage. He wiped his eyes, and they stayed dry. "You're a smart guy, Augs. Really smart. But you're wrong about this, and I thought you were my friend. The only part you got right was Genesis asked me to get rid of some stuff for her. She emailed me. She told me Cal had stolen some of her underwear out of her locker at SportsPeak. That's what I was doing when you caught me the first time. And yeah, I came back later. I burned it for her because—because I loved Cal, but it wasn't right what he did to her. Let's go. You can take me to the police. I didn't do this, and I'll tell them that too."

"I don't think we're going to do that," Wayne said from behind Auggie. Auggie turned. Wayne stood in the doorway. He'd healed since the fight with Theo, the marks of it gone except for a slight crookedness to one of his fingers that hadn't been there before.

"Wayne, thank God," Orlando said. "You need to call Mom and Dad and have them get that lawyer you used. Augs is crazy, and not his usual kind of crazy that's neurotic and sweet."

Wayne's eyes were so dark they were almost black. His gaze fixed on Auggie, unwavering. Auggie could feel his pulse in his throat, a sudden lightheadedness.

"Orlando," Wayne said, still staring at Auggie, "go get that tie from my closet, the one I wear for athletic signings."

"What? Why? Wayne, Augs thinks I killed Cal. You need to call Mom and Dad and—"

"Everything's going to be ok, and I swear to God I'm going to take care of you, but you need to do exactly what I say right now: go get the tie from my closet." When Orlando didn't move, Wayne screamed, "Go get it!"

In his peripheral vision, Auggie saw the sudden pallor in Orlando's face, the way the thick brows scrunched together.

"Do you want me to tell him?" Auggie said. "Or are you going to?"

"You're done," Wayne said.

"You killed Cal."

"One more word, and I'll make you be quiet."

"Let him talk." Orlando's voice was sharp. It echoed weirdly through the apartment.

"This is your chance, Wayne. This is your chance to show Orlando that you can be a good brother. Bail him out like you did after we found your shit under his bed. Tell him what you did. Take responsibility for it, and the craziness can end. Otherwise, the police are going to get a rifle with Orlando's prints all over it. Are you going to let that happen to him?"

"Augs, what are you talking about? I thought you just told me I was the killer."

"The last time things looked bad for you, Wayne stepped up. I thought he'd do it again if he knew how seriously in trouble you were. We made sure he got a front row seat to the accusation. Was I wrong, Wayne?"

"I knew it," Orlando crowed. "I knew you didn't really think I was a murderer!"

Wayne's silence sent goosebumps crawling up Auggie's arms.

"I'm going to handle this," Wayne said in a dead voice. "Pee— Orlando, I'm not going to let anything happen to you. But I need you to help me. This is a family problem. We can solve it as a family."

"Things would have been different if Deja had lived," Auggie said. "Isn't that right, Wayne?"

"Orlando, do what I told you."

"She was coming to tell you the good news: she was signing with a big university. She was walking here from her house, carrying the letter of intent, to tell you, when she was shot and killed. She knew you and Cal would be happy; the university had been courting her, and there was big money in it for all of you. That's what you and Cal had been fighting about for weeks, isn't it? Whether Deja would stay local and play for Wroxall or go big and earn you both a lot of money."

Wayne let out a broken breath.

"You loved her," Auggie said.

"I didn't care about the money," Wayne said. His eyes were fixed somewhere past Auggie. "I didn't care where she played. I wanted her to do what was best for her, for her career. She was the one who was talking about staying here so we could build a life together. Cal—Cal couldn't see anything except the money. He was always broke. He was always hitting me up for a loan so he could score. He thought I was putting her up to it, thought I was forcing her to choose Wroxall and stay local, but I wasn't. I just wanted her to do what was best for her."

"Cal never touched Genesis, did he?"

Wayne shook his head. He was still staring at something invisible to Auggie. His throat moved reflexively. "I thought it was her. Deja. We did that sometimes, after a tournament. Messed around at SportsPeak. We didn't have a lot of places we could be alone, and it was fun and hot. The lights were off. By the time I realized it was Genesis and not Deja, it was too late."

"You did that to her?" Orlando said, his voice rising.

"I didn't mean to! But it would have worked out. We would have figured out a way to handle it."

"No," Auggie said. "Cal was running your business into the ground. He couldn't keep his head straight. He couldn't clean up his act. His dealer was coming around, selling to your athletes. He was going to ruin everything."

"We were going to—I was going to buy him out. It was the only way to save the business." Wayne laughed suddenly and covered his mouth. "What the hell am I talking about? Let's get this over with."

"What happened that night?" Orlando said. "Don't take one fucking step until you tell me what the fuck you did to Cal."

Wayne's shoulders dropped. "Deja called. She was upset because she'd had another argument with Nia. Nia was using. PED shit. Deja said that was the last straw; she wasn't going to stay in Wahredua, couldn't stand to stay here. She said she had good news. She'd changed her mind about Wroxall. She knew how badly Cal and I had been fighting, and she knew he'd want to know right away. I told Cal she was coming over to talk about it, that she was bringing the letter. Then she—" His voice broke, and for a moment, the grief in his face was infinitely deep. "She never came. And Cal thought I was lying. Or hell, who knows what he thought? He picked a fight again. I only hit him once, and he went down. For this one, awful moment, I thought it was a gag. I looked it up later; they're called one-punch kills. They're not even that uncommon."

"And then you went to the basketball expo," Auggie said.

"I had to. I didn't know Deja was—I didn't know what had happened to her. Then those girls came and knocked on the door. First Sadie, then Nia. Sadie went away, but Nia wouldn't leave. She wanted to talk to Cal. Wanted to fight. And I was standing in the kitchen, with Cal on the floor, and it was like I was waking up. I started to realize what had happened, what—what Cal had made me do. I'd be finished. My whole world would come crashing down, just when I thought Deja and I could finally have a life together."

"Your car was here. That's the BMW Sadie saw: yours, not Genesis's, not Orlando's."

Wayne nodded mechanically. "Nia finally left, but I knew she and Sadie had seen my car, seen Cal's, and I knew, eventually, when people wondered what had happened to Cal, they'd start thinking about it. I drove out to the expo, checked in at the hotel, took pictures, posted a couple on social media, and drove back. I left my phone there so the cell records would look like I was in the hotel. Then I waited until it was late, took Cal to his car, and drove him out to that rest stop. I left him there. I ditched his car back in Wahredua, close enough to walk, and then I got in mine and went back to the hotel.

"The rest was like you said. I thought I could make people think Nia got shot by a Volunteer. And nobody would ask questions about that bitch dealer. I left the gun at Genesis's house, but I wiped it down. I thought I did, anyway. And I was the one sending those emails to Orlando; I made up that email account and pretended to be Genesis. I knew I needed to get rid of some of Deja's clothes, things she'd left in the apartment, but I couldn't do it myself. It was going to kill me to do it. I asked Orlando to take care of it; I knew he'd do anything for her."

"You son of a bitch," Orlando shouted. "You son of a bitch! You killed Cal!"

He charged, bulling into Wayne and sending both of them stumbling into the hallway. For a moment, it looked like Orlando had the upper hand. Then Wayne twisted free, grabbed Orlando's hair, and brought his knee up into Orlando's face. Bone crunched, and Orlando collapsed on the floor, his nose and mouth bloody.

Wayne was breathing hard as he looked up at Auggie.

"Theo," Auggie shouted. This had been part of the plan too, in case Wayne turned on them. Theo's performance earlier had been the perfect reason to separate. Now he could come up behind Wayne and neutralize him.

But no one moved in the apartment.

"I already took care of your fuck buddy," Wayne said with a grin that was all teeth.

Beyond Wayne, at the other end of the hall, the door to Wayne's bedroom was open. No one moved inside.

"Theo!"

"Shut the fuck up." Wayne advanced toward Auggie, stepping over Orlando without seeming to see him. "We're going to go for a ride now. I am not going to let you ruin everything."

"Everything is ruined," Auggie said, backing up until his back hit the dresser. "Everything in your life that you loved is ruined. Orlando will never forgive you. Your family will never forgive you. You've lost the business. You've lost Deja."

"The game's not over until it's over," Wayne said. "Fourth-quarter comeback. Bottom-of-the-ninth win. I'm not letting it end like this, not when I've worked so hard."

He was three feet away and coming closer.

"I get that," Auggie said, "but you don't understand how badly—"

When Wayne grabbed him, Auggie lunged forward instead of pulling away. His fist connected with Wayne's throat. Wayne's eyes bulged, and he wheezed and stepped sideways.

Darting around him, Auggie broke for the hall. Wayne hit him from behind. It wasn't some brilliant, technical move; he just clubbed Auggie as hard as he could between the shoulder blades, and Auggie smashed into the jamb. White light and pain erupted in his head. He tried to recover. His hip checked the wall, and he stumbled again. Then Wayne caught up, raining blows onto Auggie's back and shoulders and head until Auggie went down. He hit the floor less than six inches from Orlando, and a distant part of Auggie's brain was surprised to see Orlando's eyes open and staring at him.

"You little faggot," Wayne wheezed. He knelt on Auggie's back, and Auggie felt something pop and then a sharp pain. Big hands closed around Auggie's neck, tightening, and an alarm sounded inside Auggie. No air. He couldn't get any air. He arched his back, trying to buck Wayne off, but Wayne was much bigger and had him pinned. Blackness fuzzed the edge of Auggie's vision. He reached back, clawing at Wayne's face, and for a moment, the incredible pressure closing his throat eased.

Auggie gasped raggedly for air. He couldn't move because Wayne's weight still pinned him to the ground, but he could breathe. Then the hands were back.

"Don't let him do this, Orlando," Auggie shouted as he pried at the fingers. "Don't let him—"

The haze of black static came more quickly this time. He raked his nails on Wayne's hands and arms. He tried to get his face again. He remembered diving as deep as he could when Fer had taken him to the beach the first time, the ocean water black and stingingly cold. The tremendous pressure in his head.

And then the weight on him was gone, the pressure was gone, and Auggie was sucking in breaths of air. He flopped onto his back, crying, the pain in his throat so great that he couldn't bring himself to shout for help. Somehow, though, he sat up.

Orlando had Wayne in some sort of wrestling hold, and to judge by Wayne's contorted expression, it wasn't a comfortable one.

"Hey, uh, Augs," Orlando said, the casual words belied by the strain in his voice. "Could you, um, call the cops? He's really strong."

24

The cops had Theo in for questioning most of the night, while Auggie and Orlando went to the hospital. By the time John-Henry and his partner, Upchurch, had finished interviewing Theo, it was close to dawn.

John-Henry followed him out into the steel-gray light of the parking lot. "Just between us, Theo, we tracked down the collectibles."

"What?"

"The collectibles, the ones that Wayne claimed Cal sold to pay for his drugs. We think Wayne dumped them at the basketball expo— chucked them in the trash to make it look like Cal had either run off or been robbed. Someone dug them out of the dumpster, and when he sold one, the owner of the pawn shop logged it on a received-property database. We just saw that it had been flagged. A couple of uniformed guys are going to meet up with the local police and get the full story, but we think we'll be able to tie it to Wayne."

"That's good, John-Henry."

"I know this is pretty inappropriate, but have you heard anything from Cart?"

Theo shook his head.

"He's missed all his shifts this week. He left a message with dispatch saying he quit, but it was so strange that they kept him on rotation just in case it was a joke."

"Fuck."

John-Henry put a hand on Theo's shoulder. "That's not your trouble to carry. I know it doesn't help, me saying that, but I thought you should hear it."

"You're right," Theo said. "It doesn't help."

He walked to the hospital. The morning was cool. The air was wet. Dew dimpled the blossoms of a bed of tulips. From the Wahredua Family Bakery came the smell of yeast and hot oil—the day's doughnuts, already getting started—and an old Chevy rolled past him, a pair of steel balls hanging off the tow hitch, their rattle oddly musical when the Chevy went over a speed bump.

The hospital gift shop would still be closed, so Theo stopped at a twenty-four-hour Walgreens and bought flowers and a cheap glass vase. When he got to the hospital, he navigated and lied until he found Auggie's room. Auggie was asleep. The flowers were daisies. He put water in the vase. He added the contents of whatever was in the little packet of nutrients and preservatives that came with the flowers, clouding the water. Then he sat in one of the vinyl-backed chairs and fell asleep.

He was on the floor, his arms tied behind his back. Somewhere far off, Luke was yelling, calling his name. Only then the voice was Auggie's.

Theo jerked awake.

The morning light made him squeeze his eyes shut. When he opened them again, Auggie lay on his side, watching him. Bruises covered his neck in grape-sized blotches. With one of those waking-up noises that couldn't be helped, Theo wiped his mouth, checking for drool. A yawn caught him. When he finally managed to talk, all he could think of was, "Hi."

"Hi," Auggie said with a smile.

"How are you? Wait, don't answer that. Does it hurt to talk? Just nod your head."

"It's ok. My voice sounds funny, and it's not exactly pleasant."

"How's your head?"

"Ok."

"How's your—"

"I'm fine, Theo. I just want to get out of here. How are you?"

"Me? Jesus, he barely touched me. He caught me by surprise and hit me pretty hard. While I was still out of it, he gagged me and tied me up; I'm surprised he didn't stomp my face in just to get revenge."

"I guess being quiet was his top priority."

"Thank God." Theo's gaze dropped; he wadded up the plastic wrapper that had come with the flowers. "Guess I let you down again, huh? Right when it mattered the most."

"You were there with me. You trusted me to do something dangerous and important. Things didn't go like we planned, but you didn't let me down."

"Great." He was staring at the crumpled plastic. "Now I've immediately stopped feeling so fucking awful."

"Hey Theo?"

He didn't look up.

307

"You know how people sometimes get student loans for school?"

It came out of nowhere, his face hot, his eyes prickling. He nodded and wiped his cheeks.

"What's wrong?"

"Nothing." Theo took a shuddering breath. "Student loans, yeah, you just have to—" The next wave crashed over him, and his shoulders caved. He pressed fingers against his eyes.

Auggie sat up, pushing back the blankets. Theo waved furiously for him to stay, his whole body shaking, as he choked out, "I'm fine. God, I could hear you. I could hear you, hear what he was doing to you, and I couldn't do anything. I was so fucking useless. Again."

From the next room came a woman's voice. "And how are we doing today, Mr. Hobarth? And how are we doing today, Mr. Francis?" Laughter that the woman—the nurse?—probably imagined in her head as tinkling. "And what are we going to watch today, Mr. Hobarth? And what are we going to watch today, Mr. Francis?" Clip-clop, clip-clop. "Let's see that arm today, Mr. Hobarth. No, no, no. Now don't be a sourpuss. It's just your old friend Mr. Blood Pressure Cuffy-Wuffy."

Theo's eyes were sticky and burning when he finally managed to bring himself down. He tilted his head at the voice and said, "It's like a bad kid's show.

"Jesus," Auggie said, covering his face. "Where's my old friend Mr. Weefle Injection?"

Theo's laugh was wet and short, but it felt real. "I'm sorry. I'm sorry about this. I'm going to go."

"I guess you didn't sleep much."

"They had me at the station all night. The only good news is John-Henry thinks they're going to drop the assault charges from earlier this year. He didn't come out and say it directly, but he made it sound like the county wouldn't have much interest in prosecuting me anymore. Have you talked to Orlando?"

Auggie shook his head. "I didn't, you know. Sleep much either." He didn't say anything. He just lay there, his Adam's apple moving under the bruises, his eyes dark and steady.

Theo shucked his boots. He climbed up onto the bed, and then they both had to squirm around until they were stretched out together, Auggie with his head on Theo's chest, Theo's arm around him.

"My arm's going to be pins and needles."

Auggie made a sleepy noise that sounded like he might not be too bothered by that fact. Then he roused, his chin digging into Theo's chest, and said, "Student loans?"

"Why do you care about student loans?"

"I think—I think that's what I'm going to have to do." He chuckled, turning his face into Theo's chest. "Fer's furious, and rightly so. The Civic is totaled. I've blown so much money on stupid shit. I keep getting in trouble." Auggie shook his head. "He's going to try to lock me in my bedroom after this. I'll be lucky if he lets me out before I'm forty. And—and I think Fer might need some help too, in his own way. He's so stressed. He's carried our family since he was a teenager, and I don't think he's been happy in a long time. I can do this for him, you know? Take one thing off his shoulders."

"That's really thoughtful of you."

"What about a job application?"

"What?"

"A job application."

"I'm not hiring."

Auggie poked him.

"Jesus, ok, stop. I seem to remember that you don't have the time or inclination for a job."

"Could you, you know, help me fill out my first one?"

"They're pretty self-explanatory."

More poking.

"Fine, yes. Damn it, I think you punctured a lung."

"Will you be a reference?"

"Absolutely not."

"Just tell them how amazing and wonderful and smart and brave and strong I am. Oh, and that I'm dependable, reliable, a natural leader, a problem solver, and that I can definitely remember to clock in and out."

Theo's fingers played with the buzzed hair on Auggie's nape. "I'll figure out something."

As though someone had flipped a switch, Auggie's breathing evened out. In the silence that followed, Theo heard flies buzzing. He heard the sound of blows, the fear bleeding into Auggie's voice, the call for help that he couldn't answer.

Auggie's hand was surprisingly cool when it touched his cheek and thumbed away tears.

"Sorry," Theo mumbled.

"I thought we said crying is ok," he said in a voice sandy with sleep.

"It is. I'm all cried out now, promise."

But he wasn't. And then, sometime later, he was. And he slept. And his last thought was that God must be real because Mr. Cuffy-Wuffy hadn't interrupted them.

25

The week of finals, Auggie tried four times before he caught Dr. Kanaan in her office. When she answered, she was wearing a loose hijab, a Wroxall sweatshirt, and joggers. Her running shoes had mud on them.

"Yes?" Her thick eyebrows drew together as she studied Auggie. "I'm sorry, are you—"

"No, I'm not in one of your classes. My name is Auggie Lopez. I'd like to talk to you; I'll only take a minute."

"I'm sorry, Auggie. The end of the semester is exceptionally busy, and I'd prefer that you made an appointment."

Auggie shook his head. "I don't think this can wait."

Down the hall, a pair of boys who looked distinctly like freshmen was waiting for the elevator. One of them was bragging about having finished all his finals. The other was obviously trying to cram, flipping notecards.

"It's about Theo Stratford."

"I'm really not sure—"

"This conversation would be better in private."

Dr. Kanaan's face was blank as she stepped aside. The office was lined with shelves, and although every available inch was filled with books, sleek modern furniture and the open window combined to make the room still feel comfortably spacious. Auggie shut the door behind him.

When they were seated, he pulled out his phone and displayed the registration page for the course Shakespeare in the World. He handed it to Dr. Kanaan. She looked at it and passed the phone back.

"I don't understand. If you're interested in enrolling in the course, you'll need a pink slip, and you'll have to discuss that with the instructor. The waitlist is exceptionally long, and if you're hoping I'll be able to make an exception for you, I'm afraid I can't."

"The waitlist isn't just exceptionally long," Auggie said. "The waitlist is unbelievable. You have two hundred people trying to add a single section of Shakespeare in the World."

"I'm sure the department will consider adding another—"

"Dr. Kanaan, I'm going to be frank: when was the last time any university anywhere had a waitlist of two hundred people trying to get into a class called Shakespeare in the World?"

For the next ten seconds, Dr. Kanaan rearranged things on the desk: a stapler, the cable for a MacBook, a foam apple that was probably one of those stress toys. She looked like she was thinking about squeezing the hell out of that apple.

"You said this was about Theo Stratford."

"That's right."

"I think you'd better explain yourself and then go, Mr. Lopez."

Auggie tapped a few more screens until he got to the Instagram hashtag he'd created, #hotguysreadshakespeare. He'd spent the last few weeks building the tag around Theo, occasionally adding comments where he talked about the Shakespeare in the World class he'd taken. To Auggie's surprise, many of Theo's former students had chipped in, adding their own testimonials. The hashtag had taken off after that, with people posting pictures of other hot guys who, presumably, read Shakespeare. Sometimes, it seemed a little bit like a stretch. There was one of a guy in yoga pants, his hair in a man bun, and there was absolutely no indication at all that he was reading Shakespeare. He just had great abs.

"What is this?" Dr. Kanaan said.

"This is free marketing. I've got a lot of followers, Dr. Kanaan. I'm happy to send them your way. Most people's lives would be improved by taking a class from Theo, although you could tell him not to be such a bitch with the participation points. I've let people know that Theo will be teaching Shakespeare in the World next year. Fall and Spring semesters. That's why you have two hundred people lining up to take a course that, in the last four terms, has had an all-time high of twenty-six students."

Dr. Kanaan was silent for a long moment. "Theo's situation—"

"No," Auggie said.

"And I suppose that if the department doesn't give Theo instructional opportunities, you're going to tell your followers to take a different class."

"Of course not. But I am going to post his evaluations. And then I'm going to post the evaluations of every other instructor in the department, beginning with Dr. Wagner. And then I'm going to start a #freetheo campaign."

"That doesn't make any sense. He's not imprisoned."

"It doesn't have to make sense. That's the beauty of social media."

"This is blackmail, Mr. Lopez."

"No, this is an opportunity. You have a phenomenal instructor who could help your program grow. Your department has mothballed him because they're afraid he's toxic. Here's your proof that he isn't. Give him two sections each semester until he graduates, and you'll get two more years of free marketing from me. Theo gets to teach and build his CV. You get increased enrollment, which means better numbers for the dean, which means more funding, more professorships, etc."

"I'll have to talk to the chair. This will take time."

"Not too much, I hope. People want to finalize their course registration."

When Auggie left, he had the distinct impression that Dr. Kanaan didn't like him. His hands were shaking, and as he rode down the elevator, a huge, sloppy grin broke out. He thumped his head against the metal paneling of the car.

"Fuck yes," he shouted, and the words echoed in the elevator's metal box.

He still had a couple of finals that he needed to study for, so he headed across the quad toward the Sigma Sigma house. The campus was sharply divided between the kids who had finished (or who had given up) and the ones who hadn't. A boy was showing another boy how to fly a drone, the two standing shoulder to shoulder as they looked at the controls. A girl was teaching what looked like a hula-hoop class to several middle-aged women, all in leotards. A guy and a girl were making out in the shade of an oak tree. A pair of women, their hair shaved, their heads tattooed in blue geometric designs, were quizzing each other with flashcards. A cute kid with a mop of curly hair sat with his eyes closed, quietly conjugating Spanish verbs out loud.

"Augs!"

Auggie put his head down and walked faster.

"Augs, wait! Hold on!"

Sighing, Auggie stopped and looked over his shoulder. Orlando was jogging after him. Scabs still marked where the skin had split on his nose and lips, but the bruising had faded. The wind pulled at his dark curls. When he came to a stop, he wrapped his arms around himself, looking everywhere but at Auggie's face.

"I'm sorry—"

"I'm sorry—"

They both laughed uncomfortably.

"Me first," Auggie said. "I'm sorry we used you as bait. We legitimately thought Wayne would confess because he'd already done it once, when we found all the money under the bed. I'm sorry I made up that fake email and made you think Genesis wanted you to help her again. And I'm really, really sorry about Wayne. I will totally understand if you hate me."

Orlando pushed some of the thick, coarse curls away. With what looked like a lot of effort, he met Auggie's eyes. "You found who killed my brother. And yeah, it was my other brother. But Augs, you're never going to know what that means to me. Thank you."

"Well, you did kind of save my life, so I think we're even."

"My parents will still pay you, you know. They don't want anybody to think they won't cover their debts."

Auggie just shook his head. Someone on the quad was playing the panpipes, the music shrill and grating. "No, that wouldn't be right."

"You found Cal's killer—"

"No. But thank you."

After a moment, Orlando said, "I'm sorry about everything, Augs. I'm sorry I dragged you into that mess. I'm sorry I wouldn't listen to you and Theo when you tried to tell me something was wrong. I'm sorry Wayne hurt you. Are you ok?"

"I'm fine."

"Is Theo ok?"

"I guess."

"What's that mean?"

"He's fine, he's just—he's just Theo being Theo." The words exploded free before Auggie could stop them. "Half the time it's like he's holding on to me for dear life, and the other half it's like he wants to pin my mittens to my sleeve."

A huge grin bloomed on Orlando's face.

"What?" Auggie said.

"Nothing."

"No, what?"

"I just always forget how dumb you are."

Auggie slugged him.

"Jesus, Augs, watch it." Orlando rubbed his shoulder, his grin getting even bigger. "You're getting some legit guns."

And right then Auggie realized that he loved Orlando. Maybe not in the way he'd thought when they'd met, not romantically, instead like one more dumbass brother. But he still loved him, and it couldn't have left him more shocked.

To cover his surprise, he asked, "How's, you know, stuff with your family?"

"Ok. I mean, not ok. Not at all, actually. My parents aren't talking to me. They're pretending they're all wrapped up with Wayne's defense, but really, they're just furious I made them look bad. Chris and Billie spent the whole day Wayne got arrested telling me how amazing I was, and now they've gone over to Pammy's side and tell me every chance they get how I've ruined our family." Orlando knuckled at his eyes. "I've been talking about it a lot with my therapist. I guess I think, maybe, um, they haven't treated me very well."

Auggie nodded.

"And I think maybe I need a little space from them. They've been in my head for a long time. My whole life, really. And I think I've got some bad behaviors from trying to be someone they'd love. So, sorry again. For being so weird and messed up."

"You're not weird and messed up."

Orlando burst out laughing, and then Auggie started laughing too.

"Ok," Auggie said, "but you're not any weirder or more messed up than the rest of us."

"Thanks, Augs. But I am. I know it. It's ok. I'll have plenty of time alone to figure things out."

"You're not alone. You know that, right?"

"Yeah, sure. Anyway, that's not why I came over here. I want you to meet someone."

"What?"

"Come on. I want you to meet someone."

Before Auggie could protest, Orlando set off across the quad. Auggie trailed after him. A blond boy was sitting next to a line of hawthorns, his arms loose around his knees. He had strong features: a prominent nose, a broad forehead, eyes so pale blue they were like ice. When he smiled, he was attractive but not precisely handsome, although Auggie couldn't have explained exactly why.

"This is Augs," Orlando said, dropping onto the ground. "Auggie. The guy I was telling you about. Auggie, this is Ryan."

They said hello. Auggie sat. Ryan kept throwing nervous smiles at Orlando and then trying to catch Auggie's gaze in quick glances.

"Augs knows everything about poetry," Orlando said. "That's why I thought you guys would hit it off. He totally helped me pass my business writing class. Augs, Ryan writes the best poetry in the entire world. You're going to love it!"

"Really?" Ryan asked. His voice was quiet, with a soft accent that sounded like it might be from somewhere in New England. "Who's your favorite poet?"

314

"I don't know anything about poetry. Orlando's just impressed that I know where to put commas sometimes."

Ryan laughed.

"And Augs is super strong too," Orlando said. He launched himself onto Auggie, bearing him down toward the ground, and Auggie had to fight him off, laughing. "See?" Orlando said when they finally separated. "He's, like, the strongest person I know."

"Are you insane?" Auggie said, feigning a kick that made Orlando squirm away. "What the hell is wrong with you?"

"Hold on, I just saw this girl from chem class." Orlando shot to his feet and ran across the quad, shouting, "Miriam, hold up!"

"Oh my God," Auggie said, covering his face. "This is the worst setup ever."

"He's not exactly subtle, is he?" Ryan said. He looked like he was fighting a smile.

"Not even close. I'm surprised he didn't strip me down to my boxers and put me on parade."

"So you wear boxers," Ryan said, his smile slipping free.

Auggie grinned. "What about you?"

"You'll have to try a little harder to find out."

Face hot, Auggie said, "No, I meant, what about you, like—oh my God."

Ryan's smile got bigger.

"I meant, Orlando totally made that up about me knowing a lot about poetry. Did he—I mean, do you—are you, like—" Sweat popped out along Auggie's forehead. "You know what, I'm just going to go over there and kill myself."

Laughing, Ryan nodded. "I write poetry."

"Oh. Cool. I'm going to be totally honest and tell you that I know almost nothing about poetry. I mean, I'm double majoring in English, and I like reading Shakespeare, even though I don't understand half of what I read."

"People always say that," Ryan said. "But the best part about poetry is you don't always have to pin down a meaning. It's more important to just feel a poem. The sounds, the images, what it does in your gut."

"Wow. I've never heard someone talk about it like that. That's pretty . . . cool."

Ryan blushed. It was a crazy blush, running through his face like wildfire.

"I'd like to hear some of your poems sometime," Auggie said.

"Yeah." Ryan smiled and nodded. "They're not very good, but ok."

Auggie opened his mouth, but his phone buzzed. He thought about ignoring it. And then he thought about Fer going nuclear if Auggie missed any sort of contact.

"I'm sorry, I've just got to check this."

Instead of Fer, though, Theo's name showed on the screen.

"Just a second," Auggie said. "I'm really sorry."

"It's fine."

"Hello?"

Instead of a voice, though, the call buzzed with ambient noise.

"Theo?" Someone farther down the quad was laughing, and Auggie put a hand over his ear. "Theo, are you there?"

Mumbled words. The only one Auggie could pick up was "spinning."

"I'm coming over." He disconnected the phone.

When he looked up, Ryan was watching him, a quizzical look on his face.

"My friend," Auggie said. "He's going through a rough patch."

"He's lucky he's got you."

"I'm not sure he feels that way. Could I—would it be weird if I got your number? Basically I'm trying to avoid any sequence of events that involves Orlando wrestling me just so I get to see you again."

Ryan laughed. He took Auggie's phone and entered his number. "Next time," Ryan said, "you have to tell me something about you. You can't just be a super-hot guy who loves Shakespeare and wants to hear bad poetry."

Wrinkling his brow, Auggie said, "I can't?"

26

Everything was going fine until the texts from Cart. It was early afternoon, the sun spinning dust motes in the stillness of the living room, oblong panels of light stretching across the boards. The windows were open. The smell of hot tar filtered into the house; a crew was busy patching the road, talking, shouting, the occasional beep of heavy machinery backing up. Theo had finished a draft of his thesis chapter on *Romeo and Juliet*. He'd decided to celebrate by removing the couch cushions and vacuuming up the various types of crumbs that had fallen behind them.

When the first text came, a mixture of surprise and relief made him take it literally.

I hope your happy.

It was the first communication from Cart since the birthday party—the first sign that Cart was even alive after vanishing completely. Theo had to sit down, forgetting about the missing cushions, the springs hard under his ass. He was still typing out a reply when the second text came.

you are a faggt andi hat faggotes

Theo stopped composing his message. He knew he was clutching the plastic case too tightly; he could feel it flexing, and then the sliding cover for the battery popped free.

you ruined my lif you fuckinng qurrr ihate you som uch

And, of course, there wasn't anything to say to that, so Theo picked up the cover for the battery and tried to slide it back into place. He couldn't. Then he could, but the plastic pinched his finger, and he swore and threw the phone across the room. It hit the wall, gouging the plaster, and cracked against the floor. Then it buzzed again.

Sucking on his finger, he retrieved the phone. He read every message as they came in. At least a dozen of them. A part of him understood that Cart was drunk or high, was hurting, was humiliated, was saying things that came out of a place of terrible pain. And another part of him could hear the words in Cart's voice: *You ruined my life. You ruined my life. You ruined my life.*

Since Cart had left, he no longer bothered with the electrical boxes or the shower curtain rod or the hollow-core door. He took the brown plastic bottle of Percocet (thank God for refills) and a fresh joint out of the drawer in the entertainment center. He put down two of the pills with a Big Wave; he'd kept them stocked in the fridge in case Cart decided to show up one day. Then he put down another. Upstairs, he smoked the joint in bed and drank another Big Wave. At some point, it seemed like a good idea to throw the half-empty bottle. For a frozen instant, it made a star of beer and broken brown glass against the wall. He was convinced he watched the whole thing in slow motion.

It wasn't just Cart. It was Auggie, while Theo was tied up and gagged and listening, unable to do anything. It was Ian, and it was Lana, the car spinning. Theo wasn't sure, but now he thought maybe the radio had been on, and while the tires had screamed across asphalt, Elton John had been singing "The Bitch is Back." It was Luke, who had died alone in the loft, where Theo had knelt and picked straw out of his hair.

"There's no straw in my hair," Luke kept saying back, and he was grabbing Theo's wrists, struggling with him. "Will you just lie still, for fuck's sake? Do you need to go to the hospital? Jesus Christ, Theo, what the fuck were you thinking?"

So he told him. He told him everything he'd been thinking. He didn't sleep, but he went somewhere. When he and Luke had both been teenagers, they had gone hunting one weekend in November. They had camped by a lake that didn't have a name, and in the morning, Theo had woken to find the tent empty. Luke was gone. He had stumbled into cold gray light to pee on a tangle of winter-brown honeysuckle. Luke was gone. The buck he had gotten the day before was still hanging in the tree, and his shoulder was bruised where the rifle had kicked back. Luke was gone. Theo had gone to stand by the lake. That water was the same color as the light. That was where he went.

When he jerked up from the bed, his face was hot, and the room was dark. He was breathing too fast. Hyperventilating, a small part of his brain supplied.

"It's ok, it's ok. You're ok."

"Auggie?"

"Yes, God, you just about gave me a heart attack." The darkness made Auggie an outline. His fingers scratched pleasantly through Theo's hair. "Lie down."

When he woke again, the room was empty. Theo made his way downstairs and was surprised to see the back door open, with a morning breeze blowing pleasantly through the screen door. Beyond the line of oaks, the horizon was a shingle beach of gray clouds. He peed. He showered. When he came out of the bathroom with a towel around his waist, Auggie was letting himself in through the back door, a bag full of takeout containers in one hand.

"Morning," Auggie said, easing the screen door shut. "I couldn't find anything except beer and peanut butter, and I thought you might need something to eat."

In the line of oaks, a waxwing sang its plaintive cry. Theo's skin pebbled, and he opened his mouth.

"I love you."

Color rushed into Auggie's face, and he bit his lip. He opened his mouth. He closed it. He bit his lip again. That expressive mouth.

Drops of water cooled on Theo's shoulders. He pushed back wet hair. "Please say something."

Auggie gave a one-shouldered shrug, but his face lit up. At night, Theo had read, the human eye could see a star from a billion lightyears away. "I love you too."

Theo crossed the room and kissed him. Auggie made a soft noise. The takeout bag hit the floor. His hands were firm on Theo's hips, and he kissed back.

Then he pushed Theo away.

Theo reached for his face, but Auggie caught his hand.

The smell of sausage and maple syrup wafted up. Then Theo laughed quietly. "Ok. Got it."

"Theo, I love you more than I've ever loved anyone."

"Right. You love me, but you're not in love with me. We're better as friends. I had my chance and I blew it. It's ok, Auggie. I've heard them all before; you're not going to hurt me."

Auggie watched him

"Oh fuck," Theo said, covering his eyes. "Who the fuck am I kidding?"

He was surprised when fingers closed around his wrists, pulling his hands away from his face. Surprised, too, by the resolve in Auggie's expression.

"I love you, Theo. But—but I'm twenty. And I just spent a year chasing this horrible guy and letting him abuse me and mess with my head. And I'm scared that I won't be able to be what you need. That I won't be able to help you when you're so set on not being helped. I'm scared somehow I'll do things wrong, and you'll—" He cut off, biting his lip.

"If you think I'd hurt you—"

"No. Not that. But—" It was terrifyingly adult, the determination in Auggie's face. "But I don't think you know what you want either. I think you've gone through the two worst years of your life, and I think you want anything that you think will make you feel better. Me—"

"I want you because I love you."

"—or pills, or booze, or weed, or a closeted boyfriend who will keep you just busy enough that you don't have to face how much pain you're in. You were stoned out of your mind last night, Theo, telling me all the guilt you carry around, telling me every bad thing you think you're responsible for. You're killing yourself with it."

Theo twisted free. "Thanks for telling me. Thanks for solving the big riddle."

"Someone needed to. This is hard for me. This is terrifying for me. But people care about you, Theo, and we want you to know we're worried about you."

"Yeah? So, what, there's a whole gang of fucking adolescents talking about the fact that my daughter is disabled and my husband is dead and I'm hooked on pills and whatever else you just said, and you drew the short straw? Thanks, Auggie. Next time, put it in a fucking card."

Auggie's chest rose and fell rapidly. His cheeks were flushed. Of all the times to cry, now seemed like a good one to Theo, but Auggie's eyes were dry.

"Well?" Theo said.

"I don't know what you want me to say."

"I don't want you to say anything. I want you to get the hell out of here."

Auggie bent toward the toppled bag of takeout.

"Leave it, for fuck's sake." More words burst free: "What the fuck do you know about anything? You are so fucking stupid you let that guy roofie you, and now you want to tell me how I need to fix my life."

Auggie pushed out through the screen door. It clapped shut behind him, rattling in the frame, and his steps moved away across the back porch.

Theo kicked the bag of takeout. Containers slid across the floor. One flapped open, spilling sausage links onto the linoleum. Fighting the urge to break something else, Theo went upstairs. He dressed. He went downstairs. His movements were automatic: the entertainment center, the drawer, the brown plastic bottle. He remembered the lake, the still-water light of dawn. And then he crossed the room, his feet slapping the floor, and threw open the front door.

Auggie was sitting on the porch steps, toeing a weed in the flowerbed below him, his hands on his knees. He looked over his shoulder, and his face was blank. The sun was rising behind him, a crown of light picking out clumps of hair that stood up where he had slept on it.

Working his jaw, Theo stepped out onto the porch. Dirt and grit clung to the bottom of his feet. The uneven edges of boards bit into his soles. A morning late in spring, the smell of dew and pollen and wet earth and lilacs just starting to bloom.

"I don't know what to do. I don't even know where to start."

Auggie stood and squared his shoulders. "Then we'll figure it out together."

INDIRECTION

Keep reading for a sneak preview of *Indirection*, book one of
Borealis: Without a Compass.

Chapter 1

"STAKEOUTS DON'T REQUIRE CHEESE," SHAW SAID to his partner, boyfriend, and best friend since college, North McKinney. They were sitting in a Ford sedan on a quiet block of Kingshighway. On one side of them, Forest Park opened up, where puddles of safety lights illuminated February-bare branches. On the other side stood businesses, churches, Barnes-Jewish Hospital, condominium buildings, and the glowing façade of The Luxemburg. Still nothing.

"It's not cheese." North's voice was low and deep, with the heat of a fire about to catch. He rattled the can for emphasis.

"It's got cheese in the name."

"No, it's got cheez in the name." North traced the letters with one finger. "See? That's so they can't get sued for false advertising."

"That makes it even worse. You understand that, right? It's probably full of benzoates and carrageenan and that's not even getting started on what dairy does to your body."

"It's not—"

"Because of your dairy allergy."

North's jaw tightened before he spoke again. "That's what I'm trying to tell you: I'm ninety-nine percent sure there's no dairy in this. None. It has cheez, Shaw. Not cheese. So I'm totally safe."

"I really think—"

"No."

"I'm just going to—"

"No," North rumbled, and when Shaw reached for the can, North planted a hand against Shaw's head and shoved him against the driver's window.

"It's killing you," Shaw said, trying to knock North's arm away. "By 2038, I won't have a boyfriend anymore."

"It's going to take that long? God, I need to start buying this in bulk."

"North, I absolutely forbid you to—"

The can's hiss interrupted Shaw. One-handed, North sprayed a mound of the artificial cheez onto a cracker balanced on his knee. The mound got bigger. And bigger. North didn't stop until the pyramid of cheez started to topple, and then he scooped up the cracker and shoved it in his mouth. He grinned, displaying the cheez foam between his teeth, and crunched loudly. Then he coughed.

Shaw watched him for a minute as the coughing continued and tears ran down North's face. North was getting plenty of air. He was also white-knuckling the can of cheez spray as though he thought Shaw might take advantage of this moment of weakness.

"Don't worry," Shaw said, putting his fingers to his temples. "Master Hermes just recognized that I'm now a level-five psychic. I'll dissolve the cracker with my mind, and while I'm in there, I'll fix that acid reflux you've been—"

"Don't you fucking dare," North croaked, swatting Shaw's hands away from his temples. He managed to swallow, cleared his throat, and in a raspy but more normal voice continued, "First of all, that psychic stuff is bullshit Master Hermes sells you when he has to pay the vig to those Bosnian guys he borrowed from."

"Oh, he didn't borrow it. The spirit of George Gershwin showed him where—"

"And second of all, even though I know it's not real, don't you ever fucking dare use that juju to mess around inside me."

"A lesser man would point out that a couple of nights ago you were begging me to mess around inside you."

"And third of all, I don't have acid reflux. I got food poisoning from that fucking toxic nacho cheese—"

"Dairy allergy," Shaw murmured.

Whatever North had been about to say, he didn't finish because instead he screamed with what sounded like frustration. Softly.

Movement at The Luxemburg's front door drew Shaw's attention. In the flood of lights illuminating the building's exterior, Chris Hobson might as well have been standing on a stage. He was in his late twenties, close to North and Shaw's age, cute but on the verge of being rat-faced. He was an investment wunderkind at Aldrich Acquisitions, the company owned and run by Shaw's father, and he'd been responsible for helping Aldrich Acquisitions become a principal investor in several highly valued biotech startups. He was also, Shaw and North were pretty sure, a thief.

"He's moving," Shaw said, taking out his phone. He sent the same message to Pari, their assistant, and to her nonbinary datemate, Truck.

Kingshighway was a busy road during the day, but late on Saturday, the flow of cars was irregular. Twice that night an ambulance had pulled into Barnes-Jewish, sirens screaming, and once a Silverado had pulled to the curb ahead of Shaw and North, breaking the crust of old snow so that a troop of frat boys could pile out and piss on the sidewalk. Chouteau boys, undoubtedly—the same college, just up the road, where North and Shaw had met. Other than that, though, the night's entertainment had consisted of Shaw trying to tap into his past lives and North trying to see how many crackers he could sandwich together with spray cheez.

Now, though, Hobson had emerged, and it was time to work.

Hobson turned up the street, walking toward the portion of St. Louis known as the Central West End. It was a ritzy area, with Chouteau College, Washington University, and the hospital creating anchor points for people with way too much money. It had trendy bars and coffee shops, fancy restaurants, and even a handful of clubs. If Hobson stuck to his usual routine, he'd be going to the Jumping Pig, a hipsterish bar that offered pork infusions and bacon-themed everything. If Shaw had to guess, he'd say it would be closed in a couple of months, but for now, it was Hobson's go-to.

As though on cue, Hobson went east at the end of the block.

Shaw and North waited a tense ten minutes; the only sounds were their breathing and the cars whipping past, the whisper of slush churned by tires. Then a message came from Pari: an image of Hobson backing through a men's room door, his hands on Truck's waist.

HE'S TOUCHING MY DATEMATE!!!!!!

"You're never going to hear the end of that," North said, grabbing the door handle. "You know that, right?"

Shaw sighed, nodded, and got out of the car.

At the next break in traffic, they jogged across Kingshighway, cutting at an angle so they reached the sidewalk at the end of the block. Pari was coming towards them along the cross street. Her long, dark hair was bundled up under a ski cap, and she wore a quilted down coat that came to her knees. The bindi today was raspberry colored.

"He's touching my datemate!" was her first, screeching announcement.

"I think it's sweet," Shaw said. "Having a bisexual villain. I think that's really kind of nice. And progressive. Don't you think, North?"

Pari's head swiveled toward him.

"I mean—" Shaw tried again.

North groaned.

"You think it's sweet? You should have seen Truck's face. That...that new-money prick was groping Truck through hir jeans. Truck was so scared!"

"Truck offered to spank my monkey—those were hir words, by the way—this week, Pari. Twice. Ze's not exactly a sexual shrinking violet."

"We're getting into the weeds here," North said.

"I'm sorry," Pari said. "I'm sorry, did I hear you correctly? Are you slut-shaming my datemate? Ze's level of sexual activity is none of your business."

"Well, it's kind of my business when we're talking about my monkey."

"Let's not—" North tried.

"Truck is an unbelievably generous lover," Pari said, shaking the set of keys she'd lifted from Hobson.

"So is North!"

"That's really not—" North said.

"And Truck is extremely well endowed."

"So is—"

"Ok," North said, grabbing the keys from Pari's hands. He caught Shaw's arm and dragged him down the block toward The Luxemburg. Over his shoulder, he called back, "Let us know if we need to hurry."

"I've seen North when he wears those cutoff gray sweatpants," Pari screamed after them. "He might as well have been holding a measuring tape for me."

"Jesus Christ," North muttered.

"It's very difficult to have a conversation with her because she's so—"

North growled and shook Shaw by the arm. "Don't. Start. You two were fucking made for each other."

By then, they were getting close to The Luxemburg. North released Shaw's arm, and Shaw stumbled a few steps before catching himself. He set off toward the condo building, glanced back, and said, "I don't want you to feel bad, so I just think I should tell you that I think you look really good in those gray cutoffs. They make your whole, you know, business area look very impressive."

"I'm going to murder you," North stage-whispered. "Get the fuck in there so I can be done with this nightmare."

"Very bulge-y."

North packed a snowball faster than Shaw expected, and it caught him in the back of the head as he ran toward the condo building. He was still shaking snow out of his hair, the snowmelt trickling down his nape, when he stepped into the lobby.

It was about what he had expected from The Luxemburg's outside: tile and wainscotting, coffered ceilings, lots of white paint. A mural of the 1904 World's Fair covered one wall; in the bottom-right corner, a young lady looked like she was having an indecent relationship with a waffle cone, although Shaw would have to inspect further to be certain. On the other side of the lobby, a security desk marked the midpoint between the front doors and the elevators.

Two women stood behind the desk: one was white, in a security uniform, a hint of a pink-dyed curl slipping out from under the peaked cap. The other was black and wore scrubs. An ID clipped to the waistband identified her as Dr. Holloway. The women had been looking at something on a phone, and now they both turned their attention to Shaw.

"Hi," Shaw said, wiggling out of his sherpa cloak. "I'm—" He'd gotten his arm stuck, and it took him a moment to get it free. "I'm Max. I'm here to see my cousin. Oh, I like your nails!"

The women exchanged a look as Shaw approached the desk. "Sir," the woman in the security uniform said. Her nametag, now that Shaw was closer, read Weigel. "You said you're here to see your cousin? What's the name and unit number?"

"I told my boyfriend I wanted to get rainbow-painted cat claws for Pride," Shaw said wistfully, staring at Weigel's nails, "and he told me no. Oh, you've got a tattoo! Is it a rose?"

"It's a carnation," Weigel said, rotating her arm to display the underside of her wrist.

"For purity," Holloway said and started to laugh until Weigel slapped her leg.

"My boyfriend won't let me get any tattoos. Or piercings. I told him I wanted to get my nipples pierced, and he said he'd break up with me. He said he's the only one allowed to touch my body."

"Boy," Weigel said, drawing out the word. "What'd you tell him?"

"Oh, I know he just wants what's best for me. Davey's so sweet. He picks out what I'm supposed to wear—well, not my cloak. He told me I couldn't have this, but I bought it anyway. But he made me wear this stuff." He gestured at the long-sleeved tee and jeans. "And I have to hide the cloak at Mom's. But I can't tell her about Davey because when I said something about the diet Davey put me on, she just about lost her mind."

Holloway narrowed her eyes at him; she was picking at her weave with one hand. "You ain't nothing but skin and bones. Why're you on a diet?"

"Davey likes it when he can count my ribs. He says that's when I look best for him. Oh, Coca-Cola. That's my favorite! I don't know when the last time was that Davey let me have one."

"Like a giant, white baby," Holloway murmured to herself.

Weigel held out an unopened can of Coke, but instead of taking it, Shaw moved around the desk. "Hey, you've got all sorts of cool stuff back here. Do you really watch all those screens?"

"You know you shouldn't be back here," Weigel said.

"Leave him alone," Holloway said. She reached out and caught some of Shaw's hair. "Now don't tell me Davey makes you wear your hair like this?"

"Oh." Shaw let his expression fall. "I was, um, really bad. One time. And Davey cut my hair. It was for my own good. You know, he had to teach me a lesson."

"Child," Weigel said. "Why don't you call Davey and tell him to come down here?"

"Do you want to see what my hair used to look like? It was really long. Oh, that's a picture of a mole on Davey's back that I think might be cancerous. And that's a carousel horse, but the carousel's gone, so I guess maybe it's just a regular horse now. But out of wood. And that's—"

"Just a giant baby," Holloway said to herself again, both women turning away from the lobby to face Shaw, leaning closer to look at the pictures on his phone. He glanced up just once, over their heads, as North sprinted silently across the tile. Then he went back to the patter, dragging it out until North rode the elevator up and Shaw guessed that several minutes had passed.

"Anyway," Shaw said, "I guess I'd better go see Chris. Chris Hobson. He's my cousin; he lives in 8A."

"Sweety pie," Holloway said, "you got to get this Davey out of your life. He's got some bad energy."

"I say call him," Weigel said. "Get him down here and let the two of us talk to him for a few minutes. That boy won't ever trouble you again."

"And drink that Coke," Holloway said. "I think I've got a Kind bar in my purse. You're too thin; don't listen to that boy."

"Drink that Coke right up," Weigel said as she grabbed the desk phone. "What's your cousin know about all this?"

"Oh, he and Davey don't get along at all. That's the whole reason I came over tonight; Chris wants to talk about it."

The women exchanged knowing looks.

"Uh huh," Holloway said, fluffing Shaw's hair again. "Listen to your cousin, Max. You're too pretty to waste on a jerk like Davey."

"Mr. Hobson? Yes, I've got your cousin Max—yes, sir. I'll send him right up."

It took a little longer, but Shaw finally managed to extricate himself and ride the elevator up. He found the door to 8A unlocked, and when he stepped inside, North was waiting near the landline phone where he'd answered the call from the security desk and told them to let Shaw into the building.

"What the absolute fuck was all that fuckery?"

"I got a Coke!"

"You've got an abusive boyfriend named Davey? Jesus fucking Christ, Shaw. I didn't say you couldn't buy that stupid fucking cloak. My exact words were, 'I don't think you'll wear it very much, so I don't think it's worth the money.' And I didn't say you couldn't get tattoos or have your nipples pierced. I said maybe you should think about the fact that you don't like needles and having the script of *Memento* tattooed over every inch of your body might be a decision you regret in a few months."

"I—"

"And if you say one fucking word about that Coke, I'm going to lose my fucking shit."

North's shit looked pretty lost already, so Shaw just sipped the cola and nodded. "It's been a hard night. Your penis. Those cutoffs."

North's fists clenched at his sides. Then he turned slowly and stalked down the hall.

The condo looked like it had come straight out of a CB2 catalogue: sinuously modern furniture, glass and teak, the occasional bleached wicker and white-varnished rattan piece. It even smelled store-bought, like all-purpose cleaner and artificial lavender. Sliding glass doors opened onto a balcony overlooking the park: asphalt ribbons, the arched backs of stone bridges, winter-brown grass rippling like water.

Shaw and North pulled on disposable gloves and moved quickly through the unit. They couldn't toss the place the way they normally would have, but they still managed to work efficiently, dividing the rooms without speaking, each man methodical in his search.

North found the safe hidden on the bookshelf. It had a cover designed to look like a row of books, and it was surprisingly good—from a distance. With the cover pulled back, a keypad and lock were visible. They tested keys on the lock until one of them turned, and the safe's door swung open.

"Computer," North said as he drew several external hard drives from the safe.

"Got it," Shaw said, already powering up the laptop. A login screen appeared, and Shaw typed in the Aldrich Acquisitions administrator password—provided courtesy of his father, who also happened to be their most valuable client. After an uncertain flicker, the screen changed, and Shaw had access to Chris Hobson's computer.

After scrolling quickly through the files, Shaw said, "Nothing obvious."

"It's corporate espionage," North said as he plugged in the first external hard drive. "He's been smart enough so far not to leave a trail of bread crumbs. That's why we're here."

"So far," Shaw said with a smirk. A new window popped up, showing the contents of the hard drive that North had just connected. "Porn."

"Tentacle porn," North corrected.

"You really shouldn't judge—oh." Shaw cut off when North double-clicked one of the files. He covered his eyes and then peeked between two fingers. "I didn't know he could fit so many inside him."

North was already disconnecting the drive. He plugged in the next one.

"This is it," Shaw said as he looked at the files.

"Make a nice, obvious folder to stash it all. Something like 'Chris's Secret Stuff – DO NOT TOUCH.'"

Instead, Shaw burrowed into the computer's main drive, created an unnamed folder, altered the properties so that it was hidden, and copied over the contents of the hard drive. It was a lot of data, and it took several minutes. While they waited, he sent a text to their contact at Aldrich Acquisitions—a woman named Haw Ryeo.

Everything uploaded.

Haw didn't respond, but Shaw knew how things would go: Hobson's computer, which was technically company property, would be inspected immediately. The stolen files and documents would be found, providing grounds for a warrant. In their search of the condo, the police would find the hard drives. Hobson would go to prison, and Aldrich Acquisitions would maintain control of millions of dollars' worth of intellectual property.

"Done?" North asked.

Shaw nodded.

While North disconnected the cables and returned the hard drives to the safe, Shaw powered down the computer. They locked up the condo, took the fire stairs, and let themselves out through a service door. Shaw sent another text, and Pari met them on the same street corner.

"He touched Truck's butt," Pari informed them as she accepted Hobson's keys.

"Get back there and claw his eyes out," North said. "Just make sure you put the keys in his pocket while you do."

Pari's grin was vicious; she practically ran toward the Jumping Pig.

Shaw followed North across Kingshighway again. This side of the street was dark, and the air from the park smelled like wet wood and mulched leaves. In the distance, a few artificial lights looked like silver brads fixing the trees against the night sky.

"Is this how you thought things were going to be?" Shaw asked as they approached the Ford.

"I thought it went pretty smoothly."

"No, I mean—corporate work, planting evidence, tracking down the mistresses of high-level executives."

"Is this a morals thing? Are you feeling guilty?"

"What? No. He stole that stuff; we just gave them a way to prove it. No, it's just—I don't know, I didn't think this is what we'd be doing."

"It's work, Shaw. And we're good at it." North opened the door and rested one arm on the roof of the car. "We're fucking fantastic at it."

"Right."

"And Borealis is doing great."

"Right."

"So?"

After a moment, Shaw shrugged and got into the car.

Chapter 2

WHEN THEY PULLED UP in front of North's Southampton duplex, Shaw had one thing in mind.

"Huh?" North said. And then he grunted and spread his legs. "Oh."

The borrowed Ford rumbled quietly beneath them. The inside of the car smelled like the air freshener—shaped like a cluster of cherries, although smelling more like Laffy Taffy than anything else Shaw could name—and like the American Crew gel North still wore in his textured thatch of blond hair. He was hardening rapidly under Shaw's touch, and he leaned back in the seat, eyes hooded as he watched Shaw impassively. Normally his eyes were a remarkably light blue, the predawn color of fresh snowfall, or like light caught on the rim of a sheet of ice. Tonight, in the darkened interior of the Ford, with his pupils blown wide, they might as well have been black.

He made a sound in his throat and tried to spread his legs farther. His knee thumped the door panel.

"This is when you invite your beautiful, sexually prodigious, unbelievably generous boyfriend inside," Shaw whispered, his fingers tracing the length of North's dick through the denim.

North made another of those noises, but he was still relaxed against the seat. With one hand, barely more than a flick of his fingers, he beckoned Shaw closer.

Grinning, Shaw leaned over the center console. North's movement was minimal, only a few inches, making Shaw come to him. He moved toward North's mouth for a kiss.

At the last moment, though, North veered, his mouth coming to Shaw's ear, and at a normal volume he said, "What about Davey?"

"Ow!" Shaw reared back so fast that he hit the car's headliner. "North, what the hell?"

"I just remembered your crazy, abusive, controlling boyfriend Davey. I just wanted to make sure he was ok with us messing around."

"You are really taking that the wrong way."

North just watched him through hooded eyes. His erection was still visible through the jeans.

"I just took a few details and, you know, made something else up."

"Uh huh."

"You and Davey have absolutely nothing in common."

"Uh huh."

"He was a total figment of my imagination."

"Uh huh." North reached down, pretending to adjust himself, although his hand lingered long enough to suggest something else. "Except those details that you took from real life."

"North, come on!"

"Night, Shaw."

"Hey, hold on." Shaw caught his wrist, drawing North's hand to the bulge in his own jeans. He let out a satisfied noise and rutted softly against North's palm. "It's been almost a week," Shaw whispered. "And last time, we didn't even get to do a sleepover."

"We're not ten, Shaw." But his fingers curled possessively, rubbing slow and hard against Shaw's dick.

Shaw made another of those appreciative noises; he didn't miss the flush speckling North's throat. Leaning over the console again, he stroked North and found him, if anything, even harder than before. "Please? I want you to fuck me."

The rumble in North's throat was almost a growl. "Is that what you need, baby?"

Shaw nodded.

"Say it," North ordered.

"I need it. I need you to fuck me."

North's grin was sharp and sudden. "Then ask Davey."

"North!"

North's grin got bigger.

Shaw slapped his erection.

"Holy Christ, Shaw!" North folded, covering himself. "What the fuck?"

"You're being a brat."

"Did you just fucking spank my cock? And not even in the fun way, I might add?"

"Quit being so mouthy," Shaw said, "and take me inside and fuck me."

"You're a fucking monster."

Shaw turned off the car and withdrew the keys from the ignition. "Now, North."

North grumbled the whole way to the front door. He let them inside, and the puppy—North's puppy—was there, waiting for them. He immediately started yipping, dancing around their heels, clawing at North's legs.

"Hello," North cooed. "Gotta take care of him first."

"He's a fucking cockblock," Shaw called after him. "This is worse than having children. Children you can just lock in their rooms when daddy needs some dick."

North pointed at the ceiling and glanced back long enough to reply softly, "Keep shouting; I'm sure Mr. Winns is interested in what daddy needs."

Face hot, Shaw locked the door behind him and headed into North's bedroom. He left the sherpa cloak on a chair, kicked off the engineer boots, and climbed onto the bed. A few minutes later, North was there too, toeing off his Redwings, rucking up the sweatshirt he'd worn. He peeled it off, exposing the dense slabs of muscle, the old scar on his side, his chest and belly covered by thick blond fur. He crawled between Shaw's legs, ran his hands up Shaw's thighs, and kissed him. Then he pulled back, palming Shaw through his jeans, a smirk plastered on his face.

"Why are you being so mean to me tonight?"

"Keep whining," North said, eyebrows shooting up, "and you're going to find out how mean I can be."

Huffing a breath, Shaw reached for North's waistband. He unbuttoned the jeans, worked the fly down, and pulled out North's dick. North shivered and let out a breath. Shaw stroked him slowly, watching North's eyes glaze.

Then Shaw's gut twisted.

North was tugging on Shaw's shirt, trying to turn him out of it, his fingers warm and rough.

"Just a second," Shaw said.

"What?"

"Just a second. I've got to, um, clean up first."

North studied him, kissed him, and fell onto his side. Swatting Shaw's thigh, he said, "Hurry, mister. Now who's being mean?"

Shaw did what he needed to do. Perched on the toilet, he suddenly felt hyperaware that none of the guys in the books he liked ever had to deal with this situation. When he'd finished, he opened the door and called to North, "Just gonna take a quick shower." He stepped under the hot water, found the bar of hemp-milk soap he'd stashed so that he didn't have to use the chemical-laden Irish Springs stuff that North bought in bulk, and cleaned himself up. His hair looked like a cumulus cloud after he toweled it, but North seemed to like his hair more the longer and wilder it got, so he left it the way it was and padded into the bedroom naked.

North was asleep on the bed, jeans still around his thighs, the puppy curled up in the crook of one arm. He yapped at Shaw once.

"I don't know what you're complaining about," Shaw muttered as he walked around to North's side of the bed. "You got exactly what you wanted."

"Shaw?" North mumbled.

"Let's get you out of these," Shaw said, helping North free of the jeans.

"Just give me five minutes. Gonna fuck you…" He made a sleepy noise. "…can't walk."

Sliding under the covers, Shaw found North's hand and squeezed it. Then he kissed him. By the time he was reaching to turn off the lamp, North was asleep again. And in the morning, when Shaw woke, North had already left for work.

Chapter 3

"SHE DOESN'T LOOK like a romance author," Shaw said, studying the picture on the website. It showed a woman still on the young side of middle age, trim, her hair in a severe black bob. She had a cigarette holder in one hand, a wisp of smoke artfully photoshopped into the image, and she wore elbow-length gloves. "If anything, she looks like Audrey Hepburn. Or a flapper. Or Audrey Hepburn playing a flapper."

It was Wednesday, and although Shaw had taken Sunday off (North hadn't), Monday and Tuesday had been nonstop with the work Aldrich Acquisitions sent their way. It wasn't just the investigations that kept North and Shaw busy; it was the paperwork. Shaw's father had mostly kept out of the arrangement, at Shaw's insistence, and although Haw was a reasonable woman, corporations still apparently required massive amounts of paperwork, documentation, and evidence—all of it carefully organized and presented. After their first job, North had insisted on doing the paperwork himself.

Today was a paperwork day. The Borealis offices occupied the main floor of the house Shaw owned in Benton Park, and they consisted of two main areas: the outer office, where Pari pretended to be an administrative assistant and where Truck and Zion occasionally completed reports for the part-time jobs they did for Borealis; and the inner office, where North and Shaw worked. The inner office had seating for clients and two desks, placed side by side in the center of the room. North's was immaculate: a large, high-definition computer monitor, a lamp, and a stacked chrome inbox-outbox combo that looked like something Don Draper might have used. Shaw's desk did not quite reach the level of immaculate, although it was definitely cleaner than it had been. It currently held a series of four Twinkies that had been dissected to various degrees and pinned open against their cardboard sleeves; volumes one, three, and six of the *Encyclopedia of Environmental Analysis and Remediation,* a Vitruvian Man coffee mug full of water and green onions, and the LP for *The Best of Gallagher,* which was currently being used as a plate for a piece of a child's birthday cake. Shaw didn't remember who the child had been, but the cake still looked edible.

"North?"

North was typing something in a spreadsheet, checking figures against a page he held.

"North, I think she might be lying."

"Hmm."

"I think she might be lying, the woman who called us. She doesn't look like a romance author at all."

"Uh huh." North pecked at the keyboard.

"North!"

"Look at this. It's the middle of February, and we've already billed more than we did in the whole first quarter of 2018. And that's not even counting jobs like last night."

"North, I'm trying to tell you something."

After one last, lingering glance at the spreadsheet, North looked over. "That's her?"

"That's what I'm trying to tell you: I think this is a ruse."

"A ruse."

"A con."

"A con."

"A scam."

North sighed. "Ok. Let's hear it."

"She doesn't look like a romance author at all."

"And just because I feel like my life won't be complete until I hear this: what is a romance author supposed to look like?"

"Well, you know." Shaw gestured vaguely. "A corset. Fishnet stockings. Stiletto heels. Would it kill her to wear a bustier?"

"I don't—"

"Or one of those vinyl bodysuits. And maybe a whip!"

"I think you're thinking of a prostitute—"

"Sex worker."

"—or dominatrix." North pointed to the screen. "This lady just looks like she has too much time on her hands, and maybe she likes playing dress-up."

"Says the man who just ordered an adult Naruto costume—" Shaw cut off at the noise North was making. "I mean, right, yes, whatever you were saying."

A knock came at the door, and a moment later, it opened.

"Ms. Maldonado is here to see you," Pari said, all sweetness and light with a prospective client standing behind her.

"Thank you, Pari."

"And Truck asked me to tell you that hir job is taking hir to East St. Louis."

North nodded; he was obviously trying not to make a face. "Please remind hir that we only reimburse legitimate expenses."

"Ze knows," Pari said, her smile turning brittle.

"That means—"

"Ze knows. We all know."

"All right," Shaw said. "Great. Thank you, Pari. Thanks so much. Ms. Maldonado?"

A soft voice answered, "Yasmin," and then the woman and Pari traded places, and Yasmin Maldonado moved into the office. She had a skunk stripe of gray roots where her hair was parted, and she looked thinner than she had in the picture. She wore a MICHIGAN IS FOR LOVER'S sweatshirt, snow pants that crinkled every time she took a step, and ratty Reeboks. The only thing consistent with the picture was the smell of cigarette smoke that moved with her.

They took a few minutes getting her settled, exchanging introductions, and her eyes roved around the office before settling on the LP with its slice of birthday cake. With what looked like a great deal of effort, she dragged her gaze up to look at North and Shaw.

"I know you're going to think I'm fangirling, but I just can't believe you're willing to take this case. The gay detectives! This is so exciting!"

"Well," North said with a sidelong glance at Shaw, "there might have been a miscommunication. I'm interested in hearing about the job you want us to do, but I have to be honest and tell you we're very—"

"Very interested," Shaw said. "Very excited about a chance to do some work with the LGBTQ community."

Yasmin nodded. Then her mouth widened into an O. "You mean us! Oh, right. Yes, that would be great. I mean, you're gay! It would be fantastic."

"Right," North said with another of those sidelong looks. "We're definitely gay."

"And you're boyfriends," Yasmin said, clasping her hands.

Another of those sidelong looks. Shaw discreetly rolled his chair back a few inches and kicked North in the ankle. "Why don't you tell us," Shaw said, ignoring North's murderous glare, "what's going on? You mentioned death threats. Against you, in particular? What's been happening?"

"Well, I don't care what anyone says: we can't cancel the con. We can't. I won't. I'm not going to let some pathetic nobody terrorize us into ruining a wonderful time for hundreds of people."

"You're talking about the..." Shaw checked his notes, which he now saw were written on the back of a Jack in the Box receipt. "Queer Expectations Convention? Is that right?"

"Yes. The premiere gay romance literature convention in the world."

"The only," North coughed into his fist.

But Yasmin had heard him, and she shook her head. "Oh no, there's another. Gay Romance Literature. Very...hoity toity. Noses in the air. Not like us; we just want to have fun."

"And this con, Queer Expectations, it's being held in St. Louis this year?"

"That's right." Yasmin squirmed to the edge of her seat, snow pants crinkling. "A few weeks ago, I started getting emails. 'I'm going to get my revenge.' 'You're all going to pay.' That kind of thing. Then the physical letters started showing up. They had the words cut out of magazines, you know. They said the same kind of things. I brought them, in case you want to see them." She gestured to a folder on her lap. "And I checked in at the hotel Monday; Tuesday morning, I had another one. Someone had slipped it under the door while I was asleep. It's crazy. The whole business is insane. And of course, someone leaked it, and our guests are going wild. We already have a lot of people who suffer from anxiety, and this is going to put them in the ground. It really will."

"I'm not sure," North said slowly, "what you want us to do. This sounds like something you need to take to the police."

"I tried! They're not interested. Actually, if I'm being frank, they looked at me like I'm crazy. Very homophobic. It's probably because we're in Missouri."

"The Metropolitan Police aren't always my favorite people, but they wouldn't ignore a credible threat."

"But they did. I mean, they are. They talked on and on about being careful and keeping an eye out for anyone strange or unfamiliar. It's a romance convention! We're all strange! And we love it that way. I tried to explain to them that something horrible is going to happen, but they just won't listen."

"Did the messages you received have any specifics?" Shaw asked.

"Like what?"

"Well, anything, really. Any details."

Yasmin made a face, opened the folder, and spread a half dozen pages on the desk. They were all as she had described them: cut-out words pasted onto copy paper, spelling out a variety of threats: *I'm going to get you, No one is safe, Watch your back*. Shaw sighed and looked at North.

"Oh no," North said. "You're the one who opened this particular door to Batshit Land."

"The problem," Shaw said, "is that even if the police wanted to help, there's nowhere for them to start. You might be the intended target, but you might not—this one says, 'I'm watching all of you.' There's no sign of when or how someone might be in danger. We're even making the assumption that this is connected to the con. You're giving the police a black hole of possibilities, and they'd need limitless resources in order to even try to make a difference."

"But they can't do this. You're not allowed to threaten people."

"You're right; harassment is against the law, but it's a misdemeanor. Unless you can give them a viable suspect, they just don't have the resources to run down something like this."

Yasmin stared at them, mouth agape, her breath stirring invisible eddies with the smell of cigarette smoke. "Fine. Fine. That's why I'm here, isn't it? I'm going to hire you: private detectives. Gay private detectives."

"If I have to hear about how gay I am one more time," North said to Shaw, "I'm going to shit a unicorn."

"We're not gay detectives," Shaw said to Yasmin. "We're detectives who happen to be gay. And this isn't a gay detective agency. It's a detective agency that helps the LGBTQ community."

"Or anyone who can pay."

"Well," Yasmin said, "I fit both those criteria. I can pay, and I'm part of the LGBTQ community. I mean, I'm straight, but I write about gay men. I'm an ally."

"We know," Shaw said. "And we're really grateful. And we're looking forward to reading your books."

North cleared his throat.

"We really are," Shaw said. "I think North got a little chub just looking at the cover for *Spankin' Angels*, and I really liked the description of *Marcus the Marquis*, especially the part about the Prince Albert—"

"What Shaw is trying to say, in perhaps the most backassward way possible, is that we can't take this case. We'd like to help you, and I'm sorry this is upsetting for you, but you're asking us to do something impossible. We don't have the resources to provide security for an entire convention. Your best bet is to do what the police recommended: remind people to be vigilant, keep hotel staff and security in the loop, and immediately inform the police if anything suspicious happens."

"What if I have a suspect?"

"You just said you have no idea—"

"We had to ban a convention-goer last year. She was way too aggressive with the men who attended. Objectifying. Sexualizing. She hired a young man, a hustler, to seduce a very well-known author, and then the police got involved because it was a vice sting. It was awful. We had to tell her she was never welcome back at Queer Expectations."

"Why didn't you mention this to the police?" Shaw said.

"Because...because I didn't think of it at the time."

"Very convenient," North said.

"I didn't! A friend just told me that Leslie—she's the woman I'm talking about—Leslie is planning on crashing the con. And sitting here, listening to you, it all suddenly clicked."

"What a wonderful coincidence," North said.

"Exactly," Yasmin said, straightening in her seat with excitement.

"No," Shaw said. "He's being sarcastic."

"Oh." Yasmin's expression fell, then she brightened again. "I can pay you to see if Leslie really is in the area. That's something you can do, right? You can just try to find her. Come to the convention. See if she's hanging around. And if she's not, if she's safely back in Utah or wherever she normally is, your job is done, and you get paid. Although I really hope you'll attend the whole convention because you'll be our local celebrities."

"Would you give us a moment?"

"What? Oh, yes. Of course. We can even pay you for your time at the convention. Your hourly rate. You really don't understand— everyone will be so excited."

When the door shut behind her, North spun in his chair to face Shaw. "No."

"Hold on."

"No way, Shaw. This is amateur hour. We might as well be investigating a high-school mean girls club. Samantha told Sarah who told Megan that the boys' swim team stuffs their speedos."

"First of all, you would know, because I remember freshman year you bragging about that water polo player and telling me, quote, 'Turns out I like the taste of chlorinated balls.'"

North made a disgusted noise. "Shaw, we've got four open jobs from Aldrich right now. Four. I honestly don't know the last time I slept more than six hours in a night, the paperwork keeps piling up, and on top of that, we've got independent clients who are willing to pay obscene hourly rates for us to take pictures of cheating spouses. This is a fan convention for romance readers. Gay romance readers. How are they going to pay us? In poppers?"

"Actually, that's not a bad—"

"This is what we've worked incredibly hard for, Shaw. This. What we've got right now. We built Borealis from nothing, and it's finally paying off. Why can't we just enjoy that things are good right now?"

"We didn't start Borealis to get rich," Shaw said quietly.

"Speak for yourself, you fucking trust-fund baby."

With a shrug, Shaw waited, holding North's gaze.

Outside, a diesel truck lumbered past the house, engine grumbling as the driver struggled to shift up.

North let out a wild growl. "Fine. Fine. Just shut the fuck up. If you say one more fucking word, I'm going to lose my mind."

"All I said was that you like chlorinated balls and that you might want our clients to pay us in poppers."

"You got what you fucking wanted, Shaw, like you always do."

"You—"

North stabbed a finger at Shaw. "Not one. more. fucking. word."

Shaw shrugged again.

Wiping his face, North stood. He bent, caught Shaw's hair, and kissed him. Then he gently tugged on the hair, turning Shaw's head, and whispered, "If you ever tell anyone how easily you just made that happen, you're going to need a truckload of poppers to handle what I'll do to you."

"Is that a bad thing or a good thing? It kind of sounds like a good thing."

North scowled, released Shaw, and headed for the door. As he pulled it open, he said, "Ms. Maldonado? We'll take the job. The contract is standard, and we do require a retainer—" North cut off, and when he spoke again, his voice was tight and hard. "I'm with a client."

A man's voice, familiar, carried back to where Shaw sat: "North, North, North. Is that any way to greet your uncle?"

Acknowledgments

My deepest thanks go to Wendy Wickett. Many people caught the occasional typo during serialization and graciously let me know about it, but Wendy proofed every single chapter. She not only caught my mistakes, but she made suggestions for clarity and accuracy, and the book as a whole is much, much stronger for it. I'm incredibly grateful for her clear, careful reading of this manuscript!

About the Author

Learn more about Gregory Ashe and forthcoming works at
www.gregoryashe.com.

For advanced access, exclusive content, limited-time promotions,
and insider information, please sign up for my mailing list at
http://bit.ly/ashemailinglist.

Made in the USA
Monee, IL
09 January 2022

88543852R00204